*I*n a large town in Germany, many years ago, there lived a poor cobbler and his wife. All day long the cobbler would sit in his tiny shop, mending boots and shoes and sometimes making new ones to order. In a little garden beyond the city gate, the cobbler's wife grew fruit and vegetables, which she sold at a stall in the market. So fine was her produce, and so beautifully displayed, that her stall was always crowded with customers.

The couple had a son called Jacob, a sturdy and handsome boy, who would sit with his mother in the market and help the customers

carry their purchases home. Jacob
rarely returned from these trips
empty-handed; sometimes he was
given a coin, sometimes a titbit from
the kitchen, or, at the very least, a
bunch of flowers from the garden.

One day the cobbler's wife was
sitting as usual in the market with
several baskets of vegetables, fruits,
herbs, and seeds. Little Jacob sat
beside her calling out, "Buy, ladies
and gentlemen, buy our beautiful
cabbages, fragrant herbs, apricots,
apples, and early pears."

An old woman came hobbling
across the square. She was dressed
in rags and had an ugly, pointed

face, full of wrinkles, with red-rimmed eyes and a sharp, hooked nose. She leaned on a stick and dragged herself along with difficulty, her legs barely supporting her.

The cobbler's wife had sat in the market place every day for sixteen years, and never before had she seen this strange figure. She shrank back as the old woman hobbled up to her.

"Are you Hannah, who sells vegetables?" asked the woman in a harsh, grating voice.

"Yes, I am Hannah," she replied. "What can I do for you?"

"I'll look and see if there is anything I want," said the woman.

She bent over the basket and began to rummage with her ugly hands, pulling out the delicate herbs and holding them to her nose with spider-like fingers.

Hannah was annoyed to see the rare herbs she had laid out with such care treated in this way. But she had a peculiar horror of the old woman and dared not protest.

"Bad stuff, very bad," muttered the old woman as she finished turning over the contents of the baskets. "There's nothing here that I need. Fifty years ago everything was much better. You have very bad stuff, very bad!"

These words angered young

Jacob. He called out boldly, "You nasty old woman! You turn over our best herbs with your ugly fingers; you crush them and hold them to your long nose. No one who has seen you will want to buy them! You say our goods are bad, but let me tell you that the Duke's cook himself buys from us and no one else!"

The old woman stared at Jacob and with an unpleasant smile said, "Don't you like my long nose, little boy? You shall have one just like it. It'll grow right down to your chin."

She began poking about among the cabbages again. Pulling out the best ones, she squeezed them

then threw them back into the basket, repeating, "Bad stuff, bad cabbages!"

"Don't shake your head like that," said the boy in distaste. "Your neck is as thin as a cabbage-stalk. If it broke, your head would fall into our basket and no one would want to buy from us again."

"So you don't like my thin neck, eh, little boy?" croaked the old woman, grimacing horribly. "Then you shan't have any neck! Your head shall sit straight on your shoulders so that it won't roll off your little body."

"Don't talk such nonsense to the boy!" cried the cobbler's wife.

"If you want to buy something, hurry up, before you drive all my other customers away."

"Very well, just as you wish," exclaimed the old woman angrily. "I'll have these six cabbages, then. But I can't carry them. You'll have to send the boy with me to help. I'll pay him well."

Jacob didn't want to go, for he was afraid of the old woman. He wept and pleaded with his mother not to send him, but she told him sternly that it would be wrong to let an old woman carry such a load. So Jacob tied the cabbages up in a large cloth and set off across the market place.

The old woman walked very slowly, and it was nearly an hour before they reached the outskirts of the town. They came to a halt outside a small, crumbling house. The old woman took a rusty hook from her pocket, pushed it into a little hole, and the door flew open. Jacob stood rooted to the spot by the sight that met his eyes.

Inside, the ceilings and walls were of marble, the furniture of rare ebony, richly inlaid with gold and precious stones, while the floor was of glass so smooth that Jacob slipped and fell several times as the woman led him into the house. In one of the rooms she stopped, and taking a silver whistle from her pocket, blew it sharply.

At once a crowd of guinea-pigs came hurrying down the stairs. To Jacob's amazement, they walked on their hind legs and wore nut-shells on their feet. They were fully clothed and on their heads they wore hats in the latest fashion.

"Bring me my slippers, you rabble!" shrieked the old woman, shaking her stick at them so that the animals squeaked with fright. "How long am I to be kept waiting?"

The guinea-pigs scurried up the stairs again and were back in a flash carrying a pair of coconut husks lined with leather, which they slipped neatly onto the old woman's feet. Immediately she stopped limping, threw away her stick, and ran across the glass floor, dragging Jacob after her. She took him into a large room that looked like a kitchen from the number of strange utensils everywhere, although the furniture — beautiful mahogany

tables and upholstered armchairs—
was more like that of a drawing-room.

"Sit down," ordered the old woman.
She pushed Jacob into one of the
armchairs and pulled up a large table
so that he could not get out.

"Just sit and rest for a little while;
you have carried a heavy load. You
look hungry. I shall make you a soup,
such a soup as you will remember to
your dying day!"

She blew her whistle again. The
guinea-pigs reappeared, this time
wearing aprons over their clothes,
with wooden spoons and kitchen-
knives stuck in their belts. They
were followed by several squirrels
in wide turkish trousers and green

velvet caps. Obviously the squirrels were scullions, for they whisked about the room fetching bowls, saucepans, eggs, butter, and flour and lining up everything by the hearth. Then the old woman began to prepare the soup.

The fire crackled, the contents of the saucepan bubbled away and a wonderful smell filled the room. The old woman ran hither and thither, with the squirrels and guinea-pigs at her heels, pausing every now and again to poke her nose in the pot. At last the soup was ready. The old woman lifted the saucepan from the fire and poured the soup into a silver bowl, which she put in front of Jacob

saying, "Now, little boy, eat up your soup and it will make you into a fine fellow. You'll become an excellent cook; but the herb — no! — that little herb you'll never find. Why ever didn't your mother have it in her basket?"

Jacob did not understand what the old woman was talking about and began to eat with relish. The soup was delicious. He had always enjoyed the meals cooked for him by his mother, but nothing had ever tasted quite as good as this.

When he had finished eating, the guinea-pigs lit Arabian incense, and soon the room was filled with clouds of blue smoke. The smoke grew

thicker and thicker. It dulled the boy's senses and he lost consciousness. He came to for a moment and cried out that he must return to his mother. Then he dozed again and finally fell into a deep sleep.

Strange dreams visited him. He dreamed that the old woman took away his clothes and dressed him in a squirrel skin. He found that he could jump and climb like a squirrel, and he joined the guineapigs and the other squirrels as the old woman's servant. Jacob's first job was that of shoe-cleaner, which meant that he had to rub the old

woman's coconut-husk shoes with oil and polish them. As he had often performed similar tasks at home, he worked quickly and well.

After a year, he was promoted: with some of the other squirrels he was given the job of catching sunbeams and sifting them through a sieve to make bread for the old woman, who had no teeth.

After another year, he rose to the rank of gatherer of drinking water. This did not mean digging a well or catching rainwater in a barrel. It was a far more delicate task. Jacob and some of the other squirrels had to collect rose-dew in brazil-nut shells, and this served as the old woman's

drinking water. She drank a great deal, so the water-carriers were kept hard at work.

Another year passed, and Jacob was given the job of cleaning the floors in the house. As they were made of glass, every breath was visible and keeping them clean was no mean task. Jacob and his fellow-workers tied old rags to their feet and slid about the floors until they shone like mirrors.

In the fourth year, he progressed to the kitchen. The office of cook was an honourable one, reached only after considerable training. Jacob went through every job, from scullion to head pastry-cook. He learned how to prepare appetizing dishes and sauces from a hundred and one different ingredients, and how to make soups from every herb and vegetable under the sun. After seven years in the service of the old woman, Jacob had acquired such skill as a cook that he surprised even himself.

Then one day, as the old woman prepared to go out, she ordered Jacob to pluck a chicken, stuff it

with herbs, and have it roasted
by the time she returned. Jacob
obeyed her instructions: he wrung
the chicken's neck, scalded, plucked,
and cleaned it. Then he went into
the pantry to fetch the herbs for the
stuffing. There he caught sight of a
cupboard that he had never noticed
before. Its door was slightly ajar
and Jacob saw that it was full of
boxes which gave off a strong but
pleasant smell. He opened one of
them and found a herb of strange
shape and colour. It had blue-green
leaves and a red flower with yellow
edges. He noticed at once that the
flower had the same smell as the
soup the old woman had cooked

when he first came. The scent was
so strong it made him sneeze. He
sneezed and sneezed and sneezed —
until he woke up.

Jacob found himself lying
in the old woman's armchair and
looked around him bewildered.
Then he remembered how he had
come to be there and clapped his
hand to his forehead.

"What wondrous dreams I had!"
he cried. "I was an ugly squirrel. I
made friends with guinea-pigs and
became a great cook. How Mother
will laugh when I tell her! Oh dear,

though, she's bound to be cross with me for falling asleep in a strange house instead of helping her in the market."

He jumped up, eager to leave. After such a heavy sleep he felt as stiff as a board, his back ached and he could not move his head; he had to laugh at himself for being so drowsy. At every step he staggered and banged his nose against a cupboard or a door. The squirrels and guinea-pigs frisked around him as though they wanted to go with him. He told them to come, for they really were delightful little creatures, and for part of the way they did indeed hop along behind

him; but after a while they turned back and Jacob heard their faint squeaks dying away in the distance.

Jacob reached the town and began to make his way through the crowded streets toward the market square.

As he went by, he heard people saying on all sides, "What an ugly fellow! Where has he sprung from? What a long nose he has! What has become of his neck? Look at his bony hands!"

Jacob looked round for this strange creature but could not see

him. He would have liked to have gone in search of him, but remembered that he must hurry back to his mother.

Jacob's heart beat faster as he reached the market place. His mother was sitting there and still had quite a few vegetables in her basket, so he could not have slept for long. But he could see from a distance that she looked sad. Her chin was cupped in her hands, and as he drew near he saw that she was paler than usual. For a moment he did not know what to do; then he plucked up courage and touched her hand saying, "What is the matter, Mother? Are you angry with me?"

His mother turned and gave a horrified shriek.

"What do you want, you monster? Go away! What a cruel joke!"

"But, Mother, what's wrong?" asked Jacob in surprise. "Don't drive away your own son!"

"I told you to be off!" exclaimed Hannah angrily. "You won't get anything out of me, you misshapen creature."

"Mother, are you ill?" asked the boy, anxiously. "Take a good look at me. I am your son, Jacob."

Hannah called her neighbour. "Look at this repulsive little man! He is driving all my customers

away; and on top of that he is making fun of my misfortune. He says he is my son — shame on him!"

Stall-keepers from all over the market ran up and scolded Jacob — and market women know how to use their tongues, as you can

imagine. They told him off roundly for ridiculing a poor woman whose son, a lively, good-looking boy, had been stolen from her seven years

before. In the end, they flew at him and drove him away.

Poor Jacob could not make out what was happening. He was convinced that he had been with his mother at the market that very morning and had gone with the old woman to her house.

When he saw that his mother would have nothing to do with him, Jacob's eyes filled with tears. He left the market and walked sadly along the street to the shop where his father mended shoes.

"I'll see at least whether my father knows me," he said to himself.

He reached the shop and stood at the threshold, looking in. His father

was bent over his workbench, stitching away at a shoe. He was completely absorbed in his work and did not notice Jacob. After a minute, however, he glanced up and, in a startled voice, exclaimed, "Good gracious, what's that? Whoever is that over there?"

"Good evening, master!" said Jacob, stepping into the shop. "And how are things with you?"

"Bad, bad, old chap!" replied the cobbler, and Jacob saw with a sinking heart that his father, too, had failed to recognize him. "I'm not so handy at my work as I used to be. I'm all alone and getting old, and I can't afford an assistant."

"Haven't you got a son?" asked Jacob.

"I had a son once," replied his father. "He was called Jacob and would have been twenty now. If only he were here it would be a different tale. I'd be making new shoes, not mending old ones. But that's the way of the world."

"What became of your son?" asked Jacob, his voice trembling.

"God only knows," replied the cobbler. "Seven years ago he was stolen from us in the market."

"Seven years ago," echoed Jacob, faintly.

"Yes, old fellow, seven years ago.
I remember it as though it were
yesterday. My wife came home
that day in tears: the boy had
disappeared. She had not seen him
all day, although she had searched
the whole town for him. He was a
handsome boy and my wife was
very proud of him. She often used
to send him to the houses of her
rich customers with vegetables.
That was all right; he never
returned empty-handed. But I
used to say, 'Be careful, the town
is large, and there are many wicked
people in it; keep a strict eye on the
boy!' And it happened as I had
feared. One day an ugly old woman

came to the market, complained about our produce, and in the end bought so much that she couldn't carry it all herself. My wife sent the boy with her — and that was the last we saw of him."

"And this happened seven years ago?"

"It will be seven years in the spring. We had the town crier tell everyone about the boy's disappearance. We asked from house to house. All our friends searched with us, but in vain. Some say the old woman was a witch who comes to the town once every fifty years to buy herbs and vegetables."

As the cobbler talked, Jacob began to realize what had happened. He had not dreamed it — he had really served the wicked witch for seven years as a squirrel. Anger and grief overcame him. The old woman had stolen seven years of his youth from him — and what had he gained in return? He had learned to clean shoes made of coconut husks and to polish glass floors, and he had been taught to cook by guinea-pigs.

Jacob stood wrapped in thought, brooding over his fate. The cobbler interrupted his reverie by asking, "Wouldn't you like a pair of boots, or perhaps," he added with a smile,

"a shield for your nose?"

"What's wrong with my nose?" asked Jacob. "Why should I need a shield for it?"

"Each to his own taste," replied the cobbler, "but I tell you, if I had a nose like yours, I'd have a shield made for it. I have a nice piece of chamois leather here that would do the job. Mark you, it will be expensive, for it'll take at least a yard, but I'm sure you'll be satisfied. As it is, you must knock your nose against everything around you."

Jacob was struck dumb. He felt his nose; it really did seem flat and unusually long. So this was what

the old woman had done to him! This was why his mother had not recognized him, and why people had called him repulsive.

"Master," he begged, "lend me a mirror, so that I may look at myself."

"Goodness me!" exclaimed the cobbler. "With a figure like yours you shouldn't look in the mirror too often. You'd better get out of the habit, it can't do you any good."

But Jacob persisted. "Please let me look in your mirror," he said. "Believe me, I'm not asking from vanity."

"Leave me in peace! I haven't got a mirror," said the cobbler. "If you

must look at yourself, go to the barber's shop," and he returned to his work.

Jacob crossed the street and went into the shop of the barber, who had known him since childhood.

"Good evening," he said. "I'd like to have a look in your mirror, if I may."

"Certainly," said the barber. "You are such an attractive chap, so well built, so tall, slim, and handsome; you have a neck like a swan, the hands of a queen and a nose without equal in this world. Possibly you are a little vain, but never mind. Have a look by all means; look as long as you like."

He laughed and all his customers joined in. Jacob stood in front of the mirror and tears welled up in his eyes. No wonder his mother and father hadn't recognized him! For the mirror reflected a terrible image: little narrow eyes, a huge nose reaching to the chin, a head set deeply between the shoulders, and the body of a child. The arms were as long as a man's, but with rough, misshapen hands and long yellowy-brown fingers. Little Jacob had become deformed and ugly. Everything he had found fault with in the old woman's appearance, she, through witchcraft, had inflicted on him.

"Well, have you gazed your fill?" asked the barber. "Now, listen, I have a proposition to make to you. I have been losing trade lately to my competitor because he has brought in a giant to attract customers. How would you like to come and stand at my door and invite people in? You would do well out of tips and I would give you free board and lodging."

Jacob was deeply offended by the barber's suggestion. He stalked out of the shop, leaving the barber and his customers staring in amazement.

The old woman might have crippled his body, but his mind

remained fresh and alert; what is
more, he had acquired wisdom.
It was not his lost looks he was
lamenting, but the fact that his
own father had driven him from
his threshold. He decided to try
again with his mother.

He went to the market and
begged her to listen to him calmly.
He reminded her of the day he
had left with the old woman. He
recalled a number of incidents
from his childhood. He described
how he had served the woman for
seven years as a squirrel, explaining that she had bewitched him
because he had laughed at her.

The cobbler's wife did not know

what to think. Everything the strange fellow had told her about his childhood corresponded with that of her own son, but as soon as he mentioned the squirrel and the witch she interrupted him, saying that witches didn't exist. Finally, she said that she would have to consult her husband. She packed up her produce and asked Jacob to go with her.

When she reached the cobbler's shop, she said to her husband, "Listen, this little man claims to be our lost son, Jacob. He told me that seven years ago a witch stole him and changed him into this monster."

"He did, did he?" said the cobbler angrily. "You wretch! I told you only an hour ago that we'd lost our son. So, you were bewitched, were you? Just you wait, I'll bewitch you!"

And, seizing a bunch of leather straps, he leapt at Jacob and beat him mercilessly until the poor man wrenched himself free and ran off weeping.

Night was falling and little Jacob, cold and hungry, wandered the streets of the town in search of somewhere to rest his head. No one spoke to him, no one offered him a bite to eat or a bed for the night, and eventually he sank down

exhausted on the steps of a church and went to sleep.

*I*n the morning Jacob was woken by the first rays of the sun. He pondered on his fate. How was he to keep body and soul together when his own mother and father had turned him away? He was too proud to work for the barber, to display himself like a clown, but what else could he do? Then he remembered that at the witch's house he had mastered the art of cookery. He felt certain he was good enough to hold his own with

the best and decided to make use of his skill.

The Duke, who ruled the country, was a well-known gourmet. He loved a good table and his cooks were famous all over the world. Jacob made his way to the Duke's palace. At the gate, the guards roughly demanded to know what he wanted. Jacob said he wished to speak to the head cook. They laughed, but let him come in and led him through several courtyards. Everywhere Jacob's misshapen appearance aroused great curiosity. Servants turned to stare, laughed aloud, and joined the guards, so that by the time Jacob reached the

main entrance to the palace a whole procession had formed behind him. On all sides the shout went up, "A monster! A monster! Look!"

The Duke's steward strode up, brandishing his long ivory staff.

"What's all this noise about?" he cried. "Don't you know the Duke is resting?"

The steward dispersed the crowd with his staff and asked Jacob what he was doing in the palace. When he heard that Jacob wanted to speak to the head cook, he said, "Surely you need to see me. You want to become the Duke's court jester, I suppose?"

"No, sir, I do not," replied Jacob

emphatically. "I am a cook. I can prepare the rarest dishes. Please take me to the head cook so that I may have a chance to prove my worth."

"As you wish," replied the steward, "but you are a foolish lad. As the court jester you would have no work to do, plenty to eat and drink, and a wardrobe full of fine clothes. Still, if you insist, I'll take you along."

Jacob thanked the steward and followed him through the corridors of the palace to the room of the head cook. Bowing low before him, the little fellow said, "Sir, do you require a skilled assistant?"

The head cook looked him up and down, then burst out laughing and exclaimed, "What! You want to be a cook? You could never reach the top of the stove, not even if you stood on tiptoe! Whoever sent you to me was pulling your leg."

The head cook guffawed until his belly shook, and all the servants laughed with him.

Jacob was not to be put off. "You won't miss an egg or two, will you?" he said. "And perhaps a spoonful of syrup, a drop of wine, a little flour, and some spice? If you let me have them, I'll show you what I can do."

"All right, then," said the head

cook. "It will give us all a laugh, anyway. Let's go into the kitchen."

They passed through several rooms and corridors until they came to the kitchen. It was a huge room, equipped with every imaginable utensil. Fires burned in twenty hearths, and a clear stream of water,

which also acted as a fish tank, flowed down the middle of the room. All the ingredients a cook uses regularly stood on marble shelves, while on both sides of the room, doors opened off into store-rooms, which were stocked from floor to ceiling with every delicacy under the sun.

Scullions ran hither and thither, clattering pots and pans. But when the head cook entered, the noise stopped at once and they all froze to the spot like statues. The only sounds were the crackling of fires and the murmuring of the stream.

"What does the Duke desire for breakfast today?" the head cook asked the first breakfast-maker.

"Crab soup with spiced dumplings," came the reply.

"Good," said the head cook. He turned to Jacob. "You heard what the master desires. Let's see you try your hand. You'll be lucky if you make a success of the dumplings, though; that's our secret."

They were all amazed when
Jacob replied calmly, "Nothing
could be simpler. Bring me some
fresh vegetables, crab meat, Indian
spices, wild boar dripping, a little
red pepper, and an egg. And for the
dumplings I shall need four kinds
of meat, a little wine, duck dripping,
and a certain herb called stomach's
consolation."

The head cook looked impressed
in spite of himself.

"Well, well," he said. "You seem
to know something about this
after all. But, as they say, the proof
of the pudding is in the eating.
We shall see what you make of all
these ingredients."

Everything was brought and made ready, but, as the cook had predicted, Jacob was too small to reach the top of the stove. Two chairs were placed together and a marble slab laid across them. Jacob climbed up and prepared to show what he could do. The cooks, scullions, and servants gathered round to watch. When Jacob had mixed the ingredients, he put them into a pot on the stove and announced that they must be left to cook until he gave the word. Then he counted up to five hundred, clapped his hands, and cried, "Enough!" The pot was removed from the stove and Jacob asked the

head cook to pass judgement.

The cook picked up a golden spoon, walked solemnly to the pot, spooned up a little of the soup, and tasted it. He half-closed his eyes. Everyone waited with baited breath for the verdict. Then he smacked his lips and cried, "Excellent! Upon my soul, excellent!" He turned to the steward. "Would you care to taste it, sir?" he said.

The steward bowed, took the spoon, tasted the contents, and beamed with enthusiasm.

"All honour to your art, head cook," he said, "you are a master, but you have never prepared a dish quite like this."

At that moment the Duke's chamberlain entered and announced that the Duke was waiting for his breakfast.

The head cook gave orders for the soup and dumplings to be sent up. A little later a servant came in with the message that the head cook was to go to the Duke at once. The cook quickly changed into his best clothes and accompanied the servant.

The Duke had just finished eating and was wiping his whiskers.

"Head cook," he said, beaming, "I have always been satisfied with you,

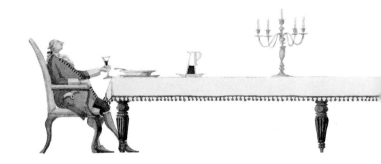

but I have never eaten a breakfast like the one you served today. Tell me, who cooked it?"

"My lord, it is a strange story," replied the cook.

He told the Duke of Jacob's appearance that morning, how he had asked to be taken on as a cook and allowed to prepare the breakfast as a test. The Duke was very surprised. He sent for the little man and asked him who he was and where he came from. Jacob could not say that he had been bewitched, but he told the Duke truthfully that he

had neither a father nor a mother and that he had learned to cook from an old lady.

The Duke asked no further questions, but said, "If you will enter my service, I will give you fifty ducats a year, a set of best clothes, and two pairs of trousers, besides. In return you will cook my breakfast every day and instruct the under-cooks in the preparation of my lunch. You will hold the rank of first assistant under the head cook. In my palace, it is a custom for new servants to be given a name by me. I shall call you Long-nose."

The newly-christened Long-nose threw himself to the ground before

the powerful Duke, kissed his feet, and promised to serve him faithfully.

Long-nose was well provided for and did honour to his position. As for the Duke, he was a changed man. In the old days, he had been known to throw bowls and trays at the cooks' heads. Once, he had hurled a roast leg of veal at the head cook with such violence that the latter had fallen badly and was forced to stay in bed for three days.

With Jacob's arrival the Duke's rages ceased. He had the table laid five times a day instead of three in order to take advantage of his little cook's miraculous skill. Not once

did he find cause for complaint; the dishes were always exquisite, the meals were varied and the Duke put on weight visibly. Many a time he would send for the head cook and Long-nose, sit them down one on each side of him, and with his own hand feed them with the daintiest morsels from his table. This was the highest favour he could bestow.

Long-nose became the marvel of the city. The noblest gentry begged the Duke to let their servants learn cookery from him. The ducal treasury did quite nicely out of this arrangement, for each of them paid half a ducat a day for the tuition.

*T*hus, Long-nose lived in contentment and prosperity for two years. Day followed day in calm succession. Only the thought of his parents continued to grieve him.

Now, it so happened that Long-nose was very good at shopping. Whenever he had time, he would go to the market himself to buy poultry and fruit. His appearance no longer provoked jeers and mockery; rather it inspired respect, and the market women thought themselves lucky if he so much as bent his nose over their goods.

One morning he was walking about the market looking for the fattened geese of which his master was particularly fond. He passed up and down several times and then stopped at a stall where some beautiful geese were displayed. They were just what he wanted. He bought three, together with a coop, which he swung onto his back, and then set off on his return journey. As he went along, two of the geese gobbled loudly, but the third, to his surprise, merely sighed from time to time, almost as though it were a human being.

"Perhaps she's ill," thought Long-nose. "I'll have to kill her soon and cook her."

To his astonishment, the goose replied to his thoughts in a clear voice:

"If you stab with a knife

I will give you a peck,

If you wring my neck

You take your own life."

Long-nose started and nearly dropped the coop. He set it down on the ground and cried, "A talking goose, by all that's wonderful!"

After he had recovered himself a little, he said, "But not so wonderful as all that. After all, I was once a squirrel. I'll wager," he

said to the goose, "that you haven't always been a goose."

"You are right," sighed the bird. "Once I was the daughter of a powerful wizard. I little thought then that I should end up in the Duke's oven."

"Have no fear of that!" cried Long-nose. "I should never dream of cooking such a rare bird. As soon as we get to the palace, I'll smuggle you up to my room and you can stay there until we decide what to do. If anyone asks questions, I'll say I'm fattening you up on special herbs. But don't worry," he added hastily, as he saw a tear beginning to form in the

goose's eye. "You'll be quite safe with me, as I'm an honest man and the Duke's second cook!"

Long-nose was as good as his word. He kept the goose, who told him her name was Milushka, in his room, and fed her on titbits from the kitchen. Whenever he had a spare moment he would spend it with her, and they passed many happy hours in conversation.

Milushka told him how her father, the wizard Thunderclap, had quarrelled with a wicked witch, who in revenge had changed his daughter into a goose and brought her to this faraway place. In return, Long-nose told Milushka his own

story. The goose listened attentively and said, "I know a little about magic; my father taught my sisters and me something of his art. I think I know what happened in your case: the witch put a spell on you with the aid of an herb. If you can find the same herb you will be able to break the spell."

This was not much comfort to Long-nose, for where was he to look for the herb? Nevertheless, he thanked Milushka, and felt a glimmer of hope.

At this time the Duke was entertaining a prince from a neighbouring country. He sent for Long-nose and said, "The time has come, my friend, for you to demonstrate your mastery of your art. My honoured guest is a connoisseur of fine cooking. I want you to astound him with your dishes, so that he will envy my table. If you value your head, see that you do not serve the same dish twice. Spare nothing, and give of your best."

The little cook bowed low, saying, "My lord, it shall be as you

wish. I will do everything in my power to please this prince."

Long-nose sharpened his wits. He spared neither himself nor his master's purse and spent whole days in the kitchen harrying the cooks and scullions.

At every meal the Duke read satisfaction on the face of his guest and he was extraordinarily pleased with Long-nose.

On the fifteenth day of the visit, the Duke called Long-nose to his table and presented him to the Prince, who said, "You are indeed a wonderful cook. The whole time I have been here you have not repeated a single dish and

everything has been served exquisitely. But, tell me, why have you not yet given us that queen of dishes, sovereign pie?"

Long-nose was dismayed, for he had never heard of sovereign pie. But he thought quickly and replied, "I had hoped, Your Highness, that we should long enjoy the honour of your presence at my master's court, and I had planned to serve this dish on the day of your departure."

"And have you been saving it for my departure, too?" laughed the Duke. "Why haven't I been treated to this rare dish? See that it is on the table tomorrow!"

"As you wish, my lord," said

Long-nose and withdrew.

His heart was heavy, for he did not know how to make the pie. He went up to his room and, weeping bitterly, told Milushka of his misfortune.

"Have no fear," she said. "Sovereign pie was often served at my father's table and I think I can remember what went into it. Even if it isn't exactly as it should be, their lordships will never notice."

Long-nose jumped for joy and listened carefully while Milushka described the recipe. Then he set to work. He made a small amount to begin with and asked the head cook for his opinion of it. The cook

tasted it and praised the new dish to the skies. The next day, Long-nose made some more of the pie, placed it on a silver dish, garnished it with flowers, and sent it to the Duke's table. He then changed into his best clothes and went up to the hall. The head carver was just slicing the pie. He handed a portion to the Duke and to his guest. The Duke took a good mouthful, turned his eyes up to the ceiling, swallowed it, and cried, "Well, well, this really is the queen of dishes, and Long-nose is the king of cooks! Don't you agree, my friend?"

The Prince took a small morsel, chewed it thoughtfully for a moment, and then a crafty smile crept over his face.

"It is certainly well prepared," he said, pushing his plate away, "but something is missing from it."

The Duke frowned formidably, and reddened with anger.

"Why, you dog!" he shouted at Long-nose. "How dare you serve your master like this! I'll have your head cut off!"

"But my lord," Long-nose defended himself, "I prepared the pie according to the rules of my art and I am sure I left nothing out."

"You lie, you scoundrel!" roared

the Duke. "I'll have you chopped into little pieces and roasted like this pie!"

Long-nose, fell to his knees in front of the Prince.

"Have mercy, noble sir," he cried, "and tell me what the pie lacks. Do not let me die."

"It won't help you much if I do, my dear Long-nose," said the Prince, with a laugh. "I knew yesterday that you wouldn't be able to prepare the dish as my cook does. You need a special herb to give it the right flavour, and that you will never find."

The Duke was furious.

"I must have it at all costs," he

raged, his eyes flashing. "I swear on my honour as a nobleman that you will be served with this dish tomorrow, or else you will see this fellow's head impaled on the palace gate." He turned to Long-nose. "Go! You have twenty-four hours."

The little cook returned to his room where Milushka was waiting for him. The poor goose was very apologetic, having failed to remember the herb in the recipe. She said that it was very rare and only blossomed at night by the light of the full moon.

"There is a full moon tonight," Long-nose cried hopefully.

"In that case," said the goose,

"there is no time to lose."

She asked if there were any old chestnut trees near the palace, for it was there, near the roots, that the herb was usually to be found.

"Yes," replied Long-nose, feeling his spirits begin to rise again. "Near the lake, two hundred paces from the palace, there is a row of chestnut trees."

"Come quickly, then; we'll go and look for it," said Milushka.

Long-nose picked up the goose and they left the palace.

At the gate they were stopped by the guard, who said that he had strict orders not to let Long-nose leave the grounds.

"But surely I can go to the garden?" he asked.

This the guard permitted, for the garden was surrounded by a high wall and there was no fear that he would escape. When they came to the garden, Long-nose put Milushka gently on the ground and she waddled in front of him toward the lake, where the chestnut trees grew. He followed her with a heavy heart. This was his last hope. If they failed to find the herb, he decided he would fling himself into the lake rather than face his cruel punishment. For a long time the goose searched under the chestnuts, turning over every

leaf with her beak, but in vain.

Just as Long-nose was about to give up the search in despair and abandon himself to his fate, he caught site of a huge old tree looming black in the moonlight at the other end of the lake. They set off toward it, the goose hopping and flying ahead and Long-nose following as fast as his legs would carry him. All at once the goose stopped, flapped her wings joyfully, poked her beak into the long grass, and pulled up a plant. She handed it to her companion saying, "Here is the herb! Look, it's growing everywhere; you will be well stocked."

BRING ME A BOOK™

This Book Has Been Chosen For You by Kay Goines

LITTLE
LONG-NOSE

WILHELM HAUFF

illustrated by

LAURA STODDART

CANDLEWICK PRESS
CAMBRIDGE, MASSACHUSETTS

Long-nose stared at the herb. The short stalk bore a flame-coloured flower with yellow edges. A sweet scent came from it, reminding him of the day of his enchantment.

"I think this is the very herb that transformed me," he cried. "I shall try it straight away."

"Wait!" said Milushka. "Pick some of the flowers, but then we must go back to your room. You can try out the power of the herb when you have gathered together your money and possessions."

They made their way back to the palace. Long-nose was trembling with excitement. He tied his possessions into a bundle and heaved a deep sigh.

"Now, at last," he said, "perhaps I shall rid myself of this curse."

He breathed deeply the scent of the magic flower.

A powerful shudder passed through his limbs; he felt his neck stretching, his nose shrinking, and his whole body straightening.

The goose watched him in amazement. "How handsome you are," she cried.

Jacob, deeply moved, clasped his hands in prayer. Then he turned to Milushka and said, "To you I owe my freedom. I shall repay my debt by taking you back to your father.

He will surely be able to free you from your spell."

The goose thanked him and wept tears of joy. They slipped out of the palace undetected and made their way toward the coast, where they boarded a ship for Milushka's country.

Do I need to relate how they safely reached Milushka's home, where the wizard Thunderclap lifted the curse on his daughter;

how Jacob took his
departure, richly rewarded;
how he returned to his
home town and to his
parents, who were overjoyed
to learn that this handsome
young man was their long-lost son;
how with the gifts he had been
given by Thunderclap he bought a
large shop and lived in happiness
and prosperity?

I shall tell only this: that after
Jacob's disappearance from the
palace, a desperate search took
place. Everyone joined in the hunt
for the Duke's little cook. The
Prince accused the Duke of hiding
Long-nose in order to save his best

cook from death, and of failing to keep his word. The quarrel led to a war between the two states, the greatest in living memory. When peace was finally declared it was celebrated with a huge feast attended by both rulers and their

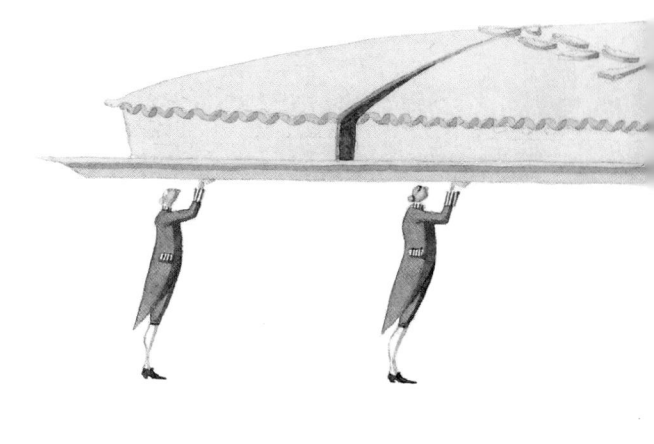

courts, at which the Prince's cook
served on gold platters a delicious
sovereign pie, which everyone
enjoyed very much.

Which only goes to show how
trivial events may have great and
far-reaching consequences.

In memory of
Amy Wingate-Saul
L. S.

Other Candlewick Treasures:

The Canterville Ghost
Elsie Piddock Skips in Her Sleep
The Lord Fish • *Rikki-tikki-tavi*
A White Heron

This text is based on translations by
Jean Rosemary Edwards and Percy E. Pinkerton

Illustrations copyright © 1997 by Laura Stoddart

First U.S. edition 1997

Library of Congress Cataloging-in-Publication Data
Hauff, Wilhelm, 1802-1827.
Little Long-nose / Wilhelm Hauff ; illustrated by Laura Stoddart.
— 1st U. S. ed. (Candlewick treasures)
Summary: After unwisely insulting a disagreeable old woman in
the market, Jacob is persuaded to help carry her purchases home
and unknowingly falls under a spell that lasts seven years and
drastically changes his appearance.
ISBN 0-7636-0327-9
[1. Fairy tales. 2. Dwarfs—Fiction.] I. Stoddart, Laura, ill.
II. Hauff, Wilhelm, 1802-1827. Dwarf Nose. III. Title. IV. Series.
PZ8.H293Li 1997
[Fic]—dc21 96-29534

2 4 6 8 10 9 7 5 3 1

Printed in Italy

This book was typeset in Truesdell.
The pictures were done in watercolor.

Candlewick Press
2067 Massachusetts Avenue
Cambridge, Massachusetts 02140

Walter Leuthold

African Ungulates

A Comparative Review of Their Ethology
and Behavioral Ecology

With 55 Figures

Springer-Verlag
Berlin Heidelberg New York 1977

Dr. WALTER LEUTHOLD
Zurich, Switzerland,
formerly Research Zoologist
and Acting Chief Biologist
Kenya National Parks

ISBN 3–540–07951–3 Springer-Verlag Berlin Heidelberg New York
ISBN 0–387–07951–3 Springer-Verlag New York Heidelberg Berlin

Library of Congress Cataloging in Publication Data. Leuthold, Walter, 1940–. African
ungulates. (Zoophysiology and ecology; v. 8). Bibliography: p. Includes index. 1. Ungulata—Behavior. 2. Ungulata—Africa. 3. Mammals—Behavior. 4. Mammals—Africa.
I. Title. QL737.U4L48.599′.3′045.76.44535.

Typesetting, printing and bookbinding: Zechnersche Buchdruckerei, Speyer.

Preface

This book has been written mostly within sight of wild African ungulates, at the research center in Tsavo East National Park, Voi, Kenya. While this had many positive aspects, there were also a few drawbacks. The main one of these is the fact that Voi is not exactly at the hub of scientific activity, even if we restrict ourselves to African ungulates. Thus, whereas I had felt initially that I was sufficiently familiar with ethological work on these animals to write a useful review, it soon became woefully evident that this assumption was erroneous. Over the last few years studies on African ungulates have proliferated and results are being published in journals almost all over the world. My location in East Africa was sometimes less than ideal with respect to access to the most recent literature, and I depended to a considerable extent on the goodwill of colleagues in giving or lending me relevant papers. I am happy to report that I received a great deal of support and cooperation in this respect. Nevertheless, I may have overlooked some important papers inadvertently; their authors should not feel slighted by such omissions, which only reflect availability of literature to me.

Readers may also notice a considerable geographical bias in favor of East Africa, at the expense of other African regions, particularly South Africa. This results mainly from my personal background, for while I have been fortunate enough to live and work in East Africa for close to ten years, I have not visited other parts of Africa. On the other hand it is fair to say that, at least until quite recently, most field work on African ungulates was carried out in East Africa.

One or two practical points may be noted here: (1) Crossreferences to different sections of the text are made by means of the section numbers given in the Table of Contents and the respective section headings. (2) Scientific names of the ungulates mentioned in the text are given in the Systematic Index, alongside the English names. (3) The frequent reference to national parks and other protected areas has necessitated the use of the abbreviations "NP" for national park and "GR" for game reserve.

It is a pleasure to acknowledge the valuable cooperation and assistance extended to me by many colleagues who talked or corresponded with me, sent me their reprints and reports, or drew my attention to research workers and literature previously unknown to me. Over the years, I have benefited considerably from discussions with numerous colleagues, among whom I wish to mention specifically Drs. R. D. Estes, P. J. Jarman, J. B. Sale and F. R. Walther. I am grateful to Prof. J. D. Skinner (Pretoria) for his valuable services with respect to literature from Southern Africa, and to Messrs. R. Underwood (Pretoria) and J. C. Hillman (Nairobi), who made available unpublished material from their studies on eland. I particularly wish to thank Dr. M. R. Stanley-Price, for a time my "next-door neighbor" to the east (some 80 km away), who not only lent me several unpublished theses in his possession, but very kindly undertook to read the first draft of this book and made numerous useful suggestions for its improvement.

The following kindly provided photographs for inclusion in this book: Mr. J. Bernegger, Dr. J. H. M. David, Dr. and Mrs. I. Douglas-Hamilton, Dr. R. D. Estes, Dr. S. C. J. Joubert, Prof. and Mrs. H. Klingel, Dr. H. Kruuk, Mr. and Mrs. D. L. W. Sheldrick. (Photographs not otherwise identified are my own). I am also grateful for the use of several of the splendid drawings by Dr. Fritz Walther. A number of figures were drawn by my wife Barbara, who also did the first critical reading of the text. For permission to reproduce figures previously published elsewhere I am indebted to Messrs. A. A. Balkema (Cape Town/Rotterdam), Blackwell Scientific Publications (Oxford), E. J. Brill (Leiden), IUCN (Morges), P. Parey (Berlin and Hamburg), Institut Scientifique de Madagascar (Paris). I am also grateful to the Springer-Verlag, and to Dr. K. F. Springer personally, for the understanding shown for my problems.

The Trustees and Director of the then Kenya National Parks permitted me to write this book while being in their employment as research biologist in Tsavo National Park. Mr. M. B. Owaga, Secretary at the Tsavo Research Project, ably undertook the laborious task of typing the final manuscript.

On the more personal level, I wish to thank my wife and children for their patience and forbearance shown on the many evenings and week-ends when I was "unavailable".

Perhaps the greatest debt of gratitude I owe to the one who first introduced me to the fascinating world of African ungulates and who played an important part in my professional and personal education; regrettably, he died prematurely, of a malicious ailment, some months ago. In grateful recognition, I wish to dedicate this book to the memory of Helmut K. Buechner.

January, 1977

Voi, Kenya, and
Zurich, Switzerland   WALTER LEUTHOLD

Contents

Introduction

The mammalian fauna of Africa, and particularly its ungulate component, has evolved to a variety and multitude unparalleled elsewhere—at least in recent times—both in terms of different species and of sheer numbers. Its diversity and profusion have greatly impressed Western man ever since he began invading and colonizing Africa, and continue to do so to the present day. Until quite recently, large tracts of land, with their natural habitats and their wild animals, have remained relatively unaffected by "civilization", but the latter is advancing inexorably in all directions, and truly "wild places" become ever harder to find. Yet, at the same time, Western man experiences a growing need for just such places, to escape from his overpopulated and polluted surroundings and to re-establish some long-lost contact with "nature." The recent upsurge of tourism in many African countries bears witness to this need, and the African ungulates contribute a large share in attracting this tourism, which provides substantial earnings for the host countries.

During the last few decades, the survival of large assemblages of wild animals in natural surroundings has become increasingly threatened by the unchecked expansion of the human population and its activities. Several forms of ungulates, as well as other animals, have become endangered or even extinct, particularly in the southernmost parts of Africa, where man's impact has been especially severe.

This development has attracted the attention of conservationists all over the world, who have called for the establishment of national parks and similar reserves containing representative portions of the highly varied habitats of Africa and their associated fauna. Fortunately, these calls have not fallen on deaf ears, and many African statesmen have taken an active interest and positive action with regard to conservation moves in their countries. While the colonial governments did—rather belatedly in many cases—set up national parks in the territories under their administration, many additional parks and reserves have been created by the new African governments after their independence. This fact is often overlooked when people in Europe and America call for more protective measures, conveniently forgetting their own past sins in this respect. More direct assistance to African countries, most of them economically poor, from the so-called developed nations to increase conservation measures where necessary, should be accorded high priority, in the interest of all mankind.

Various problems, i. e., ecological imbalances, etc., in national parks, have demonstrated that, to achieve its aims, conservation needs to be based on a substantial fund of scientific background knowledge, both ecological and ethological. The latter is especially necessary for purposes of animal husbandry, either involving captive animals in zoos, safari parks, etc., or in the context of game

1

ranching. Zoological parks and similar institutions play an increasingly important role in the preservation and breeding of endangered species, including ungulates. In the circumstances of captivity, where man is in close contact with originally wild animals, he must be able to understand and interpret their behavior, both to prevent accidents to himself and to cater for the animals' well-being. Game ranching is often considered to be a potentially important form of land use and meat production in areas unsuitable for agriculture or conventional ranching (though this remains yet to be proved in practice), the main argument being that indigenous ungulates are better adapted to local conditions than exotic species such as cattle and goats. Behavioral factors may have an important bearing on productivity under semidomestic conditions, and knowledge of the behavior of certain ungulates under natural conditions is therefore essential in this context.

Apart from these practical aspects, there have always been purely scientific interest and curiosity that have spurred man on to pursue ethological studies of African ungulates and other mammals. Research into behavioral adaptations to environment and into social structures of various species may contribute ultimately to a better understanding of man's own behavior and sociology.

As a result of the relatively recent awakening of conservation-oriented interest in the large mammal fauna of Africa, there has been a "flurry" of field research in the last two decades. Numerous studies of individual species have been undertaken and their results published in various scientific journals. There have, however, been few attempts at relating the various different studies together in a unified framework. This book is intended to help to fill this gap, at least with regard to the ethology of ungulates. Rather than giving detailed descriptions of the behavior of individual species—which are available in the original papers—I have tried to emphasize the comparative point of view and to stress the adaptive aspects of ungulate behavior, particularly in an ecological context. Not the least of my hopes is that this book, by summarizing information not easily accessible to many, will contribute toward the conservation of the magnificent African ungulate fauna.

Part 1
General Background

Chapter 1

African Habitats

The great variety of African ungulates, and other mammals, is doubtless related to the almost infinite diversity of habitats on this continent. In turn, the variety of habitats is linked to the fact that Africa extends over about 60° latitude, almost equally far north as south of the equator, and consequently over a number of different climatic zones. The latitudinal spread is matched by the altitudinal one, ranging from sea level to almost 6,000 m above sea level (Mt. Kilimanjaro).

In the following, "Africa" means the entire African continent less its extreme northwest portion, the area known as Barbary (to the north of, and including, the Atlas mountains). The present-day mammal fauna of that area is closely allied to that of Eurasia and cannot be considered as truly African, in a biogeographical sense, although this may not always have been so (cf. Bigalke, 1968). Figure 1 shows Africa's main biotic zones, i.e., climato-vegetational complexes that can be usefully distinguished in biogeographical and ecological discussions. With considerable oversimplification one can say that the vegetation of Africa is arranged in "concentric belts of increasingly dry and sparse vegetation" around an equatorial belt of lowland evergreen forest (Moreau, 1966). Deviations from this general pattern are caused primarily by the surface relief, in particular by the relatively high elevations of large parts of eastern and southern Africa. Keeping this in mind, we may distinguish the following broad vegetation types:

Lowland Forest. This is evergreen forest with a closed canopy in areas of year-round high rainfall and humidity, as well as relatively minor fluctuations in temperature, both on an annual and a daily basis. In the main, these forests are confined to low-lying equatorial regions of Central and West Africa, primarily the Congo Basin and the West African coast and its immediate hinterland, with a noticeable gap between 0° and 3° eastern longitude, the so-called "Dahomey Gap." Elsewhere, similar forest types occur locally under suitable conditions, e.g., along the coast of eastern and southern Africa or in the vicinity of lakes and rivers where the groundwater table is high.

Montane Forest. While structurally similar to lowland forest, montane forest is associated with a considerably cooler climate and marked fluctuations of daily temperatures. The hills and mountains that it covers, usually above about 1,500 m a.s.l., are often shrouded in mist and clouds; this perpetual moisture is largely responsible for the profuse development of arboreal lichens, and some other epiphytes, that often characterize these "cloud forests." Higher up, the forests gradually merge into bamboo thickets and other vegetation types of the Afro-Alpine zone. Montane forests are widely distributed, in many isolated "islands," over much of Africa, particularly the eastern half (Fig. 1).

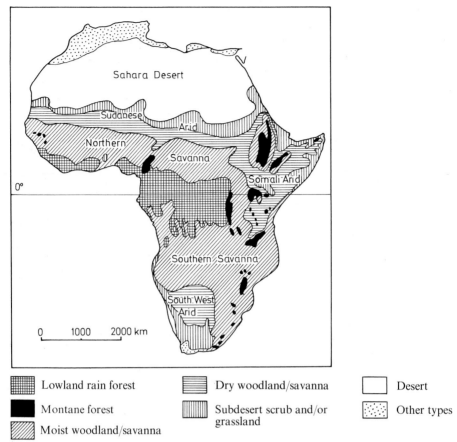

Lowland rain forest	Dry woodland/savanna	Desert
Montane forest	Subdesert scrub and/or grassland	Other types
Moist woodland/savanna		

Fig. 1. The main biotic zones and vegetation types of Africa (after Davis, 1962; Cloudsley-Thompson, 1969)

Savanna. This rather loose term embraces a great variety of habitats, all characterized by an interspersion of grasslands with varying densities of trees and/or bushes. Climatically, savannas occur in a wide range of conditions, from subhumid zones bordering on lowland forest to semi-arid ones adjacent to subdesert. The moister savannas comprise relatively dense woodlands with a thick tall-grass understorey, as for instance the "miombo" *(Brachystegia)* woodlands of south-central Africa. At the other extreme are dry woodlands composed mainly of relatively small trees and with only a poorly developed understorey, exemplified by the *Commiphora-Acacia* woodlands ("thornbush") of northeastern Africa. At their fringes, these woodlands merge into subdesert scrub vegetation.

Pure Grassland. This vegetation type is largely confined to some higher areas of southern Africa with a relatively cool climate, where few or no trees grow, but a continuous permanent grass cover exists ("high veld"). It occupies a small zone at the border between Southern Savanna and South West Arid Zone (Fig. 1). More or less extensive areas of pure grassland also occur locally elsewhere (e.g., the Serengeti Plains in Tanzania).

6

Subdesert and Desert. Characterized by low and erratic rainfall, these areas support little or no vegetation. Outside the Sahara, subdesert and desert occur in parts of the Somali Arid (Somalia, Ethiopia, northern Kenya) and South West Arid Zones (Kalahari, Namib in South and South West Africa).

This characterization of vegetation types is, by necessity, greatly simplified, and considerable diversity exists within them, particularly those lumped under the heading "savanna." Also, vegetational transitions being very gradual in most cases, boundaries drawn between vegetation types are always somewhat arbitrary.

In addition to the factors of the physiographic environment man has, through his activities such as agriculture, pastoralism and the use of fire, modified the original vegetation of many areas to a greater or lesser extent. In particular, many originally small areas of forest have been considerably reduced or completely destroyed within the last 50–100 years, e.g., along the coast of eastern and southern Africa (essentially lowland forest) or in parts of the East African highlands (montane forest). Furthermore, the southward advance of the Sahara desert over the past few decades is probably attributable in large part to human activities, although a long-term trend toward drier climatic conditions may also be involved (Cloudsley-Thompson, 1974).

Space does not permit a more detailed description of the various vegetation types of Africa; for further information I would refer the reader to Keay (1959), Brown (1965/66), Cloudsley-Thompson (1969), Hedberg and Hedberg (1968), and especially to Moreau (1966). Kingdon (1971) and Lind and Morrison (1974) deal with East Africa only, but in rather more detail.

One other aspect is, however, important in the present context: the past changes in climate and vegetation of Africa. Palaeobotanic evidence, mainly from the analysis of fossil pollen, indicates that the climate, and with it the extent of various vegetation types, fluctuated considerably during the Pleistocene (van Zinderen Bakker, 1962; van Zinderen Bakker and Coetzee, 1972). According to these (and other) authors, certain periods, probably corresponding with glacial phases of the northern hemisphere, were characterized by lower mean temperatures in much of Africa, compared to present conditions. Van Zinderen Bakker (1962) believed that the lower temperatures—in the order of 5°C less than today—were associated with increased humidity, which would have resulted in the expansion of moisture-dependent vegetation types, particularly montane forests (see also Moreau, 1966). More extensive and more recent evidence seems to indicate, however, that the reverse actually occurred, i. e., that lower temperature was correlated with more arid conditions (van Zinderen Bakker and Coetzee, 1972). Whichever view applies, repeated temperature changes appear to be well-documented and must have influenced considerably the extent and distribution of different vegetation types at different times, and that in the geologically recent past (see also discussion by Hamilton, in Lind and Morrison, 1974).

Thus, we may probably view the Pleistocene in Africa as being characterized by alternate advancing and receding of different vegetation types. These changes had important effects on the distribution of animals, including ungulates, as we shall see in Chapter 2. On a continent-wide scale, we may summarize these developments as follows: on the basis of present-day rainfall records there

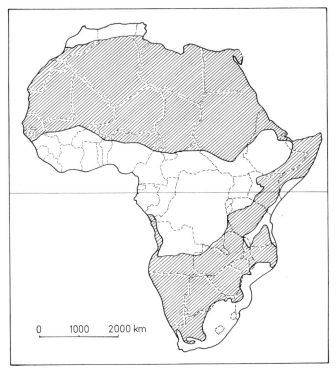

Fig. 2. The drought corridor in Africa. *Hatching:* areas with marked dry seasons, in which mean monthly rainfall is less than 10 mm in at least three consecutive months (after Balinsky, 1962)

is a relatively narrow zone, extending from South West Africa northeastward to Somalia, within which there is a pronounced dry season of at least three consecutive months with less than 10 mm average monthly rainfall (Fig. 2). The existence of this "drought corridor" (Balinsky, 1962) limits the distribution of moisture-dependent vegetation types and their associated fauna. Along with the climatic changes of the Pleistocene, the drought corridor is likely to have expanded and shrunk alternatively. During periods of its expansion, subdesert and dry savanna vegetation extended over much larger areas than before or afterward, enabling elements of the present Somali and South West Arid Zones (Fig. 1) to come into contact or even be exchanged. During moister phases, the drought corridor would have been narrowed, perhaps even interrupted in places, allowing elements of moist savanna and of lowland forest to move farther to the east (or west) and bridge the gap between the Congo Basin and the east coast. The intermediate montane forest areas (Fig. 1) would have expanded at such times and facilitated the east-west exchange. Numerous examples of disjunct distribution of both plants and animals provide indirect evidence for these past events (e.g., Balinsky, 1962; Verdcourt, 1969), and many cases of sibling species, subspecies or even conspecific populations that now occur in distant localities, separated by large unoccupied areas, can only be explained when related to past climatic changes (Meester, 1965; Bigalke, 1968; Moreau, 1966).

Chapter 2

The Ungulate Fauna of Africa

The term "ungulates," as used in this book, includes the orders Proboscidea (elephants), Perissodactyla (odd-toed ungulates) and Artiodactyla (even-toed ungulates). I have already alluded to the great variety of ungulates occurring in Africa; this has caused considerable problems for taxonomists, and the nomenclature of African ungulates is by no means settled, particularly in the family Bovidae (horned ungulates). For practical purposes, I have followed the most recent taxonomic treatment by Ansell (1971) and Gentry (1971), without necessarily agreeing on every detail. The Appendix lists the species mentioned in the text, with scientific names, in systematic order. Scientific equivalents of common names used in the text can be found in the Index. General information on distribution and biology of African ungulates is available in a number of handbooks and field guides, particularly Dorst and Dandelot (1970; see also Bigalke, 1968).

The three orders mentioned comprise a total of 90 species (a few more or less if a different taxonomy were used). Outstanding among major taxa is the family of the Bovidae which alone accounts for 75 species (see Appendix), ranging in size from the tiny royal antelope (3–4 kg) to the African buffalo (males up to 850 kg). This diversity of forms calls for some explanation. Partly, it can probably be accounted for by the sheer size of the African continent and, in particular, by the great variety of habitats occurring within it, as outlined in the preceding chapter. In addition, the climatic changes discussed above, with their effects on vegetation and animal distribution, probably favored radiation by repeatedly cutting off segments of species populations from one another. This can be inferred from the fact that there are many examples of closely related species or subspecies occurring in different parts of the continent, particularly those most affected by the drought corridor referred to above, and its changes. Such areas are primarily the Northern and Southern Savannas (Fig. 1), which may have been separated from each other by forest during moister phases, and the Somali and South West Arid Zones, lying at either end of the drought corridor. Table 1 lists pairs of corresponding species or subspecies in these areas (see also Meester, 1965 and Bigalke, 1968).

On the other hand, there are a few examples of species now occurring in widely separated areas without having developed into clearly distinct forms, e. g., the white rhinoceros, the mountain reedbuck and possibly steinbuck. Some caution is, however, necessary in interpreting distribution patterns, as present-day ranges of some species may be only small remnants of their former ranges within historical times, particularly in southern Africa where the reduction of ungulates (and other wild animals) has been especially severe.

Table 1. Pairs or groups of corresponding species and/or subspecies in northern and southern savannas and/or arid zones

A. Savannas	
Northern	Southern
Giant eland	Common eland
Kob	Puku
Nile lechwe	Lechwe (red and black)
Bohor reedbuck	Southern reedbuck
Western hartebeest	Lichtenstein's and red hartebeests
Topi/Tiang	Tsessebe (Bontebok/Blesbok?)

B. Arid zones	
Somali	South-West
Grévy's zebra	Mountain zebra (incl. Hartmann's)
Grant's (and other) gazelles	Springbok
Beisa and fringe-eared oryx	"Gemsbok" (South African oryx)
Kirk's dikdik	Damaraland dikdik

Ecologically, the great variety of habitats has generated a wide range in degrees of specialization. The majority of African ungulates live in one type or another of savanna; most of the species with the widest distribution are savanna animals, for instance the warthog, bush pig, bushbuck, waterbuck and bush duiker. Perhaps the least specialized ungulate (or shall we say the most versatile?), in terms of habitat requirements, is the African elephant, occurring from lowland and montane forests through all kinds of savanna to areas bordering on subdesert. Its geographical and ecological distribution is approximated by that of the African buffalo which, however, does not advance as far into arid areas.

On the other hand, some species show pronounced adaptation (and restriction) to rather specialized habitats; in some cases, this is coupled with a very small species range, as in the mountain nyala (upper montane forests and heathlands of Ethiopia), the lowland nyala (low-lying, near-coastal dense bush in southeastern Africa), or the Nile lechwe (swamps of the upper Nile and some tributaries). By contrast, the sitatunga has a wide distribution despite very specialized habitat requirements (mainly papyrus swamps).

A considerable number of ungulate species are restricted to dense forest, some occurring in lowland forest only (e. g., pygmy hippopotamus, water chevrotain, okapi, Jentink's, banded and some other duikers, royal antelope), others in both lowland and montane forests (giant forest hog, bongo, yellow-backed and a few other duikers). Somewhat surprisingly, no ungulate species inhabits exclusively montane forest, with the possible exception of Abbott's duiker, a close relative of the yellow-backed duiker, and the mountain nyala which, however, occurs chiefly above the montane forest zone. This lack of endemics of montane forests suggests that, perhaps, the extent of these forests fluctuated so much and until so recently that little or no radiation beyond the subspecies level took place (in contrast to birds; see Moreau, 1966).

Even in a number of cases of savanna forms one must assume that the separation of now different forms is relatively recent and that phylogenetic divergence is in an early stage. This is particularly evident in some related forms of the Northern and Southern Savannas (cf. Table 1) which are treated as subspecies by some taxonomists and as full species by others. A good example is the hartebeest, with a number of northern forms generally considered subspecies, including *major, lelwel, jacksoni, cokii* and others, and the southern representatives *caama* and *lichtensteini*. The latter is classified as a separate species in the system followed here, but other treatments are equally justifiable and have been proposed in the past (e. g., Haltenorth, 1963).

A surprising number of African ungulates are adapted to life under fairly to very arid conditions. Their specializations entail virtual independence of free water, coupled with the ability to extract sufficient water from low-quality food through metabolic processes, and in some cases high mobility, enabling the animals to take advantage of irregularly distributed rainfall. However, very little is known about the biology, including ethology, of these arid-land species, with only a few exceptions. Among those adapted to the most extreme conditions are addax, scimitar-horned oryx, dama and dorcas gazelles, whereas several other gazelles, springbok, beira, dikdiks, beisa and southern oryx ("gemsbok") occur in environments that are only slightly more favorable. It would be interesting to know more about specific behavioral adaptations in such species, but the obstacles to studying them in the wild have so far discouraged potential field workers.

Many species of African ungulates have a very limited distribution, for which often no reason is immediately apparent. Such species occur in widely differing habitats, such as lowland forest (pygmy hippopotamus, okapi, Jentink's and banded duikers), dry savanna or bush country (dibatag, Hunter's hartebeest, some dikdik species) and subdesert or desert (Speke's gazelle, beira). In most cases, apparently suitable habitat would be available over areas much larger than the species' ranges. Their restriction to relatively small areas is probably related to the climatic and faunal histories of the areas concerned which, in general, are but poorly known, as well as to the influence of man, particularly in more recent times.

An interesting phenomenon is the fact that within a few species, or higher taxa, there are pairs of related forms showing quite different adaptations, one being a forest inhabitant, the other a savanna animal. Such pairs are, within species, forest/savanna elephant and forest/savanna buffalo, and within higher taxa, pygmy/common hippopotamus and okapi/giraffe. In all cases, the savanna form shows various characteristics of higher evolution, including larger size. Unfortunately, little behavioral information is available on any of the forest forms, apart from some observations in captivity, so that no meaningful ethological comparisons can be made at present.

Obviously, it is impossible to give a complete account of the multitude of African ungulates in a few pages. The main purpose of this brief survey is to draw attention again to the great diversity of forms and the various degrees of specialization and adaptation to an almost endless variety of habitats.

Chapter 3

Ethological Research on African Ungulates

A. Historical Review

Ethology is a relatively young branch of biology; its initial efforts were directed primarily toward birds and fishes, while mammals received attention only at a later stage (cf. Ewer, 1968). It took even more time before ethologists began to study the behavior of free-ranging mammals. Despite the fascination of many European travellers in Africa with the astounding diversity of ungulates and other mammals, serious studies in the wild only started within the last two or three decades. Some of the early hunter-naturalists collected voluminous notes on the "habits" of wild ungulates, but a considerable portion of this information was biased by preconceived notions and/or subjective interpretations. This is not to say that these early writings are useless, but it is difficult for the present-day student to distinguish reliable from unreliable reports without actually engaging in extensive observations himself.

Field ethology, with emphasis on large mammals, was pioneered in Africa by Hediger (1951) who undertook a scientific mission to the national parks of the then Belgian Congo in 1948. Two Belgian scientists followed suit: Verschuren, who was Hediger's assistant on the 1948 mission, and Verheyen, but their efforts remained relatively isolated. In East Africa, field research on ungulates was stimulated originally by ecological problems in the late 1950s: the Grzimeks' work in the Serengeti and that of several American Fulbright Scholars in Uganda's national parks and in Kenya (Petrides, Swank, Longhurst, Buechner). At about the same time, a few ethologically oriented studies began (Backhaus' on giraffe and lelwel hartebeest—actually in the Congo—and Buechner's on Uganda kob), and in the early 1960s there was a veritable "upsurge" of behavioral research on East African ungulates (Estes, Klingel, Schenkel, Frädrich, and others). In South Africa, systematic behavioral work started even later. However, as many studies, both in eastern and southern Africa, were initiated within a few years, information has accumulated rather rapidly since then, and this process is still continuing, if not accelerating.

Also in the late 1950s and early 1960s, several authors began detailed behavioral observations on African ungulates in captivity (Walther, Backhaus, Kühme, Trumler, Zeeb); their studies have been valuable especially with regard to behavior not easily observed in free-ranging animals, e. g., expressive, agonistic, and sexual behavior. In particular, Walther's comparative studies have led to the formulation of a theoretical framework relating to the evolution of bovid behavior.

In recent years, emphasis in field studies has, again, been more on ecological aspects, once it was clearly recognized that successful conservation measures

12

depend on an adequate understanding of ecological processes and interrelations. This has led to the establishment of several research institutions with a more or less coordinated program of studies according to priorities dictated by ecological problems and management requirements, e. g., the Serengeti Research Institute, Tsavo Research Project, Uganda Institute of Ecology (formerly Nuffield Unit of Tropical Animal Ecology), Kruger Park Research Unit, as well as research sections in various Game Departments and other conservation agencies. In this framework, there have been fewer strictly ethological studies, but a considerable amount of behavioral information has been collected in the course of primarily ecologically oriented research.

With an increasing body of ethological knowledge accumulating, a shift gradually occurred from a phase of mainly descriptive work toward one of functional interpretation of behavioral phenomena. The widespread occurrence of territoriality among African ungulates led to questions about its adaptive significance (e. g., Buechner, 1963; Spinage, 1974), and the great diversity of ecological adaptations and types of social organization prompted enquiries into the relationships between these two aspects of ungulate biology (e. g., Jarman, 1974; Estes, 1974). These are important steps in the direction of a unified biological approach, where the unfortunate division between disciplines is reduced and the close relations existing between ethology and ecology (e. g., Geist, 1968, 1971 a, b; Leuthold, 1970c) are fully recognized. Through the approach taken in this book I hope to contribute to this development.

B. Methods of Study

As in most ethological research, the primary method of study consists of prolonged visual observation and detailed recording, augmented by such technical aids as still and motion pictures and sound recordings. An increasingly important aspect has been the quantification of the data collected, so that hypotheses can be tested by means of statistical analyses. Experiments have rarely been carried out so far, partly because much descriptive work was required at first, and partly because of the physical difficulties of manipulating wild ungulates in experimental situations.

Ease of observation is probably the main factor that has influenced the choice of species for field studies. As a result, there is now a considerable body of information on ungulates living in grassland and fairly open savannas (e. g., zebra, warthog, several Alcelaphinae, some gazelles and the larger Reduncinae), whereas we still know rather little about bush-living species (bush pig, most Tragelaphini, gerenuk and dibatag) and next to nothing about true forest animals (giant forest hog, okapi, bongo, most duikers). The matter is further complicated by the fact that the majority of ungulates living in dense bush and forest are smaller than species of the open savanna, with some exceptions on both sides. About a few large open-country species little is known because they tend to be rather shy and unapproachable in most parts of their range, even in protected areas; such species include the eland, oryx and the Saharan species addax and scimitar-horned oryx. In the last two cases, recent persecution by man is the likeliest cause for their inaccessibility, apart from conditions in their habitat; but in oryx and eland the reasons are less easily understood.

The relatively new telemetric techniques (radio-tracking, etc.) promise to make it easier to obtain at least certain kinds of behavioral information on bush- and forest-dwelling ungulates. They have already proved to be of great value in tracing the movements of such highly mobile creatures as elephants (Leuthold and Sale, 1973) and migratory wildebeest (Inglis, 1976), and their application is increasing.

A factor of great importance for the study of movements and of social relationships is the possibility of recognizing individual animals. Natural characteristics, such as the shape of horns, cuts, scars and other defects of the ears or other parts of the body, can render individual recognition possible without necessitating resort to artificial means. Better still for this purpose are the permanent skin markings of some species, such as zebra, giraffe, Tragelaphines, which are as individually distinct as human fingerprints. However, in populations of very mobile and highly gregarious animals, this method is often not reliable or efficient enough, as known individuals do not stand out in any way from their groups. In such cases it is necessary to mark animals artificially, by means of ear tags, collars, paint, freeze-branding or radio-transmitters, to make certain individuals readily identifiable. To this end, animals have to be captured, and the method of choice has for some time been drug-immobilization, although traps, nets, and other mechanical devices may be more suitable for small species. Capture techniques using drugs delivered by projectile syringes were introduced to Africa by American researchers in the late 1950s (e. g., Buechner et al., 1960; Talbot and Lamprey, 1961) and were adapted and developed for various purposes within Africa mainly by Harthoorn (1965, 1970). Their use has facilitated many behavioral studies that could otherwise not have achieved what they did.

A considerable amount of ethological information on African ungulates has been derived from captive animals. Some caution is normally necessary in evaluating the findings of such studies. The conditions of captivity may alter certain aspects of the behavior of the animals concerned. The most important thing in this context is to be aware of this possibility and not to generalize too freely from one's findings. Behavior that is employed primarily in relation to the physical environment (i.e., most or all of the behavior reviewed in Chaps. 5 and 6) is likely to be affected to a greater or lesser extent by conditions of captivity. For example, activity patterns that may be influenced primarily by food supply, weather conditions and/or predation pressure in the wild are virtually always different in captivity, where they are generally determined by artificially imposed feeding times or forced movements between outdoor enclosures (daytime) and buildings (night).

On the other hand, all behavior for which a strong innate basis is known, or can be assumed, to exist is unlikely to be seriously modified in captivity. This probably applies to certain "basic" behaviors, such as locomotion and body care, as well as to much of the social behavior, at least at the level of the individual, viz. expressive, agonistic, sexual, and maternal behavior. Basic

14

postures, gestures or movements used in these contexts are likely to be largely invariable, whether the animal showing them is wild or captive. Thus, these behavior patterns may lend themselves well for comparative studies in captivity.

However, frequencies and intensities with which such behaviors are shown in captivity often differ markedly from the situation in the wild. This has two main reasons: (1) captive animals are generally relieved of the time-consuming search for food, and of guarding against predators, so that they have considerably more time to engage in other (e. g., social) activities that take a less prominent place in wild animals, (2) the spatial restrictions of captivity often result in much more frequent social interactions, which tend to be of higher intensity, than would normally be the case among free-ranging animals. Some examples will be given in different contexts below.

Thus, to summarize, the *form* of a given behavior may well be typical (i. e., species-specific) in captive animals, but not the *frequency* with which it occurs or, sometimes, the *circumstances* under which it is shown.

Apart from the limitations just discussed, studies on captive animals offer several important advantages: firstly, the observer can usually approach his subjects much more closely than is possible with wild animals. Thus, behavior can be recorded that might escape detection in free-ranging animals, e. g., low-intensity vocalizations, relatively minor expressive gestures, etc. Secondly, the fact that the observer does not constantly have to guard against disturbing the animals under observation considerably facilitates his work; also, he can be virtually certain of keeping the animals in sight for almost any length of time. Thirdly, for comparative purposes one can often obtain observations on many different species within a short time in captivity, which might be impossible with wild animals. And finally, even if results are sometimes of questionable value, work on captive animals provides invaluable training and observational experience, particularly for the beginner, which is bound to enhance the value of any field work done later. For further discussions of observing captive animals see Walther (1963a).

In this book observations on captive animals will be quoted extensively in contexts where (1) the conditions of validity stated above appear to be fulfilled, or (2) no other information is available. Observations from captivity are identified as such.

Chapter 4

Conservation

As mentioned briefly earlier, a considerable number of national parks and other reserves have been established throughout the African continent, the great majority of them within the last three decades. The obvious aim of this development is to preserve representative areas of "original Africa," containing as many different habitats and animal species as possible. While great progress has been made in this direction, it is by no means certain that the long-term future of these protected areas is assured. Much depends on, firstly, the socio-economic and political developments in the countries concerned, and secondly on ecological trends within present reserves. National parks can only continue to exist if the human population surrounding them can be convinced that it is advantageous to keep them, for one reason or another, and economic considerations will play an important role in this context for some time to come. Within reserves, large and powerful herbivores requiring great quantities of food have the capacity to alter their habitats substantially, to the possible detriment of other species. The effects of elephant and hippopotamus populations on the vegetation of several national parks in eastern and southern Africa have, for some time, caused considerable concern.

This is not the place to discuss such problems in detail; I merely wish to point out again that continuing research is required to monitor these developments, try to find explanations for them, and suggest possible remedies. While much of the research needed is primarily ecological in orientation, there is also room for more ethological studies, particularly where social relationships and other behavioral factors are involved in disturbances of a "natural" balance. This requires continuing rapprochement and interchange of ideas between "pure" ethology and "pure" ecology; the trend has already begun, as mentioned above, and is evident from a number of recent field studies (e. g., Sinclair, 1970, 1974; Jarman, 1974; Jarman and Jarman, 1973b, 1974; Estes, 1974).

Apart from their important role in conservation, national parks and other reserves have been vital in facilitating ethological research. Not only are they the places where wild ungulates still occur in relative abundance nowadays, but prolonged protection from hunting and the frequent contacts with man (or vehicles) as a result of increasing tourism have made possible a relatively close approach to many ungulates. This, of course, is an indispensable precondition for behavioral field studies depending, as they mostly do, on visual observation of undisturbed animals. By far the greatest proportion of recent ethological field work has been conducted in national parks and game reserves, and the advance of scientific knowledge in this field owes a great deal to the existence of these protected areas, and to their creators and custodians.

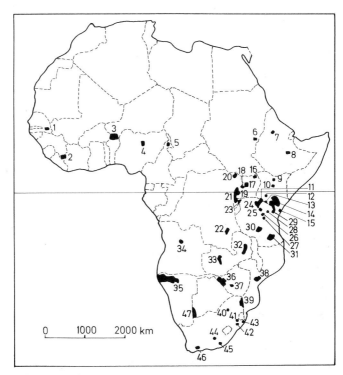

Fig. 3. Some of the better-known national parks (NP) and game reserves (GR) of Africa, including those mentioned in the text. Note that this is far from complete, and absence of markings in this map does not mean that there are no reserves in the country concerned (after Guggisberg, 1970)

Senegal:
1: Niokolo Koba NP

Guinea/Liberia
2: Mount Nimba Reserve

Niger/Dahomey/Upper Volta
3: W-du-Niger NP

Nigeria
4: Yankari GR

Cameroon
5: Waza NP

Sudan
6: Dinder NP

Ethiopia
7: Semien NP
8: Awash NP

Kenya
9: Marsabit National Res.
10: Samburu-Isiolo GR
11: Mara GR
12: Nairobi NP
13: Amboseli NP
14: Tsavo NP
15: Shimba Hills Nat. Res.

Uganda
16: Kidepo NP
17: Kabalega (Murchison Falls) NP
18: Toro GR
19: Ruwenzori (Queen Elizabeth) NP

Zaire
20: Garamba NP
21: Virunga (Albert) NP
22: Upemba NP

Rwanda
23: Akagera NP

Tanzania
24: Serengeti NP
25: Ngorongoro Crater
26: Lake Manyara NP
27: Tarangire NP
28: Arusha NP
29: Mkomazi GR
30: Ruaha NP
31: Selous GR

Zambia
32: Luangwa Valley NP
33: Kafue NP

Angola
34: Luando GR

South West Africa (Namibia)
35: Etosha Game Park

Rhodesia
36: Wankie NP
37: Rhodes Matopos NP

Mozambique
38: Gorongoza NP

South Africa
39: Kruger NP
40: Loskop Dam Nature Reserve
41: Hluhluwe GR
42: Umfolozi GR
43: Ndumu GR
44: Mountain Zebra NP
45: Addo Elephant NP
46: Bontebok NP
47: Kalahari Gemsbok NP

17

Chapter 5

Physical Maintenance Behavior

This category includes all behavior related to body maintenance, viz. feeding, drinking and elimination of waste products, and body care, viz. grooming, wallowing, etc. It is among these behaviors that many interrelationships with other aspects of a species' adaptations are particularly evident. For instance, the mode of food gathering and the degree of selectivity shown by an animal are related to body size and shape, functional morphology and anatomy of the digestive tract, mobility, habitat selection, etc. These aspects may be touched upon briefly in the following; they will be discussed more thoroughly in Chapter 19.

A. Feeding Behavior

Observers of the often complex communities of African herbivores have long been intrigued by the ways and means by which such communities maintain themselves in apparent harmony, i. e., without strong mutual competition over available resources. It is generally thought that the main principle operating in this context is that of ecological separation, based at least partly on differences in food habits of different species (e. g., Darling, 1960; Grzimek and Grzimek, 1960; Talbot and Talbot, 1962). A great number of feeding studies have been carried out to elucidate this principle, some on single species, others on several species comparatively (e. g., Stewart and Stewart, 1971; Bell, 1971; Jarman, 1971; Field, 1972; Stanley Price, 1974; Duncan, 1975; see also Hofmann and Stewart, 1972). Most of these studies have been concerned mainly with the ecological aspects of differentiated food habits. However, specific food habits are largely the result of differing behavioral responses by different animals to the same or a similar vegetation type, within a similar environment. In the following, we will discuss primarily the behavioral mechanisms that are important in the context of feeding and food habits. However, Ewer (1968) pointed out several years ago that little information is available on actual feeding behavior, and the situation has not changed much since.

Behavior related to feeding can conveniently be divided into the following aspects:

1. Mode of food gathering and ingestion
2. Degree and mechanisms of selectivity
3. Development of food habits during ontogeny.

Table 2. Classification of African ungulates according to food habits (based on Hofmann and Stewart, 1972)

Subgroup	Principal food	Species listed by Hofmann and Stewart	Other species possibly belonging to same category
1. Bulk and roughage eaters (i.e. grazers)			
a) Roughage grazers	grass throughout the year; relatively independent of free water	hartebeest, topi, fringe-eared oryx, mountain reedbuck	tsessebe, bontebok, plains (?), Grévy's and mountain zebras
b) Fresh grass grazers dependent upon water	(green) grass, some dicotyledons in dry season; drinking fairly regularly	waterbuck, kob, Bohor reedbuck, oribi, blue wildebeest, buffalo	lechwe, puku, southern reedbuck, black wildebeest, possibly sable and roan; hippopotamus, warthog, white rhinoceros
c) Dry region grazers	grass and occasionally some dicotyledons in arid zones	Beisa oryx	South African oryx, possibly scimitar-horned oryx and addax
2. Selectors of juicy, concentrated herbage (browsers)			
a) Tree and shrub foliage eaters	leaves, shoots, flowers and occasionally fruits of mainly woody plants	giraffe, bongo, gerenuk, greater and lesser kudu	nyala, dibatag, perhaps some of the dry-country gazelles; prob. okapi, black rhinoceros
b) Fruit and dicotyledonous foliage selectors	small nutritious items: fruits, leaves and shoots of forbs, shrubs and trees, rarely young grass	red duiker, bush duiker klipspringer, suni, dikdiks, bushbuck	other duikers, probably water chevrotain
3. Intermediate feeders			
a) Preferring grasses	grass, forbs and leaves of shrubs and trees; marked seasonal variations	impala, Thomson's gazelle	(elephant?)
b) Preferring forbs, shrub and tree foliage	leaves and shoots, also fruits, primarily of dicotyledons; occasionally grasses, particularly when young	Grant's gazelle, eland, steinbuck	springbok, other gazelle species, (elephant?)

I. Food Gathering and Ingestion

Herbivores are commonly divided into grazers, browsers, and mixed feeders. Grazers feed entirely or predominantly on grasses (Gramineae) and exclusively in the lower or lowest layers of vegetation; browsers feed largely or exclusively on dicotyledons and more commonly in the upper strata of vegetation (shrubs, trees), while mixed feeders derive various proportions of their diet from both categories of food plants. A more refined classification of feeding types among East African ruminants, based largely on comparative studies of stomach structure (Hofmann, 1968, 1973), has been suggested by Hofmann and Stewart (1972). It is summarized in Table 2, augmented by information on other ungulates (food habits only) where available.

Any classification of African ungulates by feeding habits will have to be qualified in various ways. Firstly, some species are more flexible than others, and food habits may differ considerably between populations in different parts of a species' range. For instance, the impala is classified as an "intermediate feeder preferring grasses" (Table 2) by Hofmann and Stewart (1972), partly on the basis of stomach structure. However, in the drier parts of their range impala are predominantly browsers, e.g., in the Selous Game Reserve (Rodgers, 1976), Tsavo National Park (pers. obs.) and South West Africa (Gaerdes, 1965). Secondly, many species show more or less marked seasonal variations in their diets, often characterized by relatively high proportions of grasses in the wet season and increasing reliance on dicotyledons, including evergreen plants, as the dry season progresses (e.g., Jarman, 1971, 1974; Hillman, 1976; Rodgers, 1976).

More recently, Jarman (1974) suggested a somewhat different classification of "feeding styles" of bovids, which is based more on the way food is collected than on what is actually eaten. One of the main differences between grass and browse as food (apart from the nutrient contents) is the dispersion of food items in the habitat. Grasses generally grow in dense "carpets" or thick bunches, while leaves and other parts of dicotyledonous plants are more widely separated. This, coupled with various morphological adaptations, largely determines the mode of ingestion and the entire way of feeding. Very generally speaking, grazers have broad, relatively undifferentiated muzzles, move slowly and over short distances only while feeding, and ingest a comparatively large quantity with each bite (examples: buffalo, wildebeest, hippopotamus, white rhinoceros). Browsers, on the other hand, have more pointed muzzles, very prehensile lips and highly mobile tongues, allowing them to pluck small individual items; they usually ingest a small quantity only with each bite and move about considerably while feeding (examples: giraffe, gerenuk, dikdik, black rhinoceros). Obviously, feeding styles are far more differentiated than this highly generalized picture indicates, and there are many intermediate types (mixed feeders). The feeding style is inter-related in many ways with various other aspects of a species' biology, particularly with spatial and social organization and with antipredator behavior (Jarman, 1974). This will be discussed more fully in Chapter 19.

Fig. 4. Gerenuk feeding in bipedal stance on hindlegs. This is normal behavior in this species (from Leuthold, 1971 c)

Ungulates show a variety of other morphological adaptations to feeding, which usually have behavioral correlates. One of the more conspicuous of these is the ability to rise up on the hindlegs and feed in a bipedal stance at a level that could not be reached on all four legs. This ability is particularly

Fig. 5. Elephant rising onto hindlegs to reach branches of tree to feed on. This is rare in the elephant (phot. J. Berneg-ger, Amboseli NP)

24

characteristic of gerenuk (Fig. 4) and dibatag, but a number of other ungulates also possess it although they may show it only rarely, e.g., dikdik (Tinley, 1969; Hendrichs and Hendrichs, 1971, Fig. 13), several gazelle species (Walther, 1968), springbok (Bigalke, 1972) and even the elephant (Plate 15 in Sikes, 1971; Fig. 13 in Croze, 1974; see Fig. 5). It is perhaps somewhat surprising that more species do not make use of the ability to rise up on the hindlegs, which at least the males must all possess for mating and which domestic goats show extensively in the context of feeding.

Digging, usually to obtain roots or bulbs, occurs in a number of ungulates employing different means: warthog use their elongated snout and nasal disk; elephants their tusks, sometimes also the trunk and/or forefeet; some bovids may also use their forefeet on occasions, for instance oryx (Shortridge, 1934; Root, 1972) or springbok (Shortridge, 1934; Bigalke, 1972). Oryx are also said to use their long pointed horns to pierce or cut pieces out of the large tubers of *Pyrenacantha malvifolia* (Icacinaceae), a stem succulent (Root, 1972). A captive eland used its horns to bend and break twigs off trees to eat them (Walther, 1966a, p. 59). Schenkel and Schenkel-Hulliger (1969, p. 56) observed a black rhinoceros pulling down an otherwise unattainable small tree with its "horns" in a similar fashion. On the whole, however, observations of ungulates using their horns deliberately in the context of feeding are very rare.

Perhaps the most specialized morphologic adaptations to feeding are found in the elephant. The combination of the highly mobile trunk and the hard hornlike tusks makes this species the most versatile ungulate, as far as the mode of food gathering and ingestion is concerned. (Both the trunk and the tusks have other functions as well, particularly in social behavior.) Perhaps as a consequence of this, the elephant as a species has one of the most varied diets of all herbivores; it also occupies the widest variety of habitats.

A few "oddities" in ungulate feeding behavior include meat-eating and bone-chewing. In some of the smaller antelope species, particularly in forest-dwelling duikers, cases of actual "predation" (e. g., killing and eating birds) have been reported, though mostly from captivity (Kurt, 1963; Grimm, 1970). A few other instances are quoted by Hediger (1951). Examination of stomach contents from wild water chevrotains indicates that a certain carnivorous tendency may be normal in this species (Dubost, 1964). Chewing of bones by ruminants has often been reported, in recent years mainly for giraffe (references in Leuthold and Leuthold, 1972) and sable antelope (Glover, 1968; Estes and Estes, 1969). It is usually assumed that, in this way, the animals obtain minerals that may be in short supply in their environment. A case of oryx eating ostrich eggs in South-West Africa (Sauer, 1970) perhaps also reflects a similar situation.

II. Selectivity

In addition to belonging to one of the generalized feeding types described above (grazer, browser, or mixed feeder), ungulates may select, to a greater or lesser degree, specific items from the vegetation available to them. Selection takes two main forms: (1) for plant species, and (2) for plant parts. Selection for plant species results in a more or less characteristic composition of a species' diet in a given habitat, while selection for plant parts appears to be aimed primarily at obtaining those components of a plant with the highest nutritive value.

Among grazers, selection for plant parts has been established through a number of quantitative studies of samples of stomach contents. Stems, leaves, and leaf sheaths of grasses differ in the structure of epidermal cells and can be differentiated microscopically on the basis of cuticular fragments (e. g., Stewart, 1965). In general, grass leaves have a higher protein content than stems (and vice versa for fiber) and are accordingly sought out preferentially by buffalo and grazing antelopes such as wildebeest, hartebeest and topi (Gwynne and Bell, 1968; Bell, 1971; Field, 1972; Sinclair and Gwynne, 1972; Stanley Price, 1974; Duncan, 1975).

Among browsers, selection for certain plant parts is more directly obvious in the field but has not been studied quantitatively. For example, gerenuk often sniff extensively over a potential food plant before actually plucking anything, or leaving it altogether. Such behavior is particularly pronounced in relation to shrubs with evergreen coriaceous leaves (e. g., some Capparaceae in Tsavo NP). The gerenuk apparently search for the youngest, most nutritious parts, mainly the tips of shoots, occasionally also flowers or young fruits. Little or no corresponding searching behavior is usually evident in relation to deciduous shrubs, in which the quality of leaves tends to be more uniform (Leuthold, 1970a).

Little is known yet on the actual mechanisms involved in food selection. The above observations on gerenuk, and some on other browsers as well as on captive antelopes (see below), suggest that olfaction is of primary importance, at least in browsers. As these animals generally feed well above ground level, searching behavior (e. g., sniffing) is easily observed, but in grazers it is much more difficult to detect. On the basis of his findings that topi select principally for grass leaves, almost regardless of their state and of species, Duncan (1975) suggested that they may respond primarily to mechanical properties of the vegetation on offer. As this kind of selection is rather important, both in relation to optimal use of food resources and to ecological separation, it would be important to obtain a better insight into the behavioral mechanisms involved.

III. Development of Food Habits During Ontogeny

While there is a considerable amount of information on what constitutes the natural diet of various ungulates (cf. Table 2), little is known on how the "proper" food habits are formed. Popular notion tends to accept that young animals "know instinctively" what to eat and what to leave, in other words implying that food selection is innate. However, animals of any given species show considerable variation in their food habits in different places (e. g., black rhinoceros: Goddard, 1968, 1970; gerenuk: Leuthold, 1970a). This means that the composition of the diet depends to some extent on what is available in any one habitat, and suggests that learning also plays a part in the formation of food habits. This assumption is supported further by the fact that most ungulates are relatively flexible in their food habits, to accommodate seasonal and local fluctuations in food supply, and that they can usually be induced to accept entirely strange foods, e. g., in captivity.

If learning is indeed important in the formation of food habits, one would expect it to be most pronounced in young animals. Experience with various—mainly captive—mammals lead Ewer (1968, p. 29) to conclude that "a young animal is usually more easily induced to accept strange foods than an adult, whose preferences are, to some extent, already determined." Also, adult animals "may be less flexible than the young and the process of changing food habits may require some time." To illustrate this, she gave an example (Ewer, 1968) of cattle in South Africa that had been raised in nearly grassless country and had "become browsers instead of grazers." When transferred to grassland areas, such cattle first lost condition until they had successfully adjusted their feeding behavior to the new vegetation type.

Thus, there is some evidence indicating that learning plays a part in the formation of food habits, but little is known of its actual importance and the mechanisms involved. When observing wild ungulates, one often gets the impression that a young animal follows its mother around as she feeds and investigates plants from which she eats, and may eventually eat them, too. This suggests that direct imitation of the mother, or perhaps another social partner, may be one mechanism by which young ungulates learn to recognize palatable food plants (cf. Fraser, 1968). This was largely confirmed in a series of experiments with two young captive antelopes, a gerenuk and a lesser kudu (Leuthold, 1971 b). The gerenuk was younger, considered the kudu as its "mother" and obviously imitated the latter's feeding to a considerable extent, so that it eventually ate several plant species that wild gerenuk apparently rejected. In another instance, a young buffalo reared in the company of black rhinoceros and elephant consumed a considerably higher proportion of browse than did wild buffalo in the same general area (though not in exactly the same habitat). This may have been a result of the buffalo calf imitating its social partners at an early age (Leuthold, 1972), the rhino and elephant being primarily browsers under prevailing circumstances.

While imitation of the mother or other companions may be one mechanism that acts to determine a young animal's food habits, it cannot be the only one. Young ungulates reared in isolation from conspecifics do not accept all plants as food but may be quite selective, as was the lesser kudu of the example mentioned above (Leuthold, 1971 b). For instance, he rejected several plant species that were eaten by wild conspecifics (Leuthold, 1971 a), but only in the dry season when choice was limited. Such species may be "second-rate" in terms of palatability and accepted as food only under conditions of food shortage. The mechanism employed in selection was obviously olfaction in the first instance; occasionally, rejection after tasting also occurred. These observations suggest that young ungulates do have a way of "knowing" what may be good food and what is not, most likely some innate "screening" mechanism based on olfaction and, perhaps to a lesser extent, on taste.

The experiments referred to were limited in number and scope, but it seems reasonable to conclude from them that a young ungulate's food habits develop through a combination of an innate screening mechanism on one hand, and learning, by imitation of a social partner or perhaps by trial and error, on the other hand. The disposition and capacity for learning probably decrease as the animal gets older.

These conclusions are still based on rather scant evidence only. Also, what has been said above applies primarily to selection of food plant species; how the mechanisms for selection of plant parts are transmitted from one generation to another is not yet understood. Particularly in grazers, one almost has to assume a genetic basis for the type of selection effected. Further research on these questions is needed.

B. Drinking Behavior

Most ungulates, as other mammals, drink directly through the mouth, sucking water in by movements of the lingual floor. The only exception is the elephant, which sucks water into its trunk, then lifts the head and empties the water into the mouth. However, very young elephants also drink directly through their mouths, in a manner similar to their way of sucking milk. Due to the shortness of their necks, they have to adopt a rather awkward posture to reach the water (cf. Plate 27 in Sikes, 1971), and they gradually change to using the trunk for drinking.

While most ungulates depend on having open surface water available, a few species are capable of obtaining water from underground. The elephant, in particular, is well known for digging holes in sandy river beds, using mainly trunk and forefeet. Ground water begins to seep into these holes, being filtered in the process, and clean water is then available not only to the elephants, but often to other species that do not dig themselves (e. g., black rhinoceros, various antelopes). Digging for water also occurs in Grévy's and Hartmann's zebras, both species of relatively arid environments, who use their forefeet (Short-ridge, 1934; Klingel, 1968, 1974a).

A number of African ungulates are apparently able to survive without drinking at all, for instance gerenuk (but see Hagen, 1975), possibly some other gazelle species, dikdik, and probably oryx. They can extract sufficient water from their food and/or have evolved special water-conserving mechanisms (see, e. g., Maloiy, 1972). Other species apparently have to obtain water at least once every few days (e. g., elephant, buffalo, zebra) and cannot do without it for long (cf. Heath and Field, 1974). These limits of physiologic tolerance greatly affect the species' choice of habitat, extent of movements and pattern of daily activity (see Chap. 6, C, I.), including the frequency of drinking.

On the local level, the frequency of drinking and its timing are influenced by a number of factors, such as climatic conditions, the distance of watering points from the main feeding grounds, disturbance by man and/or predators, and possibly conflict with other ungulate species (see Chap. 7, C, I.). However, little quantitative information is available yet in this context. Weir and Davison

(1965) recorded the times and frequencies of drinking by different ungulate species at artificial waterholes in Rhodesia. They found more or less specific temporal patterns, with some species drinking mainly or exclusively during the day (warthog, sable, roan), whereas others showed a marked peak in the evening and also drank during the night (elephant, buffalo, giraffe). Ayeni (1975) found similar patterns in Tsavo NP, with warthog, zebra and most antelopes being primarily diurnal, while elephant, buffalo, and black rhinoceros were mainly crepuscular and nocturnal in their drinking visits. Thus, the different ungulate species show a certain degree of temporal separation in their use of waterholes.

Temporal separation may be complemented or enhanced by local separation. In the case of pan-shaped waterholes, natural or artificial, the animals have little choice in their way of approach. However, in the case of rivers and lake shores, ungulates tend to be rather selective with regard to the sites they choose for drinking. Jarman (1972a) and Jarman and Mmari (1971) recorded the properties of a considerable number of drinking sites along Lake Kariba, Rhodesia, and along a small river in the Serengeti NP, respectively. They found considerable differences between various ungulate species with respect to the characteristics selected or avoided. For instance, zebra and hartebeest tended to approach water in open localities offering good visibility, whereas impala rather preferred well-wooded drinking sites affording cover. These preferences correspond to a considerable extent to general habitat preferences, but they are probably also related to the respective species' antipredator behavior (Jarman and Mmari, 1971).

Avoidance of predators is indeed an important aspect in the context of drinking, as is evident from the careful approach and general "nervousness" shown by most ungulates near watering places. Except for the elephant, all ungulates must lower their heads to ground level—or even below—for drinking, which makes them temporarily more vulnerable to predators. The extreme example in this context is the giraffe, which has to spread and bend its forelegs in order to bring the head down to the water, the whole operation being quite an elaborate procedure during which a quick reaction to a surprise attack is difficult, if not impossible.

C. Urination and Defecation

Elimination of waste products is an obligatory physiological process that occurs at certain intervals in all individuals. Behavior associated with this process has, in the course of evolution, often provided the raw material for various forms of social expression. For the moment we will, however, disregard these secondary functions (they will be considered in Chap. 8) and simply give a comparative account of the behavioral correlates of urination and defecation.

We will distinguish three aspects: (1) postures, (2) spatial and temporal distribution, and (3) associated behavior. This differs slightly from the approach adopted by Altmann (1969) who gave a detailed description of voidance behavior in mammals. However, classification of observed behavior into clearcut categories is always arbitrary to some extent, and different authors may use different classifications with equal justification.

I. Postures

Many ungulates adopt characteristic postures for either urination or defecation, or both, which can often be recognized at considerable distances in the field. These postures vary according to sex and age. The variations related to sex are generally a consequence of physical structure, i. e., the locations of the orifices involved, whereas those related to age are more commonly connected with expressive functions of the behavior concerned in a social context. For instance, in most female ungulates the urinary orifice lies directly below the anus, while in the males it is located somewhere between the midventral and the inguinal region. In virtually all bovids and equids the females urinate with somewhat arched back, raised tail and straddled hindlegs, while males generally show less departure from the normal stance. Thus, males and females often adopt distinctly different urination postures. This is not so, however, in the elephant, where the female's vulva is located between the hindlegs, and both sexes urinate in near-normal stance.

Defecation postures, on the other hand, generally differ less between the sexes, but often vary markedly between young and adult animals, particularly among males of some antelopes where secondary expressive functions may be involved (e. g., in gazelles: Walther, 1968; Leuthold, 1971 c).

While the overall range of variation is limited, the postures adopted for defecation and, particularly, urination are to a large extent group-specific. All male gazelles urinate with hindlegs extended well backward, the back inflected and the tail raised to a variable extent (Fig. 6a). In the Tragelaphines, the

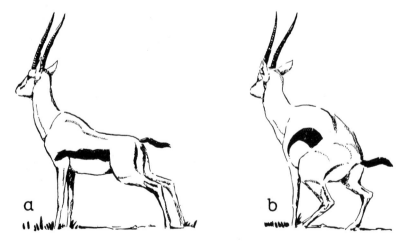

Fig. 6a and b. Urination (a) and defecation (b) postures of adult male Thomson's gazelle (from Walther, 1964b)

30

male urination posture differs little from the normal stance, while other antelopes are intermediate between these extremes. Similarly, male Tragelaphines show relatively little departure from the normal posture for defecation, only raising the tail and perhaps arching the back slightly, whereas adult male gazelles crouch low down with their hindquarters (Fig. 6b; cf. Walther, 1968; Leuthold, 1971c), as do dikdik (Fig. 7; cf. Hendrichs and Hendrichs, 1971) and, sometimes, oryx (Walther, 1958).

Fig. 7. Defecation posture of adult male Kirk's dikdik

During urination and, less commonly, defecation ungulates often give the impression of being deeply "absorbed" by the action. The head points steadily in one direction, although the animal does not appear to actually look in that direction; often the ears are laid back, in contrast to a situation of alarm or "interest" (cf. Altmann, 1969). In the absence of a pronounced urination posture this attitude sometimes draws the observer's attention to urination, e. g., in male giraffe or Tragelaphines.

One behavioral difference between urination and defecation is common to virtually all ungulates: they almost invariably stand still during urination but may defecate while walking. Walther (1964a), speaking of Tragelaphines, remarked that they "take urination more seriously than defecation," and Frädrich (1967)

31

commented similarly with reference to suids. One explanation for this difference would be that the animals might soil their legs and other parts of the body, if they urinated while walking. This is less likely to happen with feces which, in most African ungulates, are relatively dry and solid (exceptions: buffalo, hippopotamus). In addition, and perhaps as a consequence, urination often has secondary signal functions in a social context (e. g., in male–female relations, see Chap. 13, A), which defecation may not have, or only if it is performed by a stationary animal and/or accompanied by a striking posture.

In a few species, the manner of urination and/or defecation differs between social classes. Adult male hippopotami urinate and defecate simultaneously and disperse the mixture with rapid, propellerlike tail movements over a considerable area. Subadult and/or low-ranking bulls, as well as females, release their feces in the "normal" fashion (Hediger, 1951; Verheyen, 1954; Frädrich, 1967). In both species of rhinoceros dominant bulls spray their urine in several short bursts, while low-ranking bulls release it in a steady stream (Schenkel and Schenkel-Hulliger, 1969; Owen-Smith, 1971, 1973).

For further details on urination and defecation of various ungulates (and other mammals) see Altmann (1969).

II. Spatial and Temporal Distribution

With regard to the spatial distribution of urination/defecation we can distinguish two principal situations: (1) random or diffuse, i. e., occurring anywhere in the area utilized by the animal in question, (2) localized, i. e., being restricted to certain localities in which excrements usually accumulate (dung heaps, middens). This applies primarily to defecation but, as urination is often linked with it (see below), to a lesser extent also to urination.

Localized defecation by both sexes commonly occurs in dikdik, klipspringer, black and white rhinoceros; localized defecation in one sex only, usually the (adult) male, in a variety of antelopes (e. g., Grant's and Thomson's gazelles, kongoni, wildebeest, oribi), Grévy's zebra and hippopotamus. Diffuse defecation in both sexes is the rule in the Reduncinae, Tragelaphines, buffalo, giraffe and elephant. In other species, both modes of defecation may occur in different areas or in different contexts (e. g., impala, plains zebra, warthog).

The way defecation is distributed in space is often indicative of an animal's social status. In particular, localized defecation tends to be an attribute of high-ranking individuals, generally adult males, although it does occur also in females in certain species (see above). It probably functions as a means of olfactory marking and will be discussed from that angle in the appropriate context.

Temporal distribution of voidance presumably depends, in the first instance, on the rhythm—if any—of feeding and drinking, digestibility and "through-put" of food, perspiration, etc., but may secondarily be modified by other factors. For instance, in many ungulates urination and defecation often occur in close sequence ("Harn-Koten" in gazelles: Walther, 1968), so that their rates may be correlated to some extent. Urination almost invariably precedes defecation, but this does not necessarily mean that urination releases or "catalyzes" defecation.

Also, voidance in one animal often induces the same in others (allelomimetic behavior), particularly in gregarious species such as impala, or between mother and young (e. g., in black rhino: Schenkel and Schenkel-Hulliger, 1969). A change from one type of activity to another is often accompanied by urination and/or defecation; this is particularly pronounced after a period of resting (e. g., in impala). Defecation may also occur with increased frequency in the context of agonistic encounters, e. g., in gazelles ("Demonstrativkoten": Walther, 1968), again presumably with an expressive or communicatory function. Defecation may further be released when an animal happens to encounter some other dung, either its own or that of another animal, conspecific or not (see below). In female ungulates urination is often stimulated by a male investigating the perineal region (see under mating behavior, Chap. 13, A). Furthermore, feces are often released in response to sudden fright, and during actual flight; their consistency then often differs from the normal one ("Angstkot": Frädrich, 1965; cf. Altmann, 1969).

Thus, the rates of defecation and urination are influenced by a variety of environmental, including social, factors, in addition to an assumed basic physiological rhythm. It is, therefore, impossible to generalize on the temporal distribution of voidance in the different species of ungulates.

III. Associated Behavior

Under this heading we consider behavior that is not directly and functionally related to urination or defecation, but commonly or always occurs in conjunction with them. Altmann (1969) differentiated between appetitive behavior ("Appetenzverhalten") preceding voidance, such as movement to a specific locality, sniffing, pawing, etc., and follow-up behavior ("Folgehandlungen"), with similar elements involved. These two categories are here considered together.

Defecation is often preceded by pawing or scraping of the ground with one or both forefeet, e. g., in several species of gazelles, in dikdik, oribi and oryx, but not in Reduncinae or Tragelaphines. Scraping with forefeet after defecation appears to be rare; it has been recorded in steinbuck (Tinley, 1969). Scraping with the hindfeet after defecation is a feature of the two species of rhinoceros, which leave clearly visible scrape-marks at their dung heaps.

In various species, ground-scraping also occurs in other contexts, and its main function can be assumed to be expressive, particularly where it precedes defecation. If it follows afterward, it may also serve to impregnate the performer's feet with the scent of the dung (e. g., black rhino: Goddard, 1967) or, alternatively, to mark the dung or defecation site with a secretion of the interdigital glands (oribi: Hediger, 1951). However, this is generally difficult to substantiate.

That scents are important in the context of defecation is amply demonstrated by the fact that many species, particularly those with localized defecation, carefully sniff around at the place at which they eventually defecate. In fact, a number of observers have noted that the scent of any dung encountered by an animal may induce it to defecate, usually on top of the old dung. This effect can be quite unspecific, i. e., dung of a very different species may act as releaser

(Tinley, 1969; pers. obs.). For instance, a young male lesser kudu raised by us in captivity was observed several times to defecate after encountering even fairly old elephant dung and sniffing at it intensively. This releasing mechanism might well be a basic "ingredient" in the development of localized defecation. In the latter context a given animal is usually stimulated by its own dung and thus keeps adding to the "pile."

It is noteworthy that, with few exceptions, associated behavior is best developed in species with localized defecation. In many cases, the same applies with regard to pronounced, visually striking defecation postures (see below, dikdik and gerenuk). These facts further indicate that urination and, particularly, defecation have acquired important secondary functions in social communication in the course of evolution; they have been ritualized ("Kot-Zeremoniell" of Pilters, 1954). We will consider these functions in the appropriate context (Chap. 8).

IV. Specific Examples

Having reviewed general features of urination and defecation from a comparative point of view, it is perhaps useful to give some specific examples of the behavioral sequences that may occur in this context.

Black Rhinoceros. Defecation is localized; large dung heaps are formed along major trails and may be used by several different animals. A typical sequence may be as follows: a rhino approaches a dung heap, (sometimes) sniffs at it, turns on the spot, defecates, then scrapes with both hindfeet alternatively and finally walks away. The scraping movements break up the original boluses and scatter the dung to some extent; they also impregnate the feet of the animal with dung scent. In addition, they leave clearly visible marks within the dung heap. Urination is, apparently, not generally combined with defecation (Goddard, 1967, p. 143; Schenkel and Schenkel-Hulliger, 1969, pp. 77–80).

In the white rhinoceros voidance behavior appears to be virtually identical (Owen-Smith, 1971, 1973).

Kirk's Dikdik. Defecation is localized and often combined with urination in both sexes. Dung heaps, used by both male and female (and young if present), are formed near territorial boundaries (see Chap. 16, C), but not exclusively. Territorial neighbors may use adjoining dung heaps. As dikdik pairs often move together, ritualized urination/defecation may take the following course: firstly, the female approaches the defecation site, sniffs at it briefly, rarely scrapes with one or both forefeet, then crouches fairly low and urinates. Crouching a bit lower yet, she then defecates, whereupon she leaves the spot. The male, who may have been standing next to her all along, now moves to the dung pile, sniffs intensively, sometimes showing "Flehmen" (see Fig. 37). He then starts several bouts of vigorous scraping, using both forefeet alternately (e. g., five scrapes left, then five scrapes right, etc.), leaving clearly visible scratch marks. Between bouts of scraping, he sometimes turns about 180°. After several series of scraping, he urinates in a fairly low crouching posture, then crouches even lower (cf. Fig. 7) and defecates, again changing position occasionally. Then he may leave without any further action, but the entire ceremony is a very drawn-out and elaborate behavioral sequence. In the end, the female's feces are buried under soil (through the male's scraping) and under the male's dung. Both sexes adopt visually striking postures for both urination and defecation, which may have a communicatory function (Tinley, 1969, pp. 24/25; Hendrichs and Hendrichs, 1971, pp. 36–39; Hendrichs, 1975a; pers. obs.).

Gerenuk. Defecation and urination are entirely diffuse in the females, more or less diffuse but generally combined in adult males. The latter may show part or all of the following sequence: while walking along, perhaps feeding intermittently, he suddenly stops and sniffs the ground. Then he walks forward a few steps, scrapes the soil lightly with a forefoot (or both alternately), adopts the urination posture (hindlegs spread backward, back inflected, cf. Fig. 6a) and urinates. Then he moves the hindlegs forward, crouches low down (Fig. 7 in Leuthold, 1971c) and defecates on the same spot. Then he may walk away and resume his former activity. In most cases, on-the-spot investigation revealed the presence of old dung pellets on the sites of the urination-defecation ritual, but only in small quantities. No actual dung heaps have been found so far in gerenuk (at least in Tsavo NP). Perhaps the behavior just described could be interpreted as an early stage in the development of localized defecation. One gets the distinct impression that defecation is induced by the scent of the old dung that the animal encounters more or less by chance. On one occasion I observed a male scraping vigorously with both feet and then performing the combined urination/defecation on the spot where a female had just defecated (as in dikdik). Possibly, such behavior is more common than is suggested by the single observed instance.

In the dibatag Walther (1963, 1968) noted virtually identical behavior in captivity.

These examples illustrate the elaborate behavior accompanying urination and/or defecation in at least some ungulates. For further information and discussion see Walther (1967a) and Altmann (1969).

D. Comfort Behavior

This category comprises all behavior related to the care of the body, particularly its surface, including the removal of local irritations and/or ectoparasites. We can distinguish three main types of body care behavior: (1) that performed only by the animal's own body or parts of it (self- or autogrooming, e.g., shaking of entire body or of head only, ear and tail movements, biting, licking, scratching with hindfeet), (2) that involving inanimate objects of the animal's surroundings (e.g., scratching or rubbing on trees, rocks or termite hills, wallowing in dry dust or wet mud, bathing), and (3) that involving more than one individual, i.e., allogrooming (social grooming, mutual grooming).

We will first review types (1) and (2) as to their occurrence in the various ungulate groups and then discuss the findings in a comparative framework. Type (3) warrants separate treatment because of its social significance.

I. General Review of Ungulate Comfort Behavior

Ear and tail movements, mainly to ward off insects, are very widespread but relatively simple components of body care behavior and are not included in this review. The various elements of more complex comfort behavior occur in the different ungulate families as follows:

Elephantidae. Despite the versatility of their trunk, elephants show virtually no grooming movements involving only their own body. However, they frequently rub against trees, rocks, or termitaria, and bathe in rivers and waterholes; less often they roll or wallow in moist earth. In addition, they use the trunk to blow dry dust, water or wet mud over the body (Kühme, 1963; Sikes, 1971; Hendrichs, 1971; pers. obs.). These actions usually result in the elephants assuming the color of the major soil type in their environment.

Equidae (Zebra Only). Kicking and stamping with front or hind feet and local twitching of the skin are commonly employed to ward off insects. Nibbling and biting, using both upper and lower incisors, as well as scratching with a hind foot in the head/neck region are common movements of skin care. Zebras frequently rub on trees and/or termite hills (cf. Hediger, 1942/50) and wallow in dry dust. Wet wallowing and bathing are rare or absent, also licking, except in mother-young relations (Hassenberg, 1971; Klingel, 1972a).

Rhinocerotidae. Rhinos use virtually no self-grooming movements, but commonly engage in rubbing, dry and wet wallowing and bathing (Schenkel and Schenkel-Hulliger, 1969; Schenkel and Lang, 1969).

Suidae. Pigs scratch themselves with their hind feet, but this is the only autogrooming behavior commonly shown. They rub and wallow (both dry and wet) frequently. To rub the anal region, they squat on their hindquarters and move the body forward (or backward) along the ground ("Sitzrutschen": Frädrich, 1965, 1967).

Hippopotamidae. As these animals are active primarily at night, little is known on their comfort behavior on land, except that they wallow in wet mud and do not lick or nibble their bodies (Frädrich, 1967).

Giraffidae. Giraffes frequently shake the head and neck and occasionally nibble or bite the lower portions of front or hind legs. No scratching with the hind feet has been observed, except for rare attempts by young animals. They make extensive use of stiff twigs or branches to scratch parts of the neck and head, even the inside of the ear. They may also step over a brushy bush and slowly rock back and forth, scratching their belly and the inside of the legs in the process. They do not wallow or bathe, nor rub the body

36

against trees, rocks, etc. (Backhaus, 1961; pers. obs.). Little is known about the okapi.

Bovidae. Among the multitude of African bovids, particularly the smaller antelopes, we find the most varied autogrooming behavior. Most bovids ward off biting insects by foot-stamping, skin-twitching, and shaking the head or the entire body, the latter sometimes followed by a short run. They clean themselves or remove local irritations by licking, nibbling or biting (the latter mainly on legs and tail), and by scratching with the lower incisors (sides, rump, legs), with the horns (back and sides), and the hind feet (neck and head). By contrast, comfort behavior involving external objects is relatively rare in bovids. Some antelopes occasionally rub their forehead against a twig or branch; this is particularly common in horn-carrying animals, thus often males where, however, it is difficult to draw the line between "mere" comfort movements and behavior with aggressive overtones ("horning", see Chap. 12, C). Actual rubbing of the body occurs almost exclusively in the buffalo; some antelopes occasionally rub the neck or chin on the ground, particularly while lying down. Dry wallowing appears to occur only in the two wildebeest species, wet wallowing and bathing only in the buffalo. Some species of the Reduncinae, e.g., the red and black lechwe, and the sitatunga regularly enter or lie in the water, but this seems to be related more to feeding or general habitat choice than to actual comfort behavior. Waterbuck are said to enter water when sick, but this is not a normal situation (e.g., Walther, 1963b, 1964a, b, 1965a, 1966b, 1968).

This summary does not claim to be comprehensive. The references given in each paragraph are, in the main, those that describe the relevant behavior for whole groups; additional and more detailed information can be found in many single-species studies, particularly for the bovids.

What generalizations can be made from the above review? There appear to be clear-cut relationships between an animal's body shape—and hence flexibility—and its comfort behavior; also between the latter and the external covering of the skin, i.e., whether there are stiff bristles, soft fur, or no hair at all. To a large extent, these various characteristics are also tied to the animal's taxonomic position. Thus, most of the smaller bovids (e.g., gazelles, the smaller Tragelaphini and Reduncinae) are of slender build, with relatively long and mobile necks and limbs and a furry coat. They show the highest development of self-grooming, to the near-exclusion of behavior utilizing external objects. The main exceptions within the family are the buffalo and the somewhat stocky wildebeest. The other extreme is represented by the rhinoceros, elephant and probably the hippopotamus, all with very bulky bodies on stout, short legs of limited mobility, and a thick neck of little flexibility; also they all have nearly hairless skins. In these species, self-grooming is almost totally lacking, while behavior using objects of the surroundings is common in all. The suids represent an intermediate stage in most respects, while the equids fall fairly near the bovids. The giraffe deviates somewhat from this generalization, for although being long-necked and long-legged it performs few comfort movements of its body alone, but makes extensive use of external objects. Possibly other factors are important in this species, e.g., problems of remaining in balance while performing body-care movements. The same might apply to some other heavy-bodied species (e. g., buffalo, rhino, elephant), in addition to considerations regarding general mobility and/or flexibility of limbs and neck.

Thus, comfort behavior provides a good example of the varied and complex functional correspondences between morphology and behavior.

Two characteristics of body care behavior should be mentioned in passing: firstly, it occurs with particular frequency and intensity after prolonged periods of resting; secondly, it has pronounced allelomimetic properties, i. e., members of a group tend to engage in it simultaneously (e. g., Walther, 1964a, 1968).

So far, we have considered mainly the functions of skin care and removal of parasites or other irritations. Comfort behavior may, however, have other effects as well. For instance, ungulates employ various behaviors that help in regulating their body temperature. The commonest is simply seeking shade, which virtually all ungulates do under certain conditions. Others are bathing and mud-wallowing, which have been mentioned above, but in another functional context. Apart from its direct cooling effect, wet-wallowing tends to leave a coat of dried mud on the animal's body, which may shield the body from solar radiation, in addition to providing protection from biting insects. Furthermore, ungulates may expose their bodies to the sun or to wind at different angles to achieve a temperature-regulating effect (see also Chap. 6, E). Perhaps the most conspicuous thermoregulatory behavior in ungulates is the ear-flapping of elephants. The dense venation of the ears, particularly their rear sides, acts as a kind of radiator giving off heat. Blood temperatures may differ as much as $4\,°C$ between different portions of the ear (Baldwin, 1971; Douglas-Hamilton, 1972; Sikes, 1971). Buss and Estes (1971) showed that elephants alter their ears' exposure to wind and the rate of ear-flapping in response to changes in ambient temperature and wind speed.

II. Allogrooming

A number of gregarious ungulates (e. g., zebra, gazelles, impala) engage in mutual grooming (social grooming). Two animals stand close together and lick, nibble or scratch (with the teeth) each other either simultaneously (zebra) or alternately (antelopes). Warthogs show "one-way" allogrooming, i. e., one animal actively grooms another which remains passive (Frädrich, 1965).

Various observers claim that allogrooming is primarily directed to those parts of the body that are difficult to reach for the individual (e. g., Hassenberg, 1971, for equids). Others say that this is not so, but that mutual grooming is concentrated near the head and that it may be mainly a form of social contact (e. g., Walther, 1964a, 1968, for various antelopes). Probably both views are true to some extent, perhaps in different degrees for different species or families of ungulates.

There is no doubt that mutual grooming is of considerable social significance. For instance, individual zebra have preferred partners with whom they engage in mutual grooming most often (Klingel, 1967). It may serve to foster and maintain interindividual bonds, and thus increase group cohesion, as is known from other mammals (examples in Ewer, 1968). Also, it is obvious that an animal derives physical "pleasure" from being groomed. This is evident from the animal's behavior while being groomed (e. g., the sometimes "trancelike" motionless stance of a captive animal being stroked by a person), and from the fact that some ungulates may adopt specific postures to "invite" grooming (Walther, 1964a, 1968; Frädrich, 1965).

Many of the observations on grooming behavior, both individual and mutual, reported in the literature were made on captive ungulates. I mentioned earlier that, in the absence of the more pressing demands of food gathering and avoidance of predators, certain behaviors tend to hypertrophy in captivity, particularly grooming, play, and sexual behavior (Hediger, 1942/50). For instance, Walther (1958, 1964a) observed frequent and intensive mutual grooming in gerenuk and lesser kudu (and other species) in captivity, whereas in several years of field observations on these two species I have never seen any real allogrooming, except in the case of mother–young relations. Occasionally, two female gerenuk rub heads together, but this does not involve any licking, nibbling or biting (Leuthold, 1971c, and unpubl.). Similarly, Frädrich (1965, Fig. 10) found that warthog in a zoo groomed (and also fought and played) much more frequently than in the wild. Thus, caution is indicated in the interpretation of observations on captive animals only.

A special case of allogrooming is the licking and cleaning of a young ungulate by its mother. This will be treated in Chapter 14.

Chapter 6

Behavior Related to the Environment

Most or all animal behavior is related to the environment in one way or another, but this chapter reviews behavioral responses to specific components or factors of the physical environment, viz. space, time, weather, etc. Relations to animals of other species, as well as conspecifics, will be considered separately (Chap. 7; Parts 3 and 4).

A. Habitat Selection

While few ungulates are highly specialized with regard to their habitat, most of them require certain specific features and, in general, do not occur in areas lacking them. The degree of specialization varies widely between species, and groups of species. To a considerable extent, habitat requirements are similar in several species within a genus or even a subfamily. For instance, all duikers (Cephalophinae) occur in forest or dense bush, with the partial exception of *Sylvicapra*, while most members of the Alcelaphinae generally inhabit fairly to very open country (savanna, grassland). Similar generalizations apply to several other taxa. This does not mean, however, that habitat requirements of closely related species are identical.

The choice of the proper habitat is perhaps one of the most basic behaviorally mediated processes in an animal's life, yet we know virtually nothing about the mechanisms involved. Two main possibilities suggest themselves:

a) As habitat requirements are often similar in related species, one might infer a genetic basis for the choice, i.e., that individual animals possess innate responses to environmental features, which guide their habitat selection.

b) Habitat selection could also be effected through intraspecific (or intrapopulation) tradition, i.e., young animals might learn the essential attributes of species-specific habitat through early experience, from the association with their mothers and/or other (older) conspecifics.

Experiments with mice (*Peromyscus* sp.) suggest that genetic determination plays an important part in their habitat selection (Wecker, 1963, 1964), but for ungulates no direct evidence is available as yet. Quite probably, genetic and traditional factors combine to enable a young animal to make the proper choice of habitat.

Some species, or populations, occupy somewhat different habitats at different times of the year. Such changes are mostly related to fluctuations in food and/or water supplies in the course of the year. They may involve relatively small-scale movements between different vegetation types, as are found in many ungulate populations (e.g., Bell, 1971; Jarman, 1972b; Simpson, 1972; Stanley Price, 1974; Duncan, 1975), or large-scale annual migrations over considerable distances, as for instance in the Serengeti area of Tanzania (see Fig. 11).

In a few species, there appear to be sex-related differences in habitat preference. For instance, male giraffes tend to occur in more densely wooded areas than females (Foster and Dagg, 1972; Moore-Berger, 1974).

There are many interrelationships between the habitat type normally occupied by a species and its size, general morphology, food habits, antipredator behavior, social organization, etc.; some of these will be reviewed in Chapter 19.

B. Space-Related Behavior

In this section we will examine the ways in which ungulates utilize the space available to them, and the attributes of that space that are important to them.

I. The Concept of Home Range

Contrary to once widespread popular opinion most terrestrial—and indeed many aquatic—animals do not roam ad libitum over vast areas, but generally confine their activities to one or several circumscribed areas in the course of the year and, mostly, their entire lifetime. While a number of earlier authors noted this fact, it was mainly Hediger (1942/50, 1949, 1951) in Europe, and Burt (1940, 1943, 1949) in America, who pointed it out more emphatically and introduced the appropriate concepts and terms into mammalogical literature. Burt (1943) defined the home range as "the area, usually around a home site, over which the animal normally travels in search of food." This definition, as Jewell (1966) noted, is unnecessarily restrictive because, firstly, not all mammals—and particularly few ungulates—have a fixed home site and, secondly, activities other than food-gathering also take place within the home range. Following Jewell (1966, p. 103) we may define the home range as follows: *the home range is the area over which an animal normally travels in pursuit of its routine activities.*

The majority of home-range studies have involved small mammals, where the home range often is a more or less compact area of fairly well-defined extent. The same may apply to the more sedentary ungulates. However, many other species undertake seasonal movements or migrations over considerable distances, making little use of some intervening areas. In such cases one may speak of several seasonal (or temporary) home ranges, with more or less fixed routes of travel connecting them (cf. Geist, 1971b). For the area encompassing this entire system Jewell (1966) suggested the term lifetime range, defined as "the total area with which an animal has become familiar, including seasonal home ranges, excursions for mating, and routes of movement." Perhaps annual home range (Jay, 1965, in Jewell, 1966) could be used in the same sense, provided that the movements in question occur on a fairly regular annual basis.

Walther (1967a, 1972b) suggested the term "action area" ("Aktionsraum") for the total range of an individual or group, preferring to limit home range to what has been called "seasonal home range" above. Personally, I find Jewell's "lifetime range" more appropriate, as it describes expressis verbis what it denotes.

At this point I wish to stress that *home range must not be treated as synonymous with territory* (see Chap. 15, C), as is sometimes done. Burt (1940, 1943) already warned against confusion of the two terms; Hediger, however, did not distinguish them. More recently, Etkin (1964) contributed to the unfortunate confusion of terms by designating as "territory" what, in effect, corresponds to home range, as defined above. He departed radically from conventional terminology when he referred to territory as an "unqualified" term (Etkin, 1964, p. 25) in comparison to home range. Quite to the contrary, home range is commonly used as the less specified term, denoting the unit of space that an animal—any animal—inhabits, whereas territory is an area of primarily social significance, with a number of specific functions (for definition and further discussion see Chap. 15, C). All members of a population have a home range, but relatively few only, of specific social status, may hold a territory.

II. Size of Home Range

To obtain reliable data on home range size requires long-term observation of known individuals. For this reason, well-documented information on wild ungulates is still rather scarce. Table 3 presents some examples of home range sizes in African ungulates. The areas given are generally annual home ranges, i.e., they include all areas used in the course of the year, regardless of the intensity of utilization. Seasonal home ranges may be only a fraction of the size of the annual ones. It is difficult to judge to what extent the data in Table 3 are directly comparable among themselves, as home range sizes may have been calculated in different ways, often not specified in the original papers, and observations made over different periods of time.

Within certain limits, small animals have smaller home ranges than large animals of similar physical constitution. This is illustrated by the home ranges of antelopes in Table 3. For instance, dikdik and bushbuck have by far the smallest home ranges of the antelopes listed, while large species such as sable and roan have the largest. Most other species fall between these extremes. Exceptions occur in migratory populations, e.g., Thomson's gazelles in the Serengeti NP (no data available). We know virtually nothing yet about some of the small forest antelopes (e.g., various duikers, suni), but it is probably safe to assume that their home ranges are among the smallest in African ungulates.

It would, however, be too great a simplification to imply that home range size increases roughly in proportion to body size. Various other factors are equally important, particularly food habits, mobility, social structure and the quality of the local habitat (see Chap. 17, A). Mobility, i.e., the propensity and capacity to cover long distances in a short time, is to some extent positively

Table 3. Home range size in some African ungulates. Figures generally represent annual or lifetime ranges for adult animals only, in km². M = male, F = female, n = number of animals on which mean is based

Species	Area	Sex	Mean	Range	n	Reference
Elephant	Lake Manyara NP	F	—	14–52	48	Douglas-Hamilton, 1972, 1973
	Tarangire NP	F	—	330	1	Douglas-Hamilton, 1972, 1973
	Tsavo West NP	M}	350	294–337	2	Leuthold and Sale, 1973
		F}	350	328–441	2	Leuthold and Sale, 1973
	Tsavo East NP	M}	1,580	1,035–1,209	2	Leuthold and Sale, 1973
		F}	1,580	525–3,120	4	Leuthold and Sale, 1973
White rhinoceros	Umfolozi GR	M	1.7	0.7–2.6	27	Owen-Smith, 1974, 1975
	Umfolozi GR	F	11.6	10–15	8	Owen-Smith, 1974, 1975
Black rhinoceros	Umfolozi GR	M	4.1	3.7–4.7	4	Hitchins, 1971
	Umfolozi GR	F	6.7	5.8–7.7	3	Hitchins, 1971
	Ngorongoro Crater	M	15.8	2.6–44.0	16	Goddard, 1967
	Ngorongoro Crater	F	15.0	2.6–26.2	13	Goddard, 1967
	Olduvai Gorge (Tanzania)	M	22.0	5.5–51.8	11	Goddard, 1967
	Olduvai Gorge (Tanzania)	F	35.5	3.6–90.7	13	Goddard, 1967
	Mara GR	M	12.1	7.1–18.6	5	Mukinya, 1973
	Mara GR	F	13.8	5.6–22.7	7	Mukinya, 1973
	South-West Africa	M + F	—	30–40	—	Joubert and Eloff, 1971
Plains zebra	Kruger NP South Africa	M + F	164	49–566	49	Smuts, 1975
	Ngorongoro Crater (sedentary)	M + F	—	80–250	—	Klingel, 1969a
	Serengeti NP (migratory)	M + F	—	>1,000	—	Klingel, 1969a
Mountain zebra	Mountain Zebra NP	M + F	—	3–5	—	Klingel, 1972a, 1974b
Hartmann's zebra	South-West Africa (seasonal ranges)	M + F	—	6–20	—	E. Joubert, 1972b

Table 3 (continued)

Species	Area	Sex	Mean	Range	n	Reference
Warthog	Nairobi NP	(F)	1.3	—	—	Bradley, 1968
	Sengwa, Rhodesia	M	1.8	0.7–3.7	10	Cumming, 1975
		F	1.7	0.7–3.4	15	Cumming, 1975
Giraffe	Nairobi NP	M	62	—	10	Foster and Dagg, 1972
		F	85	—	10	Foster and Dagg, 1972
	Tsavo East NP	M	164	12–650	60	Leuthold and Leuthold, in press
		F	162	9–480	50	Leuthold and Leuthold, in press
	Timbavati (South Africa)	M	37.4	12–72	4	Langman, pers. comm.
		F	22.9	14–44	9	Langman, pers. comm.
(Reticulated)	Samburu District, Kenya (ranchland)	M	18	14–37	8	Moore-Berger, 1974
		F	13	8.5–30	28	Moore-Berger, 1974
Buffalo	Ruwenzori NP	herd	—	10	1	Grimsdell, 1969
	Tsavo East NP	herd	—	85	1	Leuthold, 1972
	Serengeti NP	herd	—	450	1	Sinclair, 1970
Nyala	Zinave NP (Mozambique)	M	—	1.3–9.5	9	Tello and van Gelder, 1975
		F	—	0.4–3.6	3	Tello and van Gelder, 1975
Bushbuck	Nairobi NP	M	0.0056	—	—	Allsopp, 1971
		F	0.0025	—	—	Allsopp, 1971
	Ruwenzori NP	M	0.24	0.15–0.35	4	Waser, 1975a
		F	0.12	0.06–0.20	5	Waser, 1975a
Lesser kudu	Tsavo East NP	M	2.2	0.8–4.3	8	Leuthold, 1974
		F	1.8	0.4–3.5	8	Leuthold, 1974
Eland	Nairobi NP and adjacent plains	M	41	6–71	41	Hillman, 1976
		F	134	34–360	19	Hillman, 1976
Waterbuck	Ruwenzori NP	F	6.5–7	—	25	Spinage, 1969a
Bohor reedbuck	Serengeti NP	M	—	0.25–0.6	—	Hendrichs, 1975b
		F	—	0.15–0.4	—	Hendrichs, 1975b

Species	Location	Sex				Reference
Roan antelope	(Zambia)	F		77	1	S. Joubert, 1974
	Kruger NP	(F)		60–100	—	S. Joubert, 1974
Sable antelope	Shimba Hills, Kenya	M		6.5	1	Estes and Estes, 1969
		F		7.6	1	Estes and Estes, 1969
(Giant sable)	Luando GR, Angola	F		12–20	2	Estes and Estes, 1974
Hartebeest	Maralal, Kenya	M		2.6	1	Ables and Ables, 1971
	Nairobi NP	M		6.7–10.3	5	Gosling, 1974
		F		3.7–5.5	4	Gosling, 1974
Topi	Serengeti NP (woodlands)	M	1.6	0.9–2.7	6	Duncan, 1975
		F	1.5	0.7–2.7	5	Duncan, 1975
	Serengeti NP (western plains)	M+F	ca. 180	—	—	Duncan, 1975
Impala	Maralal, Kenya	M	3.4	1.1–7.3	7	Ables and Ables, 1969
		F	2.7	1.2–4.6	3	Ables and Ables, 1969
	Nairobi NP	M		2.0–5.0	—	Leuthold, 1970b
		F		0.9–5.7	—	Leuthold, 1970b
	Serengeti NP	M+F	ca. 5		—	M. V. Jarman, 1970
Thomson's gazelle	Ngorongoro Crater	M+F	ca. 9		—	Walther, 1964b
Gerenuk	Tsavo East NP	M		4.1–6.4	4	Leuthold, 1971c
		F		2.4–4.5	3	Leuthold, 1971c
Kirk's dikdik	Serengeti NP	M+F		0.025–0.12	—	Hendrichs and Hendrichs, 1971

correlated with body size, but not consistently. As an exception from the rule, Thomson's gazelles in the Serengeti NP undertake almost as extensive annual migrations as the much larger wildebeest. But hardly any species below the size of Thomson's gazelle is known to make wide-ranging movements, while many of the larger species regularly move over considerable distances (e. g., eland, wildebeest).

Another factor interrelated with home range size is the size of social groups normally formed by a species. Solitary animals (e. g., black and white rhino) usually have smaller home ranges than similar-sized gregarious ones (e. g., buffalo, elephant). This is self-explanatory if we view the home range primarily as a reservoir of resources (see below). Home range size may also differ between males and females (Table 3).

The factors discussed so far are attributes of the animal itself, physical or behavioral. Of course, the quality of the habitat is of utmost importance in determining home range size. If an animal can satisfy all its needs the year round in a small area, it is likely to have a small home range. If there are large fluctuations in, e. g., the food supply, the animal may be forced to exploit a larger area or to move elsewhere temporarily, establishing two or more seasonal home ranges. For herbivores, rainfall pattern and vegetation type are probably the primary determinants of home range size, as well as the availability of open water for those that depend on it. This is well illustrated in Goddard's (1967) work on the black rhinoceros. Table 3 shows considerable differences between Ngorongoro Crater and the nearby Olduvai Gorge, Tanzania, the latter being more arid (annual rainfall 400 mm vs. 650 mm in the Crater). Even within Ngorongoro Crater home ranges varied between about 3 km² and 15 km² in different vegetation types (Goddard, 1967, p. 135). The elephant is another good example of this point (Table 3). In Manyara NP, Tanzania, an area with ca. 750 mm annual rainfall, a high water table, year-round water supply, and evergreen vegetation ranging from groundwater forest to dense *Acacia* savanna, cow/calf groups had home ranges of 15–52 km² (Douglas-Hamilton, 1972). In Tsavo East NP, with very irregular rainfall of 250–500 mm per year, restricted water supplies and largely deciduous woodlands, home ranges of four cow/calf groups over eight months measured between 1,200 and over 3,000 km², while in Tsavo West NP, under more favorable conditions, two cow/calf groups had home ranges of 330 and 440 km² (Leuthold and Sale, 1973).

From the above it is clear that home range size depends on a variety of factors, partly attributes of the animal itself (including species, sex, and age), partly characteristics of the local environment. The latter interrelationships will be discussed further in Chapter 17.

III. Internal Anatomy of the Home Range

It was primarily Hediger (1942/50, 1949, 1951) who pointed out that an animal's home range should not be viewed as merely a piece of ground on which the animal happens to be, but as a living space with an internal organization relevant to the animal's needs. He distinguished between "objective space" ("Umgebung"),

46

meaning the portion of habitat utilized by an animal (ecologically defined), and "subjective space" ("Umwelt"), comprising the sum total of localities and features of significance to the animal (psychologically defined). Following these concepts, Ewer (1968, p. 64) stated that "a home range ... [does not] necessarily mean a continuous area enclosed within defined boundaries," but "... may consist essentially of a number of places which are of importance ..., linked by a series of pathways."

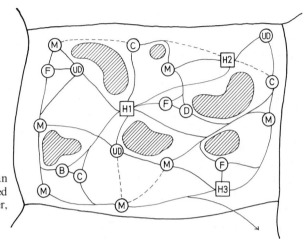

Fig. 8. Diagram of mammalian home range with different fixed points, trails, etc. (after Hediger, 1942/50)

——: Major trail
----: Minor trail
H1: First-order home
H2: Second-order home
H3: Third-order home
F: Feeding place/area
UD: Urination/defecation site

M: Marking site
D: Drinking site
B: Bathing site
C: Place for comfort behavior (e.g., tree or termite mound for rubbing)
⬚: Obstacles affecting alignment of trails (rocks, bush clumps, etc.)

Heavy solid line: home range boundary; note that this representation assumes exclusive use of the area by its occupant(s), but this situation is relatively rare in African ungulates (see Chap. 16)

This is the essence of Hediger's widely reproduced schematic representation of a home range (Fig. 8). Its main features are localities (or areas) where the animal engages in specific activities, called "fixed points" ("Fixpunkte"). A network of more or less regularly used "pathways" or "trails" ("Wechsel") links the fixed points (Fig. 9). Important among the latter are one or several homes (burrows, etc.; applicable to very few ungulates only), feeding areas, drinking and bathing sites, localities for urination and/or defecation, places for comfort behavior, e.g., trees or termite hills for rubbing (Fig. 10), dry and wet wallows. In connection with ungulates it is perhaps not appropriate to call a feeding area a fixed point, but otherwise Hediger's model is useful and widely applicable, apart from the fact that Hediger called the area involved a territory rather than a home range.

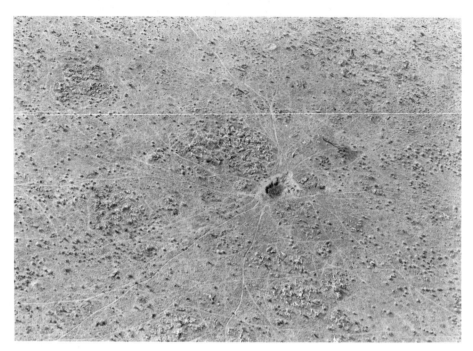

Fig. 9. Animal trails converging on a fixed point, in this case a dried-out waterhole (aerial photograph from Tsavo NP)

Fig. 10. Fixed point and trail in home range of elephant and/or rhinoceros: a termite mound, extensively used for rubbing, and major trail leading to a river *(left background)*

48

The main implication of the model is that not all parts of the home range are of equal significance to its inhabitant(s), but that certain portions or places are used more than others. This has since been confirmed for a variety of (mainly small) mammals. For instance, Adams and Davis (1967), through continuous observations of California ground squirrels *(Citellus beecheyi)*, found considerable variations in the utilization of different parts of the home range; as a result, they coined the term "internal anatomy of the home range" which I have chosen to head this section. For further discussion see Kaufmann (1962, 1971), Grubb and Jewell (1966), Robinette (1966), and the reviews by Sanderson (1966) and Jewell (1966).

Hediger's own observations (1951) in the national parks of the then Belgian Congo were pioneering in this field and provided some of the first examples of the internal anatomy of home ranges in African ungulates. He pointed out that home ranges (and territories) of different species overlap widely and that any one environmental feature may have the same or a different significance to animals of different species. For instance, a tree may be used as a source of food (elephant, giraffe), a facility for comfort behavior (buffalo, warthog), a shady resting place (rhino, elephant and others) and, among nonungulates, as a home (squirrels, birds) or an observation post (primates, birds). Termite hills may fulfil similarly diverse functions. One often finds well-worn trails, probably used by different species, leading from various directions and over considerable distances to a prominent tree or termite hill that usually shows signs of heavy utilization (Fig. 10). For further details see Hediger (1951, 1967) and Walther (1967a, b).

In some herbivores the inner organization of the home range may be ill defined, to the point of being virtually nonexistent. This applies particularly to species that do not use external objects for comfort behavior, are independent of open water, and urinate and defecate more or less randomly. Two such species are the lesser kudu and the gerenuk, in which I have found no obvious signs of a well-defined structure of the home ranges. In particular, no fixed points are evident, with the possible exception of the gerenuk's urination/defecation sites and, perhaps, their antorbital marking points. Nevertheless, these animals inhabit clearly defined home ranges (Leuthold 1971 c, 1974).

Among African ungulates, only warthogs occupy spatially fixed homes, in the form of underground burrows. These are generally assumed to have been dug by aardvarks *(Orycteropus afer)* originally. They serve the warthogs not only as resting places and shelters, but as veritable "climate chambers" (Geigy, 1955; Bradley, 1971; see Chap. 14, A). Bush pig and giant forest hog are reported to rest in the same places in thickets repeatedly, and also to build nests for their young (Frädrich, 1967). Hippopotami may resort regularly to the same resting places in the water (Hediger, 1951; Verheyen, 1954). Little corresponding behavior is yet known in other ungulates, but the "stamping grounds" of territorial males in some species (e. g., blue wildebeest: Estes, 1969), or certain resting areas that are used repeatedly (e. g., hartebeest: Stanley Price, 1974) could perhaps be regarded as equivalent to "homes."

IV. Functional Aspects of Home Range

We can conceive a home range, firstly, as an area containing all the resources (food, water, shelter, etc.) needed by the animal and, secondly, as an area with which the animal is familiar and within which it usually feels "at ease." The resource aspect helps us to understand why larger and/or gregarious herbivores generally have bigger home ranges than smaller and/or solitary ones (cf. Table 3). In the present context we are primarily concerned with behavioral phenomena, and the following discussion is limited to this aspect.

A commonly expressed opinion (e.g., Jewell, 1966; Ewer, 1968) assumes that the chief advantage of having a circumscribed home range lies in the animal's being thoroughly familiar with the area and its features. This familiarity is believed (1) to ensure knowledge of and access to the available resources, and (2) to facilitate escape from predators. While this concept sounds entirely plausible, there is as yet little direct evidence to support it. Metzgar (1967) showed that white-footed mice *(Peromyscus leucopus)* unfamiliar with the terrain on which experiments were conducted suffered considerably higher losses from predation than those that knew the area intimately. These conclusions may well have wider applications, possibly to ungulates as well.

Some indirect evidence also supports the above concept of home range. For instance, various mammals appear to be ill at ease when outside their normal surroundings; they move about very cautiously—if at all—and are easily frightened, even to the point of blind panic (e.g., Jewell, 1966; Ewer, 1968, p. 65). White-tailed deer *(Odocoileus virginianus)*, when transplanted to a new area, scattered in all directions from the site of release (references in Robinette, 1966). It is quite possible that some translocation projects failed primarily because the animals involved could not cope immediately with the exigencies of their new surroundings, lacking familiarity with them (see, e.g., Hanks, 1968, on puku).

Various observers have noted also that it is difficult to drive deer and prong-horn antelope *(Antilocapra americana)* outside their home ranges (e.g., Etkin, 1964, p. 24; Robinette, 1966); the animals tend to circle back rather than leave their familiar surroundings, thus demonstrating a considerable degree of attachment to the area. We may, therefore, restate the earlier definition of home range (Chap. 6, B, I) and say that it is *the area that an animal is familiar with and does not leave voluntarily.*

An offshoot of the apparently strong attachment to a given home range is the phenomenon known as homing, i.e., the propensity and ability of animals forcibly removed from their home range to return to it, often in the face of very adverse circumstances. Spectacular cases of homing ability have been reported for white-tailed deer in North America, with individual males covering distances of 430–540 km in 9–12 months (Glazener, 1948; in Robinette, 1966). I know of only two documented cases of homing in African ungulates, both involving relatively short distances. Four male Uganda kob translocated over 15–22 km returned to their home ranges within 5–8 days (Leuthold, 1966b). A female puku in Zambia covered about 24 km between the point of relase and her original home range, having apparently traversed long stretches of normally

50

unsuitable habitat (Hanks, 1968). In various other cases, however, transplanted ungulates settled down in new surroundings, e.g., Grévy's zebra and Hunter's hartebeest introduced into Tsavo NP in 1962 (Sheldrick, pers. comm.; pers. obs.), black rhinoceros released in Nairobi NP (Hamilton and King, 1969). Thus, the factors governing homing, as well as the stimuli responsible for successful orientation, remain largely unknown (cf. discussion in Leuthold, 1966b).

As a result of the strong attachment to a given locality and the ability to return to it from far away, geographically continuous populations are often subdivided into localized segments (home range groups) that do not generally intermingle and may even form more or less exclusive breeding units. An organizational pattern of this kind has been demonstrated in the Uganda kob (Buechner, 1963; Buechner and Roth, 1974); it is likely to apply to a greater or lesser extent to various other species (cf. Laws, 1969a, 1970, on elephants; but see also Leuthold and Sale, 1973). The formation of relatively isolated breeding units, through behavioral characteristics, may have important implications from the genetic and evolutionary points of view (see Chap. 18, C).

V. Movements and Migrations

While many ungulates are relatively sedentary (cf. sizes of home ranges in Table 3), others undertake regular or irregular movements involving, in some cases, very considerable distances. If such movements follow a more or less regular, predictable pattern, both in space and in time, they are usually called migrations.

As a rule, all major movements are dictated by changes in environmental conditions, primarily in availability of food and/or water. Thus, they are usually related to the pattern of rainfall. A well-known example of fairly regular seasonal migrations is that of the wildebeest, zebra, and gazelles in the Serengeti ecosystem (Fig. 11; see Grzimek and Grzimek, 1960; Brooks, 1961; Talbot and Talbot, 1963; Walther, 1972a, and others). In these circumstances it is generally possible, within limits, to predict where major concentrations of the species mentioned are to be found at any given time (Pennycuick, 1975).

In other situations, where rainfall is more erratic both in spatial and temporal distribution, as well as in quantity, large-scale movements may occur unpredictably. This is particularly pronounced in subarid and arid areas. The most famous case is that of the mass movements ("treks") of springbok that formerly took place in southern Africa (Cronwright-Schreiner, 1925, in Bigalke, 1966; Child and Le Riché, 1969). Because of the huge numbers involved and the often staggering losses incurred in the course of a trek, these movements have been likened to lemming irruptions. As a result of the drastic reduction of springbok numbers and range, only relatively small-scale treks occur nowadays from time to time (Bigalke, 1966). Oryx ("gemsbok") in South-West Africa, as well as some antelopes living in the southern part of the Sahara (e.g., Addax, Dama and Dorcas gazelles), are said to undertake irregular (or possibly regular) movements governed mainly by rainfall (Dorst and Dandelot, 1970), but no detailed studies have been carried out yet in these areas. Radio-tracking of elephants in Tsavo NP has shown that some individuals and, by implication, their groups

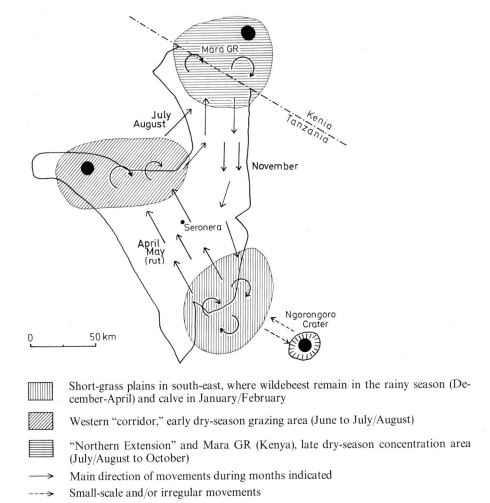

Fig. 11. Schematic representation of the migration system of blue wildebeest in the Serengeti area, Tanzania (after Norton-Griffiths, 1972; and Pennycuick, 1975)

▦	Short-grass plains in south-east, where wildebeest remain in the rainy season (December-April) and calve in January/February
▨	Western "corridor," early dry-season grazing area (June to July/August)
▤	"Northern Extension" and Mara GR (Kenya), late dry-season concentration area (July/August to October)
⟶	Main direction of movements during months indicated
⇢	Small-scale and/or irregular movements
⌢	Local movements during "stationary" phases
●	Nonmigratory local populations
—	Serengeti NP boundary

or herds utilize areas more than 100 km apart in the course of a year, concentrating temporarily in areas of green vegetation produced by local rainstorms (Leuthold and Sale, 1973). On a smaller scale, giraffe undertake seasonal movements over 10–30 km between areas of deciduous woodland and evergreen riverine forest in Tsavo NP (Leuthold and Leuthold, in press). Further examples will be given below (Chap. 6, D, II).

From the behavioral point of view, it would be interesting to know the mechanisms of sensory perception and orientation that trigger and govern such

52

movements. It is often assumed that the animals involved possess the ability to perceive even very local rainstorms over considerable distances. This is suggested by circumstances in the Tsavo elephant study and also by the fact that the otherwise quite regular migratory pattern in the Serengeti may be disrupted, even temporarily reversed, by out-of-season rainfall. We know even less about mechanisms of orientation. Circumstantial evidence and studies on temperate-zone ungulates (e.g., Schloeth, 1961a; Geist, 1971b) suggest that knowledge of normal migration routes, as well as the location and extent of seasonal home ranges, is acquired through tradition, particularly in long-lived species such as the larger antelopes and the elephant (cf. Chap. 11). However, this alone does not explain the performances observed in some ungulates, least of all the remarkable homing abilities.

C. Time-Related Behavior

It has long been recognized that the various activities of animals are not equally distributed in time but that there may be more or less distinct phases in which certain activities predominate. The sequence of these phases is generally termed the activity pattern. Such patterns are evident in relation to the 24-h day/night rhythm but, on a different scale, may also develop in relation to the annual cycle. We will consider these separately.

I. Daily Activity Patterns

Although many authors have commented on the actual or supposed existence of well-defined daily activity patterns in African ungulates, factual information on them is still relatively scant. This is primarily because recording activity in free-ranging animals is very laborious and time-consuming with the methods currently available, which necessitate continuous visual observation of the animals concerned. Thus, activity studies require a high input of man-hours which many research workers—usually with limited time available—have been reluctant to provide. Many statements on activity patterns are therefore either vague generalizations, or based on a small number of observer-days only, so that conclusions drawn from the results may be of limited value. The most comprehensive activity studies published to date (mid-1976) are those by Jarman and Jarman (1973a) on impala and by Walther (1973) on Thomson's gazelle. Much of the following discussion is based on these papers (which will not be quoted in all instances below).

A further restriction imposed by visual observation concerns the investigation of nocturnal activity. Many studies have been limited to daytime recording only while, in some cases, night observations have been made during periods of full moon. However, Gaerdes (quoted in Joubert and Eloff, 1971, p. 31) stated that greater kudu, oryx, and other antelopes were more active during

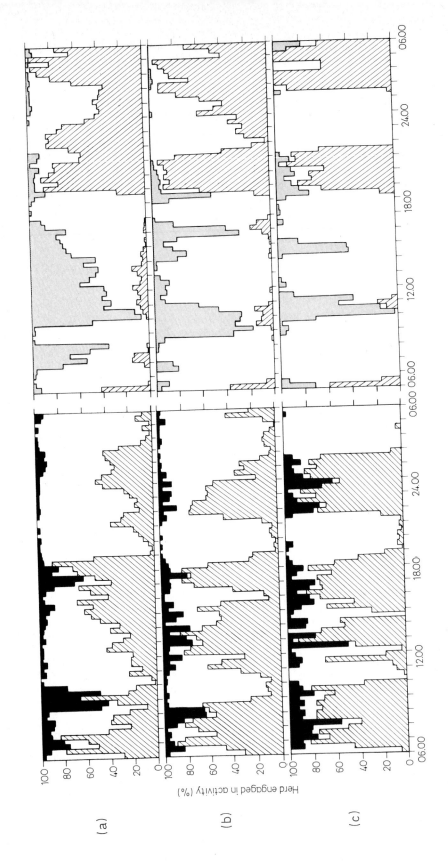

Herd engaged in activity (%)

(a)

(b)

(c)

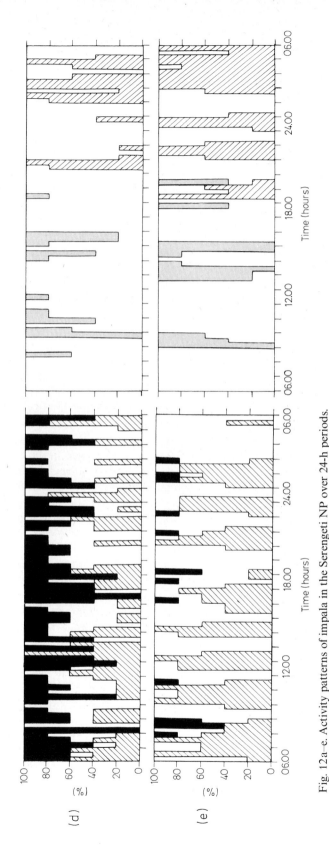

Fig. 12a–e. Activity patterns of impala in the Serengeti NP over 24-h periods.
(a)–(c): Female herds in January (a), May (b) and July (c).
(d), (e): A territorial male with females (d) and one without females (e).
On the left are "mobile" activities: feeding (*hatched*) and moving (*black*); on the right "static" activities: standing-ruminating (*dense stippling*) and lying down (*hatching*). Note the alternation of mobile and static activities in all sets, the increasing amount of feeding from set (a) to (c) reflecting deteriorating pasture quality as the dry season progresses, and the great difference in the amounts of moving between (d) and (e) resulting mainly from the difference in the "social environment" (from Jarman and Jarman, 1973a)

periods of full moon than in dark nights, although he gave no supporting evidence. Walther (1973) comments similarly with respect to Thomson's gazelle, and even the otherwise markedly diurnal warthog was sometimes found feeding in moonlit nights (Shortridge, 1934). In a recent study of feral hogs *(Sus scrofa)* in the USA, Kurz and Marchinton (1972), using radio-tracking, found that the animals moved about significantly more in moonlit than in dark nights. Erkert (1974) studied the influence of moonlight on the activity of several mammal species (though not including any ungulates) and found definite relationships which, however, differed in various ways between the species studied. These findings point out the major shortcomings of observations made under full-moon conditions. The recent development of night-observation equipment and the increasing use of telemetry promise to overcome the technical problems encountered up to now. Only then will it be possible to obtain an unbiased picture of 24-h activity patterns and a realistic interpretation of their functional aspects.

Bearing in mind these limitations, we may now examine and discuss activity patterns found in recent field studies and some of the factors influencing them.

In contrast to man, and some other primates, which generally observe a period of complete inactivity at night, most ungulates are active, to varying extents, during both day and night. Almost the only ungulate species with a clear-cut day/night rhythm is the warthog, which is active for 8–12 h in the daytime and spends the remainder of the 24 h in a burrow, presumably resting (Frädrich, 1965; Bradley, 1968; Clough and Hassam, 1970). The hippopotamus observes a similar but inverse rhythm, spending most of the daytime in the water, though not entirely inactive, and moving onto land to feed during the night (Hediger, 1951; Verheyen, 1954). In both cases the change in activity is combined with a pronounced change of environment. However, in most other ungulates, periods of various activities such as feeding, moving, social interactions, etc., are interspersed with resting phases spread throughout the 24 h (Fig. 12).

Popular opinion holds that most wild ungulates are active (feeding, moving) mainly in the early morning and late afternoon, with a long period of inactivity in the middle of the day. However, detailed studies show that this view is only partially correct and, at any rate, far too simplified. There are marked differences, in this respect, between ruminants and nonruminants, although evidence substantiating this for African ungulates is as yet rather scant. In ruminants, the specialized feeding/ruminating routine precludes long periods of complete inactivity, particularly deep sleep (Balch, 1955), and some food intake is necessary at relatively short intervals to "keep the system going." From various studies of ruminants a marked, though not necessarily regular, alternation of feeding and ruminating phases is evident, when weather conditions are not extreme (see below) and there are no disturbances. Ruminants therefore often show a—sometimes only minor—peak of feeding activity around midday, and also near midnight, for example waterbuck (Spinage, 1968), hartebeest (Stanley Price, 1974), topi (Duncan, 1975), gerenuk and giraffe (Leuthold and Leuthold, unpubl.), as well as impala (Fig. 12) and Thomson's gazelle. This contrasts to some extent with certain nonruminants that may show prolonged periods of inactivity, or at least nonfeeding activity, in the middle of the day, e.g., black rhinoceros (Goddard, 1967; Schenkel and Schenkel-Hulliger, 1969; Joubert and Eloff, 1971), elephant (Hendrichs, 1971; pers. obs.), warthog (Clough and Hassam, 1970; Cumming, 1975).

Several species, ruminants and nonruminants alike, show a marked resting phase at night, or in the very early morning, including considerable periods of lying, and even short bouts of actual sleep, e.g., the elephant (Hendrichs, 1971), plains zebra (Klingel, 1967), as well as some of the species mentioned above (cf. Fig. 12).

A major conclusion emerging from different studies is that activity patterns of a given species (or even individual), while perhaps showing certain basic trends as outlined above, vary considerably from day to day (cf. Table 12 in Walther, 1973), as well as between seasons. This suggests that activity patterns can be modified by a great variety of influences, and a number of recent studies have included attempts to identify the operant factors and assess their effects. For instance, the activity patterns of the same individually known male gerenuk in Tsavo NP on three different days, at different seasons, showed considerable variations, both in the temporal distribution (Fig. 13) and the overall proportions

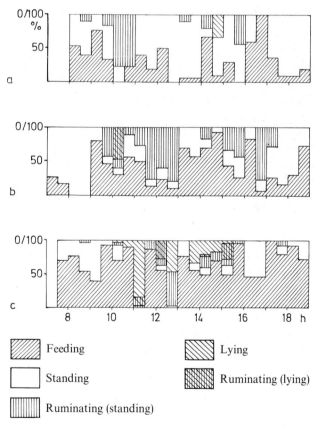

Fig. 13a–c. Diurnal activity patterns of an individually known male gerenuk in Tsavo NP on three different days: (a) 3 February 1972, (b) 24 August 1972, (c) 29 August 1972 (for weather conditions see Table 4)

(Table 4) of the different activities. In this case, the principal influences are clearly weather conditions, as indicated in Table 4. On a very hot day, in February, the gerenuk fed only little, particularly in the middle of the day, but spent most of his time just standing, much of it in the shade of trees or shrubs. By contrast, on the cooler days in August he was feeding considerably more and, accordingly, spent much less time standing, virtually none of it in shade. On the third day it rained repeatedly and, as gerenuk tend to lie down during rain (see Chap. 6, E, III), lying made up a much higher proportion of time than on the other two days. On all three occasions this male was in the company of 3–4 females, so that the social environment (see below) can be regarded as essentially the same.

This example emphasizes just one of the many factors that can influence activity patterns, though perhaps one of the more important ones: the weather. Many observers have commented on the various ways in which weather and climatic conditions affect the activity of African ungulates. This may happen either directly, through day-to-day changes in weather, or indirectly, through the seasonal effects of climate on habitat conditions. Apart from the weather and its daily and seasonal variations, a number of other factors can also affect ungulate activity patterns in various ways, for instance certain characteristics of the species concerned (e. g., thermoregulatory mechanisms, dependence on free water) and/or of the individual (sex, age, reproductive state, etc.), as well as the social environment and external disturbances (e. g., predators). In the following, I will review information on the effects of these factors on activity patterns. I should emphasize that, although each factor is considered separately, two or more may act simultaneously—sometimes in opposite senses—and the resultant activity pattern will reflect a compromise accommodating the different influences.

Daily Weather. Many generalized statements indicate that ungulates tend to be less active, i. e., spend more time resting, in hot and sunny than in cool weather. The day-to-day changes in weather conditions thus appear to influence the activity pattern mainly in connection with thermoregulation, e. g., by affecting the amount of time an animal spends in shade. The above example of the male gerenuk (Fig. 13; Table 4) gives some indication of this effect; Jarman and Jarman (1973a) present more extensive and more refined data on this point.

The most detailed work to date on the interrelationships between weather factors and activity patterns is that of Lewis (1975) and, although he observed ungulates under a semidomesticated regime (they were penned at night), their reactions to environmental conditions can probably be regarded as typical of the species concerned (eland, oryx, buffalo). Lewis' major findings, backed up by impressive quantitative data and statistical analyses, are that activity patterns vary mainly in relation to the "heat load" acting on the animals. The precise manner in which heat load manifests itself varies between species, partly as a function of morphological traits (e. g., body size, characteristics of skin and/or fur) and thermoregulatory mechanisms. Thus, for one species solar radiation may be the most important single factor, whereas for another it may be ambient

Table 4. Summary of weather conditions and proportions of various activities of the same male gerenuk on three different days in Tsavo NP (cf. Fig. 13)

Date	Season	Weather	Shade temperature (°C)			Proportions of different activities (% of total time of observation)			
			08 h	14 h	18 h	Feeding	Standing	Lying	Ruminating
3. 2. 72	short dry (hot)	hot, little wind	22.0	32.0	30.5	31.7	66.8	1.5	11.5
24. 8. 72	long dry (cool)	fairly warm, windy	20.0	29.5	26.5	39.3	58.7	2.0	24.1
29. 8. 72	long dry (cool)	cool, windy, light rain	21.5	25.0	22.0	63.1	24.5	12.4	8.8

temperature or thermal reradiation (examples in Lewis, 1975). The overall effect is, usually, a reduction of "mobile" activities (feeding, moving) under conditions of high heat load, and a corresponding increase in "static" activities (standing, lying). Heat load is generally highest around midday and/or in the early afternoon, and a phase of reduced mobile activities occurs in that part of the day fairly regularly and predictably (Figs. 12 and 13), within certain limits. In male gerenuk and female giraffe in Tsavo NP we found significant negative correlations between daily maximum temperatures and the proportion of daylight hours spent feeding (corresponding correlations did not, however, emerge for female gerenuk and male giraffe, for which we have no immediate explanation; Leuthold and Leuthold, unpubl.). In wild animals, daytime reductions in feeding time can probably be compensated for at night to a certain extent; more information on this point is, however, needed.

Other weather factors may also influence ungulate activity. For instance, rain causes virtual cessation of mobile activities in several species (e. g., impala, gerenuk, Thomson's gazelle) and may even induce them to lie down (cf. Fig. 13, Table 4 and below). Under different circumstances, e. g., after a period of hot weather, rain may have a stimulating effect and increase mobile activities, such as running or jumping "games," at least temporarily (e. g., Lewis, 1975). Strong wind, which sometimes precedes rainstorms, may have a similar effect, e. g., on impala (Jarman and Jarman, 1973a).

Climate/Seasons. Seasonal changes in activity patterns are governed primarily by the availability and quality of food and/or water. A marked dry season—where this occurs—usually confronts herbivores with a dual stress: (1) food and water may be in short supply quantitatively, and (2) what food is available is often of low nutritive quality. Thus the animals require more time than during a rainy season to achieve a nutrient/water intake sufficient for growth, reproduction, or even just maintenance. If, in addition, the dry season coincides with a period of hot weather (which, however, need not necessarily be so), thermoregulatory considerations may necessitate curtailment of mobile activities in the daytime, which means that less time is available for feeding.

Impala of the Serengeti NP may spend up to an hour daily in moving to and from water, and actually drinking, "and this at a time of year when feeding time would seem to be at a premium" (Jarman and Jarman, 1973a, p. 85). Hartebeest in Nairobi NP also move to and from localized water sources every 2–3 days during the dry season (Stanley Price, 1974). Apart from the reduction in feeding time, these movements involve additional energy expenditure, at a time when energy intake (particularly the nutritive quality of the diet) is already relatively low. An unknown quantity in this context is the extent to which daytime reduction in feeding time can be compensated for at night, but the possibilities of such compensation are likely to be limited, particularly in ruminants which generally have to maintain a certain balance between food ingestion and rumination.

Considering all these adverse circumstances, it is not surprising that the total nutrient intake of some herbivores falls even below the level required for body maintenance during the dry season, and the animals have to utilize reserves stored in the body during more favorable times—they "lose condition," as has been documented in, e. g., hartebeest (Stanley Price, 1974), topi (Duncan, 1975) and impala (Jarman and Jarman, 1974).

Apart from the fluctuations in quantity, seasonal variations in food quality also affect ungulate activity patterns, particularly in ruminants. For instance, young plants contain much less fiber than mature ones; this is especially marked in grasses. Young grass is broken down more easily and passes through the digestive system more quickly than mature grass; there is a similar difference between leaf and stem material. The seasonally different abundance of young grass and grass leaves therefore affects the length of feeding and ruminating "bouts" and their distribution throughout the day (for details see Stanley Price, 1974; Duncan, 1975; and Lewis, 1975).

In addition to these general considerations, specific local conditions may also account for certain modifications of daily activity. Some ungulate species occupy different vegetation types at different seasons, which may affect the feeding routine and therefore the overall activity pattern. However, while seasonal movements between different vegetation types are well documented (see Chap. 6, D, II), little factual information on concomitant changes in activity patterns is available (but see Duncan, 1975). In a few cases, seasonal occupance of certain vegetation types is, additionally, coupled with daily movements between different vegetation types, which results in overall seasonal differences in activity patterns (e. g., in hartebeest of Nairobi NP: Stanley Price, 1974).

Where reproduction is markedly seasonal, as in many ungulate populations of southern Africa, as well as in wildebeest and some other Alcelaphinae in tropical Africa (e. g., Duncan, 1975; Estes, 1976), the activity patterns are bound to vary considerably between seasons, being affected by synchronized rutting, calving, etc. However, little quantitative information is available as yet on this point (but see Duncan, 1975, on topi).

Species Characteristics (Morphology, Physiology, etc.). The somewhat unusual basic activity patterns of warthog and hippopotamus have already been mentioned, as have the constraints imposed on ruminants by their specialized mode of food "processing." The degree of dependence on free water can also influence basic activity patterns, through the need—or lack of it—to move to and from water (see above). So will species-specific mechanisms of thermoregulation (e. g., shade-seeking, wallowing, bathing, etc.) and the extent to which a given species is affected by heat load (cf. Lewis, 1975). The general mode of feeding is also important in this context: browsing entails more movement and smaller intake per bite (see Chap. 5, A, I). Thus, a browser requires more time for ingesting a given amount of food than a grazer. For instance, the eland studied by Lewis (1975) consistently spent more time feeding than either oryx or buffalo, both grazers. On the other hand, the generally higher quality of browse may allow the browser to fulfil its energy requirements with a smaller quantity of food than the grazer; also, less rumination may be needed for dicotyledonous food than for grasses. Thus, the combined time of ingestion and rumination may be similar in browsers and grazers. Some species show marked seasonal variations in the composition of their food by grass/browse (e. g., impala); this could also affect their activity patterns seasonally.

Characteristics of social grouping in a species may also indirectly influence the activity pattern in individuals through what is usually called contagious behavior or social facilitation. In gregarious species the activities of individuals in a group or herd are often synchronized to a considerable extent, as animals tend to adopt the activity of their neighbors. Such behavior is particularly pronounced in impala (Schenkel, 1966a; Jarman and Jarman, 1973a), but Walther (1973) also found marked synchronization of activities in Thomson's gazelle, and it may indeed be widespread among gregarious species. In elephant groups coordination of activities is usually even more pronounced, in accord with the generally high degree of cohesion within family groups (Douglas-Hamilton, 1972; pers. obs.).

Age. In very young antelopes that lie hidden for much of the time (see Chap. 14, D, II) the activity pattern differs sharply from that of adult animals. Even when older, the young of several species form "crèche" groups (Chap. 14, E) that are fairly well coordinated within themselves, but differ in their activity pattern from adult animals. In particular, they may spend considerably less time feeding as long as they are still being suckled.

One type of activity that is characteristic of, and often confined to, young animals is play (Chap. 14, D, IV), which tends to occur in bouts in the morning and evening (Jarman and Jarman, 1973a; Walther, 1973).

Sex. Several studies have shown that females tend to feed longer than males, at least during daylight hours, e.g., in warthog (Bradley, 1968; Clough and Hassam, 1970), giraffe (B. Leuthold, unpubl.), waterbuck (Spinage, 1968), topi (Duncan, 1975). Conversely, males may spend more time lying down, or otherwise inactive (e. g., giraffe), or in mobile activities (e. g., topi, impala). Some of these differences are interrelated with the factors considered in the following two paragraphs.

Reproductive Condition. Lactating females tend to spend more time feeding than nonlactating ones, e. g., in waterbuck (Spinage, 1968), impala (Jarman and Jarman, 1973a) and other species (e. g., Lewis, 1975). Females in advanced pregnancy often leave their herds and presumably adopt a different activity pattern (prepartum isolation; Chap. 14, A). Females with very small young that they may have to suckle several times a day behave similarly.

Social Factors. Male Uganda kob on arena territories (Chap. 16, E) feed and rest less than those on single territories. The latter spend more time in mobile activities when females are present than when there are none (Tables 6 and 7 in Leuthold, 1966a). Similarly, territorial male impala are more active, with herding, mating, and other social behavior in the presence of females, and consequently feed and ruminate less than when they are alone (Fig. 12; see Table 3 in Jarman and Jarman, 1973a; also Ables and Ables, 1969). These differences reflect the cost of territorial status, in terms of energy expended in return for exclusive mating rights (Chap. 18, B).

Another situation where social status affects the activity pattern involves adolescent males in territorial antelopes. While still small, young males remain within the herd of their mothers. As they grow up, they are increasingly harassed

62

by the adult male on whose territory the maternal group happens to be. Thus, they have to be constantly on guard and have to move out of the adult male's way time after time. This could result in less time (and "security") being available for feeding and resting; the entire process may play a part in regulating the survival of young males (Jarman and Jarman, 1973b).

External Disturbances. Although this may appear self-evident, disturbances caused by, e.g., the passage or presence of predators, including man, can also modify an animal's, or a group's activity pattern. Often this is difficult or impossible to assess quantitatively, but occasionally relevant data can be obtained. For instance, a male Uganda kob on a single territory (Chap. 16, E) showed a considerably higher proportion of "standing/walking" than normal (21% vs a mean of 8% found in other observations), when two lions were in the vicinity (Leuthold, 1966a). In areas frequently disturbed by man some normally diurnal ungulates adopt a predominantly nocturnal activity pattern (e.g., the warthog: references in Shortridge, 1934).

In summary, there are many factors that can, and do, influence the daily activity patterns of ungulates, and the resultant variations, both between individuals and from day to day, often render it difficult to make valid generalizations. Nevertheless, the results of various studies suggest the existence of a basic activity pattern in most, if not all, African ungulates, which may be governed partly by endogenous factors and partly by such regular features of the environment as the day/night rhythm. Both Walther (1973) and Jarman and Jarman (1973a) feel that dawn and dusk (i.e., marked changes in light intensity) act as major determinants of the activity patterns in Thomson's gazelle and impala respectively, as there are important and fairly consistent differences between diurnal and nocturnal activity (Fig. 12; see also Young, 1972, on impala movements). This basic pattern appears to be adapted, firstly, to the species' mode of feeding (e.g., alternation of food gathering and rumination); secondly, to its physiological requirements (thermoregulation, water dependence); and thirdly, to its overall antipredator strategy. In the latter context, Jarman and Jarman (1973a) point out that the activity patterns of gregarious antelopes living in savanna or open woodland, such as impala, waterbuck, etc., are characterized by a reduction of mobile activities early and late in the night, when their most important predators are active. These species rely mainly on eyesight for early detection of predators, and on rapid flight to escape. By contrast, a number of more or less solitary species, which depend more on hiding from predators (freezing, see Chap. 7, C, III), tend to be more crepuscular or even nocturnal in their feeding and other mobile activities (examples: dikdik, reedbuck, bushbuck).

II. Annual Patterns

Annual patterns of animal activities are generally governed by more or less regular changes in certain environmental factors, such as temperature, precipitation, light (photoperiod), through their effects on distribution and abundance of resources or on the animals' physiology. This is too complex a subject to be treated extensively in the present context; therefore only a few major points will be mentioned.

The main aspects of an animal's life history that may be profoundly influenced by seasonal changes in the environment are home range and movements on one hand, and reproduction and associated behavior on the other hand. We have already dealt with some of the regular and irregular migrations and movements known in African ungulates; further reference will be made below (Chap. 6, D, II). As for reproduction, the principal question is whether or not there is a well-defined breeding season. If there is, this can have far-reaching consequences for the population involved. The entire social organization (see Part 4) may undergo pronounced changes between breeding and nonbreeding seasons. The animals involved may spend the different seasons in different areas, with different habitats. However, all this does not usually alter the behavior of animals per se, but only the temporal sequence and the frequency with which certain types of behavior (mating, mother-young, territorial, etc.) occur. An interesting subject of study is the way in which a given species behaves under different conditions, i.e., under seasonal and nonseasonal reproductive regimes, and the social and ecological implications (see, for instance, the impala study by Jarman and Jarman, 1973b, 1974). Some of these questions will be discussed further in Chapter 17.

D. Space-Time Systems

So far, we have considered behavior related to space separately from that related to time. In reality, the two are closely interwoven. Hediger (1942/50) coined the term "space-time system" ("Raum-Zeit-System") to circumscribe the tendency of many animals to engage in certain activities at certain times and in certain places. He distinguished between the "lesser" space-time system, denoting daily routines of activities and movements, and the "greater" space-time system, integrating events of the annual cycle with their spatial correlates. While we have to be careful not to view such systems as being rigidly fixed, many observations confirm the validity of the concept in general. Some examples are given below.

I. The Daily Space-Time System

The daily space-time system circumscribes what an animal does when and where during a day. The concept implies a general routine of an animal moving about its home range on a more or less regular time schedule and performing certain activities at specific locations, the fixed points (Fig. 8). The following examples illustrate the extent to which this corresponds to reality in African ungulates.

The daily space-time system is perhaps most marked in those (few!) ungulate species that show a clear-cut separation of diurnal and nocturnal activities. For instance, the hippopotamus spends the daylight hours in the water and moves onto land at night to graze. Well-worn trails and numerous defecation/marking sites attest to the frequent use of the same paths to move to and from the nocturnal feeding areas, implying considerable regularity in these movement patterns (Hediger, 1951; Verheyen, 1954). Warthog may adhere to a similar though perhaps less regular routine, but in contrast to hippopotamus they usually spend the night in a "fixed point," the burrow.

In other ungulates, differences between diurnal and nocturnal activity patterns are less pronounced, and their daily space-time systems are therefore less rigid but nevertheless clearly recognizable. Zebra in Ngorongoro Crater move over a more or less closed daily circuit, which includes a "sleeping area" where they spend the night partly resting, partly feeding, as well as daytime feeding and resting grounds, drinking sites and wallows (Klingel, 1967). They may cover the circuit on a very similar schedule on consecutive days, showing a considerable degree of routine. Similarly, impala (Jarman and Jarman, 1973a), Uganda kob (Leuthold, 1966a), topi (Duncan, 1975), and probably some other species as well, have special resting areas to which they return night after night, at least over a limited period of time. These are usually in open areas with short grass which, presumably, afford some protection against the undetected approach of predators.

Particularly striking differences in habitat utilization between day and night were found in bushbuck which showed virtually no overlap between diurnal and nocturnal distributions (Waser, 1975a). Habitats used at night contained more open vegetation types, and, again, the inference is that such behavior has primarily antipredator functions.

Walther (1973, p. 96 and Table 15) gives another good example of a fairly rigid space-time system, in Thomson's gazelle. Similar activities occurred in the same locations at about the same time every day and night. This system was adhered to, with minor variations, for about three months during a stationary phase in the otherwise migratory population.

Bull elephants in the Serengeti drank and bathed regularly in the afternoon, although not necessarily in the same places (Hendrichs, 1971, Table 18). Black rhinos wallowed preferentially between 16.00 and 18.00 h, presumably at "fixed points" (Goddard, 1967). In the dry season, a herd of giraffe (though not always the same individuals) in Tsavo NP regularly moved between daytime feeding and resting areas in relatively open vegetation, and riverine forest which they entered in the evening and left again the following morning (Leuthold and Leuthold, unpubl.; we do not know, however, if they spent the entire night in the forest). Moore-Berger (1974) reported similar movements in reticulated giraffe.

Thus, a marked tendency to adhere to a daily space-time system is evident in several species of African ungulates. On the other hand, some observers also point out the great variability of such patterns (e. g., Schenkel and Schenkel-Hulliger, 1969, for black rhinoceros). Obviously, the feasibility of following a routine pattern depends to a large extent on local environmental conditions. It may be possible to maintain a relatively fixed space-time system for a certain period, but changes may be necessary from time to time to accommodate a variety of influences, such as day-to-day variations in the weather, disturbances

(e. g., predators), social factors (e. g., rutting activities), as well as seasonal changes in the availability of resources. As in other contexts, flexibility may be vital and adaptive, and the daily space-time system should not be viewed as rigidly fixed but rather as a general framework that can be adapted to specific external circumstances.

II. The Annual Space-Time System

The annual space-time system integrates events of the annual cycle with their spatial correlates, e. g., temporal migration patterns with migration routes and seasonal home ranges. Again, the regularity with which such systems are adhered to may vary considerably between animal species, areas and consecutive years, primarily in response to environmental conditions.

A well-known example, and one of relative constancy, is the migration system in the Serengeti area (cf. Fig. 11), where the major stations and events for white-bearded wildebeest are as follows:

December to March fairly stationary phase on the southeastern short grass plains, where calving takes place (mainly in January); April to June gradual movement northwestward through the Seronera area, with rutting "on the move"; July to September in the relatively moist long-grass woodland areas of the western and northern Serengeti and adjacent Mara Game Reserve in Kenya; October to November return migration to the southeastern plains (Grzimek and Grzimek, 1960; Talbot and Talbot, 1963; Norton-Griffiths, 1972; Pennycuick, 1975).

The entire migration "circle" entails travelling over a minimum of some 1,500 km, not counting the day-to-day movements undertaken in the course of feeding and other activities, nor any "side trips" or doubling-back movements. The latter occur frequently in response to local rainstorms, which cause many minor differences in the migration pattern from year to year. Talbot and Talbot (1963, p. 55) state that "the movements are highly irregular" and "no two years' or seasons' movements necessarily will be alike." Nevertheless, a certain degree of regularity, and predictability, is a feature of the Serengeti wildebeest migration.

Parts of the Serengeti zebra population follow a pattern similar to that of the wildebeest, while other species undertake less extensive movements (Grant's and Thomson's gazelles, eland). In addition, entirely sedentary populations of most species, including wildebeest, exist in certain areas (e. g., the west) of the Serengeti NP (Fig. 11).

The Serengeti migration system is perhaps extreme in its spatial extent and in the numbers of animals involved, but fairly regular movements between well-defined seasonal ranges are characteristic of many ungulate populations, both in Africa and elsewhere. Where the animals do not cover large horizontal distances, they often move between different altitudinal zones and/or different soil and vegetation types. Generally they tend to follow the "catenary sequence" (Bell, 1971), spending the wet season on high, well-drained ground (hills, slopes) and moving into valleys (riverine and lacustrine flats, etc.) in the dry season, and back again later. On the higher ground the vegetation often consists of relatively short grasses and/or deciduous woodlands, whereas in the valley bottoms tall grasses and/or evergreen bush and forest predominate, providing a food supply during the dry season.

Such seasonal movements across the catena have been described in some detail by Bell (1971) for the western Serengeti, by Jarman (1972b) for the Zambezi Valley, and by Simpson (1972) for greater kudu in three areas of southern Africa; they appear to be rather widespread, at least among the more mobile ungulates. On a small scale, corresponding movements occur even among otherwise very sedentary species, such as lesser kudu and gerenuk in Tsavo NP (Leuthold, 1974, and unpubl.). These species also move from areas of deciduous bush/woodland toward, and into, riverine areas with evergreen vegetation as the dry season progresses. Stanley Price (1974) and Duncan (1975) concluded that the main causative factors underlying seasonal movements in hartebeest and topi were the structure and condition of the grass sward, with regard to its suitability as food.

The regularity of the temporal and spatial movement patterns depends largely on climatic conditions, particularly the occurrence and distribution of rainfall. In areas with relatively regular and reliable rainfall, the extent of movements and the locations involved may vary little from year to year. In areas with highly irregular rainfall only parts of the space-time systems may be reasonably predictable, usually the dry-season ranges. This apparently applies to both elephants and giraffes in Tsavo NP, where individuals or groups tend to occupy the same dry-season ranges (generally riverine areas) in subsequent seasons, but the rainy-season ranges may differ substantially from year to year, depending largely on the spatial and temporal distribution of rainfall (Leuthold and Sale, 1973; Leuthold and Leuthold, in press).

Thus, in correspondence to what was said above about the daily space-time system, we may consider the annual space-time system as a generalized framework, the details of which are "filled in" in response to prevailing environmental conditions in any one place and at any one time.

E. Influences of Weather on Behavior

Earlier (Chap. 6, C, I), we have discussed the influence of weather on daily activity patterns. This is probably by far the most important way in which the weather affects ungulate behavior. However, some ungulates show fairly specific reactions to certain weather factors; I will describe some of them below, on the basis of information from the literature and some personal observations.

I. Sunshine and Temperature

As a general response to hot weather many ungulates seek shade and/or remain inactive during much of the day (see Fig. 13 and Table 4). In cases where no shade is available, the following alternative behaviors may be shown: Thomson's gazelles sometimes move to higher ground where wind may provide some cooling effect (Brooks, 1961; of course, this is not always possible). Bontebok and blesbok adopt a characteristic posture, with head held low and oriented toward the sun (Fig. 14), and even follow the sun's movement in the course of the day, like needles of a compass. This has been interpreted as exposing the smallest possible area of the body surface to the sun (David, 1973; Du Plessis, 1972).

Fig. 14. Group of bontebok facing the sun in characteristic head-low posture (from David, 1973)

Conversely, in cool weather—particularly in the early morning—Thomson's gazelles may actually seek insolation by orienting and exposing their bodies in such a way as to "catch" a maximum of solar radiation (Walther, 1973). The effect of such behavior can be enhanced by movement from bushy areas into open grassland.

II. Wind

As just mentioned, Thomson's gazelles may seek exposure to wind, for its cooling effect, in hot weather. Elephants sometimes extend their ears sideways, while facing downwind, so that the underside with its dense network of superficial veins is directly exposed to the wind. This may obviate the need for ear-flapping, the relation of which to wind speed has been referred to earlier (Chap. 5, D, I).

On the other hand, a cold wind can reduce activity to the point of many animals lying down for extended periods (Brooks, 1961; Jungius, 1971; Walther, 1973). This probably helps to conserve heat, as less body surface is exposed to the wind. Some antelopes also tend to turn their back into the wind, which presumably has a similar effect.

In addition to causing heat-loss, wind is important to ungulates as a vector of scents and sounds providing information about the environment. Animals at rest, when perception of and/or attention to visual stimuli may be lowered, often orientate themselves so as to pick up a maximum of information from the wind. However, if the wind becomes strong, its acoustic effects on the vegetation (rustling, etc.) make it more difficult for the animals to identify specific sounds, e. g., to perceive the approach of a predator. Under such circumstances Thomson's gazelles (Brooks, 1961) and southern reedbuck (Jungius, 1971) were found to be particularly wary and difficult to approach. Similarly, impala were "nervous and excitable" on windy days (Jarman and Jarman, 1973a), as were wildebeest (Talbot and Talbot, 1963). Of course, it is difficult to establish with certainty the exact reasons why animals are "jumpy" in windy conditions.

Information conveyed by the wind may also play a part in triggering long-distance movements to areas offering favorable feeding conditions. Elephants, as well as other ungulates, appear capable of perceiving localized rainfall, or its effect on the vegetation, over considerable distances and may then move to the areas affected (Leuthold and Sale, 1973). Brooks (1961) surmised that the annual changes in monsoon winds might be involved in the timing of the migrations of Thomson's gazelles in the Serengeti and other areas.

III. Rain

Light rain appears to have little effect on the behavior of ungulates, but heavy rain may disrupt their activities and elicit a variety of responses. Feeding is usually suppressed altogether. Several antelopes adopt a fairly specific "rain posture," in which the back is arched, the head and neck are drawn in and the animal usually stands quietly, facing downwind, until the rain is over. In the wild, this has been recorded in Thomson's gazelle (Walther, 1973), impala (Jarman and Jarman, 1973a; pers. obs.), and Uganda kob; in captivity in Tragelaphines, several gazelles and blesbok (Walther, 1964a, 1968, 1969b; "Unbehaglichkeitshaltung"); it probably occurs in many other species.

Thomson's gazelles (Brooks, 1961; Walther, 1973), impala (Ables and Ables, 1969) and gerenuk (B. Leuthold, pers. comm.) often lie down during heavy rain (see above, Fig. 13 and Table 4). This behavior probably serves to reduce heat loss. Warthog enter their burrows during rain (Clough and Hassam, 1970; pers. obs.), which may have the same function.

Another response observed occasionally consists of breaking into wild flight at the onset of heavy rain. The flight may come to an end quickly, e. g., in Thomson's gazelle (Walther, 1973), or it may continue for some time and gradually change into a playful bout of activity with much gamboling, e. g., in Uganda kob (pers. obs.; see also Lewis, 1975). Similar behavior sometimes occurs in response to sudden gusts of wind, e. g., in impala (Jarman and Jarman, 1973a).

Rainfall indirectly affects the movements of ungulates in their daily space-time system, e. g., when dry river beds become flooded or when loamy soil gets waterlogged. Thomson's gazelles are said to move from areas of "black cotton soil" to higher, well-drained ground after heavy rain (Brooks, 1961). Of course, the delayed effects of rainfall on vegetation condition influence herbivore movements to a very considerable extent.

To sum up, weather factors affect primarily thermoregulatory behavior, activity patterns, and movements. The factors treated separately above may act simultaneously and produce a variety of combined effects, so that it may be difficult to identify the part played by each factor individually. Some recent studies on physiological adaptations to heat and solar radiation, mainly on confined antelopes, have yielded interesting results (e.g., Taylor 1969, 1970a, b; Finch, 1972, 1973), but much more research needs to be done, particularly on free-ranging ungulates and their behavioral responses to different weather conditions.

Chapter 7

Relations with Animals of Other Species

Most ungulates share their habitat, to a greater or lesser degree, with a variety of other animals, with which a multitude of relations may exist. We can very broadly categorize such relations—from the point of view of the ungulate—as positive, neutral, or negative. A relationship is positive when the ungulate involved derives some benefit from the association or interaction. A neutral relationship is one in which it neither gains nor loses anything, whereas a negative relationship may have adverse effects on the ungulate concerned. While making this distinction we should, however, not view these categories as rigid; circumstances may shift the balance of a given relationship toward the positive or negative side.

We can further distinguish between relations involving only ungulates, of different species, and those involving ungulates and less closely related species (carnivores, birds, etc.). Many interspecific relationship may be important ecologically but show few or no behavioral manifestations (e. g., ungulates–dung beetles); I will confine this review to ethologically relevant cases.

A. Positive Relations

I. Ungulate-Ungulate

Mixed aggregations of several ungulate species are a striking feature of many African herbivore communities and have often been commented on by observers. However, I know of no field study primarily concerned with the factors underlying their formation, and we can only speculate on their functional aspects. The frequent occurrence of interspecific associations suggests that factors are involved that go beyond similarities in habitat and resource requirements and resultant chance aggregations. Also, it appears that some species are more inclined than others to participate in multispecies associations. This tendency may be linked with intraspecific grouping behavior, i. e., species that generally form large herds join animals of other species more readily (e. g., zebra, wildebeest, oryx, eland, impala), whereas those living solitarily or in small groups do so less often (e. g., bushbuck, lesser kudu, gerenuk; Elder and Elder, 1970; Leuthold and Leuthold, 1975 a). This is, however, a broad generalization that requires substantiation.

Estes (1967, p. 197) said that "a positive association is demonstrated when isolated members of one species join members of another species" and explained this tentatively by assuming that a "need for social contact" inherent in gregarious species led isolated individuals "to seek the companionship of other herbivores" in the absence of conspecifics. It is indeed common to see a single individual, most often an adult male, of oryx, hartebeest, Grant's gazelle, etc., in a mixed association (Henshaw, 1972; Leuthold and Leuthold, 1975 a). Klingel (1967) noted that zebra often led the way in mixed zebra-wildebeest herds on migration, while the wildebeest tended to wait until zebra had "pioneered" a river crossing or other critical point. These observations suggest a definite benefit for at least one of the parties involved in some interspecific associations.

Other possible benefits may be less obvious, e.g., increased protection from predators. The fact that ungulates living in open country tend to form larger herds than those in more "closed" habitats is usually interpreted, at least in part, as an antipredator device (e.g., Eisenberg, 1966; Jarman, 1974; see Chaps. 18 and 19). Conceivably, a comparable effect could be achieved if several small groups of different species coalesced into a larger association. In this context it is important to note that alarm calls (see Chap. 8,B,I) of many African ungulates are suprisingly similar, either a type of snort or a barking sound. Some ungulates react to another species' alarm call, and even to the posture of alertness (e.g., Estes, 1967; Bradley, 1968), which is an important prerequisite for mutual association to be effective as an antipredator device.

In Tsavo NP we observed zebra associating with giraffe relatively frequently (Leuthold and Leuthold, 1975 a). Possibly, zebra profit from the giraffes' superior capabilities of visual detection of predators in bush country, but we were unable to confirm this suggestion. However, when approached by vehicles, the zebra often stampeded and thereby induced the giraffes to run too, although the giraffes by themselves normally tolerated a closer approach. Similar observations of interspecific stimulation into flight were made in other cases and also by other authors (e.g., Henshaw, 1972).

In summary, I wish to emphasize again that very little is known as yet on the nature and functional aspects of multispecies ungulate associations. Many may be fortuitous assemblies at localities offering conditions favorable to several species, but others may convey specific advantages to one or several of the parties concerned. In addition to the antipredatory aspects just discussed, other ecological benefits may be involved, as in the case of grazing successions (Vesey-Fitzgerald, 1960; Bell, 1971). The theory of grazing successions states that one herbivore species, through its impact on the vegetation, makes available certain portions of this vegetation to other species. For instance, large ungulates such as elephant or buffalo, may "open up" areas of tall coarse grass to smaller species by their feeding and trampling; whether such relationships are really ecologically important remains to be proved, however. As Estes (1967) pointed out, "no obligatory associations between ungulates are known, and any existing association is usually purely temporary."

II. Ungulate–Other

Perhaps the most common interspecific association involving other mammals is that between impala, bushbuck or some other antelopes on the one hand,

and certain monkeys, particularly vervets *(Cercopithecus aethiops)* or baboons *(Papio* spp.), on the other hand (e.g., Elder and Elder, 1970; Henshaw, 1972; pers. obs.). This relationship may be commensalistic, or perhaps mutualistic, albeit transitory, with two main aspects involved: facilitation of feeding, and/or antipredator responses. The latter can generally only be inferred from circumstantial evidence. Morgan-Davies (1960) stated that impala entered thick bush, which they normally avoided, when accompanied by baboons, implying that the impala felt "safer" in the presence of baboons. Other examples are quoted by Elder and Elder (1970). Various authors have also pointed out that the ungulates and primates involved in such associations react to each other's alarm calls (which may actually sound quite similar).

A purely commensalistic relationship, with the ungulates on the profiting side, is better documented. Monkeys feeding in trees drop leaves and fruits that are sometimes collected and eaten by ungulates aggregating under the trees (e.g., Morgan-Davies, 1960; Elder and Elder, 1970). In one instance, a number of baboons were feeding on the ripe fruits of a wild fig tree (probably *Ficus sycomorus* L.) in Tsavo NP, dropping quite a few figs in the process. Under the tree were about a dozen impala, a male and two female waterbuck and a male lesser kudu, all gathering fallen fruits. When the baboons left, the antelopes continued to search for fruits for a while, before moving off slowly (Leuthold, 1971e). Here, the association between ungulates and baboons was rather one-sided, but in other cases the two aspects mentioned above may be combined. Eisenberg and Lockhart (1972) reported corresponding observations on axis deer *(Axis axis)* and langurs (*Presbytis* sp.) in Ceylon.

Probably the best-known association between ungulates and a nonmammal is that involving two species of oxpeckers *(Buphagus africanus* and *B. erythrorhynchus)*, small birds of the starling family (Sturnidae). This is generally thought of as a real symbiosis—in the sense of "proto-cooperation" (Odum, 1959)—the birds deriving most or all of their food from the ungulate's body surface in the form of ticks and other ectoparasites, the removal of which is presumably of some benefit to the ungulate. In addition, oxpeckers have a sharp hissing alarm call that is usually assumed to alert the host animal, although this function may be overrated. Nevertheless, Schenkel and Schenkel-Hulliger (1969) documented various types of reactions by black rhinoceros to the oxpeckers' alarm call (see also Attwell, 1966). On the other hand, the "tick birds" may also be a nuisance to the ungulates they attend, either when poking with their bills into ears and eyes or, more seriously, when they keep open or even enlarge superficial wounds and prevent them from healing (fairly commonly seen in rhinoceros). In this respect, the birds may be considered as partially parasitic, as they actually eat some flesh from wounds. Oxpeckers frequent a variety of the larger ungulates, from about impala-size upward (including warthog), being particularly common on rhinoceros, buffalo, and giraffe (this varies somewhat between locations). A notable exception is the elephant, which is hardly ever host to oxpeckers. Also, hartebeest and most species of the Reduncinae are said not to be attended or not to tolerate the birds (Attwell, 1966; Jungius, 1971). For a review of oxpecker–host relations see Attwell (1966).

A similar but looser relationship exists between some ungulates and a few other bird species, e.g., the piapiac (*Ptilostomus afer*, Corvidae) and the cattle egret (*Bubulcus ibis*), although in these cases it is more difficult to see what benefits may accrue to the ungulates. Probably these associations are merely commensalistic, the birds catching insects attracted to the ungulates or disturbed by their passage through the vegetation. With respect to man, the presence of cattle egrets can, in fact, be detrimental to their hosts, as the white birds are visible over long distances and may reveal an otherwise concealed game animal to a hunter.

Both cattle egret and piapiac actually perch on large ungulates, whereas a few other insectivorous birds only seek their vicinity at times, notably the drongo (*Dicrurus adsimilis*), catching insects attracted to, or disturbed by, the ungulates. Here again, there may be no benefits of any consequence to the ungulates.

Hediger (1951) noted an association between the hippopotamus and a cyprinid fish (*Labeo velifer*), which sometimes attached itself temporarily to the hippo's body. It possibly removes algae or other deposits from the skin, but it is unkown whether the hippo derives any benefit from the fishes' activity.

B. Neutral Relations

Probably the majority of nonmammalian vertebrates in an ungulate's surroundings do not enter into any significant relationship with it, even when closely associated in space, although this is difficult to prove. Perhaps one should speak of "no evident relation" rather than a "neutral" one.

Looking at associations between different species of ungulates, one may find cases in which no interaction is evident, for instance when different species congregate on feeding grounds favorable to all, but are in no way coordinated in their activities and reactions to external stimuli. An example is the mixed collection of antelopes assembling under a fruiting tree as a result of the baboons' feeding (see above). This can be considered a neutral association (Estes, 1967); such cases are however, of little interest from the behavioral point of view and will not be discussed further.

C. Negative Relations

Again, we can distinguish between interactions with other ungulates and those with animals of unrelated groups (e.g., parasites, predators).

I. Ungulate–Ungulate

Negative or adverse relations between ungulates of different species usually take the form of conflict or competition over some resources desired by both

74

(or all) species. Henshaw (1972) gave several examples of conflict, all involving elephants and several bovid species (buffalo, waterbuck, etc.). Elephants addressed aggressive behavior (head-shaking, trumpeting) to the other ungulates, which usually fled. In one case, however, a male waterbuck charged toward a group of elephants, causing them to flee! Elephants, as well as black rhinoceros, commonly charge other ungulates at waterholes, licks, etc. The likeliest explanation for such interspecific intolerance is usually actual or potential competition over a locally restricted resource (Henshaw, 1972). However, as elephants are notoriously intolerant of other animals at waterholes, even species that are unlikely to compete with them for water (e. g., marabu storks, *Leptoptilos crumeniferus*, and other birds), other explanations may have to be found for such behavior. Sheer playfulness in young elephants, or investigative behavior that might be "misunderstood" as aggressive by the animal(s) affected, may account for at least some of the "intolerance" shown by elephants at waterholes.

Fig. 15. Male sable antelope displacing a group of zebra from a waterhole; note the marked threat posture with horns presented forward (from Klingel, 1967)

Among other ungulates, instances of overt hostility seem to be relatively rare, particularly interspecific fighting. Physical combat between animals of different species sometimes occurs in the artificial conditions of captivity but is probably very rare in the wild. I know of one reliably recorded instance of a fight between a male Grant's gazelle and an oryx in Tsavo NP (filmed by Simon Trevor in "The African Elephant"); the object of the fighting was not clear. Specific threat behavior is sometimes used by one species to intimidate members of another, as in the case of a sable antelope chasing zebra from a waterhole (Fig. 15; Klingel, 1967). More often, however, one species obviously seeks to avoid a direct encounter with another one, ceding the "right-of-way" voluntarily. For instance, a group of warthog regularly left their drinking site when some zebra arrived and waited at a distance until the latter left again (Frädrich,

1965). E. Joubert (1972b) reported several cases of Hartmann's zebra displacing greater kudu and oryx from shade trees or waterholes.

For this type of relationship Hediger (1940a, 1942/50) coined the term "biological hierarchy" (as opposed to the intraspecific social hierarchy, see Chap. 15) to describe situations where different species with similar physical characteristics and ecological requirements enter into competition over food, space, water, etc. The "biologically dominant"—usually simply the larger—species normally secures access to these resources without being challenged.

II. Ungulate–Parasite

Heavy infestation with parasites can lead to alteration of an animal's behavior, but such situations would have to be described as pathological and are excluded from this review. We will only consider briefly cases of everyday occurrence, involving ectoparasites such as ticks and various biting flies. In the virtual absence of detailed studies on this subject, the following section is by necessity sketchy and partly speculative.

The main behavioral reactions to attacks by external parasites are a variety of movements serving to avoid or remove them, such as shaking various parts of the body, foot-stamping, scratching, sudden jumping or running, etc. These are essentially comfort movements, which have been reviewed earlier (Chap. 5, D, I), but they can be attributed to a distinct, identifiable stimulus. They may have further repercussions: for instance, the sudden jumps and short runs often taken by some antelopes (pers. obs. on gerenuk and lesser kudu), apparently in response to biting insects, may expose them to increased risk of predation, through temporary reduction of attentiveness and/or greater conspicuousness. Moreover, seasonal changes in abundance of blood-sucking insects may influence habitat selection by ungulates. For instance, lesser kudu and giraffe in Tsavo NP spend less time in a riverine forest during the rainy than during the dry season, and I suspect that this is at least partly because tsetse flies (*Glossina* spp.) are particularly abundant during the rains. However, it is difficult to separate this possibility from the effects of seasonal variations in the food supply outside the forest and their influence on the animals' movements and choice of habitat (cf. Leuthold, 1971a; Leuthold and Leuthold, 1972).

III. Ungulate–Predator

One of the most important environmental factors that have shaped ungulate behavior in the course of evolution is undoubtedly predation. The constant risk of being caught and eaten affects many facets of ungulate life, including escape mechanisms, activity patterns, group size and formation, mother-young relations, etc.

Kruuk (1964) distinguished between direct and indirect systems within a species' overall antipredator mechanism. The indirect system includes such behavioral and ecological traits as habitat selection, camouflage, group size, breeding pattern, etc. The influence of predation on the evolution of these characteristics is usually impossible to demonstrate directly and can only be inferred from circumstantial evidence and plain logic. Several aspects of the indirect antipredator system are closely interrelated with the type of social organization prevalent in a species; we will, therefore, defer discussion of these relationships until later (Chap. 19).

For the moment, we will look at what Kruuk called the direct antipredator system, which comprises the behavioral means that an individual animal, or group, has at its disposal to minimize its chances of being caught by a predator. As in some other instances, the separation of different components of one overall behavioral complex is somewhat artificial, as certain aspects of one may be understood only by reference to the other.

Ungulates may take certain generalized "precautions" to minimize the chances of encountering a predator in the first place. Such measures include avoidance of thickets, where predators may hide; adjusting the activity pattern relative to that of the predator, e. g., to go drinking at a time when predators are least active; to walk in single file so that, in the event of a surprise attack, individuals do not interfere with each other's escape attempts (e. g., wildebeest: Schaller, 1972). However, such precautions afford only minimal protection; the crucial test usually comes when a predator actually appears on the scene.

An important point to be made here first is that antipredator behavior, as many other types of behavior, is very flexible and may vary from one occasion to another, depending on the kind of predator involved, on the type of habitat, on sex, age and social status of the potential prey animal, etc. Thus, generalization is difficult and must be attempted and interpreted with caution.

Responses of ungulates to the presence, once detected, of a predator can take the following forms (Walther, 1969a; Smythe, 1970; Jarman, 1974; Eisenberg and Lockhart, 1972):

(1) ignoring the predator; (2) increased alertness; (3) avoidance of detection; (4) flight before or during attack; (5) threatening of and/or attack on the predator. These are not necessarily alternatives, but one response may be followed by another, depending on what the predator does. We will, however, consider each possibility separately.

Ignoring the Predator. If an ungulate, after perceiving the presence of a predator, continues with its current activity without showing obvious signs of alarm, we may say that it ignores the predator. However, this does not mean that it pays no attention at all, but merely that its behavior is not noticeably altered. Obviously, this response is feasible only when the ungulate need not fear the predator immediately, either because it has sufficient means of defense or escape, or because the predator is obviously not hunting. For instance, a lone bull elephant may well ignore the presence of a lion from which it has nothing to fear, while the same lion might cause considerable excitement (and one of the responses outlined in the following) among a cow group with calves that are potential prey for the lion. In practice, it will generally be difficult to establish whether an ungulate actually ignores a predator, or whether its vigilance is so subtle as to be imperceptible to the human observer; and indeed the difference may really be immaterial. The main point is that no overt reaction is evident.

Increased Alertness. When ungulates first perceive the presence of a predator—or any other suspect object—they usually interrupt ongoing activities and adopt postures facilitating the perception of further clues on the whereabouts and behavior of the predator. A Thomson's gazelle, for instance, stops feeding or ruminating, turns and extends the head and neck in the direction of the potential danger, cocks the ears, suppresses ear and tail movements and stands motionless and somewhat tense (Walther, 1969 a, see Fig. 16), until incoming information

Fig. 16. Alert posture of adult male Thomson's gazelle *(right)*; compare with normal posture of female on left (from Walther, 1969 a)

indicates another course of action. This may be either relaxation and eventual continuation of the previous activity, or measures to elude the predator (see below). This basic pattern applies to virtually all ungulates; the details differ somewhat, depending mainly on which senses are most important in locating potential danger. Elephants, who rely primarily on scent and hearing, lift their trunk into the air, rather in the manner of a submarine's periscope, and sample the wind; they may also extend the ears sideways. When less seriously alarmed, they may merely turn the tip of the trunk into the direction of the wind, at or near ground level.

In addition to adopting a characteristic posture some ungulates, having spotted a predator, also emit certain vocalizations, generally referred to as alarm calls. In many bovid species, as well as in the plains zebra, these calls are short snorts, produced through the nose, or sharp barks (Tragelaphines), which generally show a high degree of interspecific resemblance; this may be advantageous in mixed-species assemblages. In other species, however, alarm vocalizations are entirely different, e.g., a high-pitched whistle in the reedbucks and kobs, which is produced by forcing air through the half-closed nostrils. As the mouth remains closed and abdominal contractions are clearly visible, some early observers mistakenly assumed that these whistles originated from the inguinal glands, which are prominent in most or all Reduncinae. A variation on the theme of alarm calls is sudden cessation of all calling in species in which constant vocalizing is a normal feature, as in the large aggregations of migratory wildebeest in the Serengeti (Schaller, 1972). The sudden silence has essentially the same effect as a sudden call in otherwise silent surroundings, i.e., it arouses the attention of the animals in the vicinity.

Their attention may further be stimulated by a variety of visually conspicuous behaviors. The "alert posture" described above may by itself act as a visual signal; at higher intensities of alarm certain striking movement patterns (e.g., stotting) may be employed; these will be considered in more detail below.

Upon spotting a potentially dangerous predator some ungulates, particularly gregarious ones living in open habitat, may actually approach it and gather around it at a distance allowing safe escape in case of an attack (e.g., zebra: Klingel, 1967, Figs. 24 and 25; Thomson's gazelle: Walther, 1969a; Uganda kob: pers. obs., see Fig. 17). If the predator moves, the ungulates may follow

Fig. 17. "Fascination behavior" of Thomson's gazelles toward a single wild dog (from Kruuk, 1972)

at a distance, with heads and necks stretched forward in a posture generally adopted when approaching an unfamiliar object (exploration or "curiosity" posture). Uganda kob showed this behavior toward a crocodile moving overland, a monitor lizard (*Varanus* sp.) and a python, in all cases at close quarters, but also toward an immobilized conspecific lying on the ground and kicking with its legs. Walther (1969a) called this response "fascination behavior" (see also Kruuk, 1972). Its main function appears to be to keep the predator and its movements under close surveillance and deny it the opportunity for a surprise attack. Also, it would be difficult or impossible for the predator to single out a victim from amongst the closely assembled ungulates. An accessory function may be that this conspicuous behavior attracts the attention of conspecifics, and possibly other animals, that have not yet become aware of the predator's presence.

Where relatively large ungulates are involved, fascination behavior may acquire aggressive overtones and turn into "mobbing" or outright attack on the predator, with the apparent aim of putting it to flight (see below).

Avoidance of Detection. If a predator has not yet spotted the potential prey animal, the latter may try to remain undetected, either by "freezing" on the spot, lying down in dense vegetation, or sneaking away quietly. The smaller Tragelaphines (bushbuck, lesser kudu) typically remain standing motionless, sometimes with one leg lifted as if frozen in midmotion (Walther, 1964a, p. 397; pers. obs.). Reedbuck, steinbuck, and common duiker tend to lie down on the spot, if possible in some tall grass (e. g., Jungius, 1971), when the predator approaches, then suddenly bolt from cover directly in front of him and probably startle him in the process, thus delaying his reaction slightly. The young of many species of antelopes also lie down to avoid predation, even if the adults generally use other means of escape. However, if pressed very hard, even adult Thomson's gazelles occasionally lie flat on the ground, but this is very rare (Walther, 1969a).

In general, freezing and/or lying down as a response to predators is confined to species living in relatively closed habitats (forest bush, tall grass) and forming only small groups (see also Chap. 19).

Flight. As long as the predator is relatively far away, he may simply be watched (see above); if he approaches, he will eventually reach a point at which the ungulate starts taking evasive action. The distance at which this happens is called the "flight distance" (Hediger, 1934). During his field observations in the then Belgian Congo, Hediger (1951) measured flight distances of various wild animals under different circumstances. He already noted considerable intraspecific variation; others have since confirmed this (e. g., Klingel, 1967, for plains zebra; Walther, 1969a, for Thomson's gazelle). A great number of factors can influence the flight distance of any one ungulate, or group of ungulates:

(a) Species-specific characteristics, e. g., size of the animal(s), type of habitat and the prevalent kind of antipredator behavior used. Thus, among the Tragelaphines, bushbuck and lesser kudu often have a relatively short flight distance (from vehicles), depending more on concealment, whereas eland are notoriously "shy" and may flee at several hundred meters.

(b) Individual characteristics, such as age, sex, previous experience, and reproductive status. For instance, females with small young often have a greater flight distance than other females (e. g., Kruuk, 1972, Fig. 40; Rowe-Rowe, 1974). Adult males of many ungulates tend to be less wary (again primarily toward vehicles, but in some cases also toward actual predators) than females. Walther (1969a) has examined in detail the differences in flight distance between various age and sex classes of Thomson's gazelle.

(c) Conditions in the area concerned (this again applies to man and/or his vehicles). Thus, in a long-established national park or reserve with a high visitor frequency flight distances of ungulates are minimal (e. g., Nairobi NP, Ngorongoro Crater) in comparison with open hunting areas, or even with less frequently visited parks (cf. Rowe-Rowe, 1974).

(d) Features of the predator involved, e.g., species, sex and age, number, behavior, i.e., whether hunting or not (in general ungulates appear to be able to detect this and adjust their response accordingly). This has been emphasized particularly by Kruuk (1972) and Schaller (1972), who have had very extensive experience of ungulate-predator interactions in Africa.

While I recognize that some of the above applies primarily to relations with man and is not necessarily part of "normal" antipredator behavior, it is much easier, and more reliable, to measure or estimate flight distances of ungulates with respect to man and/or vehicles than with respect to "natural" predators. Data obtained from such observations provide at least an indication of the kind and magnitude of variations to be expected in the flight distances of ungulates vis-à-vis their predators.

When a predator approaches or oversteps the flight distance, the ungulate may react in various ways, again related to the predator's behavior. If the latter starts a chase, the ungulate will move off at full speed, attempting to outdistance the predator. The outcome of the chase will then depend almost exclusively on the speed and endurance of both predator and potential prey.

If, on the other hand, the predator does not attack, the ungulate, while trying to keep at a more or less constant distance from the predator, may show a variety of additional responses, e.g., alarm calls (see above) or specialized movement patterns such as "stotting" or "pronking," the stiff-legged jumping gait of gazelles (Fig. 18; Walther, 1968, 1969a) and some other antelopes (hartebeest: Estes and Goddard, 1967; Uganda kob: pers. obs.). Other conspicuous postures or movements, such as raising or curling the tail and displaying its white underside (where appropriate), often accompany the striking gaits. These responses are common mainly in the more gregarious species and are generally

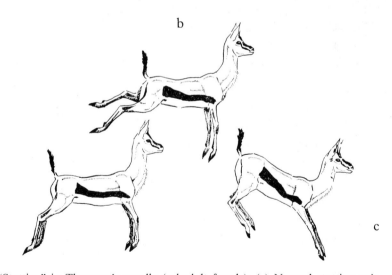

Fig. 18a–c. "Stotting" in Thomson's gazelle (subadult female): (a) Normal stotting gait. (b) Paddling with hindlegs in extremely high stotting. (c) Landing from high stotting (from Walther, 1969a)

regarded as having some signal function. One should not conceive this as a conscious effort on the part of one animal to "warn" other group members, but rather as specialized expressive behavior that usually occurs in well-circumscribed situations and elicits an appropriate response in conspecifics and, in some cases, also in animals of other species. Some of these behavior patterns may be exhibited in other contexts as well, e.g., in intraspecific social encounters in Thomson's gazelle (Walther, 1969a), while in lesser kudu the curling of the tail seems to be an automatic response coupled with running, whatever the context (Leuthold and Leuthold, 1973).

Smythe (1970) advanced the hypothesis that conspicuous movements and/or vocalizations may serve to attract the predator's attention and to induce him to give chase while the ungulate is still in a position to safely outrun the predator, thus reducing the chances of that animal actually falling prey. The predator, having given chase unsuccessfully, is less likely to molest the same animal again. At the same time, other animals may have been alerted by the displays as well as the chase itself. Thus, according to Smythe's hypothesis, which remains to be tested, conspicuous displays may have the dual effect of minimizing predation on the individual directly involved, as well as on other animals associated with it.

At the beginning of an attack, particularly by a cursorial predator, most gregarious ungulates show a strong tendency to bunch up into a dense group and try to "shelter" young animals in their midst. These measures may deny the predator the opportunity to single out an individual animal on which to concentrate the chase. Failure to isolate an individual often induces predators to abandon the chase (Kruuk, 1972; Schaller, 1972).

Specialized locomotory patterns, shown under attack, such as scattering, zigzagging, or the spectacular leaps of impala ("a herd exploding in all directions," Jarman, 1974), probably also serve to confuse the predator and make it difficult for him to single out an individual for the final chase.

If pressed hard, some ungulates may enter into water to seek refuge from pursuing predators. This occurs most often in species that are normally associated with water, such as lechwe, waterbuck, etc., but occasionally also in other species, e.g., wildebeest (Kruuk, 1972). However, in the latter species this strategy often proved ineffective, and even fatal, against spotted hyenas, who would follow their victim into the water!

Threatening and/or Attack. Instead of fleeing from a predator that has overstepped the flight distance, an ungulate, or a group, may proceed to threaten or even attack him. This response occurs either in animals that are large and strong enough, or sufficiently armed, to tackle the predator individually or in a concerted group action, or as a last-ditch effort of defense by a cornered or wounded animal ("critical reaction" of Hediger, 1942/50). Individual elephants, rhinoceroses or buffaloes may be able to keep most predators at bay, including at least single lions, and even some of the larger antelopes (e.g., oryx, roan, greater kudu) may successfully fend off lions under certain circumstances, sometimes even killing one in a desperate fight. Somewhat more commonly, several conspecifics may cooperate in warding off an attack from predators; this is known in elephant, buffalo, eland, and perhaps occurs in other species as well (Kruuk, 1972; Schaller, 1972; see Chap. 10). Kraft (1973) published a series of photographs documenting how a group of buffaloes killed one of three lions attacking them. Other similar observations are scattered throughout scientific and popular literature.

Defense of a small young by its mother (Chap. 14,D,VI) can perhaps be regarded as a special case of the critical reaction. The outcome of such confrontations is often astonishing. For instance, Burke (1974) was able to watch and photograph how a female zebra violently attacked a lioness that had killed her foal. The mare grabbed the lioness at the nape with her teeth and held on strongly for a while, despite the lioness' efforts to free herself. In the end, both zebra and lioness let go and separated, both with only minor injuries. Female warthog successfully defended their young against cheetah, at least as long as the young kept close to their mother (Eaton, 1970). Female gazelles commonly attack jackals, and rarely also hyenas, chasing their young; in such situations they often strike out with their forelegs, i.e., use different weapons than in intraspecific fighting (Estes, 1967, Fig. 1 F; Walther, 1968, 1969a). A female nyala defended her young against a bateleur eagle (*Terathopius ecaudatus*) by rearing up on her hindlegs (Robbins, 1972). Further examples of maternal defense will be given in Chapter 14.

Mobbing, i.e., active advance by a group of ungulates toward a predator, inducing him to leave without physically attacking him (described by Eisenberg and Lockhart, 1972, for axis deer in Ceylon) is difficult to distinguish from communal attack. It may be an intermediate stage between the latter and the fascination behavior described earlier and, depending on circumstances, may at some point turn into one or the other of these responses.

In view of the great variety of both predator and prey species involved, this review of antipredator behavior is, by necessity, somewhat sketchy and generalized. Many field studies on individual species, as well as some reviews, contain information on flight behavior and avoidance of predators by the species concerned. I would refer the reader primarily to Walther (1969a), Kruuk (1972), Schaller (1972), and Jarman (1974) for further details. Some additional aspects of antipredator behavior will be discussed in Chapter 19.

Part 3
Social Behavior

For the purposes of this review, the term "social behavior" will be restricted to *intra*specific interactions, in full recognition of the fact that certain relationships between animals of different species (including man) could rightfully be considered as social, too (e. g., Hediger, 1965). However, most or all such cases can be interpreted as consequences of the so-called "assimilation tendency" ("Anglei-chungstendenz": Hediger, 1940b, 1942/50): under certain circumstances an animal addresses elements of its species-specific behavior to a member of a different species, i.e., it treats the latter as a conspecific. Such situations arise most commonly—but not exclusively—in the absence of "appropriate" partners (i.e., conspecifics), as in some examples of interspecific associations treated above (Chap. 7, A, I), and in captivity, where keepers and trainers are often treated as members of a social group and can even exploit this relationship to their advantage (Hediger, 1961, 1965). Thus, most or all instances of "interspecific social behavior" can be considered as special cases of normal intraspecific relationships.

Chapter 8

Expression and Communication

Walther (1974) reviewed expressive behavior of bovids in considerable detail. He discussed various theoretical aspects, including a number of earlier attempts at defining expressive behavior unequivocally, and formulated the following definition of his own:

"Expressions which function in social communication, are the outward manifestations of an animal's momentary psycho-somatic situation. They are addressed to an actual partner (usually a conspecific) and are aimed at releasing adequate responses above the level of contagious effects, without influencing the partner mechanically and without the performer leaving the partner's sphere of action." Though minor modifications may be found desirable in the future (as it stands, it is applicable primarily to visual communication), this definition seems a useful attempt at circumscribing the behavior considered here. (As will have been noted, the term "expression" is, for present purposes, restricted to social contexts only). As there is insufficient space here to discuss many of the points raised by Walther (1974), his extensive review should be consulted by anyone with more than a passing interest in expressive behavior of ungulates.

Social interactions largely depend on the animals' ability to "understand each other," i.e., to perceive the motivational state and the "intentions" of actual or potential social partners. This is achieved through a great variety of expressive and communicatory elements that are generally called "signals." As these signals are the basis—the "tools" as it were—for all social communication, I will review them first, before dealing with different functional categories of social behavior.

We can classify signals either according to the mode of production (and perception) or according to function. Taking function first, we may distinguish four broad categories indicating, respectively, intended attraction (e. g., courting), repulsion (e. g., threat), submission, and an outside disturbance (e. g., alarm signals). The first three types of signals contain clues about the social status or "mood" of the performer and/or the probable nature of an actual or anticipated intraspecific encounter, while signals of the fourth type convey chiefly information on the animals' surroundings. Signals of the latter type may not be considered by everybody as truly social communication, but rather as individual "interjections" that may or may not acquire significance to other group members secondarily. However, this may be difficult or impossible to determine without experimentation.

More than one of the above-mentioned functions may conceivably be combined in one signal that may have different "meanings" for animals of different social classes (e. g., signals used in territorial advertizement).

A comprehensive and well-founded classification of signals according to their functions would require more detailed knowledge than we currently possess with regard to African ungulates. For this reason, I prefer to use a classification based on the manner in which signals are produced and/or perceived. This approach is chiefly descriptive; function will be mentioned additionally where it appears to be sufficiently well documented, but a knowledge of function is not essential for the purpose of this classification. Thus, on the basis of the manner or means of production we can distinguish the following types of signals:

1. Visual, i.e., postures, movements, etc.
2. Auditory, i.e., vocalizations and other sounds
3. Olfactory, i.e., scents
4. Tactile, i.e., touching and/or manipulating the body of the partner.

In the following, we will consider each of these types separately, although in many social interactions two or more of them may be combined. Such cases will be treated in more detail in the appropriate contexts later, i.e., in the sections dealing with the different categories of social behavior.

A. Visual Signals

Abilities of altering facial expressions are limited in most ungulates, but zebras (and other equids) use various combinations of ear postures, opening of mouth and baring of teeth in visual communication (Antonius, 1937; Trumler, 1959; summary in Klingel, 1972a). Most other ungulates rely on more pronounced postures and gestures; they—particularly the bovids—are "pantomimics" (Walther, 1964a).

For convenience, we may divide visual signals into static ones, consisting of a posture, expression or attitude, and dynamic ones, comprising specific movements. In both cases, either the animal's entire body or only part of it may be involved in the production of the signal. Postures or movements that have an obvious signal function in intraspecific interactions are usually called expressive movements/postures or displays.

A common form of a static display involving the whole body is the broadside or lateral display, in which the animal positions itself in front of and at right angles to the partner, or in reverse/parallel orientation. While the body remains stationary, the effect of the display may be enhanced by a specific attitude of the head or by local pilo-erection (e.g., of the dorsal crest in male Tragelaphines; Fig. 19). Lateral displays are used in both agonistic and sexual encounters (see Chaps. 12, C and 13, A); they are particularly well developed in the Tragelaphines (Walther, 1964a), both species of wildebeest (Estes, 1969; von Richter, 1972), and also in suids (Frädrich, 1967). The low-crouching defecation posture of male gazelles (Walther, 1968; Leuthold, 1971c; see Fig. 6b) can also be placed in this category. That it has a social signal function is suggested by the fact that it is usually confined to adult males and that defecation is often

Fig. 19. Broadside display of adult male greater kudu. Note erect forequarters, despite head being held low, dorsal hair crest and ventral neck mane (from Walther, 1964a)

localized and almost always combined with urination (see Chap. 5, C). Similar postures occur in oryx and dikdik (Fig. 7). Furthermore, the alert posture (cf. Fig. 16) may also have signal value in that it attracts the attention of conspecifics, and sometimes even of animals of other species. Somewhat similar in appearance is the stance adopted by territorial males of some antelope species, which has variously been called "proud posture" (impala: Schenkel, 1966a; reedbuck: Jungius, 1971) or "head-up posture" (wildebeest: Talbot and Talbot, 1963; Estes, 1969; von Richter, 1972) and is generally interpreted as a form of "static-optic marking" (Hediger, 1949), better called "advertizing". The characteristic stance of estrous zebra mares, with straddled legs and raised tail, also has strong visual signal value, attracting stallions from considerable distances (Klingel, 1967). Finally, some antelopes may lie down in an extreme form of submission ("Demutliegen," e.g., in black and blue wildebeest: Walther, 1966b; Estes, 1969).

Many displays involving only part of the body are centered on the head region. Some common forms in bovids are threat postures (see Chap. 12, C) in which the head is held forward and the horns are presented at various levels and/or angles (e.g., Tragelaphines: Walther, 1964a; gazelles: Walther, 1968), sometimes combined with specific attitudes of the ears (e.g., laid down in Uganda kob). In premating behavior more or less the antitheses of these postures are employed: the head is lifted or stretched forward (muzzle first), with horns laid back over the neck ("low-stretch" or "head-high" postures, see Chap. 13, A, I). Lowering of the head signifies submission in various species, but may also still contain elements of threat.

Attitudes of the tail too, may signal an animal's "mood" or "intention". For instance, young gerenuk lift and curl their tail over the back in a gesture of apparent submission (Fig. 20; Leuthold, 1971c). Black wildebeest hold out their

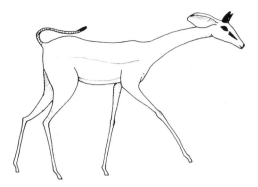

Fig. 20. Submissive posture of young male gerenuk with tail curled over back (from Leuthold, 1971c)

tails horizontally in corresponding situations (Walther, 1966b). Some antelopes have a "brush" of white hair on the underside of the tail, which may be spread in situations of excitement (e. g., in impala). Other species roll their tail upward, thus exposing the white hair, mainly in flight (greater and lesser kudu, reedbuck). While this reaction appears to be automatically coupled with running, at least in lesser kudu (Leuthold and Leuthold, 1973), it may also have signal value for conspecifics, perhaps to facilitate following other group members in flight through dense bush (this remains to be substantiated). Male hartebeest and topi hold their tail stiffly at an angle when courting females, but also in other social interactions; the expressive significance of different angles has been analyzed in hartebeest by Gosling (1975). Many ungulates raise or curl their tails when alarmed (e. g., giraffe, elephant, rhino), but it remains to be established whether this has any signal value for conspecifics or merely expresses the animal's internal state of tension.

This brings us to the dynamic visual signals. Among those involving the entire body are certain specialized gaits, such as the stotting of gazelles (cf. Fig. 18) and some other antelopes, which may have a dual function as an antipredator device (Chap. 7, C, III) and/or an intraspecific (warning) signal. Another example is the "prancing" gait used by male Uganda kob when courting females: the head is held high, with horns laid back and the white gular patch exposed, and small rapid steps are made with stiff forelegs (Buechner and Schloeth, 1965, cf. Fig. 40a). The "rocking canter" of the blue wildebeest (Estes, 1969) also belongs into this category.

Other dynamic signals involve only parts of the body. Head-shaking or nodding occurs in many antelopes, being particularly pronounced in the Alcelaphinae, especially the genus *Damaliscus* (Walther, 1966a, 1969b). Its function often comprises elements of threat, but in topi it may merely serve to coordinate the activity of group members, being exhibited particularly often when an animal begins to move.

Thrashing of shrubs with the horns, or "horning" the ground, both actions commonly performed by male bovids, are generally considered to indicate aggressive "intentions". The "weaving" (slow rhythmic sideward movements with the head held near the ground) of male Grant's gazelle (Walther, 1965a) may have a similar function, or serve as a territorial advertizing display.

Tail movements are reported to have strong signal value in both species of wildebeest where animals lash their tails vigorously from side to side when approaching a potential rival, and in other situations (Estes, 1969; von Richter, 1972). However, vigorous tail movements tend to be generalized expressions of excitement, and it is sometimes difficult to determine a function as a social signal. Similar considerations probably apply to the "flank-shaking" of Thomson's gazelle (Brooks, 1961), to which other individuals do not seem to react noticeably (Walther, 1969a).

Another dynamic signal is pawing or scraping the ground, either with one forefoot only, or both alternately, as in a number of antelopes, or with both hindfeet alternately, as in the two species of rhinoceros. In several species of gazelles (Walther, 1968) and in both species of wildebeest (Estes, 1969; von Richter, 1972) pawing is commonly associated with either urination/defecation or with aggressive displays and thus appears to have some signal value of its own in these contexts. Similarly, scraping with hindfeet, normally associated with defecation (Chap. 5, C, IV), also occurs in encounters between male rhinoceroses (Schenkel and Schenkel-Hulliger, 1969; Owen-Smith, 1973).

It is not always possible to differentiate clearly between static and dynamic signals; sometimes both types may be combined into one display. In the blue wildebeest, the "rocking canter" has been described as "basically the head-up posture set to a slow canter" (Estes, 1969). Elephants extend their ears sideways when confronted with an undetermined stimulus; this is sometimes combined with a forward rush, a "mock charge." The whole performance serves as an impressive intimidation display, both in intra- and interspecific encounters.

The above enumeration of visual signals does not aim at completeness, but merely at pointing out some of the multiple possibilities of visual communication among African ungulates. For more detailed descriptions the original publications mentioned above should be consulted, as well as the recent reviews by Walther (1974) for bovids and by Klingel (1972a) for equids.

B. Auditory Signals

Auditory signals comprise all types of communication involving sound. The great majority of these consist of vocalizations but, as we shall see, other means of sound production are sometimes employed as well.

I. Vocalizations

Strictly speaking, vocalizations include only the sounds produced through activation of the vocal cords in the larynx. However, with many sounds emitted by ungulates it is not clear whether the vocal cords are involved or not. For this reason, and for the sake of simplicity, I include a number of other sounds, such as snorts, whistles, the trumpeting of elephants (all produced by forced exhalation of air through mouth or nose) with vocalizations proper.

The exact description and analysis of ungulate vocalizations are still in their infancy (but see Kiley, 1972). Qualitative designations, such as "grunts, snorts, squeals," etc., are usually all that is available in accounts of relevant studies. Emphasis is generally placed on functional aspects, and vocalizations are classified primarily according to the context(s) in which they occur (e. g., Klingel, 1972a, for equids).

General Contact Calls. These are used primarily when members of a group are out of visual (or olfactory) contact, e. g., in dense vegetation or in the dark. For instance, gazelles are said to be "more vocal" at night than in daylight (Walther, 1968; Bigalke, 1972). Other examples are the high-pitched barks of zebra and the rumbling sounds of elephants, both often heard at night, but also by day. The elephant's contact call has sometimes been described as "stomach rumbling," but is really produced through the larynx.

Mother–Young Calls. A soft bleating sound of low pitch and intensity is uttered by many bovids seeking their dam or young. This is perhaps a special case of contact call.

Mating Calls. Male Tragelaphines (Walther, 1964a) and Uganda kob (Buechner and Schloeth, 1965) utter a low and soft bleating or grunting sound when courting females. These are audible only at close range. Similar calls possibly occur in other bovids but have escaped detection so far. Female black rhinoceros "periodically emitted a low-pitched squeal during coitus" (Goddard, 1966).

Territorial Advertisement. The grunts of male blue wildebeest (Estes, 1969), the whistling of male Uganda kob (Leuthold, 1966a), and perhaps other antelope vocalizations, probably serve this function.

Alarm. Many species of bovids utter surprisingly similar sounds when alarmed, a short abrupt snort (Alcelaphinae, gazelles) or bark (Tragelaphines). Zebra and giraffe also snort in situations of alarm. Other species produce a high-pitched whistle, e. g., the reedbucks, Uganda kob, oribi and dikdik. In the hippopotamus a hissing sound is said to be an alarm signal (Verheyen, 1954).

Aggression. Various male antelopes emit repeated grunts or snorts when chasing social rivals, e. g., after a fight (Uganda kob, gazelles, etc.). Roaring and/or bellowing sounds accompany threat and fighting in rhinoceroses and elephants; the latter may also trumpet in this context.

Distress. The young, and rarely also the adults, of many antelopes produce a loud penetrating bleat or squeal, the "distress call," when caught or severely injured. In the case of young animals, this often brings the mother near, who may try to defend the young against the predator involved (Chap. 14, D, VI). In some cases, unrelated adults also react to the distress call of a young animal, e. g., in buffalo (Sinclair, 1970, 1974).

This brief compilation of ungulate vocalizations indicates that different types of sounds may be used in different functional contexts. This view has recently been questioned by Kiley (1972) who claimed that different calls are not necessarily situation-specific but depend on the "level of excitement" of the animal involved. She based her thesis on detailed studies of vocalizations in domestic ungulates. Whether her findings and conclusions can be extended to wild ungulates remains an open question, considering the present state of knowledge.

For the moment, however, let us assume that situation-specific vocalizations do indeed occur. A striking aspect in this context is the pronounced similarity, between different species, of calls serving the same apparent function, e. g., alarm calls, mother-young calls, etc. (at least within the bovids). Such convergences may be related to a variety of factors, e. g., whether or not the calls should be easy to locate, individually recognizable, etc. (Kiley, 1972). In the case of alarm calls it may also be advantageous for them to be "understood" by all members of multi-species associations.

A great deal of research remains to be done on vocalizations of African ungulates, and their functions. While ungulates generally are not particularly vociferous animals, they utilize a considerable variety of vocalizations in intraspecific communication. Many calls are of very low intensity, audible for humans only at close range, and it is therefore quite likely that many more vocalizations occur in African ungulates than have been described to date.

II. Nonvocal Signals

Nonvocal auditory signals are rare among ungulates, the elephant being almost the only species employing them with any regularity, and only in the context of threatening or intimidation. Vigorous head-shaking makes the ears flap against the sides of the head and neck, producing a clapping sound. In situations of conflict, elephants sometimes charge into bushes and small trees, snapping stems and branches in the process. The accompanying noise is almost certainly a "calculated" part of the intimidation display. It is, however, not quite certain whether the two behaviors just described commonly occur in intraspecific encounters, or whether they would more appropriately be described as antipredator displays.

Male hippopotami eject water through their nostrils and splash about considerably during agonistic encounters; again, the noises made by the water appear to be essential parts of the displays, enhancing their intimidating function (Hediger, 1951).

Eland, particularly adult males, produce a clicking sound in a joint of the foreleg when walking; this may have a function in social communication (Underwood, 1975; Hillman, 1976).

III. Combined Visual-Auditory Displays

Sometimes vocalizations are accompanied by striking postures or movements, and the combination of different signals may form an integrated display. A good example is the "roaring display" of the impala (Schenkel, 1966a; Leuthold, 1970b; M. V. Jarman, 1973): an adult male walks or runs about, with head extended forward and the white underside of the tail fanned, uttering a series

93

of harsh roars. The function of this display is not entirely clear; in some cases it may be a form of territorial advertizement, but may also serve other functions (Warren, 1974).

A threat display of elephants consists of a rush forward, with ears extended sideways, often accompanied by trumpeting. Similarly, a black rhinoceros emits puffing sounds while rushing forward in attack. Again in the hippopotamus, a form of threat combines a lunge forward with much splashing in the water. In all these cases, the effect of the displays is probably enhanced by the combination of visual and auditory elements.

C. Olfactory Signals

Circumstantial evidence indicates that olfaction plays a prominent, and often the principal, role in the interactions of many ungulates with their environment. Among African species, the elephant, rhinoceroses and most forest-dwelling bovids (e. g., duikers) appear to rely primarily on their sense of smell for orientation, etc., as well as in social contexts. However, olfactory communication among mammals (reviewed by Eisenberg and Kleiman, 1972; Ralls, 1971; Ewer, 1968; Johnson, 1973) is relatively inaccessible to human research, particularly in the field. Experimental analysis, including the identification of active components of pheromones has begun only recently (Hummel, 1968; Müller-Schwarze, 1969, 1971). Generally, the functions of olfactory signals can only be inferred from circumstances, i.e., the observable behavior of the animal(s) involved. In the following, I will describe some ways and means of olfactory communication in African ungulates, as far as information is available to date. Comments on functions are, for the most part, speculative as much remains unknown, or at least unproved, about them.

Mammals produce and/or deploy olfactory signals mainly in the following ways:
1. The scent emanates from the animal's body and is detectable only in its presence.
2. The scent is carried by the animal's urine and/or feces, and its spatial distribution depends on the pattern of urination/defecation.
3. Odoriferous substances, produced by special glands, are deposited in the environment in various ways.

Categories (2) and (3) are commonly referred to as *scent-marking* or *olfactory marking*. The deposits can convey certain information about the originator even in his absence.

I. Scents Emanating from the Body

Ungulates encountering each other closely, either for the first time or after a period of separation, tend to sniff various parts of each other's body extensively, preferred areas being the nose/mouth, the genital and the perineal regions

(Schloeth, 1956). In this way scents emanating from an animal's body are being tested; they probably convey information about individual identity, physiological condition and other characteristics of the bearer. For instance, female antelopes certainly recognize their young primarily by scent, as naso-nasal and naso-anal contacts are particularly frequent between a female and her young after a period of separation. A female sometimes rejects a strange young only after olfactory contact, having "provisionally" accepted it on sight (cf. Hersher et al., 1963). Similarly, the young also recognize their mothers olfactorily; this is very evident in cases of young ungulates being raised by humans: a hand-reared antelope often will not accept food from a strange person unless the scent of the familiar "parent" is presented at the same time (Walther, 1966a, 1969b; Leuthold, 1967).

Olfactory examination is also pronounced in male-female contacts, particularly in premating behavior, where it presumably serves to determine an individual's reproductive condition (Chap. 13, A, I).

Some mammals discharge scents from specialized glands when frightened (see Eisenberg and Kleiman, 1972). Virtually nothing is known about such "alarm substances" in African ungulates. Possibly the dorsal gland of the springbok serves this or a similar function, as a fan of erectile hairs surrounding it is often spread open on alarm (Bigalke, 1972). Further research in this field might well uncover more cases of this nature (cf. Müller-Schwarze, 1974).

The effectiveness of olfactory signals emanating from an animal's body diminishes rapidly with increasing distance so that, in general, fairly close contact is required for them to fully serve their function. In this they differ from the signals discussed in the following two sections.

II. Urine and Feces as Scent-Bearers

Urination and defecation, whether scattered or localized, are perhaps the most generalized forms of scent-marking, i.e., the deposition, in the environment, of materials bearing scents that identify the producer and may convey certain information about him (see Altmann, 1969; Eisenberg and Kleiman, 1972). Evidence for marking functions is, however, merely circumstantial in most cases, and experimentation in the field or in captivity is needed to elucidate the role of urination and defecation in social communication.

Earlier I have reviewed the modes of urination and defecation in African ungulates (Chap. 5, C). The circumstances surrounding particularly localized urination/defecation (postures, associated behavior) suggest that it has some social significance. This is borne out by a few specific observations, for instance that male white rhinoceroses of different social status use different modes of urination (Owen-Smith, 1971, see also Chap. 16, F).

The olfactory importance of feces is further underlined by the fact that an encounter with old dung, either of the same or even another species, often elicits defecation immediately (see Chap. 5, C, II). This is probably the reason why one sometimes finds dung of two or more species piled on top of each other (e.g., Tinley, 1969, pers. obs.). The significance of this is not properly understood.

Thus we can assume that in many ungulates scents attached to excretory products act as signals in social communication. This is probably more pronounced in species with localized defecation/urination, where the signal function is often emphasized by the visual effects of postures and associated behaviors. Examples are dikdik, several gazelles, wildebeest and some other Alcelaphinae, Grévy's zebra, hippopotamus, black and white rhinoceros. (In an interesting experiment, Goddard (1967) demonstrated that a black rhinoceros was able to follow the scent trail produced by rhino dung being dragged along behind a car). In species with random (scattered) urination/defecation, the communicatory function of scents emanating from excreta may be less important, though not necessarily irrelevant. Giraffe, buffalo, elephant, most Tragelaphini and Reduncinae appear to belong to this category, as far as current knowledge indicates (cf. Walther, 1967a). In plains zebra, some individuals defecate and/or urinate over the excreta of others, which implies some olfactory (possibly marking) significance, even though voidance generally occurs at random. Since no space-related marking function is evident, Klingel (1967, 1969a, 1972a) considers these activities as a "behavioral relic" inherited from possibly territorial ancestors, or alternatively as a "pre-adaptation" toward the eventual development of territoriality and a related marking function.

Whether the relevant odoriferous substances are contained in the excreta themselves or whether they originate from special glands and are attached to feces or urine on passage is not known for African ungulates.

At least two species have developed an unusual mode of apparent scent-marking in which urine is first transferred to a certain part of the body and then deposited elsewhere. The male eland rubs his forehead, with a dense mat of bristly hairs, on the ground after urinating, and then applies the wet "mixture" to trees, etc. (Walther, 1966a; Hillman, 1976). The male Nile lechwe urinates onto his chest and neck and then "marks" the female with his urine by laying his neck on her rump (only observed in captivity so far; Walther, 1966a).

III. Marking with the Products of Scent Glands

The most obvious instances of scent marking are those involving specialized skin glands, the secretions of which are deposited in the environment in various ways. Ungulates possess a considerable variety of cutaneous glands (reviews by Pocock, 1910; and Schaffer, 1940). From the functional point of view, we can distinguish two classes of glands, according to the ways in which their products are deposited:
1. Indiscriminate deposition on the substrate
2. "Deliberate" deposition at selected sites only.

The first category includes interdigital and inguinal glands that may come into contact with the substrate wherever the animal moves or lies down. The deposition of secretions is subject to little or no control by the animal, as far as is known. Some authors (e. g., Walther, 1964b, with respect to gazelles) have suggested that the secretion of interdigital glands is applied to the substrate when the animal scrapes the ground with a forefoot, an action often combined with ritualized urination/defecation (Chap. 5, C, III), but this remains to be proved. To my knowledge, no documented information on the functions of interdigital and inguinal glands is available. For this reason we will not consider them further here.

The second category comprises almost exclusively the antorbital glands present in many bovids. They generally consist of a pit in front of the eye with a round or slit-shaped orifice. Their secretions are deposited in small droplets or lumps on prominent objects, such as dry twigs (dikdik: Hendrichs and Hendrichs, 1971; various duikers: Rahm, 1960; Aeschlimann, 1963; Ralls, 1971, 1974; gerenuk: pers. obs., see Fig. 21), grass culms (Thomson's gazelle: Walther,

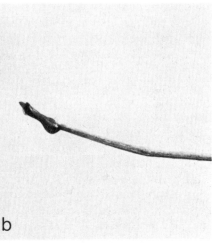

Fig. 21a and b. Male gerenuk marking with antorbital gland (a), and droplet of secretion at end of twig (b)

1968; oribi: Hediger, 1951; Gosling, 1972)—in captivity sometimes on the horn tips of conspecifics (Dittrich, 1965)—or spread more diffusely over an area on the ground or a tree trunk, as in hartebeest and wildebeest (Estes, 1969). Head-rubbing resembling the marking actions of the species mentioned also occurs in some species that have no obvious skin glands on the head, such as some Tragelaphini (Walther, 1964a; pers. obs.) and the impala (Schenkel, 1966a; Leuthold, 1970b). However, in adult male impala M. V. Jarman (1973)

97

recently found diffuse glandular areas on the forehead, the secretory activity of which changes with the social status of the individual. Similar discoveries may yet be made in other species.

While most species use twigs, etc., for marking as they find them in their environment, male oribi apparently prepare their own marking sites by biting off long grass culms at the appropriate height (Gosling, 1972), and similar behavior has also been observed in topi (Duncan, 1975).

The actual behavior involved in antorbital marking is similar in all species practicing it: the animal approaches the marking site (which may carry an old deposit already), sniffs and sometimes licks it, turns the head to one side so as to introduce the tip of the twig or culm near or actually into the orifice of the gland and deposits the secretion with a series of gentle nodding movements (Aeschlimann, 1963, photos 6–8; Walther, 1968, Fig. 16b; cf. Fig. 21). The slow "deliberate" movements may themselves have some signal value, particularly when marking occurs, as it often does, in the context of agonistic encounters ("demonstrative marking"). Some Alcelaphinae mark by rubbing the forehead on the ground or against tree trunks, leaving a more diffuse scent mark. Hartebeest (Gosling, 1975) and blesbok (Walther, 1969b) can, however, also mark in the more precise manner described above for gazelles, etc., but in the wildebeest the antorbital glands are covered by a mat of long hair through which the secretion is applied to the ground or to a tree trunk (Estes, 1969). Again, the actions involved may also have a visual signal function, as they resemble ground horning. The situation appears to be similar in the eland (Hillman, 1976).

The temporal gland of the African elephant ("musth gland") has sometimes been ascribed a marking function corresponding to that of the antorbital glands of some bovids (e.g., Sikes, 1971). There is, however, no positive evidence for this, and current thinking tends to view the temporal gland secretion as a means of direct olfactory communication, perhaps relating to group identity, or to various kinds of excitement, but its exact function is not yet clear (cf. Douglas-Hamilton, 1972).

IV. Interindividual Marking

In a few species of antelopes, one individual sometimes deposits the secretion of its antorbital gland on another one. This is, however, rather rare. During courtship, male gerenuk and dibatag mark females on shoulders or hindquarters (Backhaus, 1958; Walther, 1958, 1963b; Leuthold, 1971c). In Maxwell's duiker, a male and a female often rub their antorbital glands together; if more than one female is present (observed in captivity only), this behavior is almost exclusively concentrated on one of them (Aeschlimann, 1963; Ralls, 1971, 1974; see also Chap. 16, C). Such behavior possibly serves to establish and maintain a pair bond, even if only for the short period of the female's estrus. Walther (1966b) also found interindividual marking in captive black wildebeest.

Male Maxwell's duikers may mark each other before starting to fight, at least in the captive groups observed by Ralls (1971, 1974, 1975). In this context, the function of interindividual marking is even less clear, except that it may indicate a motivational relationship between marking and aggression (see Chap. 12, C and Fig. 31).

Perhaps it is worth pointing out that, except for gerenuk in premating behavior, all the above cases of interindividual marking were observed in captive animals.

V. Functions of Scent-Marking

A prevalent concept of scent-marking holds that it serves to inform conspecifics that a certain area is occupied. In this view, a scent mark would amount to a "no-trespassing" sign. Some authors go as far as to treat scent-marking as synonymous with "territorial marking." However, while scent-marking is widespread among territorial ungulates, nonterritorial members of some antelope populations also commonly mark with their antorbital glands, e. g., "bachelor" males of Thomson's gazelle (Walther, 1964b) or females and juveniles of Coke's hartebeest (Gosling, 1974). On the other hand, some strongly territorial species show no overt olfactory marking (e. g., waterbuck, Uganda kob). Thus, territoriality and scent-marking are not necessarily correlated (cf. Schenkel, 1966b).

Another commonly held view is that scent-marking occurs primarily along the boundary of an occupied area. While this may apply to dung heaps in some cases (e. g., dikdik, Grévy's zebra), it has never been shown to be so for glandular marking. On the contrary, detailed mapping of marking sites in the territory of a male Thomson's gazelle revealed them to be distributed along a gradient of increasing density toward the center (Walther, 1964b, p. 877). It remains to be seen whether these findings apply to other species as well.

The prevalent scent-marking theory implies that a potential intruder is repelled by the scent marks of an area's occupant. Yet I know of no case in which such repulsion has actually been observed or demonstrated. While repulsion may manifest itself in less obvious ways than an abrupt turnabout, the fact remains that this assumed function is as yet not substantiated by field or experimental evidence, at least for African ungulates (but see Müller-Schwarze, 1974, p. 108).

What, then, are the functions of scent-marking?

The best answer to this question is that we do not really know and that what we may say in this context is largely speculative. Above all, we should rid ourselves of anthropomorphic notions of possession, fences, no-trespassing signs, etc., look at the observable phenomena objectively and be careful with our interpretation.

Trying to adhere to these guidelines, what can we say about scent-marking in mammals generally, and in African ungulates specifically?

1. It occurs commonly—but not exclusively—at or near socially important locations, such as home sites (where applicable), centers of activity (e. g., the central ares of a territory), trails, etc.
2. It is often, but not always, performed primarily by individuals of high social status (e. g., Ralls, 1974).
3. It often occurs in the context of agonistic encounters.

From these characteristics of scent-marking (Walther, 1967a; Ralls, 1971) we can conclude only that its main significance lies in a social context and that its performance may be related to social status.

Perhaps the most important attribute of a scent mark is that it can convey information about its originator even in his absence. Reactions of conspecifics depend on various factors, such as their sex, age, social status, familiarity with the locality, etc. It is quite possible that, at least to some conspecifics, a scent mark does advertize occupation of the area concerned and may have an intimidating effect, but we must remain conscious of the fact that this has not been firmly established (see also Eisenberg and Kleiman, 1972; Ralls, 1971, 1974).

Moreover, the common observation that captive animals transferred to new enclosures almost immediately set about applying their scent marks suggests that marking may be of considerable significance to the performing animal itself, perhaps not so much indicating its "taking possession" of the area but rather creating olfactorily familiar surroundings, a "home atmosphere" so-to-speak. This is known to be important, for some mammals, in the context of agonistic encounters, particularly contests over a home site, territory, etc., for instance in mice: the "resident" animal in familiar olfactory surroundings tends to have a better chance of winning a contest than a newly introduced individual (Petrusewicz, 1959). Probably related to this is the fact that, in many mammals, presentation of another individual's scent marks results in excitement and increased aggressiveness in the resident animal(s), which also tends to mark more frequently and more intensively after such stimulation (examples in Eibl-Eibesfeldt, 1967/70; and Ralls, 1971). Similar reactions occurred in captive Maxwell's duikers (Ralls, 1974) and in free-ranging Thomson's gazelles (Hummel, 1968), but it remains to be seen whether they are normal and typical of African ungulates generally (see Monfort and Monfort, 1974).

D. Tactile Signals

This category is somewhat ambiguous, as it is uncertain whether any tactile contacts constitute signals in the sense discussed above. For this reason, I will not go into details here, but simply list a few cases in which a signal function is at least conceivable:

Mutual grooming: this may serve to establish and reinforce interindividual bonds (cf. Klingel, 1967, on zebra).

Courtship behavior: some male bovids lay their chin onto the female's rump; many others insert a stiffly held foreleg between the female's hindlegs ("Laufschlag," see Chap. 13, A, I). Licking of the vulva also commonly occurs in this context. All these actions can be viewed as tactile stimuli (signals?) tending to reduce the female's inclination to flee, and/or testing or increasing her readiness to stand for copulation.

Nudging or prodding: a standing bovid may tap a lying conspecific lightly with a forefoot, apparently in an effort to make the latter rise. Also, when walking in single file, one individual may butt the one in front with horns or forehead to make it move on. Female elephants are said to "guide" their calves by pushing and nudging them with their trunk. Many female ungulates prod their newborn young with the nose or a forefoot, apparently stimulating the baby's efforts to gain its feet. Again, this is particularly pronounced in elephants (e. g., Leuthold and Leuthold, 1975b).

While it is debatable whether the term "signal" is applicable to these tactile interactions, it is certainly justified to include them under the overall heading of "communication" (cf. Eisenberg, 1966).

Chapter 9

Individual Recognition

In addition to unequivocal means of communication, another important prerequisite for various social interactions is the ability to distinguish and recognize
individual conspecifics. In many situations, it appears obvious to the human
observer that certain animals know each other individually. This is, however,
difficult to prove, and often one can do no better than to make inferences
from circumstantial evidence only.

Extensive observations on plains zebra, which live in stable family groups
(see Chap. 16, A), led Klingel (1967) to conclude that they know each other
individually. For instance, immobilized zebra often rejoined their group in a
straight line after recovery from the drug; this would be difficult to explain
in any other way. The relatively low frequency of serious fighting between
bull elephants suggests that many individuals inhabiting the same general area
know each other and their relative status in terms of physical capabilities, etc.
Among giraffe, we occasionally observed an adult bull breaking away from
the herd he accompanied at the time and heading in the direction of a new
bull approaching some distance away. The latter then changed course or even
turned around and moved off. Such behavior also suggests individual recognition,
even over some distance (although other explanations could perhaps be found).
A male Uganda kob on an arena territory (see Chap. 16, E) sometimes suddenly
moved toward the periphery of the arena, apparently to attack and drive away
another male approaching from outside the arena (Buechner and Leuthold,
unpubl.). This again suggested individual recognition and might be viewed as
a "pre-emptive attack" on a potential challenger "bent on" taking over the
same territory.

All these observations support the thesis that ungulates are able to recognize
individual conspecifics, but they do not actually prove it. The best positive
evidence comes from mother-young relations, which will be reviewed in greater
detail later on (Chap. 14). In this context, there can be no doubt that individual
recognition does occur. In other contexts, the circumstantial evidence cited above
is supported further by the following arguments:

1. Permanently stable groups, such as in zebra and elephants, as well as
more or less stable dominance hierarchies could hardly be maintained without
the possibility of individual recognition.

2. Many captive animals routinely recognize their keepers, and certain other
persons, out of any number of people (e. g., Hediger, 1965). The assumption
is probably warranted that this ability also obtains in intraspecific relationships.

These arguments, along with the observations quoted above, provide good
grounds for accepting that many ungulates do indeed possess the ability for
individual recognition.

102

The sensory mechanisms that provide this ability can, again, only be inferred in many cases. They are likely to vary between species, depending on how important each sense is to a species in intraspecific communication, and also according to external circumstances. Conditions of visibility permitting, zebra may be able to discriminate visually between individually characteristic stripe patterns. If separated by relatively long distances, or in the dark, they resort to frequent calling and can apparently distinguish each other's voices. At close range, individual scent may provide the basis for mutual recognition, especially between mares and foals (Klingel, 1967). Visual cues may also have been important in the cases of giraffe and Uganda kob mentioned above. However, in the majority of ungulates, voice and scent probably play a larger role in individual recognition. Several observers have commented on individual variations in the voices of the species they studied (e. g., Estes, 1969, for blue wildebeest; Douglas-Hamilton, 1972, for elephant) but, overall, little clearcut evidence is yet available from field studies. Voice differences apparently enable domestic ungulates to recognize each other individually (Kiley, 1972). The high frequency of mutual sniffing, particularly between animals meeting after a period of separation (cf. Schloeth, 1956) implies considerable importance of individual scents. In mother-young relations both scent and voice are known to play a decisive role, although virtually all relevant evidence comes from observations in captivity (reviewed by Ewer, 1968, and Lent, 1974; see Chap. 14, D, III). The refusal of young antelopes to accept food from strange persons is apparently based on olfactory stimuli. Other observations on hand-reared antelopes suggest that they can also discriminate between different human voices and react positively to a familiar one (Leuthold, 1967; Walther, 1969b; Leuthold and Leuthold, 1973).

Chapter 10

Coordination and Cooperation

One of the main attributes of a "social group," as opposed to a mere "aggregation" formed in response to some environmental factor (e. g., Allee, 1958; Etkin, 1964), is that its members show a certain, albeit variable, degree of cohesion, and coordination of activities, as well as instances of cooperation. Voluntary cohesion is evident primarily in interindividual spacing patterns, which will be reviewed later (Chap. 15, B). For the moment, let us consider briefly some of the available evidence for coordination and cooperation among African ungulates, without going too deeply into theoretic aspects.

Many general statements about coordination of activities within groups or herds, particularly in the more gregarious species, can be found in the literature; quantitative evidence is, however, rather scarce. Klingel (1967) gives detailed information on movements and activity of a family group of zebra during a day. More recently, Walther (1973) and Jarman and Jarman (1973a) have provided well-documented accounts of activity in Thomson's gazelle and impala, respectively. In both of these species activities within a herd are coordinated to a considerable extent for much of the time (see also Lewis, 1975). The exact degree of coordination varies between different types of activity and also between different times of the day and/or the year. For instance, in female herds of impala "day-time coordination ranged from 58 % in January to 68 % in July and night-time coordination from 68 % in January to 76 % in July" (Jarman and Jarman, 1973a, p. 79). The degree of coordination may also vary according to the type of group (i. e., male or female, open or closed) and the nature and strength of interindividual bonds existing within the group. Thus, animals living in closely knit groups (e. g., zebra, elephants) might be expected to show a higher degree of coordination than those in more loosely structured groups or herds, as the antelopes mentioned. Among the latter, male groups generally appear less closely coordinated in their activities than female herds, although this remains to be properly documented.

How does coordination of activities arise? Walther (1973) considered three factors to be involved:

1. External stimuli, such as the day-night rhythm, and possibly endogenous activity rhythms: we have seen earlier (Chap. 6, C, I) that several ungulate species show a pronounced periodicity in their activities. This periodicity is well correlated with the day–night rhythm and is presumably a consequence of it. Thus, all animals within a group can be expected to react similarly to the same stimulus, e. g., light intensity. Some might argue that such similarity in reaction is itself a consequence of coordination of activities, rather than an element contributing to it. However, such reasoning overlooks the fact that

a similar, though perhaps less striking, periodicity is evident even in single animals (Walther, 1973; Jarman and Jarman, 1973a).

2. The "contagious" effects of certain activities, so-called social facilitation ("Stimmungsübertragung": discussion in Allee, 1958; Tinbergen, 1951): in many animals there appears to be a pronounced tendency to "follow suit" when one individual changes from one activity to another (allelomimetic behavior). This tendency is apparently strongest at the times when a change of activity is "due" on the basis of the normal daily pattern. Then the new activity spreads through a herd rather quickly, in a kind of "domino effect," so that an entire herd may change from one activity phase into another within a very short time.

3. Active interference by conspecifics: the effect of social facilitation may be reinforced by certain individuals actively approaching others, inducing them to change their activity. This occurs particularly often after a resting phase when, for instance, a territorial male gets up and walks from one female to another, causing them to get up and start moving or feeding. Such interactions are quite common among gregarious antelopes with territorial males (e. g., Uganda kob, impala, gazelles). They also tend to speed up the change from one activity phase into another and thus increase the degree of coordination within the group.

Functionally, coordination of activities probably serves mainly to ensure group cohesion. An uncoordinated group could easily fragment, if some animals fed, others moved, still others lay down, etc., and thus forfeit the benefits otherwise derived from group formation (see Chap. 18, A).

Turning to cooperation, we find that much depends on how this term is defined. If we accept a wide, relatively unspecific definition (cf. Allee, 1958), then cooperation may be said to occur commonly in gregarious ungulates. The very processes of group formation and cohesion could be considered to qualify as cooperation, as could the coordination of activities just discussed. However, it does not appear to serve any useful purpose to designate so many aspects of social behavior as "cooperation." For this reason, I prefer to use a narrower concept, one more akin to the meaning of the term in human relations (cf. Crook, 1971). Accepting this narrower definition, we find that instances of true cooperation are relatively rare among African ungulates, occurring mainly in the following contexts:

Communal Defense Against Predators. Some of the larger and well-armed bovids (e. g., buffalo, eland), as well as zebra and elephants, sometimes collectively attack lions, or other predators, and can turn them to flight, whereas a single animal might have succumbed (Kruuk, 1972; Schaller, 1972). Elephants often arrange themselves in more or less circular defensive formations (Fig. 22), with large aggressive members facing outward while weaker individuals, particularly calves, are protected in the interior of the ring (Sikes, 1971; Douglas-Hamilton, 1972). Other ungulates may behave similarly in corresponding situations.

Mutual Assistance in Rearing Young. As a rule, male ungulates do not take part in the rearing of the young, and females usually accept only their own young (see Chap. 14, D). However, lactating warthog also suckle the young of other female group members (Bradley, 1968), as do female elephants fairly

Fig. 22. Defensive circle of elephant family unit (from I. and O. Douglas-Hamilton, 1975)

commonly (Douglas-Hamilton, 1972). In the latter species, orphaned calves are readily adopted by other females of the group, or even by strangers (Woodford and Trevor, 1970). Several females, including immature ones, regularly involve themselves with the care of small calves in the group ("aunt phenomenon," cf. Crook, 1971; see also Leuthold and Leuthold, 1975b).

Assistance to Sick or Injured Conspecifics. This has often been reported of the elephant (e.g., Sikes, 1971; Douglas-Hamilton, 1972) and documented in the film "The African Elephant" by Simon Trevor. Various observers tell of instances where group members attempted to support or lift up individuals that had just been shot, had died of other causes, or had been injured. Such assistance usually involves getting the tusks or trunk under the body of the recumbent animal and trying to help it onto its feet (cf. Fig. 42). This behavior has, on occasions, prevented research workers from approaching a drug-immobilized elephant (e.g., Douglas-Hamilton, 1972). Similar assistance is regularly given to calves unable to negotiate difficult terrain, e.g., steep river banks. Less extensive assistance to conspecifics sometimes occurs in plains zebra (Klingel, 1967).

Searching for Lost Group Members. Klingel (1967) describes how members of a zebra group may search for an individual that has lost contact with its group. Whether and to what extent this also occurs in other ungulates is as yet unknown.

It is striking that the elephant features prominently in most of these examples of cooperation. The elephant is generally regarded as a highly intelligent mammal with an intricate social organization (see Chap. 16, A). In these respects, it may be comparable to primates where cooperative behavior is more widespread than among ungulates (Crook, 1971).

Chapter 11

Leadership

The concept of "leadership" is difficult to define objectively. The term has often been used loosely and is occasionally confused with dominance (e. g., Schomber, 1966). The main difficulty in defining leadership is to delimitate the circumstances under which true leadership is evident. For instance, we have seen that an individual changing from one activity phase into another may induce other group members to follow suit (social facilitation). Does the first animal thus exert leadership? Or, if one member of a group spots a predator, gives an alarm call, runs off and is followed immediately by the rest of the group, is this an instance of leadership?

I would consider the lead function in the two examples given as too fortuitous to warrant the term leadership; I prefer to restrict the latter to cases where a given individual repeatedly, even regularly, assumes a leading role, particularly in movements from one place to another, thus in fact determining the places visited and the routes taken between them by the whole group in the course of its routine activities. Or, if other group members can be assumed to know the destination, the "leader" would at least initiate the movement and determine its timing within certain limits. Furthermore, leadership may manifest itself in the context of cooperative behavior, such as group defense, as discussed above.

Leadership, as an individual attribute, is difficult to detect in gregarious animals, unless virtually all members of a group are individually known. It is probably most pronounced in species that live in closed groups of more or less fixed membership, e. g., the plains zebra or the elephant. In zebra, the highest-ranking mare usually leads the group, although the stallion (who ranks higher than all mares) can also determine the direction of movement (Klingel, 1967). In elephants, many instances of leadership shown—usually—by the largest (oldest?) cow, the "matriarch," in day-to-day movements, as well as in the more specific context of antipredator behavior (group defense, "organized retreat"), are reported in the voluminous literature on this species (e. g., Sikes, 1971; Douglas-Hamilton, 1972). Long-term interindividual bonds appear to favor the "concentration" of leadership in certain individuals.

Among Artiodactyla, leadership is often implied or assumed, but well-documented evidence hardly exists. This may be partly a consequence of the practical problems of recognizing leadership in gregarious animals, of which few or none may be individually known, particularly among females. Also, individualized leadership may be less developed in species that live in relatively large open groups or herds, and such species comprise the majority of those African ungulates that have been studied in sufficient detail to date. The only thing that is reasonably certain is that, contrary to some earlier assertions (e. g., Schomber, 1966, with

107

regard to gerenuk), males rarely if ever actively lead groups containing females. They may play a certain role in determining group movements by restricting the mobility of female groups, e.g., by "herding" them within a territory and trying to prevent them from leaving. When a female group moves within a territory, it is almost invariably led by a female, and the adult male—if he participates in the movement at all—generally follows behind (e.g., Leuthold, 1971c, on gerenuk).

The definition given above, and the examples just cited, imply that leadership tends to be the exclusive attribute of a given animal in the group. This may, however, not apply to all cases, and the "amount" of leadership exerted by different group members may vary according to the situation, as suggested by the behavior of domestic cows (Leyhausen, 1971).

The most basic form of leadership is the role played by a female in relation to her offspring. Perhaps many instances of leadership on a higher level of social integration can be viewed as analogous to, or even derived from, the mother–young relation. This interpretation is particularly likely to apply to cases in which there is reason to believe that group members are actually related, as in the elephant (see Chap. 16, A). On the other hand, a different explanation is needed for the plains zebra with its peculiar mechanism of group formation.

The primary function of individualized leadership, particularly in closed groups, is probably the maintenance of a stock of knowledge about the environment which, through the successive leaders, is perpetuated by tradition within the group (or population). Such knowledge may concern the fixed points in the home range, e.g., sources of water, minerals, etc., the distribution of food, routes for daily movements and/or seasonal migrations, but also the degree of danger posed by different predators, including man, under different circumstances; in fact, any relevant information about the environment, in the widest possible sense, that is acquired by learning. Such traditions could be maintained to a large extent through the mother-young association alone, if it is of sufficient duration; but especially in long-lived species, such as the elephant, the presence of old, experienced animals in the group provides opportunities for learning by younger animals even in relation to events that occur only infrequently. A case in point may be recurrent droughts, such as are on record in Tsavo NP, Kenya, at approximately 10-year intervals (cf. Leuthold and Sale, 1973). Traditional knowledge of exceptional food resources, watering points, etc., might conceivably be of critical survival value in such circumstances (Douglas-Hamilton, 1972).

Chapter 12

Agonistic Behavior

A. Introduction

The term "agonistic behavior" denotes all behavior shown in situations of conflict between two—or more—individuals (I limit its application to intraspecific interactions). This includes all forms of aggression, threat, and intimidation, but also "nonaggressive" responses to them, viz. defense, appeasement, and submission. The behavior involved is very complex, and the scope of this presentation does not allow an exhaustive treatment, quite apart from the fact that large gaps still exist in our knowledge of the agonistic behavior of African ungulates. I will first attempt to outline some theoretic aspects, including what has been deduced on the evolution of various facets of agonistic behavior, and then give a condensed group-by-group review with specific examples.

Before going into the details of agonistic behavior, we may briefly consider the circumstances in which it occurs. By definition, this is in situations of conflict; but what are the objects or factors generating conflict between conspecific ungulates (for interspecific conflict see Chap. 7, C, I)? We could visualize competition over food, water, home sites and other environmental resources. However, while instances of resource-related conflict undoubtedly occur, they are relatively rare and not well documented. The great majority of agonistic encounters occur in social contexts, involving competition over "social resources" such as rank, territory or access to mating partners (if "mating rights" are not a priori linked to rank or territory, as is often the case—see Chap. 18). Such competition over social resources usually involves males only; agonistic interactions between females in a social context are relatively rare, or less obvious.

Social competition is generally related to reproductive success. Agonistic behavior, as the medium through which such competition is effected, is thus an essential tool of selection and, therefore, universally important among socially organized animals.

All-out fighting is relatively rare among ungulates, and many agonistic encounters include a great deal of displaying and "irrelevant activities," in addition to or quite often instead of actual fighting. According to "classical" ethological theory, following mainly Tinbergen (1940, 1951), this is generally regarded as a consequence of conflicting motivations. For instance, aggression might be called for in a given situation, but the antagonist may present qualities that generate a certain amount of fear, so that an ambivalent motivational state results, in which behavior is shown that may not seem entirely appropriate in the situation ("displacement behavior"). Many threat and intimidation displays (see below), as well as various irrelevant activities occurring in agonistic encounters

(e. g., grooming, feeding, etc.), are accordingly considered to be derived from displacement behavior that may have become ritualized in the form of expressive signals.

Walther (1974) has recently challenged this view, arguing that it is quite unnecessary to adduce the concept of displacement behavior to explain most of the expressive—including agonistic—behavior of ungulates, or at least of bovids. According to him, many threat and intimidation displays can be regarded as fairly "pure" intention movements generated by the underlying primary motivation, i. e., aggression. The fact that an animal shows a threatening gesture does not necessarily mean that it is inhibited from fighting, but since a threat often suffices to settle a potential or actual dispute, it can be considered simply as the first of several possible steps in such a situation. If it does suffice, well and good; if not, an attack may still follow. Of course, situations of genuine motivational conflict undoubtedly do occur, but Walther makes the point that not all threat behavior need indicate such conflict.

As for the many irrelevant activities often seen in agonistic encounters, such as grooming, feeding, etc., Walther (1974) simply calls them "excitement activities" ("Erregungshandlungen") and doubts whether they have much relevance in social communication. At any rate, he questions the validity of calling them displacement behavior and, for instance, attempts to link "agonistic grazing" with biting intentions and/or behavior of "space claim." I do not feel called upon to resolve this controversy of concepts; clearly, more comparative research is needed to elucidate these problems. However, Walther is probably right in saying that too much behavior has been called "displacement" simply for want of a better explanation.

There remains a linguistic problem: no unequivocal English equivalent exists for the German term "Imponieren." While "display" alone is sometimes used in this sense, this term often occurs in various combinations (e. g., threat display, courtship display) so that it may remain ambiguous when standing alone. "Imponieren" is clearly "meant" to intimidate the opponent, to make him "shrink away," without necessarily conveying the intention of impending physical attack, as a threat generally does. Some authors have used the literal translation of the German term ("imposing"), while Walther (1974) suggests "superiority" or "dominance" display as suitable equivalents. At the risk of further confusing the issue, I propose to use the term "intimidation display," in accordance with the above-mentioned function, as has in fact been done by a few authors earlier (e. g., Estes, 1967). At the same time, I wish to stress that it is often impossible to draw a line between threat and intimidation displays but that there may be intergradations between the two, or even combinations of them, at least in some species. Furthermore, intimidation displays may also be used in a sexual context (Chap. 13, A, I), whereas threats generally are not (or then primarily by females).

We may distinguish three basic phases in agonistic encounters, according to their "intensity" and the behavior of the antagonists:

Voluntary Avoidance of Physical Conflict. One of the animals involved withdraws or signals submission, in effect conceding defeat and according the opponent uncontested access to the resource in dispute.

Mutual Displays. Both contestants engage in threat or intimidation displays and often assorted "irrelevant" (displacement?) behaviors ("excitement activities" of Walther, 1974). Neither gives way, but they avoid physical combat. This type of interaction commonly occurs between evenly matched antagonists and often seems to serve to confirm the status quo rather than to resolve a situation of actual competition (e. g., between occupants of adjacent territories).

Overt Fighting. This is a physical contest of strength, dexterity and other attributes, the outcome of which usually—though not always—settles a competitive situation in a decisive manner.

These three phases in agonistic encounters are, however, not neatly separable; rather, they represent stages in a continuum. One can readily turn into another, and long-drawn-out contests often contain elements of all three in varying sequence. In particular, actual fights are often interspersed with pauses of displaying, and many fights terminate in a phase (a) pattern when one of the contestants concedes defeat. Nevertheless, it is practical to look at the three phases separately, taking them in reverse order from above.

B. Weapons and Fighting Techniques

With the sole exception of the Equidae, all African ungulates possess specialized organs ("weapons") that they use primarily—though not exclusively—in intraspecific fighting. The various fighting techniques are related to the development of such weapons in each species, and we may therefore begin by reviewing the types of weapons present in African ungulates. Initially, I will deal exclusively with the commonest form of intraspecific fighting, that between male rivals in a social context.

In a few species, fighting organs are simply enlarged teeth: in the Tragulidae the canines of the upper jaw, in the hippopotamus those of the lower jaw, and in the Suidae those of both jaws, with those of the upper jaw usually more developed, at least in the African representatives. The elephant's tusks, used both as a fighting organ and a feeding tool, correspond to the incisors of the upper jaw. In the great majority of African ungulates fighting organs consist of epidermal structures in the frontal or supranasal regions: the keratinous "horns" without bony connection to the skull of the rhinoceroses, the skin-covered frontal ossicones of the Giraffidae, and the great variety of horns of the Bovidae, consisting of a permanent keratinous sheath over bony cores fused to the frontal bones (hence the name "Cavicornia").

Perhaps it is fitting, at this point, to emphasize that ungulate ethologists, in general, agree that the great variety of horns and tusks evolved primarily as organs employed in intraspecific (social) conflicts, rather than as defensive weapons against predators (e. g., Walther, 1958, 1960/61, 1966a; Geist, 1966). The following arguments support this view:

(a) Most horn-bearing ungulates use primarily other means to avoid or defend themselves against predators (e. g., escape, kicking with legs), although

111

they may employ the horns, too, particularly as a last resort, i. e., when cornered or wounded.

(b) The most effective antipredator weapon would seem to be a straight pointed horn of medium length. Very few extant horns actually conform to this type. Horns of some small bovids (duikers, dikdik, oribi) are shorter than would appear ideal for an antipredator device, whereas, those of the oryx are rather long (though they may be used effectively against predators). The majority of present-day horns, however, are shaped in a way that makes them less than ideally suited as an antipredator weapon (rings, curves, twists, etc.).

(c) In many bovids, and some other ungulates, females have considerably less-developed horns than males, or none at all. If horns were primarily an antipredator weapon, it would be very difficult to understand why females should be disadvantaged in this respect. On the other hand, social competition is largely restricted to males, where horns are most prominent.

Geist (1966) reviewed the evolution of "hornlike organs" and the concomitant development of different fighting techniques in ungulates. In his view, this evolution took the following course (see also Walther, 1966a): primitive ungulates possessed short pointed horns or tusks with which they aimed blows at various parts of the opponent's body, mostly in lateral—parallel or reverse-parallel—orientation. Successful strikes could inflict damaging wounds. However, as frequent occurrence of serious injuries is not adaptive, ways and means to reduce their incidence gradually evolved. These included, on the one hand, more effective defense mechanisms such as the development of a thick dermal shield in the areas most exposed to strikes; on the other hand, a reduction or inhibition of outright fighting with a concomitant increase in—particularly lateral—displays (see below). Geist's examples in this context include the mountain goat (*Oreamnos americanus*) and the wild boar (*Sus scrofa*); among African ungulates the water chevrotain, the hippopotamus and possibly the rhinoceros represent this stage. In these species serious fights may result in considerable injuries, but all-out fighting is comparatively rare. The giraffe may also belong here (Geist, 1966), but it differs somewhat in that its horns are blunt, unsuitable to pierce the skin. Injuries occasionally occur as a consequence of the tremendous force with which a combatant swings his head into the opponent's side or neck (see Chap. 12, E).

The next evolutionary stage involved a slight change in fighting technique, while the horns and tusks remained relatively undifferentiated. The blows may still be aimed principally at the side of the opponent, but the latter attempts to catch and neutralize them with his own head. Thus head-to-head contact ensues, and the horns or tusks serve to prevent the two heads from slipping past each other and inflicting wounds laterally. Apart from his main examples, *Bison* and *Bos*, Geist also mentioned the warthog, the giant forest hog and the African elephant in this context (the tusks of the suids and the elephant are, in this view, functionally analogous to the horns of bovids). Some of the smaller bovids with short, straight horns (e. g., Cephalophinae, some Neotragini) may also fight in this manner, but their behavior is not well known.

The third evolutionary stage brought an almost exclusive orientation of the attack toward the opponent's head, accompanied by a differentiation of horns into the bewildering array of sizes and shapes found in today's bovids (paralleled to some extent by the antlers of the Cervidae in a striking example of convergent evolution). The common fighting technique here is a prolonged head-to-head engagement, where the horns bind and hold the heads together and the fight becomes primarily a "wrestling match," a test of muscular strength. The significance of horns shifts from that of a weapon with which to inflict injuries to that of a device ensuring prolonged head-to-head contact. Injuries occur but rarely, and mainly accidentally, in this mode of fighting (see below).

Walther (1958) first suggested—and Geist (1966) concurred with his view—that the various "ornaments" on many bovid horns (spirals, ridges, etc.) serve primarily to increase friction, i.e., to reduce the possibility of the horns slipping apart during the fight. They provide the anchoring points against which the antagonists push and tug in their test of strength. This fighting technique is the norm in the Tragelaphini, Reduncinae (see Fig. 26), many gazelles and impala. The Hippotraginae show a slightly different form, correlated with the shape and size of their horns, resembling more a fencing match in which successive downward blows are exchanged, lasting engagements of the horns being less common. Fighting techniques of the Alcelaphinae fall somewhere between these two types.

The major feature of this third stage in the evolution of fighting techniques is that the attack is a priori directed toward the opponent's head, not toward the side as in the earlier stages. However, there is no complete inhibition of attacks on the side. In particular, when one of the antagonists slips or loses his balance and falls, the other may gore him in the side and injure him severely, sometimes fatally. Such cases are, however, exceptional and accidental only. Death of one or both contestants may also occur when their horns become so firmly wedged together that they cannot separate again (e.g., in *Tragelaphus*

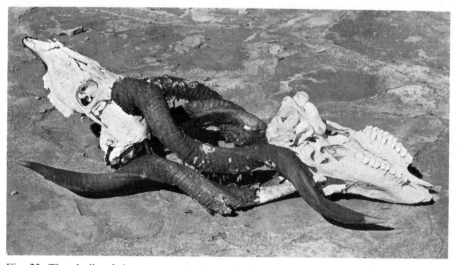

Fig. 23. The skulls of these two male lesser kudu were found in Tsavo NP with horns inextricably interlocked. One of the males must have swung around (into the air?) violently to bring the heads into this mutual orientation

spp., Fig. 23); they may then fall easy prey to a predator, or starve. This, too, is a rare event. Lesser injuries, such as cuts or horn stings, are inflicted fairly commonly; they are, however, rarely of any major consequence. Moreover, in several species the head/neck region that is most exposed to such injuries is specially protected by local thickening of the skin, a "dermal shield," as has been well documented in impala by Jarman (1972c).

Thus, there have been two major trends in the ritualization of ungulate fighting:

1. In species with relatively "crude" fighting techniques the frequency of actual combat has been reduced, while more emphasis is placed on displays ("psychological warfare").

2. In other species, fighting techniques have developed in such a way as to channel the antagonists' efforts into a mode of combat from which few injuries are likely to result ("wrestling match").

Both alternatives reduce the incidence of serious wounds and, in particular, fatal issues. But while the first one operates by reducing the amount of actual fighting, the second one allows for almost any number of fights, while displays are less prominent. For instance, male Uganda kob or Thomson's gazelle may engage in numerous fights every day without suffering any ill effects other than fatigue and, in the long run, loss of condition.

Obviously, the above categorization of fighting techniques is not fully adequate to accommodate all possibilities realized by African, and other, ungulates, but it is useful in pointing out the trends that evolution may have followed. Some species show attributes of more than one of the stages mentioned above, and indeed this is only to be expected when we deal with a group of animals as varied as the bovids, not to mention the other ungulates considered here.

So far, in this review of fighting techniques, we have considered only fighting between adult males using specific weapons, mostly in a social context. Agonistic interactions do, however, occur among other sex/age groups as well, particularly females, and also in the one major group of ungulates that possess no specific fighting organs, the equids. Among these, the plains zebra has been observed in most detail (Backhaus, 1960; Klingel, 1967, 1972a). Zebra employ a variety of fighting techniques and often use their hooves and teeth as weapons. From the relatively mild neck-wrestling ("Halskampf"), in which each contestant tries to get his neck and head over the other one's and depress him, may ensue a biting match, where the antagonists either face each other or stand in a parallel or reverse-parallel orientation, trying to bite each other's legs. As each endeavors to protect his legs from being bitten, he folds them inward and the two may end up fighting in a "sitting" position (Klingel, 1967; see Fig. 24). Sometimes, head and neck are the principal targets of bites, and biting may alternate with kicking, one or both antagonists rearing up on the hindlegs and dealing blows with the front hooves, as is common to most, if not all, equids (Hassenberg, 1971). This, according to Klingel, is the most intensive form of fighting. A further technique involves simultaneous backward kicking with both hindlegs; this is often used as a defense when one contestant is about to flee, but it also occurs in agonistic encounters between females. Thus, fighting techniques of zebra are very varied and show little ritualization, but

Fig. 24a and b. Fighting techniques of plains zebra. (a) neck fighting, (b) biting fight
(Photos R. D. Estes, from Klingel, 1967)

the hooves and the rather blunt teeth (incisors) rarely inflict damaging injuries, while really serious fights are uncommon (Klingel, 1967, 1974b).

Among "unarmed" members of many bovid species (mainly the females, occasionally also young) agonistic encounters are relatively rare and usually occur in competitive situations involving food and/or water, but also rank order, the defense of young, or the rebuttal of an importunate offspring. Such situations probably arise more often in captivity, where space is restricted, than in the wild, and the majority of observations in this context have been made on captive animals (e.g., Walther, 1958, 1960/61, 1964a). The most common aggressive behavior in such circumstances is butting with the forehead, usually not directed at a specific part of the other's body. Some females also make biting intention

115

movements ("snapping"), often directed at the other one's head, or may actually try to bite, although this is not likely to be very effective. Female Tragelaphines, in particular, also occasionally engage in a form of necking ("Halskampf") and—perhaps derived from this—may try to get the head underneath the antagonist's body in an effort to lift him/her off the feet. This technique is also common in some suids, e.g., the bush pig (but apparently not in the warthog: Frädrich, 1965). Rarely, hornless female bovids also push against each other in a head-to-head position (e.g., greater kudu in Walther, 1964a, Fig. 21a), but this may be more playful than aggressive.

In contrast to many cervids, female bovids apparently do not use their front legs in intraspecific fighting, although some may do so in interspecific encounters (Walther, 1960/61, 1964a). Kicking, biting, and necking are considered to be phylogenetically old fighting techniques that may have been retained by forms which did not develop specific fighting organs and corresponding new techniques, e.g., the equids, hornless female bovids, and some suids (for further details on this point see Walther, 1960/61, 1966a, 1968/72, 1974).

C. Threat and Intimidation Displays

Threat and intimidation displays include a great variety of signalling behaviors that convey a certain degree of readiness to fight (threat) or "determination" not to give way (intimidation). Generally speaking, threat displays involve the weapons, which are presented more or less prominently to the opponent, whereas in intimidation displays emphasis is on increasing the apparent size of the displaying animal. Furthermore, it is sometimes possible to distinguish between "offensive" threats, in which the weapons are held in a position enabling immediate attack, and "defensive" threats, in which weapons are merely ready to parry a blow, should the opponent strike. By contrast, during intimidation displays, the antagonists often adopt postures and orientations in relation to each other that would make quick attack and/or defense difficult, if not impossible. Thus, there is a qualitative difference between threat and intimidation displays, although this may not always be evident and transitions may occur, particularly in species that do not use their weapons very frequently, such as the elephant or the rhinoceros.

In view of the great variety of weapons employed by ungulates in intraspecific fighting, it is not surprising that threat displays also vary greatly between different taxa. Many bovids bring their horns slightly forward, with head held high, as do Thomson's gazelle (Fig. 25a; cf. Walther, 1964b, Fig. 4) or oryx (Walther, 1958, Fig. 21), in an aggressive threat, but hold the head and horns low in a defensive threat (Fig. 25b; for oryx see Walther, 1958, Figs. 17 and 20). Zebra bare their teeth (unspecialized weapons: Backhaus, 1960), the hippopotamus does so in the spectacular "yawn" that is generally interpreted as a threat (Fig. 25c; Hediger, 1951; Verheyen, 1954). Such presentation of weapons may occur "in isolation," but more commonly it is accompanied by ancillary gestures,

116

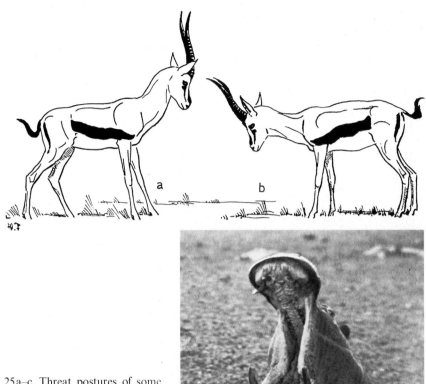

Fig. 25a–c. Threat postures of some African ungulates. (a) head-high, (b) head-low (medium) threat of Thomson's gazelle (from Walther, 1974), (c) the "yawn" of the hippopotamus

such as laying the ears back/down (marked in Uganda kob, Fig. 26a), pawing or stamping the feet, raising the tail, as well as vocalizations or, in some species, grinding the teeth. Many of the behaviors used as threat signals strongly resemble intention movements for attack (Walther, 1974), and indeed have probably arisen from "mere" intention movements through various degrees of ritualization. Most kinds of head-jerking, as well as snapping movements and the baring of teeth, are easily visualized as signs of impending attack, and often it is difficult or impossible to determine whether the movement concerned is used in its original form and function, i.e., as a "pure" intention movement, or whether it has been ritualized to the point of constituting a display of communicatory significance. Often the degree of ritualization, i.e., emanicipation from a purely aggressive function, can be inferred from the frequency with which such behavior is shown without subsequent attack and from the extent to which it is "exaggerated" in posture and/or movement.

A widespread form of intimidation is the lateral or broadside display, commonly coupled with an increase in apparent size. Mechanisms employed in this context include the overall posture of the body, often involving a stiff-legged stance or gait and/or arched back (see Fig. 19), and pilo-erection, sometimes

Fig. 26a–f. Agonistic behavior in Uganda kob. (a) Head-high threat; note tilted heads, lowered ears, and partly erect phallus in male on right. (b) Head-low threat; horns brought forward and ears lowered to the maximum, horn clashes may follow immediately from this position. (c) Facing away; heads held straight up and turned sideways, phallus partly erect.

(d) Fighting ("wrestling") with horns engaged. (e) Break-through. (f) Chase after victory

119

made more pronounced by the existence of localized hair crests or manes (e. g., in Tragelaphines and suids). Broadside displays in agonistic encounters are common among ungulates and other mammals; this, as well as their occurrence in combination with different fighting techniques suggests that they are phylogenetically old (Geist, 1966). They probably evolved in connection with the fighting methods of primitive ungulates, most of which adopt a lateral orientation, parallel or reverse-parallel, and deal out blows sideways and upward. In many more advanced ungulates, however, as Walther (1974) points out, lateral displays are not related to their current fighting techniques (head-to-head engagement); a male displaying laterally might, in fact, not be fast enough to counter a sudden attack from the opponent. Lateral intimidation displays occur, therefore, most commonly in situations where a fight is a priori not likely to arise. This may be either in species where severe fighting is generally rare, but displays are pronounced (e. g., rhinoceros), or—in other species—in the context of "herding" females or in courtship (various bovids). In the latter cases, the aggressive content of intimidation displays may be considerably attenuated.

Another prevalent type of intimidation consists of a frontal display, involving erection of the forequarters and the head and neck, sometimes being enhanced by the animal stepping on some elevated object, such as a log, termite mound, etc. (e. g., in elephant, Fig. 27, and some bovids). In this form of display, the animal can easily switch from intimidation to threat and attack, and the distinction between intimidation and threat (see above) may be blurred (e. g., in the elephant).

One display that occurs fairly commonly in some bovids is somewhat difficult to interpret functionally: in pauses between bouts of fighting, or even before fighting starts, the two antagonists stand opposite each other, with heads held high but turned sideways ("facing away," Fig. 26c). This posture has repeatedly been likened to the "head-flagging" of some gulls (see Tinbergen, 1959) and is often considered as a "peace offer" (e. g., Walther, 1958, 1964b; Jungius, 1971). Its "message" is probably rather complex; the head-high posture with horns clearly shown may well constitute a threat or intimidation display, while the fact that the antagonists do not actually face (i. e., threaten) each other, may take some of the "sting" out of the signal. One may even consider facing away as an abbreviation or relic of a broadside display (Walther, 1964b). In Grant's gazelle, this—or a very similar—posture occurs in the context of pronounced lateral display, with the antagonists standing in reverse-parallel orientation (Fig. 28). Their posture is very similar to that of, for instance, male Uganda kob in "typical" facing-away display (Fig. 26c), but their mutual orientation is different (Walther, 1965a, 1974). In contrast to animals in a true lateral display, animals in the facing-away posture are ready to parry quickly any attack that might be forthcoming. After this display, the opponents may either continue to fight, show other displays, or separate without further interaction. Sometimes, facing away may gradually turn into grooming of the shoulder and thus clear the way for "peaceful" separation. This display should not, however, be construed as indicating submission; rather, the antagonists go their way as equals after mutual facing away.

A further group of behavioral elements often shown in agonistic contexts, and which can be interpreted as having a threatening or intimidating function,

120

Fig. 27. Young bull elephant showing intimidation display ("standing tall"), enhanced by standing on a dead tree (from I. and O. Douglas-Hamilton, 1975)

Fig. 28. Intimidation display of Grant's gazelle, showing a combination of lateral display and facing away (from Walther, 1974)

121

consists of aggressive actions directed toward objects of the environment, e. g., horning or thrashing of the ground or of trees and/or shrubs. In some cases, such behavior clearly constitutes redirected aggression, addressed to an "innocuous" object—or conspecific—rather than the opponent, and probably reflects an ambivalent motivational state, e. g., a balance between aggression and fear. For instance, I once observed two bull elephants in an agonistic encounter which, however, involved virtually no actual fighting. They repeatedly advanced toward each other in threatening postures (ears extended), then stood for a while "undecided," then retreated again. During these retreats, one or both of them repeatedly grabbed a small tree with the trunk and snapped it off, or thrashed it with the tusks, in an obvious expression of "anger" or "frustration." Similar behavior is often shown by elephants in interspecific encounters, e. g., when threatening toward a vehicle (see Chap. 7, C, III). In other situations, and in other species, corresponding behavior is less obviously related to aggression. Horning of the soil, or of bushes, commonly occurs in male bovids, sometimes accompanying a potential or actual agonistic encounter, so that it may be interpreted as redirected aggression, presumably with a threat function. However, in many cases no noticeable effect of such behavior on the antagonist can be detected, and its role as a threat remains somewhat doubtful (Walther, 1974). In addition, single males quite often perform such actions alone, and their function is not clear in such situations. Perhaps they constitute vacuum activity in animals that have little opportunity to fight, or they may have a communicatory (marking) effect, through the visible traces they leave in the environment (disturbed soil, debarked shrubs), through the postures and movements involved (Walther, 1964 a, 1968), or through actual deposition of secretions from the facial glands. Nevertheless, the external appearance of these actions suggests that they are closely related to, or derived from, agonistic behavior.

The threat and intimidation displays considered so far all have obvious links to fighting behavior, past (i. e., phylogenetically old) or present. However, a feature of agonistic encounters between ungulates are the many displays or other behaviors that occur in such contexts but bear no obvious relation to fighting. I refer to the various "displacement" behaviors, some of which apparently have been ritualized to the extent of having become integral parts of agonistic display sequences. They are derived principally from the complexes of feeding and comfort (grooming) behavior. Perhaps the most common of such "irrelevant" behaviors in agonistic encounters is feeding, real or feigned, in pauses between bouts of fighting or between displays. In his detailed study of wildebeest Estes (1969) termed feeding in such situations "agonistic grazing" and concluded that it was essentially nonaggressive ("neutral"), a "face-saving" device. He left open the question of whether it was true displacement behavior or whether it could be considered as an actual display in its own right. Walther (1974) disagreed partly with Estes' interpretation and described agonistic grazing in Thomson's gazelle to illustrate how such behavior may be primarily aggressively motivated. Walther considered its function to be related to "space claim." All we can conclude from these differing observations and interpretations is that agonistic grazing probably has a variety of meanings in different species, ranging from a clearly aggressive connotation (e. g., in Thomson's gazelle) to a nonaggressive

122

Fig. 29. Two male impala showing grooming behavior during agonistic encounter

or neutral content (e. g., in wildebeest) and even to an indication of submission or appeasement (e. g., in Grant's gazelle or oryx: Walther, 1974).

Comfort movements, such as scratching various parts of the body with teeth, hooves or horns (Fig. 29), head shaking, tail swishing, etc., also figure prominently in agonistic encounters of some species, being particularly pronounced in the Alcelaphinae. Again it is difficult or impossible to decide, in many cases, whether such actions are "still" displacement behavior or "already" true displays. Estes (1969), with regard to wildebeest, favors the second alternative, while Walther (1974), rejecting much of the "displacement theory," offers no specific explanation, calling such behavior "excitement activities," on the basis of observations indicating that similar behavior may be shown in other than agonistic contexts, e. g., alarm or other "exciting" situations. He questions whether they have any significance in social communication, but such behaviors occur so markedly in specific situations that I find it difficult to deny them a communicatory function altogether. As with agonistic grazing, the degree of ritualization, the signal value and/or the "meaning" of such actions may vary considerably between species.

Other behavior commonly shown during agonistic encounters includes urination/defecation and glandular scent marking (mainly antorbital). Recent reviews (Ralls, 1971; Johnson, 1973) of scent marking have stressed its frequent association with aggressive behavior. It seems, therefore, justifiable to conclude that the basic motivation of scent marking, in many cases, is essentially aggressive, related

123

to dominance, space claim, etc. Its signal value in this context presumably stems from both the scents produced and the postures and/or movements involved (see Chap. 8, C).

Many agonistic encounters consist entirely of long sequences of mixed displays, in which clearly aggressive (threat), moderately aggressive (intimidation, marking) and essentially nonaggressive (irrelevant) elements are interspersed in variable order, without any actual fighting. This appears to be the rule when both antagonists are not strongly motivated in terms of aggression, for instance in encounters between territorial neighbors which may serve more a need for contact rather than a settlement of actual conflict (e. g., the "challenge ritual" of the blue wildebeest: Estes, 1969). In addition, there appears to be an inverse relation between the degree of ritualization of a species' fighting technique and the amount of displaying in agonistic encounters. Species with "unrefined" fighting methods and relatively undifferentiated weapons tend to display proportionately much more than species with more elaborate weapons and correspondingly ritualized fighting techniques; I have already touched upon this subject (see also Geist, 1966). Thus, display sequences can be looked upon as a form of psychological warfare, the aim of which is to gain superiority without having to engage in potentially damaging physical combat. Alternatively, such displays may also enable one of the contestants to save face and to retreat eventually without openly conceding defeat. (For further and more detailed discussion of threat and intimidation displays in bovids, see Walther, 1974).

D. Submission and Appeasement

Some agonistic encounters end in an apparent "draw," i. e., neither of the antagonists wins a decisive advantage and, eventually, they may both go back to where they came from initially. This is most common in encounters between territorial neighbors, e. g., after a border violation by one of them, where both remain on their respective territories in the end.

However, probably the majority of other agonistic encounters result in a more or less clear-cut victory for one of the contestants. In this case, the defeated animal has the choice of two basic alternatives: (1) it can remove itself from the victor's immediate vicinity by fleeing, (2) if it desires to remain nearby, it can signal its acceptance of defeat through various expressions of submission. These have the dual function of indicating subordination by the animal showing them and usually of inhibiting further aggression on the part of the superior animal ("appeasement").

While for several ungulate groups no discrete submissive behavior is yet known, some very marked and characteristic postures occur among bovids. Walther (e. g., 1966a, 1974) has repeatedly emphasized that submissive displays generally follow the principle of being the antithesis of threat or intimidation postures. Thus, if weapons figure prominently in threats, they are "hidden" in submission, e. g., by turning the head sideways, horns pointing away from the opponent, as in black wildebeest, or by holding the horns low and/or pointing backward (cf. Fig. 32), in contrast to threats, as in several gazelle species. Similarly, where threat or intimidation involves erect postures, submission is characterized by lowered head and neck, sometimes flexed leg joints making the body appear lower, and quite literally "lying low," the extreme form of submission being a prone position with head and neck stretched out along the ground. In black wildebeest, the totally submissive animal may even lie flat on its side (Walther, 1966 b).

The head-low posture has certain affinities to the defensive threat in several bovids and may thus signal a certain degree of readiness to counter any attack that might be delivered. This interpretation, however, applies primarily to animals that have weapons to "back up" their defensive threat. As the submissive posture is virtually identical in several hornless female bovids, one may have to seek another explanation for its origin. Lowering the head can also be interpreted as an intention movement for lying-down, which may have been ritualized to signal submission without the animal actually adopting a more pronounced submissive posture.

Lying-down in submission may be derived from infantile lying behavior (cf. Burckhardt, 1958); this view is supported to some extent by the fact that submissive lying-down is accompanied by vocalizations strongly resembling the juvenile distress call (Chap. 14, D, VI) in a few species, e. g., oryx and black wildebeest (Walther, 1966 b). In captive black wildebeest, this call prompted other group members to approach and, in some instances, come to the aid of the animal emitting it, as happens in the case of the juvenile distress call. One difficulty in deriving submissive lying from infantile lying is the fact that this form of submission is particularly pronounced in a species whose young do not show lying-out ("hiding," see Chap. 14, D, II) behavior, the black wildebeest. The relation between submissive and infantile lying is, therefore, not established beyond doubt.

While most expressions of submission involve mainly the head and neck, some species also use tail postures and/or movements in this context. Black wildebeest extend their tail horizontally, or may even erect and lay it over the back, the signal value presumably being enhanced by the long white tail hair (Walther, 1966 b; von Richter, 1971 a). Tsessebe hold the tail stiffly away from the body, draw in the chin and prick the ears upright (S. Joubert, 1972). Young Bontebok curl the tail upward and hold the head low in extreme submission (David, 1973). Gerenuk curl their tail upward and over their back in a submissive gesture (Fig. 20; cf. Walther, 1961; Leuthold, 1971 c).

In the wild, submissive behavior is shown most commonly by young and adolescent animals of both sexes toward adults, and by females toward adult males, most markedly in the context of sexual advances by the latter (see Chap. 13, A, II). In agonistic encounters between adult males submissive gestures are rare and, if the outcome is really decisive, the defeated animal generally tends to flee (Fig. 26 f). Indeed, speedy flight may be the only way to escape being injured, once an animal has shown signs of weakness (Estes, 1969). Flight often invites pursuit on the part of the victor, but this rarely lasts for long; it is characteristic of such circumstances that the pursuer attempts to hit or stab the fleeing opponent with his horns. Normally, however, the defeated animal escapes without serious injuries and removes itself from further attacks by the victor.

The main function of submissive behavior is to allow the inferior animal to remain in the vicinity of the superior one and to inhibit further aggression. When an animal is forced to stay near the superior conspecific due to spatial restrictions, as in captivity, submissive behavior may be more frequent and more pronounced than under circumstances permitting escape. The study of captive animals, therefore, allows observation of the entire repertoire of submissive behavior, including its extreme forms, but does not permit inferences about its occurrence in the wild. For instance, Walther (1961, 1968) fairly often observed lying-down as submissive behavior in captive gerenuk, shown particularly by a young male toward an adult male, whereas in several years my wife and I never saw a clear-cut case of submissive lying-down in wild gerenuk in Tsavo NP; young males threatened or attacked by an adult male always ran away, showing the tail curl mentioned above (Fig. 20; Leuthold, 1971 c, and unpubl.). On the other hand, an observation of Walther's (1968/72, 1974) on Kirk's dikdik indicates that extreme submissive behavior may also occur in wild animals with a high frequency: a young male lay down over fifty times during one night in response to repeated attacks from his father.

E. Systematic Review

In the following, I attempt to characterize the agonistic behavior of each ungulate group to the level of subfamily or tribe. The objective is not to describe in detail the behavior of as many species as possible (for this see Estes, in press), but rather to facilitate comparison between different taxa by emphasizing broad features. Accounts for the various groups are not equally comprehensive, depending on the amount of research conducted; also, accounts for some groups may be biased in favor of those species that have been studied most intensively. Pertinent references appear, for the most part, at the end of each paragraph.

Proboscidea. Elephants fight by pushing frontally against each other with the bases of the trunks. The tusks apparently serve to prevent the heads from slipping sideways, in a manner analogous to the horns of bovids (see above). In addition, the tusks may be used as levers to lift or depress the opponent's head. The ability of one of the antagonists to push downward from an elevated position appears to be decisive for victory. To this end, elephants sometimes attempt to make use of features of the terrain, e.g., by moving up a slope. This description is based primarily on observations of playfights; really serious fights appear to be relatively rare and have seldom been witnessed. However, deaths resulting from fights between rivals have repeatedly been reported; usually, one bull had managed to gore the other with a tusk in a vital spot, such as the chest cavity or the brain.

Threat and intimidation displays center on the head, with the ears playing an important role. Extending the ears sideways and erecting the anterior part of the body, sometimes enhanced by stepping on some elevated object (log, termite mound, etc., see Fig. 27), serve to increase the animal's apparent size and are commonly employed in both intra- and interspecific encounters. Other displays involve movements of the entire head (nodding, shaking) or of the trunk only, and a great variety of expressive nuances has been described; they are frequently combined with brief forward rushes. Agonistic encounters often include bursts of redirected aggression, such as thrashing and breaking of bushes and small trees. (Kühme, 1961, 1963; Hendrichs, 1971; Sikes, 1971; Douglas-Hamilton, 1972; Douglas-Hamilton and Douglas-Hamilton, 1975; pers. obs.).

Equidae. Being virtually the only ungulate group not possessing special weapons for intraspecific fighting, equids use primarily their teeth and hooves. I have already described fighting techniques of zebra briefly (see Fig. 24), and no further elaboration is needed here. The main points are that a considerable variety of methods is employed and that all of them show little or no ritualization (Backhaus, 1960; Klingel, 1967, 1972a; Hassenberg, 1971).

Rhinocerotidae. Agonistic encounters between rhinoceroses are characterized by a marked preponderance of various threat and intimidation displays, while actual serious fighting is relatively rare. The latter involves mainly clubbing with the head and "horns", wielded sideways, against the opponent's head and/or body. Jabbing with the anterior horn also occurs, but more often during pursuit of a fleeing antagonist. Many rhino bear wounds that could be attributed to horn jabs, but not all these are necessarily related to serious fighting; horn-jabbing also occurs fairly commonly in premating behavior. Some wounds may have causes unrelated to agonistic behavior (see Chap. 7, A, II).

Intimidation and threat displays include the following, in approximate order of increasing intensity of threat components: scraping with hindlegs (with or without defecation); head-high intimidation posture, presented frontally or laterally; stiff-legged approach and/or circling of opponents; frontal approach with the head stretched forward; forward rush with lowered head and vocalization (snorting, screaming), culminating in the two opponents standing directly opposite each other, with front horns almost touching, sometimes also accompanied by screaming. From this position, the antagonists may either proceed to fighting, as described above, or start withdrawing. During the withdrawal phase, ritualized urination and/or defecation (Chap. 5, C, IV) may occur.

This is clearly a case where relatively unrefined fighting techniques and crude, potentially lethal weapons are associated with pronounced displays that reduce the incidence of overt fighting. This description refers primarily to the black rhinoceros, but the behavior of the "white" (square-lipped) species appears to be very similar (Goddard, 1966, 1967; Schenkel and Schenkel-Hulliger, 1969; Owen-Smith, 1973, 1975).

Suidae. Of the African species, only the warthog has been studied sufficiently. However, while varying in some details, the agonistic behavior of bush pig and giant forest hog is said to resemble that of the warthog in its general

127

characteristics, so that the latter species can serve as an example for the entire group.

Warthog fight in head-to-head engagements, in which the antagonists exchange blows or press their foreheads and snouts together and push. The long curved tusks of the upper jaw, and possibly the "warts" (cutaneous excrescences), sometimes bind the heads together, thus turning the contest into a ritualized pushing match. As pointed out earlier the tusks may thus serve a function analogous to that of the horns of bovids. When the heads become disengaged accidentally, or when one of the animals turns and flees, the other may use his sharp-edged, but relatively short, lower canines to inflict cuts or more serious wounds. The lower tusks are, however, effective only in an upward blow with open mouth, which may have been the original fighting technique in ancestral forms (as it still is in *Sus*: Geist, 1966).

Broadside display is a common form of intimidation in suids (not only African species); apart from the lateral orientation, with the head turned toward the opponent (in contrast to many bovids!), it involves a stiff-legged gait and the erection of the neck mane (warthog) or the prominent dorsal crest (bush pig), and sometimes the tail as well. Other threatening or actual fighting behaviors (e. g., between females) include rushing forward, pawing with the front feet, biting or at least snapping toward the opponent (rare in warthog), pushing with the head or snout, and putting the head under the antagonist's body and lifting him off the ground (bush pig). Some of the latter behavior patterns have been observed commonly in captivity in situations of conflict, e. g., over food; it is uncertain how prominent they are in wild animals not restricted spatially. Warthogs signal submission by lowering the head, sometimes the entire body, with ears and neck mane depressed; in addition, a growling vocalization may be uttered mainly by female warthog when pursued hard by a male (Ewer, 1958; Simpson, 1964; Frädrich, 1965, 1967, 1974; Bradley, 1968; Cumming, 1975).

Hippopotamidae. Virtually no information is available on the pygmy hippopotamus, but its agonistic behavior appears to be similar to that of its larger relative, as far as can be judged from a few observations in captivity.

The hippopotami are one of the few extant ungulate groups that have apparently not developed a ritualized fighting technique but use their very damaging weapons, the lower canines, with largely unrestrained force in intraspecific fighting. They usually stand in reverse-parallel orientation and deal blows sideways and upward, with open mouth, at the opponent's body, mainly the hindquarters. Although hippo skin is proverbially thick and the areas most exposed to tusk strikes are especially protected, serious injuries commonly occur in hippo fights, and death has resulted on a number of occasions on record. Older bulls often show many scars attesting to earlier fights.

However, as in the rhinoceros, really serious fights are relatively rare, and the hippopotamus has at its disposal a wide array of threat and intimidation displays that, presumably, often serve to avert actual fighting. Such displays include the well-known "yawn" (probably a "show of weapons," Fig. 25c), the defecation display (see Chap. 5, C, I), forward rushes and/or dives in the opponent's direction, rearing up and splashing down into the water, sudden emergence at the surface, blowing water through the nostrils, as well as actual vocalizations, particularly a series of staccato grunts. Thus, again the frequency of physical combat is reduced through pronounced display sequences, while fighting techniques are unmodified, damaging, and potentially lethal. The only "defense" against injuries is the well-developed dermal shield (Hediger, 1951; Veyheyen, 1954; Frädrich, 1967).

Tragulidae. Male Tragulids use their elongated upper canines as weapons, slashing at opponents in downward strikes with mouth wide open (Dubost, 1965, 1975). Possibly, a dermal shield extending over much of the back (Dubost and Terrade, 1970) may alleviate the effects of such strikes, but the shield is present in both sexes and may equally well protect the animals from mechanical damage by the dense vegetation they habitually move through. This, at any rate, is the interpretation given by Dubost and Terrade, when first describing the dorsal shield.

Giraffidae. When fighting, two male giraffes stand in parallel or reverse-parallel orientation and swing their heads sideways toward one another's body in what, to the human observer, appears to be slow motion (Fig. 30). The intensity

Fig. 30. Subadult male giraffe "necking" (usually the two animals stand somewhat closer together)

varies greatly, from gentle head/neck rubbing to heavy blows that are audible as dull thuds at distances of 50 to 100 m. However, the horns are blunt, and the skin is very thick, particularly in the shoulder region, so that serious damage occurs but rarely, and only accidentally (e. g., bone dislocation), as a result of fighting.

At first sight, the giraffe's mode of fighting ("necking") might appear highly unusual, if not unique, among ungulates. However, if we imagine the animals in more "normal" proportions, i. e., without the elongated neck that characterizes the giraffe, their fighting consists simply of exchanging sideward blows with the head, in parallel or reverse-parallel orientation. This, as we have seen earlier, is a relatively primitive fighting technique still found in a number of ungulates (some suids, mountain goat; cf. Geist, 1966). One important difference is that, in the giraffe, no really damaging weapons are involved, its horns having broad rounded tips not suited for piercing the skin. This, and the thickness of the skin itself, may be the most important factors that allowed the species to retain a largely unmodified fighting technique. Another factor may be the giraffe's social organization, which is characterized by a dominance hierarchy apparently based on individual recognition, a framework within which the need for serious fighting seldom arises. The great majority of necking matches that one sees in free-ranging giraffes are "friendly" sparring encounters, chiefly between subadult males.

Considerable significance has been attached to the fact that necking males sometimes show penis erections and that one may mount the other in the course of necking encounters; such behavior has been called "homosexual" (Innis, 1958; Coe, 1967). However, some antelopes commonly show erections during fights and threat displays (e.g., waterbuck, Uganda kob; see Fig. 26), while mounting occurs as a dominance display in some bovids (very marked in the bighorn sheep *Ovis canadensis*: Geist, 1971 b; but also in Grant's gazelle: Walther, 1965 a, 1974). I therefore do not feel that the use of the term homosexual, with its usual (human) connotation, is justified in this context.

Threat and intimidation displays are rather poorly developed in giraffe. How-ever, in a species relying on eyesight as much as giraffes appear to do, small nuances in posture, etc., may well suffice as means of expression, even though they are not as pronounced as in most other ungulates and may easily escape detection by an observer. Raising the head, sometimes to a nearly vertical position, is a strong intimidation display. Backhaus (1961, Fig. 43) has described many more expressive head/neck postures, but we have seen little of these in free-ranging animals; perhaps they are more pronounced, or more frequently used, and thus more evident, in captivity. An obvious weapon threat apparently does not exist in the giraffe's repertoire, or if it does it is shown very rarely in the wild; perhaps this is related to the rather limited use of the giraffe's "horns" as fighting weapons (Innis, 1958; Backhaus 1961; Coe, 1967; Dagg, 1971; Mejia, 1972; pers. obs.).

Very little is known about the okapi, but a few observations in captivity suggest that its agonistic behavior, in its main features, resembles that of the giraffe (Walther, 1960).

130

Bovidae. This family includes by far the majority of African ungulates; agonistic behavior is often quite complex and rich in expressive movements and postures. Space does not permit a detailed review here; only the major characteristics will be outlined.

Bovini. Agonistic behavior of the African buffalo resembles that of other, non-African, members of the tribe (cf. Schloeth, 1961 b). Intimidation and/or threat displays include drawing in the chin, which brings the horns forward, and hunching the shoulders, which increases the apparent height, most often shown in lateral orientation (broadside display). More intensive threat is signalled by head-tossing (up and down) and snorting; the antagonists may circle each other. Fighting consists of head-to-head charges, either single clashes with the thick bosses over the forehead, or more lasting engagements with horns interlocked. Several cases of buffalo being found with horns inextricably interlocked are on record, including some females. However, serious fighting appears to be relatively rare.

Between bouts of fighting, or threat displays, one or both antagonists may thrash bushes with the horns, rub face and horns on the ground, throwing up earth in the process, and occasionally wallow in mud.

Buffalo also show a marked submissive posture, with head stretched forward and slightly lowered. Another form of apparent appeasement behavior consists of a head-high posture, with nose pointing upward, resembling an exaggerated "intention to flee," which seems to inhibit further attacks (Grimsdell, 1969; Sinclair, 1970, 1974).

Tragelaphini. The Tragelaphines' preference for closed habitats makes it very difficult to observe their social behavior in the wild. But even when this difficulty is taken into account, it appears that outright fighting is rather rare in this group. During several years of studying lesser kudu in Tsavo NP I saw no serious fights, very few other encounters between adult males and only occasional cases of playfighting among subadult males. The following account is based primarily on Walther's (1964a) detailed comparative study on captive animals.

A prominent feature in this group is a well-developed lateral intimidation display that is generally enhanced by erection of the dorsal hair crest present in all *Tragelaphus* males, and probably by the ventral neck manes of male greater kudu (Fig. 19) and nyala. Expressions of threat include, in order of increasing seriousness: head-shaking, erection of the head, lowering of the head and low presentation of the horns, in the extreme held almost parallel to the ground, pointing forward (intention movement for fighting). Soil horning may also imply a threat, as in many other bovids. Actual fighting consists of head-to-head wrestling, with horns tightly bound together, again as in several other bovid groups. The intricate horn shape sometimes leads to horns becoming so firmly wedged together that the antagonists are unable to separate again (Fig. 23), and eventually both may die (Walther, 1958, 1964a, 1966a, 1968/72, 1974; see also Tello and van Gelder, 1975; Waser, 1975b).

Cephalophinae. Conditions of observation are even worse than in the Tragelaphines because most duikers live singly or in groups not exceeding two or three animals, and in even denser habitats. Also, they are smaller and relatively rare in captivity. Males are said to be highly intolerant of other males, including their own grown-up offspring, and no fights have been described in detail until recently, when Maxwell's duikers were observed in New York Zoo. At the outset of a fight, males first press or rub their antorbital glands together (possibly mutual marking, Fig. 31). This is followed by a series of violent head-to-head

Fig. 31. Male Maxwell's duikers rubbing antorbital glands together at beginning of fight (from Ralls, 1975)

clashes, during which one or both contestants may lose balance and either fall down or be thrown into the air. One male may also jump over the other in the course of the encounter. The fights are characterized by an almost complete lack of expressive behavior (e. g., threat or intimidation displays), with the possible exception of the initial gland-rubbing which seems to be unique in this species or group. After the fight, the victor may chase the loser wildly. Whether this pattern is in fact typical of the species, and possibly of the genus and/or subfamily, or whether conditions of captivity may have effected some atypical modifications of behavior in the animals observed, remains to be established (Ralls, 1973, 1974, 1975).

Reduncinae. Agonistic techniques and displays are relatively uniform in this group. All species possess horns (in males only) that are curved to a greater or lesser extent and show pronounced ridges which, as outlined earlier, presumably serve to bind the horns together during fights. The latter consist of head-to-head engagements in which the contestants hold their faces near the ground and push vigorously against each other (Fig. 26d). Brief clashes involving single horn blows, with the opponents separating again immediately, may precede more prolonged engagements. These may last up to 20 min in Uganda kob, but are usually much shorter. Due to their specialized social system (see Chap. 16, E), territorial male Uganda kob probably fight more frequently than any other bovids.

Pronounced lateral displays appear to be entirely lacking in this group, and parallel or reverse-parallel orientations are rarely, if ever, assumed. Threat displays consist of high or low presentation of horns, held slightly forward or tilted to one side (Fig. 26a, b). The Uganda kob conspicuously lowers the ears in the threat posture (Fig. 26a, b). In pauses between fighting bouts agonistic grazing or standing with heads turned sideways (facing away, Fig. 26c) are prominent.

132

A characteristic feature of agonistic behavior in the Reduncinae—at least in Uganda kob and waterbuck—is partial or complete erection of the penis during threat displays and fights (cf. Fig. 26a, c). Whether this is a result of some form of "excitatory neural overspill" or whether penis erection has a specific signal function in agonistic encounters remains unknown (Buechner, 1961; Lent, 1969; Spinage, 1969a; Jungius, 1971; pers. obs.).

Hippotraginae. Fighting consists mainly of successive horn clashes, between which the antagonists usually separate again, but head-to-head pushing with horns engaged also occurs. While fighting, the animals occasionally *(Oryx)* or commonly *(Hippotragus)* drop to their carpal joints.

Most species show a lateral intimidation display, which is particularly pronounced in *Hippotragus* spp., where its effect is enhanced by a (dorsal) neck mane. The head is held high, with chin pulled in, ears pointing back/upward, and the tail is lifted to a variable extent. By contrast, in the submissive posture the head is held low and stretched forward, and the tail is tightly pressed against the body (Fig. 32). Prolonged lateral displaying may lead to circling, which is particularly marked in this group (it also occurs in premating behavior, see Chap. 13, A, II).

Threat displays include a head-high posture, in which the animal stands erect, with head held high and horns sometimes tilted toward the opponent (Fig. 15), and an essentially defensive head-low threat, in which the animal holds its head near the ground. Both forms of threat can be intensified by head-bobbing, at least in oryx. The head-low threat may also contain elements of submission; in fact, it is possible that different authors refer to the same posture by different names. Of course, the exact postures and their meaning differ somewhat between species, and more markedly between genera. Also, the oryx has been studied in any detail only in captivity so far.

Female sable commonly show a dominance display, in which the higher-ranking animal rubs its forehead and/or horns against the other's rump (Fig. 33). This appears to serve primarily to maintain the dominance hierarchy within female herds. Whether the antorbital glands play a specific role in this context is not yet known (Walther, 1958, 1965b, 1966a, 1968/72; Estes and Estes, 1969, 1974; Huth, 1970; S. Joubert, 1974).

Alcelaphinae. Recent field research has provided a substantial body of information on this group. All authors agree that serious fighting is comparatively rare but that a great variety of threat and intimidation displays, as well as "irrelevant activities," combine to produce complex interactions, the most striking of which are the so-called "challenge rituals" routinely performed between territorial neighbors. Perhaps this high degree of ritualization of noncombative behavior in agonistic contexts is related to the fact that the horns of at least some Alcelaphinae are relatively undifferentiated and potentially dangerous, particularly in the wildebeests.

When they do fight, all Alcelaphinae drop to the carpal joints and exchange brief horn clashes, withdrawing in between (Fig. 34a). More rarely, prolonged pushing with engaged horns may occur, with faces more or less along the ground (Fig. 34b). In the blue wildebeest, the opponents in serious fights apparently

Fig. 32. Two male roan antelopes in dominance/submissive postures; note differences in attitudes of head, ears and tail (from S. Joubert, 1974)

Fig. 33. Dominance display between female sable antelopes; the animal on the right is dominant

Fig. 34a and b. Fighting posture in bontebok (similar in other Alcelaphines). (a) before horn clash, (b) with horns engaged (from David, 1973)

attempt to get a horn tip underneath the other's head and gore him in the throat. Seemingly, there would be no inhibition from seriously injuring the adversary, if one of them ever achieved the opportunity to do so. The quickness of reaction, however, largely prevents this from happening; in addition the throat skin is very tough and further protected by the thick beard, minimizing the danger of severe injuries. Wounds inflicted with the horn tips are relatively frequent in Coke's hartebeest.

Prominent intimidation and/or threat displays include a lateral presentation, in which the opponents stand in parallel, or more commonly, reverse-parallel orientation. The tsessebe and topi, at this stage, perform a striking upward movement of the head ("head-casting," Fig. 35), during which, in high-intensity displays, one or both of the antagonists may even rear up on their hindlegs (this is one of the very few cases in which rearing-up occurs in agonistic encounters among African bovids; it is, of course, common in various species of sheep and goats). Similar but less intensive nodding movements are performed by all Alcelaphinae, also in other than agonistic contexts. From the reverse-parallel orientation, circling may ensue, as in the Hippotraginae. Standing with head

135

Fig. 35. "Head-casting" display of tsessebe (from S. Joubert, 1972)

Fig. 36. Mutual anus-sniffing during "challenge ritual" of bontebok (from David, 1973)

136

held sideways (facing away, cf. Fig. 26c) is also a common display in most or all species.

Irrelevant activities, such as agonistic grazing, comfort movements (scratching with hind feet, etc.; Fig. 29), lying down (wildebeest), ritualized to a greater or lesser extent, are very prominent in agonistic encounters among Alcelaphinae. Also, defecation occurs commonly in this context; bontebok show pronounced anus-sniffing (Fig. 36) and in wildebeest there is even a urination-Flehmen sequence in many challenge rituals (perhaps the only known instance in which Flehmen regularly occurs in a nonreproductive context). Several elements of such rituals are common to most or all Alcelaphinae.

The submissive postures, including lying down, of the black wildebeest have been described above. Tsessebe signal submission by holding their tails rigidly away from the body, with head pulled in and ears erect. Young males of Coke's hartebeest show a very similar ("head-in") posture toward territorial males. For further details of agonistic behavior of the Alcelaphinae the original literature should be consulted (Walther, 1966a, b, 1968/72, 1974; Estes, 1969, in press; du Plessis, 1972; David, 1973; von Richter, 1971a, 1972; S. Joubert, 1972; Gosling, 1974, 1975; Duncan, 1975).

Aepycerotinae. Fighting in impala is similar to that described above for the Reduncinae, i.e., pushing matches with interlocked horns, sometimes preceded by brief single clashes of horns, after which the opponents withdraw again. Threat and intimidation behavior includes an erect stance with head and horns held high and hindquarters rather low ("proud posture"), head-shaking, "volte-jumps" with lowered head and lifted tail, quick head jerks downward, pronounced tongue-flicking and yawning with head lifted and horns laid back. The latter two displays are apparently peculiar to impala, at least among African bovids (tongue-flicking also occurs in premating behavior). Facing away may be shown, too. Comfort movements, such as scratching the head and neck with a hind foot or licking parts of the body, are also prominent. When one of the antagonists breaks and flees, the other may pursue him, with tail lifted and the white hair on its underside fanned, uttering grunts and roars (Schenkel, 1966a; Walther, 1968/72; M. V. Jarman, 1973; pers. obs.).

Antilopini. Detailed observations of wild animals have been made primarily in Grant's and Thomson's gazelles and to a lesser extent in springbok; further information is available from captive animals for a variety of species from the work of Walther.

The main fighting technique of gazelles is pushing and wrestling with heads bound together by the horns, as in several other bovid groups. Particularly in the early phases of fights, or in fights of lower intensity, opponents may clash horns repeatedly, withdrawing after each clash without coming to a lasting engagement. The two methods may be used side by side, but one species may show a preference for one of them, e.g., Thomson's gazelle for quick short clashes, Grant's rather for prolonged pushing. In addition, there are specific (perhaps subgeneric) differences in the frequency of actual fighting: *thomsoni* fight very readily, *granti* do so less often. Accordingly, Grant's gazelle has a more pronounced intimidation display (Fig. 28), while "Tommies" show a less varied repertoire of intimidation and threat behavior which, moreover, is less strongly ritualized than in the larger species.

Threats consist primarily of horn presentation in various attitudes (Fig. 25): high (strong offensive threat), low (possibly more defensive, but not exclusively), angled (i.e., tilted sideways). High presentation of horns while facing sideways probably represents a transition to intimidation displays, in which an erect stance (including nose-up posture) figures prominently. Lateral intimidation, though present in several species, is less marked than in some other bovid groups (e.g., Tragelaphini, Hippotraginae). In some of the intimidation postures, particularly head-high, certain structures or patterns are prominently displayed, e.g., the white throat patch and/or the strongly developed neck muscles. The most striking intimidation display of this kind so far known in gazelles is shown by *granti*: two males stand in reverse-parallel orientation, with heads turned sideways and slightly upward, horns tilted back, neck prominently displayed (Fig. 28). They may remain in this posture for several minutes, either stationary or circling each other, until one of them finally starts walking away or until overt threatening and possibly fighting begin.

Comfort movements and/or agonistic grazing commonly occur during or immediately after encounters between potential or actual rivals, as do ritualized urination/defecation, often preceded by foreleg pawing; Thomson's gazelles may also mark with their antorbital glands in this context. Submissive postures follow the pattern outlined earlier and are shown mainly by females and young animals (Walther, 1958, 1964 b, 1965 a, 1968, 1974; Estes, 1967; Bigalke, 1972).

Neotragini. Very little is known about agonistic behavior of the species in this tribe, all of which carry short pointed horns that might be potentially lethal weapons. It seems reasonable, therefore, to assume that serious fighting is not very frequent but rather replaced by ritualized displays, as we have seen in other instances. A few observations on Kirk's dikdik lend support to this assumption: male dikdik dash forward toward each other with heads lowered, the frontal hair crest erect, but normally fail to make physical contact and retreat after each sally. Intimidation and/or threat consist of a stilted walk and bouncing jumps in the opponent's direction; ceremonial defecation commonly follows agonistic encounters. Submissive behavior includes a slinking gait with flexed leg joints and head held low, and also lying-down (Hendrichs and Hendrichs, 1971; Walther, 1974). Recent observations on the oribi present a similar picture (Monfort and Monfort, 1974).

Chapter 13

Sexual Behavior

In the overall context of reproductive behavior we may define as sexual, or epigamic, behavior the elements involved in bringing individuals of opposite sex together for mating, i.e., to ensure fertilization. Behavior related to rearing offspring, once born, is conveniently treated as a separate category, viz. maternal/filial behavior (Chap. 14).

Most ungulates living in temperate climates reproduce in a strictly seasonal pattern, usually once a year, and the season is determined mainly by external factors such as light, temperature, etc., and ultimately by the food supply. As a consequence, all members of a population come into breeding condition at about the same time. This is in sharp contrast to many—but by no means all—tropical ungulates who breed throughout the year, albeit sometimes with seasonal peaks. Each female may have her own individual cycle of estrus-pregnancy-postpartum interval, dating back to the first successful mating, perhaps modified at times by nutritional conditions. Most female ungulates experience only a short estrous period, of the order of one to three days, during which mating must take place, if conception is to be assured. Males, on the other hand, can be reproductively active at any time (contingent upon their social status in many cases); they may seek out, approach and copulate with any estrous female that happens to be present in their vicinity. The major problem here is proper synchronization of male and female activities, and a principal function of the often elaborate courtship behavior of tropical ungulates may well be to effect such synchronization, and thus ensure successful reproduction (cf. Ewer, 1968).

A major difficulty facing many ungulates is the fact that mating requires a close mutual approach, closer than would normally be tolerated in a nonreproductive situation, including physical contact which many ungulates, particularly bovids, appear to shun otherwise. A variety of behavioral mechanisms serve to overcome this difficulty and to ensure that mating can take place successfully and in an orderly fashion.

For convenience, we can divide sexual behavior into three stages:
1. Precopulatory behavior, i.e., the sequence of events leading from the initial encounter between potential mates to a state of full readiness for copulation (this is commonly termed courtship behavior)
2. Actual copulation
3. Postcopulatory behavior, i.e., any behavioral interactions between the mates that frequently or usually follow copulation.

Adopting the same approach as for agonistic behavior, I will first discuss the subject more generally and then give a brief review of sexual behavior in the different ungulate groups.

Walther (1958, 1960/61, 1968/72, 1974) has described sexual behavior of many bovid species in considerable detail and has attempted to trace the evolution of various signals and displays, and the relations of many courtship elements to agonistic behavior. The following review is based on Walther's studies and interpretations, and applies primarily to bovids. The majority of Walther's observations were made on captive animals; however, if we assume that sexual behavior consists largely of innate elements, this should not be a serious drawback.

A. Precopulatory Behavior

In any one species the sequence of events leading to eventual copulation may vary widely between different instances, depending partly on the time (in relation to physiological events) and circumstances of the first encounter between potential mates, as well as on their individual characteristics. If the female is still relatively far from peak estrus, courtship may be a long-drawn-out affair, with many different behavioral elements being shown in irregular sequence. If, on the other hand, the female happens to be in full estrus at the first encounter with a male, mating may ensue quickly, with only a minimum of "preliminaries." Thus it is necessary to observe a considerable number of instances before one can expect to have a reasonably complete picture of a species' courtship behavior (cf. Ewer, 1968).

In contrast to some other (lower) vertebrates, there are virtually no fixed sequences of male–female interactions in ungulate courtship. Males may have several action patterns at their disposal and, although certain elements may occur more frequently at one stage than at another, their sequence is not strictly determined and may vary considerably from case to case (cf. Buechner and Schloeth, 1965). Similarly, a female may respond to a given male behavior in a variety of ways.

Although rather artificial, it is convenient to treat male and female behavior separately.

I. Male Behavior

In ungulates, as in most mammals, males play a much more active role in sexual behavior than females. The first step involves locating and identifying an estrous female. The exact way in which this happens depends to a considerable extent on the social and spatial organization of the species, but we can probably assume that the main initial stimulus is usually provided by specific odors emanating from a female approaching estrus (see, e. g., Lindsay, 1965; Fraser, 1968), although other stimuli may operate as well. The male will seek out the individual concerned, be that a solitary female some distance away or a member of a herd in his immediate vicinity. In the latter case, the male may go from one female to another, sniffing each one's vulva in turn. Often, the

Fig. 37a and b. Flehmen in sable antelope (a) and Kirk's dikdik (b), near-extremes within the Bovidae

male's approach, and particularly his nuzzling the vulva, induces the female to urinate. The male usually samples the urine by letting it flow over—and perhaps into—his nose and mouth. With some exceptions (elephant and apparently the genera *Alcelaphus* and *Damaliscus*: Estes, 1972) all male ungulates then usually show the behavior known as "Flehmen" (Schneider, 1930ff), sometimes termed "lip-curl." In outer appearance, Flehmen is remarkably similar in all ungulates, as well as in some other mammal groups showing it (e.g., cats): after sampling the urine, the male lifts his head to a horizontal position or higher, with mouth slightly open, lips parted and especially the upper lip retracted to an extent varying considerably between species (Figs. 37, 40c). The nostrils appear to be at least partly closed. The animal may turn its head slowly from side to side and often licks its lips afterward. In the Tragulidae and Suidae the grimace is not at all marked and has, until recently, been thought to be lacking altogether (Dubost, 1975).

While Flehmen is essentially a male behavior pattern, normally released by the scent of female urine, females and young also show it on occasions, and it can be elicited by a variety of other scents (see Dagg and Taub, 1970).

From the circumstances in which it occurs the main function of Flehmen has long been inferred to be an olfactory test of the female's reproductive condition. Presumably, the male can detect the presence of sex hormones, or their breakdown products, in the female's urine and adjust his further actions accordingly. However, the exact mechanisms involved in Flehmen have been the subject of some controversy. Knappe (1964) suggested that the vomeronasal (or Jacobson's) organ played a role in the process. This was disputed by Dagg and Taub (1970). In the most recent and most in-depth review of the subject Estes (1972) endorsed Knappe's suggestion and proposed a model of how the Jacobson's organ may function in the context of Flehmen. These ideas, while plausible on the basis of available evidence, remain to be substantiated by more detailed observations and/or experiments.

Whatever the exact mechanisms involved in Flehmen, the associated behavior of ungulates in this context supports the interpretation that its primary function is an olfactory examination of the female's urine ("urinalysis") and, by implication, her reproductive state. Males often appear very "eager" to elicit urination in females, which led Backhaus (1961) to coin the term "Harnfordern" ("demanding urine") for this behavior. On the other hand, some female ungulates appear to increase their output of urine during estrus (Fraser, 1968), perhaps in response to the "increased demand." Often, a female moves away while the male performs Flehmen; he is usually so "engrossed" in this activity that he does not follow immediately, and the female has a chance of eluding further advances. However, even if the female does not move, the male may show no further interest in her after Flehmen; this can probably be taken as indicating that the female is not in or near estrus. Thus, many potential sequences of precopulatory behavior come to an end after the male's Flehmen ("Kleine Sexualität": Walther, 1963b, 1964a). In other cases, the male continues to seek contact with the female concerned and may even increase his efforts; this presumably signifies that the female is approaching or has entered estrus. It is usually at this point that true precopulatory behavior begins.

Having thus located a potential mate, the male must continue to approach and even touch her, in preparation for the actual mating, while at the same time ensuring that she does not run away and leave his "sphere of influence" (territory, etc.). This requires a delicate balance between somewhat muted aggression and not-too-overt appeasement. Courtship behavior, therefore, tends to

142

consist of a curious mixture of slightly aggressive and distinctly nonaggressive elements which are, however, not always neatly separable. Among the former, a prominent feature at this stage is some form of "driving" ("Treiben"), in which the male closely follows the female around. This may vary from a leisurely walk to a brisk pace and, occasionally, full gallop, depending on the species and on the degree of the female's readiness to accept the male's advances. In gazelles, in particular, this part of courtship is so pronounced, and fairly ritualized, that Walther uses the term "Paarungsmarsch" (mating march) for it. He interprets it as ritualized flight of the female from the male's "aggression," and it probably serves mainly to synchronize the partners and to bring them into proper orientation for mating. In other species, or groups, driving is less marked; the male simply follows the female around more or less closely.

Somewhat aggressive tendencies in courtship may be necessary for two reasons: (1) the male must remain active, advance toward the female and establish physical contact with her, in other words he must "move in on her" and transgress her individual distance, even in the face of evasive and/or repulsive actions on her part (see below); (2) he must also assert his superiority over the female as he will, eventually, have to subdue her—quite literally—in the process of copulation. The male's aggressiveness must not, however, be too marked, lest it defeat its purpose; aggressive behavior shown in the context of courtship therefore differs in important respects from that shown in agonistic encounters. In particular, males use virtually no threats, especially none involving their fighting weapons; instead, they rely primarily on intimidation displays in which, as a rule, weapons do not figure prominently (Chap. 12, C), or they employ more or less specific courtship-approach postures. Most striking among these is the widespread nose-forward posture, in which the male extends his head and neck forward ("low stretch," "Überstrecken") or forward-upward ("head-up posture," "Aufsteilen") when approaching the female (Figs. 38, 40a). One probably important feature of these postures is that they tend to hide the horns, which are laid back along the neck, in marked contrast to threat postures in which weapons are presented conspicuously (Fig. 25). The nose-forward posture, there-

Fig. 38. "Low-stretch" posture in courtship of bontebok; note curled tail (from David, 1973)

143

fore, amounts to a combination of slightly aggressive (close approach) and clearly appeasing (hiding weapons) tendencies (see David, 1973, for specific examples in bontebok). The effectiveness of this posture as a signal may be enhanced by certain markings being displayed prominently, e.g., a white throat patch in many antelopes (e.g., in Uganda kob, Fig. 40a). Relations to specific appeasement signals (Chap. 12, D) may also be evident in some other courtship elements. For instance, male bontebok curl their tail upward when courting (Fig. 38), which corresponds to a submissive posture shown by young animals (David, 1973). This emphasizes that some expressive gestures or postures may be used in different contexts and that their meaning may depend on the situation and the animals involved (Walther, 1974).

In the driving phase the male may show several other behaviors that are, for the most part, characteristic of courtship. A prominent gesture of this kind is the "Laufschlag" (Walther, 1958 and later), sometimes translated as "leg beat": the male lifts a stiffly held foreleg under the female's hindquarters, usually from behind but sometimes also from the side (Fig. 40d); he may or may not touch her in the process. Male Tragelaphines, who do not perform Laufschlag, sometimes place their head and neck over the female's neck or shoulders (Fig. 39). Walther

Fig. 39. Male greater kudu places head and neck over female's neck during courtship ("Halsauflegen"; from Walther, 1964a)

(1958, 1960/61, 1974) considers Laufschlag to be derived from an aggressive front leg kick, and the above-mentioned behavior of the Tragelaphines from—probably ancestral—neck-wrestling. If these interpretations are correct, elements of phylogenetically old fighting behavior have been incorporated, in ritualized form, into present-day courtship, emphasizing the relationship between agonistic and sexual behavior.

Functionally, both Laufschlag and ritualized neck-wrestling can be regarded as (1) conveying "friendly intentions" and (2) conditioning the female to tactile stimuli, in other words as testing her readiness to stand for mounting. Other gestures used by males in this context include nuzzling and/or licking the vulva, or other parts of the female's body, laying the head onto her back or rump, and possibly mounting without erection of the phallus, which often precedes mounting with erection.

The visual and tactile signals of this phase are often accompanied by soft "pleading" vocalizations uttered by the male. Due to their low intensity, these may be inaudible to human observers under field conditions, but observations in captivity have augmented the number of known examples. By their contrast to vocalizations—if any—used in agonistic encounters (grunts, roars, etc.) they further serve to convey "friendly intentions" in the context of courtship.

While there are several parallels between agonistic and sexual behavior, there is one interesting feature that sets them clearly apart, at least as far as bovids are concerned. This is the virtual absence of displacement and/or redirected behavior from courtship sequences. Whereas such elements, ritualized or not, are prominent in many agonistic encounters (see Chap. 12, C), we are hard pressed to find any that occur regularly in courtship. Perhaps this reflects the fact that both agonistic and sexual behavior are rather highly ritualized in bovids, and the behavioral repertoires corresponding to the two categories are fairly strictly separated (at least in their contemporary forms). This is generally less pronounced in other groups of ungulates.

Indeed, what has been said so far about courtship behavior applies primarily to bovids, and even within this family there are great differences between species or groups of species (see below). In other ungulate families, the overall pattern of precopulatory behavior is generally similar but considerably less elaborate. Some form of driving, i.e., the male following the female around closely, with or without physical contact, seems common to virtually all African ungulates. But the many striking postures and gestures so characteristic of courtship in various bovids are largely lacking, or at least much less developed, in other ungulate groups. In some species, elements of "unmitigated" aggression may be more prominent, e.g., in the black rhinoceros (for details see Chap. 13, D).

II. Female Behavior

Up to now, we have considered primarily the behavior of the male in courtship. However, the response of the female to the male's actions may be at least as important in determining the eventual outcome of the encounter, i.e., whether or not successful mating is achieved.

Studies on domestic ungulates indicate that, during estrus, the behavior of females differs markedly from that shown under normal conditions (e.g., Fraser, 1968). Indeed, some behavioral changes in the female, especially increased tolerance of the male's approaches and of physical contact, are an indispensable prerequisite for successful mating. In African ungulates, particularly free-ranging ones, it has rarely been possible to observe females sufficiently closely to detect such changes. The majority of relevant observations have, so far, been made in captivity (e.g., *Tragelaphus* spp.: Walther, 1964a), but some also on free-ranging animals, e.g., gazelles (Walther, 1964b, 1965a, 1968) and Uganda kob (Buechner and Schloeth, 1965). The most striking feature of such behavioral changes is usually the reduced tendency to flee from an adult male. While under normal conditions a female will generally try to evade an approaching male, she may

Fig. 40a–f. Mating behavior of Uganda kob. (a) Courtship approach with head held high, horns laid back, and short quick steps (prancing). (b) Sampling female's urine. (c) Flehmen.

146

(d) Laufschlag. (e) Mounting; note male's erect posture and clasping of female's flanks with forelegs. (f) Inguinal nuzzling after copulation

147

be considerably more tolerant in estrus, sometimes to the extent of actively "inviting" the male's attention.

Responses of females to a male's courtship advances show a broad spectrum of possible variations, ranging from complete tolerance through various forms of evasion to active rebuttal. What actually happens in any one instance depends on a number of factors, among which the female's proximity to estrus, and possibly her age and previous experience, are probably the most important. In the end, it is usually the female who, through her acceptance or withdrawal behavior, makes the choice of the male with whom she will mate. In this context, it is noteworthy that females normally repel advances by subadult and/or juvenile males and tolerate only fully adult males, if any (though it is not yet established whether this would also be done during peak estrus).

In the early stages of estrus, when a female is not yet ready to copulate, she tends to avoid the male's advances in various ways. The most drastic evasive action is obviously to run away but, while this does happen on occasions, it is comparatively rare, once estrus has begun. More commonly, a female in this situation will jump or walk forward a few steps in response to the male's approach and stop again, sometimes feeding intermittently. This evasive action is often combined with pronounced lowering of head and neck, possibly expressing submissive tendencies, sometimes also with head-shaking or head-tossing. The latter may, in turn be accompanied by snapping or biting movements ("Mundstossen": Backhaus, 1958; Walther, 1958, 1964a; "champing" in waterbuck: Spinage, 1969b).

However, if the female is really approaching estrus, the male will usually persist, and the female shows a remarkable tolerance of his repeated advances, despite her "prude play." This is manifested primarily by her evident reluctance to actually run away; she may evade contact with the male in various ways, yet stay near him. Widespread behavior reflecting this conflict situation is breaking away sideways, and turning, during the driving phase, which usually leads to the animals circling around each other in head-to-tail orientation (Paarungskreisen: Walther, 1958ff). This normally interrupts progress of courtship for a while, without actually separating the partners, and this may be the primary function of this behavior in many species. However, in some others, circling appears to have become ritualized to the extent of constituting an integral element of courtship behavior, e. g., in the Hippotraginae (oryx, sable, roan) and some Alcelaphinae (e. g., bontebok).

A more extreme way of interrupting courtship without actually leaving is for the female to lie down. This may—or may not—represent an extreme form of submission, but at the same time affords effective protection from the male's advances. This occurs fairly often in Uganda kob, possibly as an adaptation to the spatial restrictions on a lek (Buechner and Schloeth, 1965; see Chap. 16, E).

Instead of evading the male, the "unwilling" female may use threats and aggressive attacks toward him (snapping, biting intentions, butting with the forehead, kicking with hindlegs in zebra). The male usually does not retaliate with aggressive behavior but "stoically" accepts head butts, etc., while either continuing courtship or adopting an intimidation posture (e. g., lesser kudu: see Fig. 32 in Walther, 1958).

Once a female has reached full estrus, her evasive actions decrease in both frequency and intensity and may disappear altogether. Various authors report that females ready to copulate hold their tail somewhat lifted and may straddle the hindlegs a bit. Some may even "invite" the male to mate by sniffing parts of his body and/or by making attempts to mount him (e. g., waterbuck: Spinage, 1969 b). Estrous females may also mount other conspecifics, particularly other females.

Behavior associated with estrus in female ungulates can be observed particularly well in the Uganda kob, in the special circumstances of the mating arenas or leks (Buechner, 1961, 1963; Buechner and Schloeth, 1965). Estrous females spontaneously move onto the traditional, spatially fixed arenas, which results in the unusual situation that, normally, only estrous females and adult males are present together in these places. Interactions between estrous females occur commonly; they include behavior that is normally part of the male's courtship pattern, particularly mounting, but occasionally also naso-genital contact, Flehmen and Laufschlag (Fig. 40). In some cases, pronounced behavior of this sort may be a consequence of hormonal imbalance—almost certainly so in one case of a "male-behaving" female (Buechner and Schloeth, 1965, p. 219)—but mostly such behavior appeared to be a normal phenomenon accompanying estrus, as is known from domestic ungulates (Fraser, 1968).

B. Copulation

Once the male and female are sufficiently coordinated and ready to mate, actual copulation may ensue at any moment, depending mainly on whether and how well the male succeeds in inserting his phallus into the vagina. That in turn depends, at least partly, on the structure and mobility of the phallus. In bovids, with a rodlike phallus of limited manoeuvrability, a series of mountings may be required until intromission is achieved, as the male dismounts after each failure to do so. Coitus is very brief, consisting of a single powerful pelvic thrust after which the male dismounts immediately. Thus, actual copulation lasts only a few seconds, although many unsuccessful mountings may precede it. In other ungulates, particularly those with a muscularized penis capable of some movements while erect, only one mounting may be necessary, during which intromission can be achieved through "searching" movements of the penis, e. g., in the elephant or rhinoceros. In nonbovid ungulates copulation generally lasts considerably longer, from one to three min in plains zebra (Klingel, 1969c) to as long as 30–40 min in the black rhinoceros (Goddard, 1966). Frictional movements occur regularly only in the Equidae, but male suids may perform similar movements until the corkscrewlike tip of the phallus is lodged in the corresponding structure of the cervix (Fraser, 1968).

Within the Bovidae, the male's posture during coitus differs between subfamilies in a characteristic, apparently specific manner. Male gazelles carry their

149

body very erect and often do not even touch the female with their front legs during mounting; coitus is usually achieved while walking. Males of other species show various degrees of resting their forequarters on the female's body and of clasping the female's sides with the forelegs (Fig. 40e). The extreme is shown by *Tragelaphus* species where males lay their head and neck onto the female's back (e. g., Fig. 35 in Walther, 1964a; cf. Walther, 1958, 1968/72).

While most female ungulates stand for mating, the female pygmy hippopotamus may lie down, particularly when mating occurs on land (in captivity: Lang, 1972). However, both species of hippopotamus appear to mate preferentially in the water, the female being partially or wholly submerged, only lifting the head from time to time to breathe (Verheyen, 1954; Frädrich, 1967).

Most female ungulates probably experience several copulations during any one estrous period. This is, however, difficult to ascertain in free-ranging animals, and relevant data are, accordingly, scarce. Backhaus (1958, 1959) saw the same female hartebeest copulate 17 times within about seven hours, always with the same male. Again, in the unique situation of the mating arenas of Uganda kob it has been possible to record repeated matings involving the same female; they numbered up to 17—with nine different males—during daylight hours (Buechner and Schloeth, 1965). As mating on the kob arenas continues throughout the night, the total number of copulations that an individual female experiences per estrus may be considerably higher still. Multiple copulations, involving several males, are also known in the African elephant (Short, 1966).

C. Postcopulatory Behavior

Following coitus, most ungulates show a period of rest of variable length, during which they may feed, lie down, or simply stand still. Regular interactions between the mates, involving specific behavioral elements, are rare in African ungulates. A brief aggressive phase may follow copulation: female warthog sometimes behave aggressively toward the male (Frädrich, 1967), while an "outburst of aggressive activity" often occurs in male impala after copulation (Schenkel, 1966a).

Postcoital interactions are, however, regular and pronounced in the Uganda kob, and characterized by certain actions that are not, or only rarely, seen in other phases of sexual behavior: the male may lick the phallus, whistle repeatedly, nuzzle the female's inguinal region and possibly lick her udder in the process (Fig. 40f). Elements of precopulatory behavior may also occur at this stage, particularly Laufschlag, often in the form of a "pincers" movement in which the male places his chin over the back of the female from the side (Buechner and Schloeth, 1965). The sequence and frequency of the different elements are very variable, but at least some are almost always performed. The evolution of this elaborate postcoital behavior is possibly linked to the special circumstances under which mating takes place in the Uganda kob, viz. a number of small territories aggregated in spatially fixed arenas; its function, however, remains obscure.

150

D. Systematic Review

Undisturbed sexual behavior is more difficult to observe than agonistic behavior, as many ungulates appear to be rather sensitive to disturbances during courtship and mating, even in captivity, while fighting animals are often so absorbed as to be almost oblivious of their surroundings. This difficulty has led some observers to assume that most ungulates mate preferentially at night. This remains to be substantiated; it certainly does not apply in such predominantly diurnal creatures as gazelles, Uganda kob, warthog, etc. At any rate, the sexual behavior of many ungulates is still only incompletely known. In particular, most of the more solitary species living in wooded habitats have been studied exclusively in captivity so far (e. g., Tragulidae, Cephalophinae, *Tragelaphus* spp., okapi). While much of the sexual behavior probably has an innate basis (Fraser, 1968) and is, therefore, not likely to be greatly affected by captivity, conditions of restricted space and, perhaps, unusual familiarity of the sexual partners with each other do introduce some possibly modificatory elements.

Keeping these provisos in mind, we may now briefly review what is known of the sexual behavior of African ungulates. Space precludes an exhaustive account for each species or group; emphasis is placed on those aspects that are important from the comparative point of view. For a number of species, the known repertoire of courtship and mating behavior had to be pieced together from several sources, involving both wild and captive animals. Pertinent references are cited at the end of each paragraph.

Proboscidea. Precopulatory behavior of the elephant is rather simple, consisting of driving and some elements of physical contact. During the driving phase, the cow may run away a short distance. When the bull catches up, he may butt her hindquarters slightly with his tusks or inspect her vulva with his trunk (this latter action, however, occurs more commonly in relation to anestrous cows, on initial contact, than during actual courtship). In a more advanced stage, the bull places his trunk and/or entire head on the female's back. He may then mount, usually only once, and insert his flexible penis into the vaginal orifice. Copulation lasts from $^1/_4$ to 2 min. The mates then separate without further interactions, until a new courtship sequence is begun. A given female may mate repeatedly, and with several bulls, within one estrous period (Kühme, 1961, 1963; Short, 1966; Buss and Smith, 1966; Sikes, 1971; Douglas-Hamilton, 1972, 1975).

Equidae. Precopulatory behavior of zebras includes driving, naso-genital contacts, Flehmen, grooming of the mare's rump, shoulders and neck by the stallion, the male laying his head on the female's rump and mounting without erection. In captive Grévy's zebra, there may be a fairly violent driving phase, the stallion kicking the mare with his front hooves and biting her in the neck, shoulders and forelegs, uttering a bellowing call at the same time. However, some of this may be a captivity-induced anomaly.

151

In plains zebra precopulatory behavior is most pronounced in matings with young mares, but much less elaborate, or even absent, in relation to adult mares.

Copulation involves frictional movements and is said to last from one to 3–4 min in plains zebra, but only a few seconds in Hartmann's zebra. It may be repeated at intervals of 1–3 h in peak estrus. During coitus the males of some species (e. g., Grévy's zebra in captivity) bite the female's neck or shoulders. There seems to be little or no postcopulatory interaction.

Estrous female equids may adopt a special "invitation" posture ("Präsentieren"): they turn the hindquarters toward the stallion, straddle the hindlegs and lift the tail sideways. This posture is especially pronounced in young female plains zebra, where it has strong visual signal value and attracts stallions who then try to abduct the young mare from her family group. In addition, females assume a characteristic facial expression while the male mounts ("Rossigkeitsgesicht"): the ears are laid back/down, the eyes half closed, the mouth is fairly wide open, with lips retracted upward, and may make slight chewing motions (Fig. 11 b in Klingel, 1974 a). The expression strongly resembles the equine threat; sometimes mares show biting intentions or actually bite the stallion during courtship (plains zebra: Trumler, 1958, 1959; Klingel, 1967, 1969 c; Hartmann's zebra: E. Joubert, 1972 b; Grévy's zebra: Zeeb and Kleinschmidt, 1963; Klingel, 1974 a. Reviews: Hassenberg, 1971; Klingel, 1972 a).

Rhinocerotidae. Whilst the black rhinoceros is generally solitary, apart from mother–young associations, a male may accompany an estrous female closely for several days. Initially the female tends to attack the approaching male, who then sometimes shows elements of agonistic displays but usually retreats; eventually the cow tolerates the male's presence, even in close proximity. Precopulatory behavior is comparatively simple, including mainly naso-genital contacts, the urination-Flehmen sequence, attempts by the male to lay his head onto the female's rump and mounting without erection. In the early stages, nose-to-nose contact and occasional bouts of mutual horning may occur, as well as horn jabs by the male against the female's hindquarters or flanks. The initial mountings without erection are characterized by the distance kept by the male, i. e., the lack of contact between his pelvic area and the female's body (cf. Fig. 6 in Goddard, 1966). These mountings may be repeated frequently, over a protracted period, and probably serve to test the cow's readiness to stand for actual copulation which is a rather prolonged affair, lasting from 20 to 40 min. During coitus, the bull shows certain rhythmic actions, such as changes in the position of his forelegs and the attitude of head and tail; these may be associated with a sequence of ejaculations. No postcopulatory behavior is reported; the two partners usually begin to feed or lie down after mating. Sexual behavior of the white rhinoceros appears to be largely identical (Goddard, 1966; Schenkel and Schenkel-Hulliger, 1969; Schenkel and Lang, 1969; Owen-Smith, 1973, 1975).

Suidae. Of the African suids only the warthog has been studied in sufficient detail. There is a pronounced driving phase, during which the male follows the female closely in a fast walk or trot, trying to establish and maintain naso-genital contact. Simultaneously he utters a series of low rhythmic grunts "resembling the chugging of an outboard engine" (Frädrich, 1967). With increasing excitation the calls may be accompanied by snapping motions, and resultant sounds, of the lower jaw. Tongue-flicking and copious salivation usually occur in this context. When the female stops, the male rubs his snout on her flanks and back, and this "massage" appears to induce the female to stand still, almost rigidly. Then the male may mount, resting his chin on the female's back and clasping her flanks with his forelegs. Both partners remain quiet during copulation, which lasts about 10 min. There is no regular postcopulatory interaction except, as mentioned earlier, occasionally some aggression by the female toward the male. As far as is known, the sexual behavior of the warthog closely resembles that of other suids, including the domestic pig. Male suids regularly smell the female's urine but perform only a "rudimentary," hardly noticeable Flehmen (Simpson, 1964; Frädrich, 1965, 1967, 1974; Bradley, 1968; Cumming, 1975; see also Dubost, 1975).

Hippopotamidae. The semi-aquatic habits of the two species of hippopotamus render detailed behavioral studies difficult, and most observations on sexual behavior are from captive animals. Only scant precopulatory interactions are known: the male pygmy hippo "smacks his lips" (Lang, 1972), apparently in response to odors emanating from the estrous female. He is also reported (Schneider, 1934, in Estes, 1972) to perform Flehmen (could this be the same as "lip-smacking"?). He then approaches the female and attempts to place his head on her back. If copulation occurs on land, the female lies down, perhaps partly forced down by the male. Both species, however, mate preferentially in the water, the female being largely submerged, only lifting her head from time to time to breathe. Copulation is said to last up to one hour (pygmy hippo), and repeated copulations may occur over a period of two to three days. No postcopulatory behavior is known (Verheyen, 1954; Frädrich, 1967; Lang, 1972).

Tragulidae. Precopulatory behavior of the water chevrotain is simple, consisting of a driving phase during which the male repeatedly utters a series of low calls. These apparently induce the receptive female to stand still in a somewhat rigid posture, head held low. The male approaches and licks her genital area. After repeating this sequence several times, the male mounts and copulates, laying his head and neck onto the female's back. Much of this sexual behavior is similar to that of the Suidae and, like them, *Hyemoschus* shows only a "rudimentary" Flehmen grimace (Dubost, 1965, 1975).

Giraffidae. The giraffe has generally rather few expressive movements or gestures, and this applies to sexual behavior as well. Males of almost all ages frequently induce females to urinate, by naso-genital contacts, and then show Flehmen, but this is rarely followed up by further interactions. If a female is in estrus, she is "guarded," i.e., constantly followed closely, by one adult male who attempts to keep other males at a distance. Phases of leisurely "driving" alternate with feeding or just standing. Mounting and copulation may occur with few, if any, specific preliminaries, except for some mounting intention movements, which consist of raising the head high, with nose upward. Sometimes the male lifts one foreleg slightly, in a gesture reminiscent of Laufschlag (Innis, 1958; Backhaus, 1961; B. Leuthold, unpubl.).

Mating behavior of the okapi appears to be somewhat more elaborate, resembling that of some antelopes with less developed courtship patterns. In particular, male okapi regularly use a relatively violent form of Laufschlag in much the same manner as some bovids (Walther, 1960).

Bovidae. The general review of the ungulate sexual behavior above has centered mainly on the bovids. The following notes will, therefore, concentrate primarily on pointing out the differences between the subgroups within the family, and on emphasizing the features that characterize each of them.

Bovini. Sexual behavior of the African buffalo is relatively simple and similar to that of other (non-African) members of the tribe (cf. Schloeth, 1961 b). Naso-genital investigation, urination and Flehmen occur as preliminaries much the same way as in most other bovids. If a female is nearing estrus, an adult male associates closely with her (tending, guarding, cf. "Hüten" of Schloeth, 1961 b). As courtship progresses, the male repeatedly lays his head onto the female's rump, probably testing her readiness to stand. This may be followed by mounting. Actual copulation is very brief, as in cattle and most other bovids (Grimsdell, 1969).

Tragelaphini (mainly genus *Tragelaphus*). Precopulatory behavior includes a driving phase with a very pronounced nose-forward posture ("Überstrecken"), in which the male comes alongside the female and often rubs his cheeks on her sides, shoulders and neck. This may be accompanied by low pleading calls and rapid "gasping" movements of the mouth. Ritualized "neck-fighting", in which the male places his neck over the female's neck and shoulders (Fig. 39), is possibly a functional equivalent to Laufschlag, which *Tragelaphus* species do not perform. Laying the head on the female, particularly on her rump, may also be an intention movement for mounting, in which the male's head and neck rest on the female's back, while the forelegs clasp the female's flanks to a greater or lesser extent. No pronounced postcopulatory behavior has been reported (Backhaus, 1958; Walther, 1958, 1964a; Leuthold and Leuthold, 1973; Tello and van Gelder, 1975).

Cephalophinae. Virtually nothing is known on this group of mostly solitary, bush- and forest-dwelling antelopes, except that driving with naso-genital contacts, including licking and/or biting by the male, and Laufschlag occur in courtship (Aeschlimann, 1963; Walther, 1968/72; Ralls, 1973).

Reduncinae. In this group, precopulatory behavior is relatively uniform, with increasing elaboration (addition of more elements and repetition of others) in the approximate sequence: reedbuck—lechwe—waterbuck—Uganda kob. Common elements are a relatively weak form of driving, with the male in nose-forward posture (this may be accompanied by low-intensity vocalizations), naso-genital contact and Flehmen, Laufschlag and mounting without erection. The waterbuck, in addition, places his chin on the female's rump and may rub her hindquarters with his head; these actions are apparently not performed (at least not regularly) by the other species. In the Uganda kob (Fig. 40) driving is attenuated even

154

further, possibly as a consequence of the small size of the mating territory. The male carries his head very high, exposing the white throat patch, and makes small rapid steps with stiffly held forelegs ("prancing," Fig. 40a). A peculiarity of the nile lechwe appears to be a kind of marking behavior: the male lowers his head, urinates between his forelegs onto the long hair of the lower neck and then rubs the wet neck-mane on the female. The mounting posture is medium-upright, the male partly supporting his body on the female's, carrying the head erect and clasping the female's flanks with his forelegs. Regular postcopulatory behavior occurs only in the Uganda kob, as described earlier (see also Fig. 40). (Reedbuck: Jungius, 1970, 1971; lechwe: Lent, 1969; de Vos and Dowsett, 1966; Nile lechwe: Walther, 1966a; waterbuck: Backhaus, 1958; Kiley-Worthington, 1965; Spinage, 1969b; Uganda kob: Buechner and Schloeth, 1965; Buechner et al., 1966; pers. obs.).

Hippotraginae. On the whole, the sexual behavior of this group is quite similar to that of the Reduncinae, with the following main differences: during driving, the nose-forward posture is less marked; mutual circling (Paarungskreisen) is apparently a regular component of the precopulatory sequence; there may be bouts of playful fighting between male and female at the beginning of courtship (e. g., oryx; note that both sexes bear horns in this group, in contrast to the Reduncinae). Flehmen (Fig. 37) and Laufschlag are pronounced; the mounting posture is medium-erect. No postcopulatory behavior is known (Backhaus, 1958, 1959; Walther, 1958; Estes and Estes, 1969; Huth, 1970; Buechner et al., 1974).

Alcelaphinae. Courtship behavior in this group is somewhat less elaborate than in most other antelopes. The male shows a pronounced nose-forward posture when approaching a female in a characteristic slow prancing gait (mainly *Damaliscus*) with the tail held stiffly away from the body or curled over the back (Fig. 38). This may be accompanied by rapid "bleating-grunts," at least in topi. Driving is not pronounced, and Laufschlag is rare or absent. Flehmen apparently occurs only in the wildebeest (where it is also prominent in agonistic encounters between males), but not in *Alcelaphus* and *Damaliscus*. This is rather surprising in view of the otherwise universal occurrence of Flehmen among bovids. The mounting posture is somewhat less erect than in the preceding groups, the male pressing his muzzle onto the female's back. Copulation is brief and not followed by any further interactions (*Alcelaphus*: Backhaus, 1958, 1959; Gosling, 1975; *Damaliscus*: David, 1973, 1975; Lynch, 1971; Jewell, 1972; S. Joubert, 1975; *Connochaetes*: Estes, 1969; Watson, 1969; reviews: Walther, 1966a, 1968/72, 1974).

Aepycerotinae. A singular characteristic of the impala's precopulatory behavior is the marked tongue-flicking ("empty licking") that the male shows during his approach in the nose-forward posture. This may lead to licking of the female's genital area, if she tolerates the approach. Urination and Flehmen may follow, but also occur at other stages. Impala show Laufschlag very rarely. Once the female remains quiet, only walking a few steps occasionally, the male starts mounting, which may be repeated several times until intromission is achieved. The mounting posture is fairly erect, the male may or may not rest his body on the female's but does not clasp her flanks. After copulation the male often shows an "outburst of aggressiveness," including roaring displays, but otherwise no distinct postcopulatory behavior (Schenkel, 1966a; Jarman and Jarman, pers. comm.; pers. obs.).

Antilopinae—a) *Antilopini*. Within the genus *Gazella* precopulatory behavior is, in essence, relatively uniform, the main differences between species arising from different emphasis or different degrees of elaboration of the component elements. After the initial approach in nose-forward posture, often followed by the urination-Flehmen sequence, there is a pronounced driving phase, in which the male remains in the nose-forward posture or may lift the head higher still ("head-up" posture), walking closely behind the female. This may alternate with Laufschlag and a more extreme form, a sequence of rapid steps with stiffly held forelegs, the "drumroll" of Thomson's gazelle (this is somewhat reminiscent of the "prancing" gait in the Uganda kob). In Grant's and Soemmerring's gazelles (Subgenus *Nanger*) Laufschlag is reduced to an almost rudimentary form; male Grant's regularly—and Soemmerring's occasionally—carry their tail raised well above the horizontal. Later in the driving phase, the partners may move so close together and so well coordinated as to give the impression of being one animal ("Paarungsmarsch" of Thomson's gazelle). Males may utter low vocalizations during the driving phase.

Male gazelles mount while walking, and this applies even to coitus. The mounting posture is extremely erect, the forelegs dangling loosely, usually bent at the carpal joint, without touching the female. No regular postcoital behavior is known.

Mating behavior of the springbok is very similar, except that vocalizations in the driving phase are rather loud ("a series of loud grunting bellows") and the tail is normally erected vertically, or even curled forward, at least in the advanced stages of courtship.

Gerenuk are generally less active, the driving phase being less pronounced, whereas Laufschlag is very prominent, being highly ritualized and executed rather slowly and gently. A peculiarity of this species—otherwise found only in the dibatag—is that the male marks the female on hindquarters or shoulders with the secretion of his antorbital glands (see Chap. 8, C, IV). (Gazelles: Walther, 1958, 1964b, c, 1965a, 1968; springbok: Bigalke, 1972; gerenuk: Walther, 1958; Backhaus, 1958; Leuthold, 1971c).

—b) *Neotragini*. Kirk's and Phillips' dikdik are the only species in this group about which at least something is known. The male approaches the female in nose-forward posture (cf. Fig. 4 in Tinley, 1969) and may lick her genital area. Due to the proboscislike structure of the nose and upper lip, the Flehmen grimace is not as pronounced as in other bovids, but it definitely occurs (Fig. 37). Laufschlag ist also performed in dikdik (as well as klipspringer). The mounting posture is fairly erect, and the male does not lean onto the female's body, nor touch her with the forelegs. After copulation the male may lick his still-erect penis *(phillipsi)*, then resume normal activities (Ziegler-Simon, 1957; Simonetta, 1966; Hendrichs and Hendrichs, 1971). Monfort and Monfort (1974) state that the oribi does not perform Flehmen.

156

E. Functional Aspects

Fraser (1968) cites a number of studies (all on domestic species) indicating that the presence of an adult male can influence (particularly speed up) the occurrence and manifestation of behavioral estrus in some female ungulates. He goes on to say (p. 61): "It would seem, therefore, that the induction of estrus in a variety of ungulates is due not only to endogenous and central stimulation, but also to exogenous and peripheral stimulation by odor, sound, sight or touch" (see also Ngere and Dzakuma, 1975). It is uncertain whether these findings are applicable to free-ranging wild ungulates in their natural surroundings. Quite possibly, the effects observed in the studies quoted by Fraser may have been connected with the unnatural situations in which domestic ungulates are often kept, e. g., complete segregation of sexes, etc.

However, the possibilities indicated by the above-mentioned studies cannot be discounted entirely without serious research into these questions. Most field observations in this context suggest that male ungulates initiate precopulatory behavior "in earnest" only when females already show signs of incipient estrus, as determined by the male through Flehmen. However, the frequent "checking" by the male of many females in a herd (Chap. 13, A, I) could conceivably provide a specific stimulus for the final induction of estrus, once the female has attained the physical condition necessary for ovulation. On the other hand, it is well known that estrus can occur spontaneously, i. e., without specific stimulation by the male (e. g., in hand-reared females). Thus, the possible role of the male before the advent of estrus remains unclear.

Interpretations regarding the function of the sometimes complex premating "ceremonies," too, can be no more than speculative at present. The inference commonly made is that they serve to coordinate and synchronize male and female, both behaviorally and physiologically, but this remains to be substantiated in detail.

Discussing the elaborate postcoital behavior of the Uganda kob, Buechner and Schloeth (1965) hypothesized that it might increase oxytocin release, and consequently stimulate uterine contractions that might be essential for transporting spermatozoa upward in the uterus. This, too, is highly speculative, and it seems that current scientific methods are not adequate to enable us to find immediate answers to the various open questions with regard to connections between sexual behavior and physiology.

Chapter 14

Maternal/filial Behavior

A common feature of parent–young relationships in ungulates is the fact that the male normally takes no part in rearing the young. On the contrary, adult males sometimes represent a real danger to small young, e. g., in the hippopotamus (Verheyen, 1954). In the few cases where the adult male occasionally defends the young against predators (e. g., in zebra), this behavior can be better explained in terms of social organization in general than in terms of true "paternal" behavior. Thus, it is normally the female exclusively that cares for the young (an apparent exception was recently found in sable; see Sekulic *et al.*, 1976).

Complex behavioral interactions between mother and young lead to the establishment of a strong individualized relationship, commonly called the mother–young bond. The main function of this bond, as far as we can see, is to create conditions favorable for the survival of the young and its eventual integration into the specific community. A variety of behaviors of both mother and young contribute to fulfilling this function, at various stages of infancy, and the aim of the following review is to describe and interpret such behavior in African ungulates, as far as it is known. Functional aspects will be mentioned occasionally in passing, but will be discussed more fully in the concluding section of this Chapter.

Various observers have commented that female ungulates become particularly wary and secretive around the time of parturition and while the young is very small (see Chap. 7, C, III). Mainly for this reason, there are still large gaps in our knowledge of mother–young relations and, for many species, virtually all available information comes from captive animals. Lent (1974) has provided a comprehensive review of mother–young relations in ungulates, which should be consulted by everyone interested in this subject.

A. Prepartum Behavior

Female ungulates approaching parturition show various behavior patterns that can be interpreted as preparations for the imminent birth of a young. The most remarkable of these is the nest-building of suids, unique among ungulates. Bush pig and giant forest hog are both said to make a nest of grass in a thicket; the female creeps inside to give birth, and the young remain there for their first few days (Astley Maberly, 1960). Opinion is divided as to whether or not warthogs build a nest. Bradley (1968, 1971) affirms it, having found "a floor covering of dry grass" in a burrow opened up by him (1971, p. 149).

158

On the other hand, a "nest chamber" inspected by Geigy (1955) contained no nesting material, only some loose sand. Thus, nest-building behavior may vary within the species (see also Cumming, 1975).

The warthog differs from the other suids in that it uses an underground burrow, in which the female gives birth and where the young spend their first few days. The burrow acts as "a veritable incubation chamber" (Geigy, 1955) in that it greatly reduces fluctuations of temperature, compared to outside (Bradley, 1971), and may actually maintain a temperature and humidity higher than those prevailing outside. The use of a burrow and the prominent nest-building activities of most suids (Frädrich, 1965, 1967) are easily understood when related to the condition in which the young are born. Suids are regularly polytocous, their young are smaller and less advanced at birth than those of other ungulates, the majority of which are monotocous. Neonate suids have been characterized as being of the "larval type" among mammalian young and apparently depend to some extent on an external source of heat, or at least on a mechanism of heat conservation, during their first few days ("poikilothermous postnatal phase": Koller, 1962, in Frädrich, 1967). A nest or burrow serves this function, as does the marked tendency of young suids to lie close together in direct contact, often in a "heap."

At least rudimentary nest-building behavior may occur in the hippopotamus, too, which is said to select a secluded spot, clean away plant material and trample the soil prior to parturition (Verheyen, 1954).

While nest-building behavior is characteristic of the Suiformes only, the great majority of parturient female ungulates show a pronounced inclination to isolate themselves from conspecifics. This seems to be almost universal among gregarious ungulates, including domestic species (cf. Fraser, 1968), and it is perhaps more appropriate to name only those species that do not do so: plains zebra may give birth in the presence of their family group, or at least the stallion (Klingel and Klingel, 1966; Klingel, 1969c). However, during the first few days after parturition the mother is very aggressive toward all other zebra, including group members, and prevents any contacts with the foal. This behavior may be viewed as a functional equivalent of isolation (see below). African elephants have often been reported, particularly in the older hunting literature, to isolate themselves and/or move to traditional "calving grounds" for parturition (e. g., Blunt, 1930). More recent observations, however, suggest that this is largely hunters' lore. Several accounts of elephant births indicate that other group members, indeed the entire family group, may be present or nearby while a cow gives birth (Poppleton, 1957; Sikes, 1971; Douglas-Hamilton, 1972; Leuthold and Leuthold, 1975b; Fig. 42). As in zebra, this is probably related to the existence of stable, closely knit family groups and the associated behavior of communal defense. African buffalo also tend to give birth within the herd (Grimsdell, 1969); they, too, are capable of communal defense against predators. By contrast, in most other gregarious bovids preparturient females show more or less pronounced isolative behavior. The only major exceptions are the two species of wildebeest which, rather than separating from conspecifics, remain with their herds (black wildebeest: von Richter, 1971a) or may actually congregate together on calving grounds, usually on short-grass areas (blue wildebeest: Estes,

1966). In these species, lack of isolation appears to be correlated with high mobility of local populations, extreme precocity of neonates, even by ungulate standards, and a short, highly synchronized calving season (Estes, 1976).

Isolation of the pregnant female from conspecifics is often combined with a preference for a different habitat type: various species tend to seek the concealment offered by woody vegetation (e. g., bush clumps) or tall grass, as is well documented for kongoni (Gosling, 1969) and impala (M. V. Jarman, 1976). The movements associated with prepartum isolation often attract the attention of other conspecifics. For instance, territorial male impala try to prevent the departure of a female from the herd as a matter of course and therefore often interfere with a female's attempts to move away. Additionally, the scents emanating from a female about to give birth appear to resemble those of an estrous female and tend to arouse sexual interest among attendant males. Thus, the preparturient female is often "pestered" considerably by males before she succeeds in evading their attention (M. V. Jarman, 1976). Alternatively, other group members, perhaps including her own previous offspring, sometimes follow a female attempting to leave the herd, as a consequence of mere allelomimetic behavior.

Prepartum isolation often involves severance of the bond between the female and her previous young. Various authors have noted an increase in aggressiveness of the female toward her adolescent offspring shortly before the birth of a new young. Sometimes this hostility is temporary only, and the older young may join both mother and neonate later on. If the neonate dies soon after birth, the association between a female and her previous offspring may become quite close again; in some cervids, yearlings may even be suckled again in this situation (references in Lent, 1974). Talbot and Talbot (1963) indicate that this may also occur in the blue wildebeest; von Richter (1971 a, b) records it in black wildebeest, and Walther (1964 a) describes a similar situation among captive sitatunga. In other cases, the separation of the older offspring from its mother may be final, particularly if the new young survives.

Aggressive behavior of highly pregnant females toward their older young, with or without subsequent re-acceptance, has been noted in the black rhinoceros (Schenkel and Schenkel-Hulliger, 1969; they state that such behavior occurs but that they did not observe it themselves), plains zebra (Klingel, 1967; he speaks of "loosening" of the mother–young bond, but only in relation to male young), Hartmann's zebra (E. Joubert, 1972b), warthog (Bradley, 1968), blue and black wildebeest (Talbot and Talbot, 1963; von Richter, 1971a, b). In other bovids, the older young may already have separated from its mother by the time the next one is due; this applies particularly to young males who sometimes join "bachelor" herds soon after weaning (e. g., in Uganda kob: Leuthold, 1967).

In some other cases, the parturient female showed little or no hostility toward older offspring. Several adolescent hartebeest aged 9 to 11 months accompanied their mothers into isolation and were present during parturition (Gosling, 1969). A female reedbuck obviously tried to "shake off" a yearling when approaching parturition but showed no overt aggression (Jungius, 1970). Young elephants remain with their mothers up the age of puberty (males) or even permanently, i. e., until one of them dies (females). Several siblings may be born during this period, but the members of the family remain together at all times, at least under normal conditions (Douglas-Hamilton, 1972, 1975; Leuthold and Leuthold, 1975 b).

B. Parturition

Parturition is an event that happens only rarely, and at long intervals, in the life of each individual female. Observations of this event can, therefore, be expected to be infrequent; they are most likely to occur when many females give birth at about the same time in about the same place. Until recently, most data on parturition in wild ungulates concerned, not surprisingly, highly gregarious seasonal breeders such as wildebeest and, outside the tropics, caribou (*Rangifer tarandus*). However, some recent intensive field studies have yielded a considerable amount of new information on parturition and associated behavior, particularly those of Gosling (1969) on Coke's hartebeest and of M. V. Jarman (1976) on impala.

The scarcity of observations on parturition has led many people to believe that most wild ungulates give birth at night. Records from zoo animals and domestic species tend to confirm this assumption. According to Dittrich (1970), the majority of African antelopes kept at Hannover Zoo gave birth at night or in the early morning. Fraser (1968, p. 113) states that "more births occur in domesticated ungulates during the hours of darkness than in the remainder of the day." However, in the circumstances of captivity, this may well be a secondary phenomenon, arising from the activity cycle imposed by man. Female ungulates tend to be particularly wary and susceptible to disturbances around the time of parturition; for both zoo and domestic animals the night is the time of least disturbance. Thus the notion that wild ungulates give birth mainly at night requires substantiation.

In this context many authors attribute to female ungulates the ability to postpone parturition within certain limits. This ability would be of obvious adaptive value in the wild, e. g., in relation to predation, but its existence is difficult to prove.

Extensive reviews of parturition and associated behavior in mammals generally have been given by Naaktgeboren (1963) and Naaktgeboren and Slijper (1970; see also Lent, 1974). In the following I will touch on a few selected aspects on which information is available for African ungulates, preferably from the wild.

I. Time of Day

Few observers of free-ranging African ungulates have been able to witness more than one or a very few parturitions. However, those who did, or otherwise recorded the time of parturitions, have provided some interesting information in relation to what has just been said about time of day.

In wildebeest of Ngorongoro Crater "most births occur in the forenoon" (Estes, 1966), while on the neighboring Serengeti Plains the majority of births appeared to take place at night, and some in the early morning (Watson, 1969). This divergence may be related to differences in the patterns of predation prevailing in the two areas (Watson, 1969). In Coke's hartebeest of Nairobi National Park, Gosling (1969) found that births occurred throughout the day, with a suggestion of a peak soon after midday (the data may be biased by the uneven temporal distribution of field observations; this may apply to other sources as well). Spinage (1969b) reported five cases of parturition in wild waterbuck taking place in the early morning. M. V. Jarman (1976) found a marked peak around midday in the number of births of impala in the Serengeti. Interestingly enough, captive impala in Hannover Zoo gave birth primarily during the day (Dittrich, 1968), apparently in contrast to most other antelope species and zebra (Dittrich, 1970, see above). Six eland births in captivity all took place during the day (Kirchshofer, 1963), as did a number of giraffe births listed by Backhaus (1961).

More records on wild animals are clearly needed before general conclusions regarding the "normal" time of parturition can be drawn. Also, as the example of wildebeest shows, intraspecific variation may be quite pronounced, in accordance with local conditions (e. g., predation, etc.).

II. Position and Behavior During Parturition

While it is often difficult or impossible to predict parturition, both in wild and captive ungulates, several observers have noted a marked restlessness of the female shortly before and during the early stages of parturition. This may manifest itself in "aimless" walking about and frequent changes of position, e. g., from standing to lying and vice versa, or turning from one side to the other while recumbent. Many female bovids carry their tail somewhat raised, and a bulge of the vulva may be evident. A female elephant repeatedly walked backward a few steps, and several times lowered her abdomen, by bending her hindlegs, so as to nearly touch the ground with her vulva, which was partially everted (Leuthold and Leuthold, 1975b). However, there is great individual variation, and some animals show few, if any, signs of impending parturition.

The position adopted to give birth appears to be species- or group-specific to a considerable extent. Suids normally lie flat on one side (Frädrich, 1967; no observations on African species, though), as does the hippopotamus, but the pygmy hippo (captive) is said to remain standing as a rule (Lang, 1972). While both species of hippopotamus give birth more often on land, the large species, in particular, may also do so in the water. The neonate then makes paddling movements with its legs, which bring it to the surface to take its first breath (Hediger, 1951, 1961; Verheyen, 1954). Pygmy hippos born in the water in a zoo have repeatedly drowned, but this may have been related, in some way, to the conditions of the enclosure in which the animals were kept.

Equids also lie on their side (Fig. 41) and may kick their legs vigorously during labor (Klingel and Klingel, 1966). Some of the larger ungulates habitually

Fig. 41. Position of female plains zebra during parturition; note young still enveloped in amniotic sac (from Klingel and Klingel, 1966)

give birth while standing, e. g., the elephant (Lang, 1967; Leuthold and Leuthold, 1975b) and giraffe (e. g., Hediger, 1961); as a result the young may drop from as high as 2 m in the case of giraffe. Most bovids lie down during at least part of the birth process, but often change position, from the side onto the brisket and vice versa, and sometimes stand up in the final phase so that the young also falls to the ground. During the expulsion stage, the female may undergo convulsions of the entire body and kick vigorously with outstretched legs, as described in detail for Grant's gazelle by Walther (1965a, 1968) for Coke's hartebeest by Gosling (1969), and for impala by M. V. Jarman (1976). In addition to these observations on wild animals, the course of parturition in various captive antelopes has been recorded by Hediger (1961), Kirchshofer (1963), Walther (1968), D. Altmann (1971), as well as in the general reviews quoted earlier.

C. Postpartum Behavior

Immediately after the complete expulsion of the young some female ungulates lie quietly for a short while, apparently exhausted (e. g., impala: M. V. Jarman, 1976). Soon, however, most female bovids, giraffe, zebra (see below) and rhinoceros get up (if they were recumbent during parturition), turn around and start licking the neonate, in many cases consuming part or all of the fetal membranes and/or amniotic fluid in the process.

At about the same time, the young makes its first movements and attempts to stand up, often succeeding in a surprisingly short time. The "record" is probably held by wildebeest whose young may be able to walk or even run, albeit unsteadily, within 10 min or less after birth (Talbot and Talbot, 1963; Estes, 1966).

Licking of the young, while most intensive immediately after birth, often continues at intervals during the first few hours. Initially, the entire body of the young is licked, starting from the head; gradually, the female tends to concentrate on the anogenital region, which is customarily licked during suckling in the first few weeks of the young animal's life (see below). Apart from removing the remains of membranes, amniotic fluids and mucus, the intensive licking appears to have an important additional function in stimulating the neonate's movements. For most newborn ungulates it is vital to gain their feet and a measure of muscular coordination within as short a period as possible after birth. If a newborn young does not make vigorous attempts to stand up, the mother often prods or nudges it with her muzzle or forefoot, apparently to induce it to move, if licking alone does not have this effect. The few accounts available (e. g., Poppleton, 1957; Leuthold and Leuthold, 1975 b) suggest that such behavior is particularly pronounced in elephants which cannot lick their young for anatomic reasons. Here the mother, and sometimes also another cow, manipulates the newborn with trunk, tusks and a forefoot (Fig. 42). In another case, a female elephant is said to have sprinkled sand over her newborn young, which presumably promoted drying up of the amniotic fluid (Young, in Sikes, 1971, p. 168).

Such intensive care-giving (epimeletic) behavior characterizes the "active type" among ungulate mothers (Hediger, 1954/55) and has been described for free-ranging Grant's gazelle (Walther, 1965 a), impala (M. V. Jarman, 1976), hartebeest (Gosling, 1969), wildebeest (see above; and Watson, 1969), waterbuck (Spinage, 1969 b), zebra (Klingel and Klingel, 1966; Klingel, 1969 c), in addition to elephant, as well as for numerous captive ungulates (e. g., Hediger, 1961; Kirchshofer, 1963; Walther, 1968).

Most female bovids, and apparently also giraffe (Hediger, 1961), usually eat part or all of the afterbirth (chorioallantois and placenta). When it appears, many females bend their head and neck around and attempt to grasp it with the mouth, pulling it out and consuming it as it emerges (Fig. 43). In other cases, the afterbirth may be picked up from the ground and eaten, as are most or all traces of amnion, amniotic fluid, blood and mucus. This behavior appears to have a strong innate basis, as it occurred even in a hand-reared primiparous female impala in Tsavo National Park (pers. obs.). The net result is that the birth site is "cleaned up" thoroughly; the whole behavioral complex presumably serves to reduce the chances of predators being attracted to the birth site by the smell of the "byproducts." In wildebeest, expulsion of the afterbirths is delayed for two to three hours, and most of them are apparently taken by vultures, hyenas and jackals (Estes, 1966; Watson, 1969). A captive wildebeest, however, ate at least part of the afterbirth (Hediger, 1961).

Female zebra, in common with other equids, do not consume the placenta (Hassenberg, 1971; Klingel, 1972 a), whereas rhinoceros may do so, at least

Fig. 42a and b. Postpartum behavior in female African elephant. (a) Using trunk and forefoot to remove the foetal membranes. (b) Lifting the newborn off the ground in endeavors to make it stand up (from Leuthold and Leuthold, 1975 b)

partially (Schenkel and Lang, 1969). The female zebra observed by the Klingels (1966) remained recumbent for 13 min after parturition, while the foal struggled and succeeded in freeing itself of the membranes and in standing up briefly.

Fig. 43. Female impala pulling afterbirth from vulva before eating it. Newborn young *(foreground)* is still wet (photo by D. L. W. Sheldrick)

Similar periods of quiet lying (probably exhausted) often occur in the domestic horse, too, and the foal has to break the amniotic sac by its own actions (Fraser, 1968). Female elephants may pick up parts of the fetal membranes and wave them about in the air with their trunk; in two closely observed cases the mother of the newborn also ate at least part of the membranes and/or placenta (Leuthold and Leuthold, 1975b; Poppleton, 1957). Other females also "played around" with the membranes, but did not eat them. In addition, the mother and one or two other cows scraped the soil vigorously at and around the birth site (after parturition); perhaps these were attempts to "bury" the membranes (see also Sikes, 1971).

The "passive type" in maternal behavior (Hediger, 1954/55) is exemplified by the suids, but little is known on the African species. Female pigs do not lick their young and make no efforts to remove fetal membranes, nor do they stimulate the neonates' movements. Eating the afterbirth seems to be the exception rather than the rule (Frädrich, 1967). The hippopotamus resembles the suids in its behavior, but postpartum licking may occur (Verheyen, 1954); both species are normally monotocous.

Once the young (of the more "precocial" type) has gained its feet, it will usually make its first sucking attempts. All newborn ungulates appear to have an innate "vague idea" about where to look for milk. Bovids and equids start searching preferentially in angles between horizontal and vertical planes, mainly of the mother but—especially in captivity—also of other objects in their surroundings. Initially, they often try to suck in the angle between the female's forelegs and chest but eventually, by trial and error, they end up at the udder and quickly learn to find it straightaway in later attempts. The mother is sometimes said to "guide" the young toward the udder, but this may be little more than a "byproduct" of her efforts to lick the young's perineal area. Perhaps experience improves the female's performance in this respect, as in others. Many observers have commented that primiparous females often fail to accept their young or to show the appropriate care behavior. Two female impala that were probably primiparous initially shied away from their newborn young, and avoided their sucking attempts for some time (M. V. Jarman, 1976). In later parturitions such problems are comparatively rare. Sometimes, also, the young of primiparous females weigh less than the normal average, and their survival chances in the wild may be relatively low. These observations have given rise to the opinion that the first parturition may be little more than a "trial run" to perfect both the physical and behavioral performance of the female (e. g., Heck, in Hediger, 1961; cf. Frädrich, 1967). This view gains some support from the fact that the first young of each of three pygmy hippopotami in Basel Zoo were born dead or died shortly after birth (Lang, 1972). Whether this is really a general rule remains to be determined.

D. The Mother–Young Bond

I. Imprinting

The first suckling usually marks the successful establishment of a mother-young relationship which, however, requires more time to develop fully. Numerous observations on both captive and wild ungulates (excluding suids) indicate that this relationship, or bond, is individualized and exclusive, probably as a result of a two-way learning process partly corresponding to the "imprinting" first described for birds by Lorenz (1935). During a "critical period" both mother and young learn to recognize each other's individual characteristics; in the young this normally takes longer than in the mother. For the latter, postpartum licking may already provide olfactory and/or gustatory stimuli on which individual recognition of the young and the formation of the mother-young bond will be based (Tschanz, 1962; Lent, 1974). Once the bond is established, it is difficult, if not impossible to substitute either of the partners. Experimental evidence for this comes mainly from work on domestic ungulates (summary and references in Fraser, 1968), but there is no reason to believe that the situation is different in wild species. A few observations on captive ungulates support this view (cf. also Haas, 1959; Tschanz, 1962). For instance, a young male lesser kudu obtained within a few hours after birth became very tame and later showed all signs of being imprinted on us. In marked contrast, a young gerenuk estimated to be about 24 h old when captured behaved very "obstinately" toward us and repeatedly tried to run away, but immediately accepted the then three-month-old male kudu as "foster mother." We interpreted this as indicating that the young gerenuk had already become imprinted on certain generalized features of his natural mother but not yet on her specific and individual characteristics (Leuthold and Leuthold, 1973).

The bond resulting from this imprinting process can be very strong, even in relation to unnatural "parents," e.g., humans. A seven-month-old female Uganda kob that I had reared returned from a herd of wild kob, which she had joined temporarily, in response to my appearance and calls (Leuthold, 1967).

The exclusiveness of the mother–young bond is often reinforced by the aggressiveness of the females toward strange young, e.g., in wildebeest (Talbot and Talbot, 1963; Estes, 1966); this is also the rule in captivity, although exceptions do occur (e.g., Walther, 1964a; Dittrich, 1970).

II. Spatial Aspects

There is a fairly clear-cut dichotomy in the behavior of female ungulates and their young with regard to spatial relations. In some species the young follows its mother, and her group, in close contact as soon as it is able to walk and run, often within minutes or hours of birth. If it becomes separated from the mother by any great distance, it generally has little chance to survive. Such isolated young tend to follow any large object moving away from them, i.e., cars, people, or other animals. Species showing this behavior belong to the "follower" type ("Nachfolge-Typ": Walther, 1965a); they include zebra, rhinoceros, elephant, but only a few bovids such as the two wildebeests, some other Alcelaphinae (mainly *Damaliscus* species) and the African buffalo.

Virtually all other bovids are "hiders" ("Abliege-Typ" of Walther), the young of which characteristically spend long periods lying alone in seclusion ("lying-out": Gosling, 1969) while the mother may feed a considerable distance away (Fig. 44). The term "hiders," introduced by Lent (1974), is perhaps not entirely appropriate, as it might imply a "purposeful" action on the part of the mother. However, contrary to popular belief, the mother participates little or not at all in the choice of the young animal's lying place, as Walther has repeatedly emphasized and Lent also acknowledges. Nonetheless, for want of a more suitable alternative and to avoid further complication of the issue, I will use Lent's term. "Hiding" thus refers to the behavior of the young animal, not to that of its mother.

As mother–young interactions are very similar in all hider species, I will give a generalized description of the behavioral complex. After the immediate postpartum period, usually including the first suckling session, the young starts moving slowly away from the mother ("die grosse Wanderung": Walther, 1965a) and eventually lies down in a place of its own choice. In making this choice the young apparently reacts to several sign stimuli, such as "something vertical," a slight depression or a "roof" of dense vegetation (e.g., Walther, 1964a). The active role of the young in this context has repeatedly been confirmed, in the

168

Fig. 44. Thomson's gazelle fawn in hiding; note curled-up position, ears depressed, and lack of flight reaction which made close-up photograph possible (from Kruuk, 1972)

wild in Grant's gazelle (Walther, 1965a), Coke's hartebeest (Gosling, 1969), water-buck (Spinage, 1969b), reedbuck (Jungius, 1970), gerenuk (pers. obs.) and in captivity in a variety of species (e.g., Walther, 1964a, 1968; Leuthold, 1967; Leuthold and Leuthold, 1973). The female may "supervise" the process, but only rarely seems to influence the baby's choice. She then moves away from the hiding place and may feed or rest several hundred meters away, up to one km in the case of waterbuck (Spinage, 1969b) or gerenuk (Leuthold, 1971d). While some authors say that the female keeps the hiding place under constant surveillance, this is clearly not so in other instances. Perhaps this varies with the age of the young, between species and/or individually between females.

Female bovids appear to have a very accurate memory of their offspring's hiding place and, as I have suggested earlier (Leuthold, 1971d), the latter may well serve as the "medium" through which the mother–young bond becomes initially established, before the two can recognize each other individually. The following observations support this view: one morning, a newborn lesser kudu found by laborers in the bush was brought to me. The same evening I returned it to the location where it had been found. Although it had been in human hands for about eight hours and had been touched by several persons, and although the mother had been thoroughly disturbed in the morning, she later (presumably at night) came back, found and re-accepted the young (Leuthold, 1971d). Walther (1966a, p. 154) performed an interesting experiment with captive Dorcas gazelles: in the mother's absence, he made her young move from its hiding place to another one about 80 m away. On her return, the mother immediately went to the original site and became very agitated when the young failed

169

to respond to her calls. Taken to the new hiding place, she appeared extremely "puzzled" and behaved in a rather unusual way. In this case, individual recognition was already effective, but the experiment clearly shows the great significance of the hiding place, and the mother's memory for it, in the mother–young relationship. It further proved—which had been Walther's objective in the first place—that the mother could not locate the young by following a scent trail that might have been left. We will return to this point later.

Apparently, the female determines the frequency of nursing and thus largely the young animal's activity pattern. Nursing may occur fairly often during the first few days but is soon reduced to as little as two or three times a day (Table 5), most commonly in the morning and evening, and perhaps once in the middle of the day. Possibly, one or two sessions take place at night but little information on this is available (but see Hendrichs and Hendrichs, 1971, on dikdik). When "nursing time" approaches, the female wanders toward the hiding place, sometimes casually while feeding, sometimes in a more "purposeful" manner. She rarely, if ever, goes directly up to the young but stops some 10–30 m away and calls. The vocalizations used are of very low intensity and have often escaped the notice of human observers; however, numerous recent records from captivity and some involving wild animals (e. g., Grant's gazelle, Uganda kob, waterbuck) suggest that calling in this context is more or less universal in bovids of the hider type. The young normally responds to this call by getting up and, sometimes, may call in return (e. g., our hand-reared lesser kudu commonly did so); it then usually approaches the mother. If it does not see her yet, she may attract its attention with a visual signal, such as a slow head-bobbing, as described for Grant's gazelle, some *Tragelaphus* species and blesbok by Walther (1964a, 1965a, 1969b). When the young reaches the mother, there may be brief naso-nasal contact, whereupon it usually starts sucking rightaway.

With minor variations, this generalized description applies to all species of the hider type, which includes the great majority of the Bovidae. In some gregarious and highly mobile species, such as oryx and eland, hiding behavior may be less pronounced than in their relatives. Apart from the actual lying behavior, hiding is characterized chiefly by the short duration of mother–young contacts in the first few days or weeks of the young one's life, sometimes as little as $\frac{1}{2}$–1 h per day (cf. Fig. 4 in Lent, 1974).

By contrast, in the follower type the young constantly accompanies the mother closely, except for the times when it is resting, but even then it is never far away and, characteristically, will join the mother in flight at the appearance of danger (e. g., a predator).

Young giraffes show certain features of both hiders and followers, although the latter tendencies prevail overall. When very young, they usually stay close to the mother; they certainly do not "hide" as, e. g., young gazelles. Yet at quite an early age, perhaps from two weeks onward, small young are often found alone, with no adult animal in sight. They may spend the greater part of the day alone, the mother joining them only for nursing sessions in the morning and evening, and sometimes also around noon. When other females with small young are in the same area, they often join up and the young may form a "crèche" group (see Chap. 14, E); in giraffe, this apparently happens

earlier than in some bovids, particularly when their larger size and longer maturation are taken into account (Mejia, 1972; pers. obs.).

In the Suidae, the situation is somewhat more complex. Young suids are
born in a less advanced state than other ungulates and require a nest, burrow,
and/or the presence of the mother to keep warm. However, once this period
(in warthog up to a week) is over, the young follow the mother closely, although
they may still spend occasional resting periods in the burrow (Frädrich, 1965).
While Lent (1974) considers these first few days in the burrow as the analog
to the hiding phase in bovids, I am more inclined to characterize warthog,
and probably other suids, as follower types that are "born prematurely," i.e.,
in a state in which they are not yet capable of showing normal following behavior.

III. The Sensory Basis for Individual Recognition

I have already dealt with this question in a more general context (Chap. 9)
and, as far as I know, the remarks made there are applicable to the mother–young
relationship as well.

Circumstantial evidence from field observations suggests that olfactory and
auditory signals are most important for mutual recognition between mother
and young, while visual cues figure prominently only in a few species (e.g.,
zebra: Klingel, 1967, 1969c). I have already mentioned the calls that the female
utters when "collecting" the hiding young; in follower types there may be almost
constant vocal contact between females and their young at certain times (e.g.,
in wildebeest). The essential role of olfactory information is implied by the
frequent, almost obligatory, naso-nasal and naso-anal checking of the young
by the mother and, less often, vice versa. Perhaps the relative importance of
the different senses changes as the young grows older; e.g., visual recognition
may become more important eventually.

Some observations on captive ungulates support the conclusions drawn from
field studies. Newborn antelopes appear to have a general tendency to react
to calls, but there is no clearcut evidence that knowledge of specific mother
calls is innate. Rather, the young gradually learn to discriminate the mother's,
or "foster mother's," calls from other noises and, eventually, from calls of other
conspecifics. Captive young antelopes clearly distinguish their "foster parent's"
voice from other human voices. A corresponding learning process leads to discri-
mination of individual odors to the extent that, after being fed by a given
person for some days, a young antelope may refuse to accept food from another
person. This potential rearing problem can be circumvented by presenting the
"parental" odor, e.g., with a piece of clothing of the person concerned (details
in Walther, 1966a, 1969b; Leuthold, 1967; Leuthold and Leuthold, 1973; further
references in Lent, 1974).

IV. Suckling and Associated Behavior

Position. In most ungulates the normal position adopted for suckling is nearly
reverse-parallel, the young standing at an acute angle to the female, particularly

in the early stages. When the young grows older, it sometimes also attempts to suck from behind, reaching between the mother's hindlegs. In the African buffalo, this position seems to be the rule rather than the exception (Grimsdell, 1969). Both mother and young usually stand during suckling; older young sometimes drop to their "knees" (carpal joints). The female may hunch her back slightly and, in a few species, she may also lift the hindleg on the side of the young (e. g., dikdik: Hendrichs and Hendrichs, 1971; impala: M. V. Jarman, 1976), which facilitates access to the udder.

The above generalized description applies to all bovids, giraffe and okapi, zebra and rhinoceros. Older calves of the latter species lie down to suck as they cannot easily kneel down for long.

In the elephant, the suckling position differs considerably on account of the pectoral location of the mammary glands. Calves stand facing forward at an acute, sometimes nearly right angle behind the female's foreleg and suck with the mouth, curling the trunk up- and sideward.

Female suids and hippopotami generally lie on their side for suckling, the young also lying at about right angles to the mother. However, young warthog accompanying their mother outside the burrow will often suck in a standing or "sitting" position, the mother normally standing (Fig. 30 in Frädrich, 1965). Peculiar to the hippopotami is the fact that they often suckle under water; the young have to come to the surface from time to time to breathe (Hediger, 1951; Verheyen, 1954).

Behavior of the Female. In species of the hiding type, a female will collect her young in the manner described above. Prior to suckling, she usually checks its identity through brief naso-nasal and more pronounced naso-anal contact. The latter is normally a "prelude" to extensive licking of the baby's perineal area, which apparently stimulates urination and defecation. Many observations, both from the wild and from captivity, indicate that, as a rule, the female consumes both urine and feces as they are produced. If the young is a male, the female inserts her head between his hindlegs and drinks the urine from the penis. The characteristic postures adopted in this context permit determination of the calf's sex at a considerable distance (Walther, 1965a).

This may all happen while the young is sucking, but often also afterward. The female may proceed to licking other parts of the young animal's body, including head and neck (for details see Walther, 1964a, 1965a, 1968; Spinage, 1969b; Gosling, 1969; Jungius, 1970).

In follower-type ungulates, the cleaning and grooming behavior of the female is considerably reduced or even absent, except for the first few hours after birth. Naso-nasal and/or naso-anal contact prior to nursing seems to be the rule, particularly in the more gregarious species; it undoubtedly serves for individual recognition. It is in this context that the normal exclusiveness of the mother–young bond manifests itself most clearly, strange young usually being rejected by the female. The only exceptions to this general rule are the elephant and the warthog (and possibly other suids), apart from a few observations in captivity which may, however, be atypical (e. g., Walther, 1964a; Dittrich, 1970). In the elephant, young calves may be suckled by any lactating female in the family

172

group, although the constant close contact between mother and young calf probably makes it rare for the latter to suck from another female. It may also happen that a cow elephant suckles two of her own consecutive calves simultaneously (Sikes, 1971; Douglas-Hamilton, 1972). In warthog, too, females within a group suckle each other's young more or less indiscriminately (Frädrich, 1965; Bradley, 1968).

Only rarely, if ever, does a suckling female engage in any other activity, such as feeding; normally she just stands still or performs the licking/grooming described above. An unusual deviation from this general rule was reported recently for gerenuk: a young was sucking while the female was feeding in the bipedal stance (Hagen, 1975).

Behavior of the Young. During the hiding phase, the young is regularly collected by its mother and usually goes straight to her and begins to suck, both animals being "mentally ready" for the process. Older young that no longer hide, as well as young of the follower type, simply approach the female and try to suck; their success depends mainly on the female's reaction. When a female is walking, the young may overtake her along the side, cross in front of her neck to make her stop and then go into nursing position on the opposite side (e. g., in captive *Tragelaphus* spp., Walther, 1964a: "Abstoppen"). The young occasionally uses some elements of aggressive behavior, such as head-butting or pushing with the nose, to emphasize its "claim," at least in captivity. Vocalizations also occur in the same context; for instance, our hand-reared gerenuk commonly uttered low bleats while searching for milk in the inguinal region of the lesser kudu which it considered as its mother (Leuthold and Leuthold, 1973). Young giraffe commonly rub their head and neck on the mother's hindquarter before making sucking attempts.

While sucking, most young bovids and equids push their noses upward at intervals, which presumably aids the milk flow. As the young get older, this pushing ("bunting") becomes more vigorous and may cause obvious discomfort to the mother. This results in increased evasive action by the female and may be a contributory factor to the weaning process (Lent, 1974). Many young bovids also wag their tail sideways while sucking, but this seems to vary considerably between subfamilies and perhaps also individually.

When the mother licks its perineal region before or after nursing, the young bovid adopts a characteristic posture, with the tail lifted or curled upward, back slightly hunched, hindlegs somewhat straddled and the neck drawn in a bit (cf. Fig. 9 in Gosling, 1969). Young bovids appear to have a distinct inhibition to walk while being licked, or just touched, in the perineal region; when walking they show a reflexlike response to being touched there and usually stop immediately. This response can be exploited in captivity to stop calves from walking away (Gosling, 1969; pers. obs.).

A conspicuous behavior of young ungulates commonly associated with nursing is play. In a typical situation (a bovid of the hiding type), the sequence of events is approximately as follows: when nursing and the accompanying licking are terminated, the young starts running and jumping about, away from the mother and back to her again, or in circles around her. Various gaits and

173

capers alternate in loose sequence; the young may exert itself considerably and at times stand breathing heavily, with open mouth, before starting off again. After a while, the level of activity and "exuberance" subside and, eventually, the young walks away and looks for a suitable hiding place, where it will spend the subsequent phase of inactivity. The young of hiding-type species typically play alone, whereas in followers several young may participate in such "games" from an early age. However, black rhinoceros being a solitary species, its young also gambol around alone; it is quite exhilarating to watch the agility that the rather plump-looking baby rhino can develop in this context.

Older young of the hiding type, particularly when forming crèche groups (Chap. 14, E), often play communally, too, but at that stage play is no longer associated with nursing only, while for small young the few daily nursing periods (see below) provide the only bouts of activity, separated by long periods of resting.

Frequency and Duration of Suckling. Detailed and reliable information on frequency and duration of suckling in the wild is difficult to obtain. Females are generally wary and easily disturbed while nursing, or when about to do so, and unless the animals are either unaware of or well habituated to the presence of an observer, it is often impossible to collect unbiased data. This largely explains the scarcity of such information in the literature. Table 5 presents what I have been able to find (partly after Lent, 1974). In compiling these data, I have limited selection to observations on wild animals, as far as possible. In captivity conditions differ considerably, particularly with respect to activity patterns and spatial circumstances. Observations on captive animals may, therefore, not be representative, as is well illustrated in the case of the warthog (Frädrich, 1967).

With small young of the hiding type the mother normally determines the timing and frequency of suckling. Typically, there are two to five sessions within 24 h (Table 5), although little information is available on what happens during the night. Walther's (1968) observations on various species of gazelle in captivity largely correspond to the picture emerging from the rather scant field data. In the wild, suckling is generally recorded in the early morning and late afternoon, but further sessions may occur around midday and midnight.

In the follower species the suckling frequency may be influenced substantially by the young itself, as it is close to the mother all the time and may make frequent sucking attempts (see David, 1975, on bontebok).

In giraffe, the frequency and duration of suckling vary considerably, partly perhaps in relation to the age of the young and partly depending on social interactions within the herd (B. Leuthold, unpubl.).

During each suckling session there may be one or several suckling bouts, the length of which is variable and probably depends on several factors, such as the internal state of both mother and young, the external situation (disturbances), the age of the young and its behavior (e.g., intensity of pushing, etc.). For most of the data in Table 5 it is not clear whether the durations given refer to more or less uninterrupted suckling bouts or to the total time of suckling within one session.

174

Table 5. Frequency and/or duration of suckling in some African ungulates

Species	w/c[a]	Age of young	Frequency per 12 or 24 h	Duration of bouts[b]	Reference
Elephant	w			$\bar{x}$ = 30 sec (1–75)	Douglas-Hamilton, 1972
Black rhinoceros	w			ca. 4 min	Schenkel and Schenkel-Hulliger, 1969
Warthog	w	1–4 days	ca. 3/12 h		Frädrich, 1967
	c	1–4 days	ca. 12/12 h		Frädrich, 1967
Giraffe	w	newborn	6/24 h	>1 min	Mejia, 1972 (in Moss, 1975)
	w	ca. 1 month	3–4/12 h	$\bar{x}$ = 1.4 min (0.5–2.5, n = 17)	B. Leuthold, unpubl.
	w	7–12 months	2–3/12 h	$\bar{x}$ = 55 sec (45–75, n = 6)	B. Leuthold, unpubl.
Greater kudu	c			$\bar{x}$ = 6.8 min (1–18, n = 25)	Walther, 1964a
Lesser kudu	c	ca. 1 month		ca. 5 min	Walther, 1964a
	w			6 min, 8 min	Leuthold, unpubl.
Southern reedbuck	w	8–14 days	1–2/12 h	2.5–4.5 min	Jungius, 1970
Defassa waterbuck	w	2–4 weeks	1–2/12 h	ca. 5 min	Spinage, 1969b
	w	6 months		9 min 40 sec[c]	Spinage, 1969b
Lechwe	w	0–3 months	2–3/12 h	$\bar{x}$ = 5 min (n = 5)	Lent, 1969
Uganda kob	w	3–5 months	ca. 2/12 h		Leuthold, 1967
Hartebeest	w			21–48 sec	Backhaus, 1959
Bontebok	w	0–1 week	?	$\bar{x}$ = 54 sec (5–180)	David, 1975
	w	2–4 weeks	5–7/12 h	$\bar{x}$ = 22 sec (5–75)	David, 1975
Gerenuk	w	newborn	?	5–10 min	B. Leuthold, pers. comm.
		1–2 months	2/12 h	2–3 min	B. Leuthold, pers. comm.
		ca. 5 months	2/12 h	0.5–1.5 min	B. Leuthold, pers. comm.
Kirk's dikdik	w	0–2 weeks	4/24 h	up to 90 sec	Hendrichs and Hendrichs, 1971

[a] w = wild, c = captive.
[b] $\bar{x}$ = mean; range in parentheses, n = number from which mean is derived.
[c] = single record; "shorter periods are more common" (Spinage, 1969b, p. 44).

While the young is very small, it usually stops sucking spontaneously, presumably when it has obtained enough milk for the time being. With older young, it is often the mother who stops or interrupts nursing by simply walking on, pushing the calf's head away with the moving hindleg. Perhaps termination by the mother is related to more frequent sucking attempts being made by older young.

V. The Following Response

Immediately after birth all young ungulates show a strong tendency to follow any large object moving away from them; this tendency is equally evident in hiding as in following species. In the latter, the following response remains a prominent feature throughout the first few weeks or months and, although it becomes more specifically oriented toward the mother, a fairly strong generalized tendency to "blindly" follow a group of moving animals, or even a strange object, persists for some time. For instance, a young wildebeest, if separated from conspecifics, will follow a man or a vehicle for considerable distances in response to visual stimulation, but will shy away when it comes close enough to perceive the unfamiliar scents (cf. the behavior of the tame blesbok of Walther, 1969 b).

In hiding species, it appears that actual hiding behavior and its autonomous performance require a short period of "maturation" immediately after birth, before becoming fully operational. During this period, a strong unspecific following response is evident, too. This may be one of the "forces" initiating sucking behavior in the neonate, and the response presumably wanes after the first meal, when hiding sets in as an independent action pattern. In older young, the following response becomes restricted to some specific situations and individuals (i.e., the mother), at least while the hiding phase lasts. The mother may have a certain degree of control over the response; she may evoke it, either simply by moving off fairly fast or by special signals, such as tail wagging (e. g., in greater kudu: Walther, 1964a; waterbuck: Spinage, 1969b) or vocalizations. Suppression of the following response may be more difficult, but little information is available for African ungulates (see Walther, 1969b; for other examples Lent, 1974).

The factors eliciting the following response have been studied and discussed in some detail by Walther (1964a) for Tragelaphines, which are hiders, and (1969b) for blesbok, a follower. They include the speed and direction of movement (objects moving fast at right angles are the strongest releasers), the distance (a close object is followed more readily than a distant one), the quantity (a group is a stronger releaser than a single animal), and noises associated with the movement (clattering of hooves; vocalizations).

While in the follower types the following response is critical for survival from birth onward and is probably also instrumental in establishing the mother-young bond, its main importance for the hiding species develops later and is probably associated more with general learning processes (see below), the hiding behavior fulfilling antipredatory and bond-forming functions at an early age.

176

VI. Maternal Defense

Young ungulates are vulnerable to a much larger array of predators than their adult conspecifics. This fact has given rise to various antipredator strategies, incorporated into the complex of maternal/filial behavior. We will look at most of these later; here I will only review active defense of the young by its mother and/or other conspecifics.

Most young ungulates utter a loud distress call when caught. This usually brings the mother onto the scene; sometimes other conspecifics approach, too. The further course of action depends largely on the kind of predator involved and its size relative to the mother's. Thus, a female gazelle will physically attack jackals pursuing her fawn and may be successful in rescuing it (Fig. 1 E in Estes, 1967; Walther, 1968, 1969a). If a hyena chases a Thomson's gazelle fawn, the mother may attempt to confuse the predator or disrupt the chase by crossing repeatedly between the fawn and the pursuing hyena without, however, attacking the latter. In the case of a cheetah or leopard trying to catch a fawn, the mother shows signs of considerable excitement but no overt defensive action (Walther, 1969a). Thus, the extent of defense is, in large measure, related to the danger that a given predator presents to the mother; in other words, survival of the mother takes precedence over that of the young.

This general rule is, however, not without exceptions, and mothers defending young are often unusually bold. A female waterbuck with a newborn young threatened Spinage (1969b) at close quarters and later chased his Land Rover and tried to butt it. When catching newborn Uganda kob, for tagging or rearing, we were often approached by the mother to within 20–30 m, whereas normally female kob would flee at the sight of a man much farther away (cf. Leuthold, 1967). Female wildebeest may defend their young against hyenas and wild dogs (Estes and Goddard, 1967; Watson, 1969), although both these species are capable of killing adult wildebeest, at least when hunting in packs. In case of danger, young warthog characteristically cluster around the mother who may defend them successfully against predators as large as cheetah (Frädrich, 1965; Eaton, 1970). Further examples of maternal defense are given by Lent (1974), Kruuk (1972) and Schaller (1972).

While it is generally the mother only who defends a young animal, other conspecifics often also react to the latter's distress call, by coming closer, perhaps in a kind of mobbing response. In various instances, individuals other than the mother took an active part in the defense as well. In most cases these were other females, some of whom might have had young of their own nearby (e. g., impala: Hitchins and Behr, 1968; Grant's and Thomson's gazelles: Walther, 1968, 1969a; wildebeest: Watson, 1969). Eaton (1970) saw a yearling male hartebeest charge and chase away a cheetah about to attack a small calf. Usually, however, male ungulates do not participate in the defense of young, except in zebra, where the male is permanently attached to the group and may defend any group member against predators (Klingel, 1967; see also Chap. 16, A). In buffalo, an entire herd consisting of males, females, and young may react to a calf's distress call (Sinclair, 1970, 1974).

E. Behavioral Development of the Young

As the young ungulate grows older, its interactions with the environment undergo progressive changes, mainly related to learning processes and the increasing amount of individual experience resulting from them. Little concrete information is available on this development in African ungulates, and much of what there is comes from captive animals. To illustrate the changes occurring during a young ungulate's ontogeny, I will briefly review the flight behavior of a hiding-type antelope, which can be pieced together from various sources.

When only a few hours old, the young lies pressed to the ground, head tucked in (Fig. 44), with no visible movements except for breathing, and can be approached closely, even picked up, making hardly any attempt to escape ("freezing"). At this stage, running away would be pointless, as coordination of movements and strength are inadequate for a successful escape. As the young gets older, its freezing response is increasingly modified: it remains lying still when a predator appears in the vicinity but suddenly jumps up and runs away as soon as the latter approaches too closely. By thus startling the predator it may gain a momentary advantage. It may then run off and lie down elsewhere or, if pursued closely, utter the distress call which elicits the mother's defense reaction (if appropriate).

After the hiding phase, when the young accompanies its mother, it may initially show flight reactions quite different from hers. This is particularly evident in cases where the female is habituated to cars, or people, as in a national park, or in captivity. In Tsavo NP, I have repeatedly seen young lesser kudu react with strong alarm, even flight, to the appearance of my vehicle, while their mothers showed little or no concern. These observations suggest that there may be an innate response of "distrust" toward strange objects, which is most pronounced just after the hiding phase. Gradually, the young then learns, partly presumably from the mother's behavior and partly from its own experience, to differentiate between more or less dangerous and harmless objects in its environment. Once these young animals have "understood" that a certain object (vehicle, person) presents no danger, they may become even tamer than their mothers, as we found in lesser kudu and gerenuk in Tsavo NP. Walther (1968/72) made similar observations on captive eland, the young of which were easily frightened for some time after the hiding phase. This may present serious problems in captivity, as such animals are prone to injure themselves by running into fences, etc.

Other behavioral changes during a young ungulate's ontogeny involve daily activity and feeding. In hiding species it is mainly the mother who determines the activity pattern of the young; initially, there are two to five short bouts of activity during a day, associated with nursing and separated by long periods of quiet lying. As the young grows older, it may begin to stand up occasionally, walk about and feed a bit during the hiding periods; but it can do so only at the risk of increased exposure to predation and such independent activity of the young is comparatively rare. However, little documented information exists on this point. Gradually, the young accompanies its mother and her group for longer and longer periods, and adopts her activity pattern to an increasing extent. Nonetheless, the pattern of young animals may continue to differ considerably from that of adult conspecifics, particularly where several young join together in a crèche group (see below).

With regard to feeding, little is known in detail. Young ungulates start exploring potential food at an early age through nibbling at plants, litter, soil, etc. Some observations suggest that the formation of ultimate food habits depends, at least in part, on learning by imitation of the mother or perhaps other adult conspecifics (Leuthold, 1971b; see Chap. 5, A, III). Most important in relation to feeding is the process of weaning, after which the young animal has to collect all its food from the vegetation of its environment. Although weaning usually happens gradually, it often subjects the young to considerable physiological stress. Factors contributing to and governing the weaning process are little understood, but are thought to include an increasing reluctance by the mother to let the young suck, perhaps aggravated by the increasingly forceful pushing movements by the young which, in turn, may be stimulated by dwindling of the milk supply (Lent, 1974).

A striking phenomenon involving some young ungulates, generally of the more gregarious species only, is the formation of subgroups of similar-aged young, so-called "crèche" or kindergarten groups. Normally, such aggregations of young are clearly attached to a herd of adults containing their mothers, yet they may show a fairly different, partially independent activity pattern. Members of crèche groups spend a large portion of the day resting, presumably because they do not need to devote as much time to feeding as do the adults, being still suckled more or less regularly. Sometimes crèche groups are accompanied by one or two adult females, but the oft-asserted "guard" function of the latter remains to be substantiated. The mothers of at least some of the young in the crèche group appear to be well aware of what is going on there and may rush in immediately in case of danger, at least in impala (M. V. Jarman, 1973). Crèche formation is most pronounced in gregarious antelopes of the hider type, such as impala, Uganda kob, sable, etc. In oryx and eland, this phenomenon reaches its extreme, and one sometimes sees herds (not crèche groups!) containing more young than adult animals. Outside the bovids, crèche groups occur commonly in giraffe (Mejia, 1972; pers. obs.) and possibly the hippopotamus (Verheyen, 1954). Probably the young of most ungulate species tend to associate and interact with each other, when an opportunity arises, but in most of the species mentioned above the formation of fairly discrete crèche groups is a characteristic feature at a certain stage of their ontogeny.

F. Weakening and Dissolution of the Mother–Young Bond

Relatively little well-documented information is available on this point, as only intensive observations of known individuals over a long period of time could produce the data required. The following generalizations are probably warranted:

the manner in which the mother–young bond weakens and finally breaks down is related, on the one hand, to the social organization of the species and, on the other hand, to the sex of the young animal. For instance, young males of territorial species may be harassed increasingly by territory holders, until they finally leave their mother's group and join a bachelor herd. This is probably a common pattern in such territorial antelopes as impala, waterbuck, Uganda kob, hartebeest, etc. A young female, on the other hand, may remain with her mother's group unmolested; the break-down of her bond is probably influenced mostly by reproductive activities, both her own and her mother's. Birth of a young is always a potential breaking point for the bond with the previous offspring, and subsequent events depend to a large extent on whether or not the new young survives. There is some reason to assume that recruitment of young females into their mothers' group may be a common pattern of group formation and maintenance in ungulates, although evidence relating to African species is largely lacking, except in the case of the elephant (see Chap. 16, A). An interesting exception is the plains zebra, where adolescent mares in their first estrus are regularly "abducted" by stallions and may form the nucleus of a new family group (Klingel, 1967; see also Chap. 16, A). However, other mechanisms of group formation are conceivable, and Estes (1974) feels that the crèche groups may play an important part in this context. In his concept, the interindividual bonds developing within crèche groups may gradually supplant mother–young bonds and counteract any possible tendencies of a young female to join her mother's group. Possibly, such a mechanism operates in the more gregarious species although, again, factual evidence is still lacking, whereas in species forming only small groups and no crèches, young females may well be recruited into their mothers' social groups. This almost certainly is the case in elephants where, by contrast, adolescent males may be forcibly expelled from the family groups by one or several of the adult females (Douglas-Hamilton, 1972, 1975).

Much remains to be learned about the social processes that occur between weaning and the eventual integration of a young into the social structure prevailing among its adult conspecifics.

G. Functional Aspects

Having reviewed maternal/filial behavior in some detail, we are now in a position to consider the functional aspects of certain elements, and the entire complex, in an overall context. I have to emphasize, however, that much of what follows is conjectural and that little or no direct evidence is as yet available for the functions ascribed to certain behaviors.

Obviously, newborn ungulates are highly vulnerable to predation and, therefore, antipredatory functions have generally received most attention. However, other aspects may be of considerable importance, too, particularly the successful establishment of an individualized mother–young bond.

Prepartum Isolation. Separation from conspecifics and the change of habitat often associated with it have obvious advantages in relation to predation: they tend to reduce the risk, for both mother and young, of being detected by predators (cf. Gosling, 1969). During labor, the female's capabilities for defense and/or flight are impaired; the concealment afforded by bushy vegetation and the separation from a relatively conspicuous group may compensate temporarily for these disadvantages. In addition, parturient females and/or newborn young may even require protection from conspecifics who sometimes harass or attack one or the other, presumably because of their unusual behavior, appearance or smell, when birth occurs in or near a group (Gosling, 1969; Watson, 1969; M. V. Jarman, 1973, 1976).

Prepartum isolation may further be essential to ensure that the neonate does not contact conspecifics other than its mother during the critical period, i.e., before the mother–young bond is at least partially established. For instance, M. V. Jarman (1973) describes how newborn impala, if born near the herd, are approached closely and investigated with great "curiosity" by conspecifics, to the extent of getting confused as to their mother's identity. If, at this stage, the young attached itself to the wrong animal, its chances of survival would be substantially reduced. Seen in this context, isolation of the mother is the first link in a chain of events leading to a strong individualized mother–young bond; later steps consist of the intensive postpartum interactions and the entire complex of hiding and associated behavior (see below).

Time of Parturition. The apparently pronounced calving peak of Ngorongoro wildebeest in the morning may be an adaptation to heavy predation by hyenas, which hunt primarily at night; young born in the morning can gain sufficient strength during the day to have a reasonable chance of outrunning hyenas by the evening (Estes, 1966). By contrast, the spatial dispersion of parturitions— through prepartum isolation of females—of hartebeest in Nairobi National Park may, in itself, be sufficiently effective in minimizing predation, so that the timing of births is of secondary importance (Gosling, 1969). On the other hand, Jarman and Jarman (1973a) view the midday peak in impala births in the Serengeti also as being adapted to avoiding predators hunting during the night, notwithstanding the fact that parturitions are also spatially dispersed. Thus, local circumstances in any one area may call for different patterns of antipredator measures in different species, or even in different populations of the same species.

Hiding and Associated Behavior. The behavioral complex of hiding, and the maternal care associated with it, have for some time been considered as chiefly an antipredator mechanism (see discussions in Walther, 1968; and Gosling, 1969). The fact that the young is isolated from conspecifics, even its mother, for most of the time, coupled with the long periods of inactivity and the concealing properties of the hiding place, reduces the chances of a predator finding it visually or auditorily. Additional measures diminish the probability of the young hider being detected olfactorily: "smelly" substances are removed and consumed by the mother immediately after birth (amniotic fluid, fetal membranes) and for some time afterward (urine, feces). Kruuk (1972) recorded several instances in which hyenas passed within 2–3 m of Thomson's gazelle fawns without detecting them. Licking of the young by the mother, as well as the consumption of the fetal membranes and the afterbirth, are less developed or even absent in species of the follower type. The more pronounced maternal care in hiding species can, therefore, be viewed as primarily an antipredator measure integrated into the whole complex of hiding behavior.

With respect to some temperate-zone species, a thermoregulatory function (drying of the fur) has been attributed to maternal licking after birth (references in Lent, 1974), but this is unlikely to be important for tropical forms. Considerable evidence suggests, however, that postpartum licking and nudging are essential in stimulating the neonate's first movements and attempts to gain its feet (see, e. g., Hersher *et al.*, 1963).

In addition to the removal of odoriferous substances by the mother, the young animal's own scent-producing organs (e. g., interdigital and other cutaneous glands) are probably not yet functional at this stage. Walther's (1966a, 1968) experiment with Dorcas gazelles (Chap. 14, D, II) demonstrated that the mother was unable to find the new hiding place when the young was enticed to move from the original site; this suggests that the young did not leave a scent trail (or possibly that the mother was not prepared or equipped to follow one). Gosling (1969) also found that the interdigital glands of hartebeest are not functioning yet during the hiding phase.

Thus, hiding and all other associated actions, including prepartum isolation of the female, can be seen as a well-integrated complex of antipredator behavior. This, of course, immediately raises the question of how follower types can do without hiding. There appear to be two main possibilities of overcoming the predation problem: one strategy, exemplified by the wildebeest, relies on extreme precocity of the young, reducing the length of time they are most vulnerable to predators. The dense herds may be viewed as a substitute for vegetational cover. The timing of births within the day-night cycle further enhances survival chances of the young. At the same time, the marked seasonality of reproduction results in a temporary superabundance of potential prey, which the predators cannot "cope with" (Estes, 1966, 1974, 1976; Gosling, 1969). In other follower species the need for similar antipredator mechanisms may be largely obviated by the fact that adequate defense measures against most predators can be taken, either by the mother alone in large species (rhinoceros, hippopotamus, possibly giraffe) or by members of the group where this is a coherent unit (zebra, elephant, buffalo).

While hiding undoubtedly serves as an important antipredator strategy, this should not be viewed as its only function. As already emphasized in the context of prepartum isolation, separation from conspecifics may be essential for the undisturbed development of the mother–young bond. Hiding behavior of the young makes it possible for the mother to remain in social contact with her fellow group members without endangering the mother–young bond. The latter, as we have seen, becomes established—at least in part—through the female's knowledge of the calf's hiding place. The intensive interactions (licking, etc.) during suckling sessions gradually lead to mutual individual recognition independent of a location.

Again, other means to achieve the same end must be available to follower species, at least those that are normally gregarious. Several strategies have been adopted by different species. Female giraffe with newborn young continue to remain isolated for some time after parturition; presumably individual recognition is effected during this period. In zebra we can see a functional equivalent to isolation and hiding in the marked aggressiveness of the mother toward other zebra, including her own group members, during the first few days after the foal's birth. This aggression, keeping conspecifics at some distance from the young, probably prevents "fixation" (imprinting) of the young on an animal other than its mother (Klingel, 1969c). For wildebeest I can see no satisfactory explanation of how they deal with the problem of "mis-attachment," except perhaps for the extreme precocity of the young which makes it possible for them to follow their mothers within minutes of birth (most neonates of hiding species would be unable to do so). Possibly, the learning processes leading to individual recognition are speeded up in accordance with physical development.

The Mother–Young Bond and Prolonged Association. The primary function of the individualized mother–young bond is almost certainly to provide the young with an assured source of nutrition (particularly important where reproduction is nonseasonal and only a few females may lactate at any one time), protection (e. g., defense against predators), and guidance. This latter aspect may well be more important than is generally realized, but it is difficult to obtain documentary proof for this function. We have already seen that the young ungulate's reaction to strange objects may be influenced by the mother's behavior and that food habits may be partly learned through imitation. Other information about the habitat is also acquired mainly through prolonged association with a given adult animal, usually the mother; this may include the extent of the home range, distribution of food and water, location of fixed points and trails, migration routes between seasonal ranges, etc. Much of this kind of information is probably preserved within a population by tradition (Leuthold, 1970c). Considerable evidence confirming the existence of such traditions is available for temperate-zone ungulates, such as roe deer (Kurt, 1968), red deer and wapiti (Schloeth, 1961a; M. Altmann, 1963) and mountain sheep (Geist, 1971b), but little is known, in this context, of African species. Sinclair (1970, 1974) presented indirect evidence for learning by tradition of the extent of—and availability of resources in—home ranges of each herd of buffalo, quoting in support the work of Hunter and Davies (1963; reference in Sinclair, 1974) on domestic sheep: lambs raised with their mother adopted her home range, whereas those reared separately adopted new ranges, according to with whom they were raised. The subdivision of Uganda kob populations into units associated with different leks may be traditionally determined, as are the locations of the leks themselves (Buechner, 1963; Buechner and Roth, 1974). It would be of considerable interest to obtain more information on this subject, as it would probably elucidate further some functions of the close mother–young association observed in most ungulates.

Part 4
Social Organization

In the preceding chapters I have discussed various categories of social behavior that govern relations mainly between individual conspecifics, whether in groups or not. In the following, we will consider how these and other behaviors function to integrate individual animals into an organized society.

As a tentative definition of social organization I propose the following: *Social organization is the result of all social interactions and spatial relations among members of a single-species population.*

Social organization includes such aspects as group types, group sizes, relations of individuals or groups to space, relations of individuals to each other, spatial and other relations between different sex and age groups, etc. It provides a population of conspecifics with a definable structure, with particular reference to the use of space. It is maintained primarily through "a complex system of communication" (Eisenberg, 1966), important features of which have been reviewed earlier (Chap. 8).

While general aspects of the social organization tend to be species-specific, details are subject to considerable variation related to environmental conditions, e. g., climate, including its seasonal variations, vegetation type, etc. (see Chap. 17). In seasonally reproducing populations the social organization often undergoes cyclic changes, being usually more complex and most pronounced during the rutting season. At this time, it may be considered as the equivalent of a "mating system," a term generally used with reference to birds, and sometimes as a synonym for social organization. However, as well shall see (Chap. 19), the social organization of ungulates involves several important eco-ethological aspects additional to providing a framework for reproduction.

For general reviews of mammalian social organizations see Wynne-Edwards (1962), Etkin (1964), Eisenberg (1966), Symposia Nos. 14R (1965) and 18 (1966) of the Zoological Society of London, Fisler (1969), Esser (1971). Dealing specifically with African ungulates are Jarman (1974), Estes (1974) and Klingel (1975). A recent comprehensive review of social organization and its ecological implications in a wider context has been given by Wilson (1975).

In the following, I will attempt to define and review some terms and concepts important in the present context and then summarize what is currently known on the social organizations of African ungulates.

Chapter 15

General Patterns in Social Relations

This section discusses some ethological terms used to describe various social relationships and gives some examples of how they apply to African ungulates.

A. Gregariousness, Aggregations and Social Groupings

In terms of the tendency to associate with conspecifics, we usually distinguish between solitary and gregarious animals. This is, however, too crude, as there is a continuum ranging from essentially solitary species through those living in pairs and those habitually forming small groups or fairly sizeable herds to those commonly living in large herds numbering several hundreds. We may accommodate this situation to some extent by using qualified terms such as „essentially solitary," "moderately gregarious," etc., but it is difficult to arrive at a precise definition of the degree of gregariousness. One possible solution is to lump different species into categories of similar grouping tendencies, as Jarman (1974) has done (see Chap. 19).

The above discussion implies that the degree of gregariousness is largely species-specific. This is probably correct in a general way, but considerable variations occur within species under different environmental conditions (Chap. 17). In addition, members of different sex/age categories (often equivalent to social classes) within the same populations commonly show different degrees of gregariousness. Very broadly speaking, female ungulates tend to be more gregarious than males, although this impression may sometimes arise erroneously because females are often accompanied by their offspring (which constitutes a special case of social relationship). In many species, fully adult males tend to become solitary, or nearly so. This is usually connected with their social and/or reproductive status. Considerable numbers of solitary adult males are a normal feature in territorial ungulates (cf. Leuthold, 1970b), but also occur under other circumstances.

Throughout this book I use the terms "group" and "herd" fairly loosely (unless otherwise qualified), without attributing to them a more specific meaning than simply "a number of conspecific animals being together in the same location." Also, the difference between group and herd is no more than one of the number of animals involved, herd denoting a larger assemblage than group. In the present context, however, we must differentiate between groups or herds that constitute coherent social entities, and those that do not. The latter are generally called "aggregations," which means any number of animals being together in one place in response to some external factor (e. g., favorable feeding conditions) rather than as a result of specific social interactions (e. g., Etkin, 1964). While it is often difficult or impossible to determine whether a given grouping is a social entity or merely an aggregation, some knowledge of the species' general tendencies will help in making a decision. For instance, a herd of 400 buffalo has a high probability of being a cohesive unit (Sinclair, 1974, see also Chap. 16, A), whereas the same number of elephants would certainly be an aggregation composed of a number of much smaller social units (e. g., Douglas-Hamilton, 1972; pers. obs.). Similarly, a group of five bushbuck would most probably be an aggregation, whereas the same number of lesser kudu might constitute a cohesive social group (Leuthold, 1974, and unpubl.).

With regard to social units, we may further distinguish between open and closed groupings. Closed groups are those permanently comprising the same individuals and excluding strangers; their composition may be stable over several years except, of course, for births and deaths; in some species, young animals born into the group may eventually leave it or be expelled. It is difficult to demonstrate the existence of closed groups in the wild, as this requires individual recognition of most or all group members. In a few cases, this has, however, been possible. Perhaps the best examples are the plains and mountain zebras which both live in female groups of stable composition, each accompanied by one adult stallion (Klingel, 1967, 1969d). Stable female groups, to which adult and/or subadult males may attach themselves temporarily, exist in the elephant (Douglas-Hamilton, 1972) and in lesser kudu (Leuthold, 1974, and unpubl.). A number of other antelope species form small to medium-sized female groups that may remain stable in composition for considerable periods of time, although this has not yet been demonstrated conclusively, e. g., wildebeest (Estes, 1969), bontebok (David, 1973), Grant's gazelle (Walther, 1972a). Permanently stable groups appear to be rather rare among bovids generally, but the herds of several hundred head of buffalo are thought to remain basically unchanged for years, except for occasional splitting and rejoining (Grimsdell, 1969; Sinclair, 1974; Leuthold, 1972).

Among the more gregarious antelope species, where female herds habitually number 30 or more, these tend to be unstable in both size and composition, suggesting that they are largely open groupings. Again, this is difficult to establish with certainty, but observations on naturally or artificially marked animals indicate that this applies to impala (Leuthold, 1970b; Jarman and Jarman, 1974) and Uganda kob (Leuthold, 1966a), and probably other species with similar grouping tendencies. Groups containing only male antelopes ("bachelor herds") often vary considerably in size and composition over short periods of time, which suggests that they are essentially open. However, few long-term studies have yet been conducted on this subject, and there is some evidence that relationships between certain males may last longer than is immediately apparent (e. g., in kongoni: Gosling, 1975). Prolonged association between two or more adult males occurs fairly commonly in plains zebra (Klingel, 1967).

Perhaps the best example for open groupings is the giraffe, in which no permanent associations have become evident in several field studies (Foster and Dagg, 1972; Mejia, 1972; B. Leuthold, unpubl.; see Chap. 16, A). Males and females mix in groupings of very variable size and composition; the only factor that appears to foster a relationship between females, lasting for several weeks or months, is the presence of small young of similar ages.

In the field, it is often impossible to distinguish between aggregations and social units, and between open and closed groupings, without prolonged observations and means of recognizing many individual animals. In such circumstances, a purely operational definition of group has to be adopted, which says nothing about the nature of any assemblage encountered. It is usually this kind of data on which information on mean group size and its local or temporal variations is based (e. g., Leuthold and Leuthold, 1975 a).

B. Spatial Relationships Between Individuals in Groups

Even in highly gregarious species individuals may not readily tolerate physical contact, or even approach by others to whithin less than a certain distance, designated as "individual distance" by Hediger (1941). This term suggests a circular "sphere of influence" around the individual, but detailed studies on domestic animals have shown that the extent of this sphere is not the same in all directions, being generally largest around the head and smallest behind the animal (McBride, 1971). In recognition of these findings, McBride introduced the term "personal area" (or personal field) to replace individual distance. However, as the latter term is in general use, I retain it in the following, having made the above qualification.

According to the prevalence and extent of individual distance, Hediger (e. g., 1961) divided animals into "contact types," which readily establish and accept physical contact, and "distance types," which are intolerant of contact, i. e., tend to maintain individual distance. Among African ungulates, we may consider most Perissodactyla, the Suidae, Hippopotamidae and the elephant as being of the contact type, while giraffe and most bovids tend to be distance types. Among other things, contact types often rest in close physical contact (e. g., Suidae), while distance types maintain some spacing even when at rest. However, while the above categorization follows taxonomic lines to a large extent, individual distances may vary greatly within any one species, depending on sex/age classes, social status and the psychosomatic conditions, including type of activity engaged in at the time, of the animals concerned ("social subphase": McBride, 1971; see also Lewis, 1975). For instance, during mating and caring for young, the individual distance must become zero at least temporarily in all species. Other social interactions, such as fighting, mutual grooming, etc., also require a reduction or obliteration of the "personal field." Thus, individual distance should not be viewed as a constant for any one species, or even for any individual, but the division into contact and distance types appears to be useful and justified.

Hediger (e. g., 1961) also coined the term "social distance," being the maximum distance that members of a group voluntarily tolerate between each other; in other words, it is a measure of the spatial cohesion of the group. Again, this may vary widely within and between species and little factual information is available, but a few general rules can be observed: (1) the social distance is usually smallest between females and their young, (2) it is generally smaller between young animals than between adults (this may be a factor contributing to crèche formation—see Chap. 14,E, (3) in many species it is larger in male groups than in female herds. On this basis, the experienced observer can often tell from far away whether a given group of ungulates is composed of males or of females. This applies to elephants as well as to most bovids but not, apparently, to giraffe or zebra. Of course, this type of intragroup spacing could also be explained on the basis of differing individual distances, rather than of social distance, but the latter term is useful to describe the extent to which a group or herd can disperse without losing its cohesion.

A mechanism akin to individual distance may also operate between groups of conspecifics, possibly serving as an intergroup spacing mechanism (Brown and Orians, 1970). It might be responsible for such phenomena as the nonrandom spacing between different herds of buffalo in the Serengeti NP (Sinclair, 1974).

C. Dominance and Territoriality

As these two terms are widely, but often inconsistently, used in the ethological literature, and as the concepts underlying them are very important in the context of social organization, it is perhaps appropriate to review them first and define their meaning and use in the following discussions.

I. Dominance

While the term *dominance* might be considered self-explanatory, it can be characterized as *an attribute that provides its holder with access to certain resources in precedence over other individuals, without actual contest.*

Positions of dominance (i. e., ranks) within an animal community may initially have been determined through contest, be it actual physical combat or ritualized displays; once established, however, they are generally respected by community members without overt conflict.

Leyhausen (1965, 1971) has pointed out that dominance can manifest itself in two ways:

1. Dominance may be a fixed attribute of an individual, effective wherever it goes within its society, regardless of external circumstances. The resultant social structure is an *absolute social hierarchy*.

2. Dominance may be tied to some external condition, e. g., space (or time). An individual may be dominant over others in one place but not in another. This characterizes a *relative social hierarchy*, of which territoriality (i. e., space-related dominance) is the most important variety (see below).

For a detailed discussion and specific examples see Leyhausen (1965, 1971).

Thus, an absolute dominance hierarchy and territoriality are not totally different and mutually exclusive social mechanisms, as they are sometimes depicted, but rather different expressions of one and the same phenomenon, "two mutually complementary kinds of ranking order" (Leyhausen, 1971, p. 28). Nevertheless, their distribution within different ungulate communities provides the resultant societies with sometimes strikingly different characteristics, particularly as far as the breeding males are concerned, and a clear distinction between territorial (i.e., relative dominance) and hierarchical (i.e., absolute dominance) systems can generally be drawn (see Chaps. 16 and 18). The main outwardly manifest difference between the two is that, in territorial systems, reproductively active males are usually single and dispersed, whereas with an absolute hierarchy several males of similar status may be found together in one group or herd.

When discussing dominance, one should always specify the resource or object involved, as well as the contestants, as different systems of dominance may operate within and between different social classes (sex/age categories, etc.). Within a given species, absolute dominance may determine primarily the spacing patterns within groups, access to food, water, or preferred localities for various activities, and the degree and direction of certain social interactions (e.g., allo-grooming). Relative dominance manifests itself mainly in the context of reproduction, at least in ungulates. Males holding territories, i.e., exercizing relative dominance within a given area, commonly take precedence over all other males in mating with receptive females on their territories. Because of this connection between relative dominance and reproduction, the distribution and occurrence of the two types of dominance may vary considerably in the course of a year, depending on the degree of seasonality of reproduction. For instance, impala in East Africa tend to reproduce throughout the year (though not necessarily at a uniform rate); therefore a certain, albeit perhaps fluctuating, proportion of adult males is territorial at any time of the year. By contrast, impala in southern Africa have a distinct breeding season; during the rut, many males hold territories, but outside that period few or none do so (Anderson, 1972; Jarman and Jarman, 1973b, 1974). These changes in dominance status of adult males affect virtually the entire social organization of the populations concerned (see Chap. 17).

The qualities that determine an individual's dominance status are usually difficult to assess. Dominance is frequently related to body size, and thus also to sex and/or age. A male ranking very low within the male hierarchy of a given community may still dominate all females of that community, if he is larger in body size. Within sexes, an absolute hierarchy may be based principally on age, but also on such attributes as physical strength, experience, "temperament," etc., but little relevant information exists for African ungulates.

Dominance should not be confused with leadership (Chap. 11; see also Etkin, 1964). The latter is generally manifested in the context of movements from one location to another and often bears little or no relationship to dominance. For instance, in most antelope species adult males are normally dominant over females, yet when a group moves it is almost always a female that leads it,

191

whereas the male most often follows behind (e. g., in gerenuk: Leuthold, 1971c). To some extent, this may reflect the fact that the adult male, more often than not, is not an integral member of the group, but only temporarily associated with it. However, in plains zebra, too, the group is normally led by a mare, although the stallion may influence the direction of movements, even from the rear (Klingel, 1967).

II. Territoriality

The term "territory" has suffered a great deal from inconsistent use by different authors. A variety of definitions have been formulated over the years (e. g., Tinbergen, 1936; Noble, 1939; Hediger, 1949), but none has been universally accepted. In part, this probably reflects the fact that there is such a multitude of variations on the theme territory that it is virtually impossible to arrive at an all-embracing definition. In addition, however, semantic and conceptual differences between different authors have compounded these problems and created some confusion in the ethological literature. For this reason I consider it necessary to review the term and its meaning in some detail and to make clear the sense in which it is used below.

The simplest and most generalized definition is that of Noble (1939) characterizing a territory as "any defended area." Indeed, most other definitions include the notion of defense as the essential attribute of a territory. However, the very term "defense" has been criticized (e. g., Emlen, 1957; Schenkel, 1966b) on the grounds that it implies either a specific motivational state (a "consciousness of ownership") of the territorial animal, or aggression from outside to which the territorial animal reacts. The latter may well apply in some cases, but most often it is the territorial occupant himself who attacks any intruder in his domain and normally succeeds in evicting him. Thus, the term defense can be circumscribed as "intraspecific intolerance and a normally successful demonstration of dominance on the part of the territory holder." The term "dominance" provides the link with the preceding section; the most important point to be made here is that intolerance and dominance are restricted to a specific area, the territory, and that the territorial animal loses its dominance status as soon as it moves outside the territory (cf. Walther, 1972b). Its dominance is therefore relative, conditional on its being within a specific area.

This circumstance might, by itself, provide a useful definition of territory. However, some other aspects are often involved as well and deserve mention here. Nice (1941) described territoriality as being "based primarily on a positive reaction to a particular place and a negative reaction to other individuals," thus emphasizing that an important requisite for territorial behavior is attachment to a circumscribed area. This aspect is often neglected, or only implied, in definitions of territoriality. Furthermore, competition over territories may revolve around different resources in different species, which affects, among other things, the typical size of territories and the extent and intensity of defense.

Essential characteristics of a territory are therefore (cf. also Brown and Orians, 1970):

1. Fixation in space.
2. Dominance of the occupant(s) over conspecifics of comparable social status (exception: direct challenge over "ownership" of the territory).
3. As a consequence of (2), exclusive use of the resource(s) in question present on the area involved.

Based on these premises we may formulate the following definition of a territory (modified after Burt, 1943; and Wilson, 1971, 1975):

A territory is that part of an animal's home range from which it excludes individuals of comparable social status through active repulsion.

("animal" could be replaced by "group," if appropriate; however, no group territoriality is known to me among African ungulates).

To make this definition as universally applicable as possible, the following qualifications to the terms used in it have to be added:

1. To "exclude" does not necessarily and always mean to evict physically from the area concerned. For instance, a territorial male impala may react very differently to a group of bachelor males entering his territory, depending on circumstances, particularly on whether he is alone or with females. He will, however, not tolerate any of them mating with a female on his territory, if he is aware of such attempts. Thus, to "exclude" should, in some cases, be interpreted as "to prevent from engaging in certain activities."

2. "Individuals of comparable social status": this will vary primarily according to the resource involved; it may mean any other conspecifics, or only other adult males, to give the two extremes. The meaning of the term is therefore; "actual or potential rivals in competition for the resource in question."

3. "Active repulsion" should not be visualized as necessarily involving physical combat; well-established territorial systems can be—and indeed usually are—maintained by very subtle means that are often difficult to detect for the human observer. The main problem is that active repulsion need not be evident at all times, but it may have occurred at some point in the past and the state arrived at then may be perpetuated by such means as advertizement (visual, auditory, olfactory) or simply by neighboring territory holders knowing each other individually (cf. Wilson, 1975). Overemphasis of the combat aspect of defense may have led to some of the confusion surrounding the term "territory."

In view of these qualifications we might restate the definition of a territory as follows:

A territory is a spatially fixed area within which a given animal consistently prevents certain other individuals from engaging in certain activities.

"Certain other individuals" and "certain activities" would have to be specified in each case, primarily according to the resource involved.

In practice, Noble's (1939) definition of a territory as "any defended area" may be useful and acceptable in many instances, provided the exact connotation of "defended" is properly defined (for a recent comprehensive discussion of territoriality see Wilson, 1975).

Schenkel (1966b, p. 597) proposed to restrict the term territory to instances in which the occupant always has full sensory control over the entire area involved and can evict any intruder at any time. This amounts to a serious modification of the general definition, and its justification is questionable. One could argue, for instance, that the whole "point" of olfactory marking may be to overcome the problems of visual communication in closed habitats, or within very large territories, the territorial animal being represented, as it were, by its scent mark instead of being physically able to intervene at any given point in time and space. Under such circumstances an intrusion into one part of a territory may occur and pass unnoticed, if the occupant happens to be in another part; all portions of the territory cannot be defended equally at all times ("spatio-temporal" territory, as opposed to "absolute" territory: Wilson, 1975). Under the definition given above, such systems still qualify as true territories.

To my knowledge, Burt (1943) first pointed out the need to *distinguish clearly between home range and territory* (see Chap. 6,B,I). Several authors, among them Hediger (1942/50, 1949, etc.) and more recently Etkin (1964), did not consider this distinction necessary. They use "territory" and "home range" largely synonymously, which is somewhat unfortunate as it tends to create confusion in the literature. Whereas in many small mammals and carnivores the entire home range may be used exclusively by one individual or group, in most territorial ungulates, particularly African bovids, the territory constitutes only a part of the home range, as will be shown later (Chap. 16). Hediger's widely quoted model of a "territory" (Fig. 8) may be valid for many but certainly not all mammalian species; it would be more generally applicable as a model of a mammal's home range.

In the English-language literature the terms territory and home range are usually employed in the senses defined above and distinguished accordingly. Considerable confusion exists, however, in the German-language literature where the two terms have been used rather loosely and inconsistently. Several reasons may account for this:

1. Perhaps a preponderance of studies on mammals that do not show the dichotomy between territory and home range as clearly as many ungulates do (e. g., rodents, carnivores).

2. Possibly the influence of Hediger's studies which were pioneering in the field.

3. Some German authors—linguistic purists—do not use the word "Territorium," preferring instead the term "Revier" which, while appropriate in many cases, would seem to correspond in its meaning more closely to home range than to territory (at least in my view).

4. There is no universally accepted German equivalent for the English "home range;" different authors use different expressions largely according to personal preference: "Streifgebiet" (Leyhausen, 1965), "Aktionsraum" (Eibl-Eibesfeldt, 1967), "Heimatgebiet" (Klingel, 1967), "Aufenthaltsgebiet" (Walther, 1968), "Wohnraum" (Hediger, 1961; Kurt, 1968; Leuthold, 1971c). This multitude of terms probably tends to blur the meaning of the underlying concepts considerably.

It should become abundantly clear from the information presented in the following chapters that "home range" and "territory" must always be clearly distinguished, at least with regard to ungulates (for definition and discussion of home range see Chap. 6,B,I).

Chapter 16

Types of Social Organization in African Ungulates

The following review of social organizations refers to African ungulates only, as defined in Chapter 2. For purposes of comparison, I have attempted to classify social organizations according to the following criteria: (1) the use of and relations to space (home range, territory), and (2) the types and sizes of groups normally formed. In this context I use the term "social unit" to denote the smallest cohesive group of conspecifics (including single animals where applicable) that usually remain together, as a result of social bonds, and generally react in concert to external stimuli. Table 6 gives an outline of this classification, which is based, on the whole, on the most complex form of social and spatial organization that can occur in any one species, i.e., that normally prevalent during the rutting period, where seasonal variations take place (see Chap. 17). For each type of social organization (= SO-type) I will provide a schematic illustration of spatial arrangements, to facilitate comprehension of the essential features, and then give an account of one or several species representing each type, depending on the amount of information available.

As Jarman (1974) pointed out, "any attempt to subdivide a continuum creates problems." Thus it may be that one or the other species does not fit fully into one of the SO-types described below; the classification should not be viewed as final or comprehensive, but rather as an attempt to pinpoint similarities and differences between social organizations on the basis of the information currently available. Furthermore, one has to bear in mind that the social organization of any species, while generally following a specific pattern, may be profoundly influenced and modified by local environmental conditions. In the words of Eisenberg (1966, p. 71), "the social organization is potentially the most variable structure characterizing a given species. It is variable because it reflects the sum total of all the adjustments to the environment in terms of habitat exploitation and energy budget." We will discuss some of these variations more fully in Chapter 17.

A. Nonexclusive Home Ranges

Several social units inhabit the same or mutually overlapping home ranges without conflict (Fig. 45). A variety of different herd structures can be combined with this spatial arrangement.

SO-type 1a. No constant social units exist; individuals gather freely into groups of open membership and very variable composition. The sexes are neither

195

Table 6. Classification of sociospatial organizations among African ungulates

SO-type	Spatial arrangement	Social units[a]	Example
1a	Nonexclusive home range	± individuals; no lasting associations	giraffe
1b	Nonexclusive home range	stable groups of females and young; loose all-male groups	elephant
1c	Nonexclusive home range	stable groups of females and young, with one adult male permanently associated; all-male groups	plains and mountain zebras
1d	Nonexclusive home range	large, fairly stable herds including adults of both sexes; all-male groups	African buffalo
1e	Nonexclusive home range	no lasting associations; females and young gregarious; adult males solitary or in small groups	eland
2a	Nonexclusive home range but exclusive home *site*	small, fairly stable groups of females and young; males separate or temporarily associated with female group	warthog
2b	Nonexclusive home range but exclusive home *site*	fairly large groups of females and young; males largely separate (group cohesion unknown)	hippopotamus (?)
3a	Exclusive home range in both sexes	individuals only	water chevrotain (?) certain duikers (?)
3b	Exclusive home range in both sexes	permanent pairs	Kirk's dikdik
4	Exclusive home range in males only (territory includes ± entire home range)	a) small groups of females and young b) solitary adult males c) small groups of (mainly) subadult males	gerenuk
5a	Part of home range exclusive, in males only (mating territory)	a) wide variety of female/young groupings b) solitary adult males c) all-male (bachelor) herds	impala
5b	Arena or lek territories (small mating territories aggregated in dense clusters)	a) wide variety of female/young groupings b) solitary adult males c) all-male (bachelor) herds	Uganda kob
6	Exclusive home ranges in males, combined with absolute hierarchy	a) individual females, with young, or small groups b) single adult males (territorial, dominant) c) subordinate satellite males on same territories	white rhinoceros

a In all cases, social units listed separately here may be associated, at least temporarily, for varying periods of time.

Fig. 45. Social units inhabiting nonexclusive home ranges.
------: home range boundary, ▲: social unit

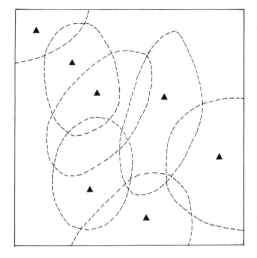

consistently segregated nor definitely associated. Adult males of similar social status within a given area probably know each other, and an absolute hierarchy appears to exist among them.

This situation characterizes the social organization of the giraffe.

The distinctive, permanent skin patterns of giraffes (Dagg, 1968), their size and—generally—relative tameness have permitted a considerable amount of sociological and behavioral data to be collected in recent years (Innis, 1958; Backhaus, 1961; Foster, 1966; Foster and Dagg, 1972; Mejia, 1972, in Moss, 1975; Moore-Berger, 1974; B. Leuthold, unpubl.; Leuthold and Leuthold, in press).

Individual home ranges can be quite large: in Nairobi NP they were on average 62 km² for adult males and 85 km² for females (Foster and Dagg, 1972), whereas our own observations in Tsavo NP indicate a mean size of about 160 km² for both sexes, with a maximum of over 600 km² (Table 3). Movements over 20–30 km in a short time are quite common (in Tsavo) and are related to seasonal changes in food supply (Leuthold and Leuthold, 1972, in press). Occasionally, we recorded movements over more than 50 km (airline distance). On the other hand, a few individuals—mainly apparently old males—tend to remain within small areas for long periods. No territorial defense has been observed in giraffes.

Giraffes are moderately gregarious, usually forming groups of 1–15 animals, larger herds being less common, though this varies locally to a considerable extent. Maximum herd sizes reported are: 18 in Transvaal, South Africa (Innis, 1958), 18 in Garamba NP, Congo/Zaire (Backhaus, 1961), 18 in Nairobi NP, Kenya (Foster and Dagg, 1972). During the dry season, 25–30 giraffes were regularly seen together near Voi in Tsavo East NP, where the largest herd noted numbered 35 (Leuthold and Leuthold, 1975a). On ranchland in Samburu District, Kenya, 17% of all herds recorded contained over 50 animals, the maximum being 175 (Moore-Berger, 1974: reticulated giraffe). In the western Serengeti NP herds are generally quite large, with a mean of 16 and a maximum of 249 recorded so far (R. A. Pellew, pers. comm.). A substantial proportion of groups (16–44 % in Nairobi NP: Foster and Dagg, 1972; ca. 40 % in Tsavo NP: Leuthold and Leuthold, 1975a) consist of single animals, mostly males.

The composition of the herds is very variable, males and females of all ages occurring together in some herds, whereas others contain primarily animals of one sex only, apart from juveniles. It is not uncommon to find several fully adult males together in one group.

Analysis of interindividual associations (e.g., Foster and Dagg, 1972; B. Leuthold, unpubl.) shows that giraffes form no permanent groups. Certain individuals may be seen together for several months, but such groupings are almost always temporary only. The most prolonged association, that between a female and her young, may persist for 1 to 1½ years, perhaps even longer in some cases. There is a marked tendency for females with small young to join and remain together for considerable periods of time. This, in turn, is related to crèche formation, which is very pronounced in giraffe. A number of small young (0–6 months old) are sometimes found together, with no adult animals in sight; the mothers may be 1–2 km away. Almost invariably, however, they return to their young in the evening or during the night. As in other ungulates, evening and early morning are the main suckling times. Suckling may continue, at least occasionally, until the young is well over a year old. Innis (1958) and Foster and Dagg (1972) characterized the mother–young bond in giraffe as particularly loose, compared to other ungulates. It may, however, be more appropriate to look at this bond as being maintained by somewhat different means than in other ungulates, e.g., through long-range visual contact not possible in other animals. When the young are 5–6 months old, they generally follow their mothers as most young antelopes do.

When a female is in estrus, she is "guarded," i.e., accompanied closely, by an apparently high-ranking bull who tries to keep other males away. (On such occasions it appears obvious to the human observer that an absolute hierarchy exists among the male giraffes of a certain area and that individuals know each other, probably visually, although this is difficult to prove objectively.) The male-female association for mating lasts for 2–3 days only (Mejia, 1972), the presumed duration of estrus. Afterward, the bull involved may again mingle peacefully with other males which he had not tolerated near the female as long as she was in estrus.

By contrast, several males can sometimes be seen following a female, or approaching her in turn, and showing Flehmen when she urinates, without any demonstration of conflict (Innis, 1958; pers. obs.). Presumably, such instances involve mainly nonestrous females and/or low-ranking (possibly younger) males that have no "serious intentions." On the other hand, Backhaus (1961) stated that Flehmen was usually the prerogative of the highest-ranking male. If indeed so, this may be more pronounced in captivity, where many of Backhaus' observations were made, than in the wild.

The peculiar fighting technique of giraffe (necking: Coe, 1967) has been described earlier (Chap. 12, E). Subadult and young-adult males commonly engage in this activity in a playful manner; serious fights are not often observed, severe injuries or even deaths resulting from such encounters must be very rare.

SO-type 1b. Social units are stable groups of females and young. The sexes are largely segregated, adult males living singly or in small loose groups, joining female groups only temporarily.

The African elephant is probably the only ungulate species with this type of social organization (outside Africa, the Asiatic elephant appears to have a very similar organization: McKay, 1973).

The literature on elephants is rather voluminous, but many of the older works are of little more than anecdotal value. A comprehensive review, including literature up to 1968, was compiled by Sikes (1971). A great deal of field work on elephants has been carried out since then, much of it related to the various "elephant problems" in national parks of eastern and southern Africa (e. g., Laws, 1969a, 1970; Laws *et al.*, 1975). In most of these studies ecological problems took precedence over behavioral aspects, but much behavioral information accrued incidentally from them. In addition, detailed investigations of the social organization of elephants have recently been conducted in the Serengeti NP (Hendrichs, 1971; Croze, 1974), Manyara NP (Douglas-Hamilton, 1972) and Tsavo NP (Leuthold and Sale, 1973; Leuthold, 1976, and unpubl.). The following account is based primarily on these four studies, plus information from Buss (1961), Buss and Smith (1966), Laws and Parker (1968), and Laws (1969a, 1974).

The basic social entity is a closely knit group of apparently related females and young, the family unit, which does not include adult males as permanent members. "The term family unit refers to an adult female and its offspring, or two or more closely related females and their offspring. These units usually number from 4 to 15 individuals, their activities are closely coordinated, and large bulls seen with them are generally attached loosely and temporarily" (Buss and Smith, 1966, p. 376). Because of the longevity of elephants it is nearly impossible to prove conclusively that members of family units, particularly the older ones, are actually related. Post-mortem examination of entire groups collected together has, however, produced circumstantial evidence on this point. On the basis of individual ages, or weights, it has generally been possible to arrange members of family units into a plausible structure of familial relationships (Buss, 1961; Laws and Parker, 1968). Family units can thus be viewed as consisting of one old cow or of (old) female siblings with their mature daughters plus all immature offspring of both sexes. If such a group increases beyond a certain size, a portion may split off and continue as an independent family unit (Douglas-Hamilton, 1972).

Individual family units rarely comprise more than 12–15 animals, although this varies locally. However, two or more family units often join up, at least temporarily, sometimes forming herds and aggregations numbering up to several hundred or even 1,000–2,000 animals. Thus, actual herd sizes observed present a rather complicated picture. Laws' (1969a) data from Tsavo NP suggested a polymodal distribution of group sizes, with a modal size of six and frequency peaks at multiples of six. This he interpreted as indicating a basic mean size of six animals for the smallest social units, larger herds being combinations of two or more basic units (and bull groups). More recent work in Tsavo NP suggests that mean group size varies in relation to certain environmental factors, such as rainfall and/or the density of woody vegetation (Leuthold, 1976; see Chap. 17, B).

In contrast to the stable cow/calf groups, bull groups are only loosely organized and change their composition frequently, sometimes several times within one day (Hendrichs, 1971). One may see groups with mainly young bulls; in other cases there are several large, apparently old bulls together, but basically bulls of any age may occur in the same group. There is no evidence of any long-term bonds between individual bulls.

In general, bull groups are rather small, averaging 2.5–3 animals (Laws, 1974), and rarely contain more than 10 individuals, although bull herds of up to 144 animals have been recorded (Parker, quoted by Laws, 1969a). A considerable proportion of bull groups at any one time consists of single animals (nearly 50 % in Tsavo NP: Laws, 1969a, and pers. obs.; ca. 35 % in the Serengeti NP: Hendrichs, 1971).

Young bulls remain with their original family units until about the time they reach sexual maturity. The age of puberty varies between different populations, depending on local ecological conditions, from about 10 to 20 years (Laws, 1969b). The time of separation from the maternal group may vary further as a result of differences in individual characteristics, behavioral and temperamental, of both the young bulls and the other group members. In some cases, a young bull may be forcibly expelled from his family unit (Douglas-Hamilton, 1972). Once separated from it, a young bull usually attempts to join another bull or a bull group, at least temporarily.

Individual bulls or bull groups sometimes attach themselves to a family unit or a larger cow/calf herd, particularly when a cow is in or near estrus. Copulation may then be attempted or successfully completed. Such attachments are, however, always temporary only, and there is no lasting association between any mature bull and any cow or cow/calf group.

Interindividual relations are evidently governed by an absolute hierarchy. With regard to family units it is generally assumed that the oldest female ranks highest, although this is difficult to determine in the field. There is considerable observational evidence indicating that the largest cow usually leads the group in movements, while the same individual often is the most aggressive, or at least the most "fussy" animal when the group is disturbed. In most cases, the largest cow is probably also the oldest in a group. Whether or not leadership, both in movements and defense, is directly correlated with rank is difficult to establish.

In bulls, rank is probably determined principally by body size and age, but more subtle properties appear to play an important role as well, such as individual traits of "character" or "temperament" (Hendrichs, 1971). Such characteristics combine to determine an individual's "social role" (e. g., Crook, 1971), in addition to his rank in the hierarchy. Circumstantial evidence indicates that any mature bull probably knows a considerable number of other bulls and their social status relative to his own. This is probably the reason why one sees generally few instances of overt aggressive confrontation between bull elephants in the field. Many of those that one does see involve relatively young bulls that have not settled their mutual social relations yet or who simply "play."

A subject of some controversy is the question of home range, site attachment and seasonal movements of elephants. The old hunting literature generally depicts elephants as roaming far and wide, over well-worn trails established by generations unnumbered. Sikes (1971) presents this view as more or less established fact without, however, adding any corroborative evidence. On p. 241 she writes: "The natural habit of the savannah or *africana* race of African elephants was to migrate seasonally from gallery forests to savannah woodland, and in some areas from higher to lower altitudes, and back again." And on pp. 244/5: "The regular long-distance directional migrations of elephants thus followed definite routes and were repeated year after year. ... Nowadays few of these routes are used, although many of them, beaten hard by years of constant use by elephants, are still clearly recognisable. The actual distances travelled by elephants on their long-distance directional migrations are not clearly known, but it is believed that on one route they used to travel from Mount Kilimanjaro to the Lorian Swamp in Kenya and back again, a distance of some 350–400 miles." This view is based largely on the often incoherent observations of early explorers and big-game hunters in Africa. In the absence of factual data confirming it, it may be considered as little more than romantically inspired conjecture.

At the other end of the spectrum is the opinion of Laws (1969a, 1970, etc.) who maintains that elephants are generally organized into discrete "unit populations" occupying a given range within which they undertake only limited seasonal movements. Referring to Tsavo NP he considered that seasonal displacements (of entire unit populations) involved no more that 15–30 km (1969a, p. 508).

The truth—as usual—lies probably somewhere in between the extremes. One has to bear in mind that, in large areas of former elephant habitat, uninhibited long-range movements of elephants may no longer have been possible in recent years, due to expanding human populations and activities. Also, specific techniques for monitoring such movements have only been developed and employed comparatively recently. Furthermore, environmental conditions induce considerable differences between different areas.

I know of only one case in which a substantial movement by an individual elephant was reliably documented before radio-tracking was widely used: a cow elephant visually marked (by cuts in the ear) in western Uganda was collected and identified $2\frac{1}{2}$ years later about 180 km (115 miles) away (Wing and Buss, 1970, p. 35).

Radio-tracking in Tsavo NP (Leuthold and Sale, 1973, and unpubl.) has revealed movements of individual elephants over 100–120 km within a few months, unanticipated by Laws' hypothesis, but at the same time a considerable degree of attachment to relatively limited dry-season ranges. A temporary subdivision of the overall population into local units is apparently effected by attachment of individuals and, presumably, population segments to discrete dry-season ranges (probably traditionally determined), but may be obliterated in the rainy season, particularly if rainfall has been irregularly distributed.

In other areas, elephant movements have not yet been studied sufficiently to permit comparison with the situation in Tsavo, except perhaps in the Serengeti NP where there are two discrete populations undertaking fairly regular seasonal displacements over 30–50 km (Hendrichs, 1971; Croze, 1974). In Lake Manyara NP, by contrast, most elephants appear to be very sedentary (cf. Table 3), although there is reason to believe that fairly regular movements formerly occurred between this park and Ngorongoro Crater, ca. 50 km away (Douglas-Hamilton, 1972). One has to be careful in generalizing about social organization and movements of elephants on the basis of the results of one or a few studies, as this species is exceptionally adaptable and versatile in coping with the exigencies of its environment.

SO-type 1c. Social units are stable groups of females and young permanently attended by one adult male. Subadult and supernumerary adult males form unisexual "bachelor" groups.

This situation characterizes the social organization of the plains and mountain zebras (but note that Grévy's zebra has a very different social system; see Chap. 16, E and F).

Social studies are facilitated by the fact that the permanent stripe patterns permit long-term individual recognition. On the other hand, zebra often occur in large aggregations where it may be impossible to identify individuals. An added difficulty is the absence of marked secondary sex and age characteristics. The following account is primarily for plains zebra, but the situation is very similar in mountain (incl. Hartmann's) zebra of southern Africa (Klingel, 1967, 1968, 1969a, d, 1972a, b, 1974b, 1975; E. Joubert, 1972b).

Zebra live in two kinds of groups: (1) family groups, consisting of one or several females and their young, with one adult male permanently attached to them, (2) stallion groups, consisting of subadult and those adult males that have no families. Family groups number from 2 to 16 animals, averaging between 4.5 and 7 members in different areas of eastern and southern Africa. Stallion groups are generally smaller, 1.6–3 individuals on average, the largest group observed consisting of ten. But the maximum size of stallion groups is difficult to determine, as different groups are not as discretely separated as the families and may join up temporarily, drifting apart again later on. Some stallions lead solitary lives.

Both types of groups are fairly stable in composition; in particular, family groups may remain unchanged for years, apart from births and deaths. Young animals generally leave their original group on attainment of sexual maturity. Young males then join bachelor groups, whereas young females are usually "abducted" by another stallion. An interesting behavioral mechanism is involved in these abductions: young mares in their first few estrous periods (at about $1\frac{1}{2}$ years of age) adopt a characteristic posture, with straddled legs and raised tail, that apparently has strong signal value. Adult stallions are attracted by this posture and attempt to "extract" the young mare from her family group. The family stallion occasionally gives chase to such outsiders and may, in the process, leave his group temporarily unattended, thus offering a chance to a third stallion to successfully drive the young mare away. The visual effect of the estrus stance of young mares (as opposed to possible olfactory cues) became evident, by chance, during immobilizing operations (Klingel, 1967). Under the influence of the drug "Etorphine" (M99) adult mares adopted a posture very similar to that of young estrous mares. Regularly, a number of stallions approached them closely and, in some cases, even tried to mount them. Older females have shorter estrous periods and adopt the typical posture only briefly, usually without attracting any other males than the attendant family stallion.

After being "conquered," a young mare does not necessarily remain with the original abductor. Several stallions may continue fighting over her until, eventually, she remains with one and either joins his original group or forms, with him, the nucleus of a new family unit. Klingel (1969c, p. 341) considers this procedure as "part of a behavioral mechanism to avert inbreeding and to encourage outbreeding. The strong personal bonds between the family members necessitate this mechanism."

The strength and durability of interindividual bonds within the family groups are demonstrated by the fact that, in the event of death of the family stallion, the group remains together and is taken over, as a whole, by a new stallion. Just how this cohesion is achieved and maintained is not entirely clear; Klingel feels that group members recognize each other visually by the stripe patterns, in addition to voice and scent. (As evidence for this he indicates that zebra separated from their group usually called only when they could not see the others, either because of obstacles in the terrain or at night). Family members, particularly the stallion, actively search for individuals that have lost contact with the group. Thus each family can be viewed as a tightly knit social unit of stable composition. Members may mingle with other groups, e. g., at waterholes, but invariably join up again with their original companions.

Within the family units, there is an absolute hierarchy in which the stallion always occupies the top position. Leadership of the group on the move is assumed by the highest-ranking mare. Young animals usually follow immediately behind their mother, being treated by the others as more or less equal in rank with her. The stallion normally brings up the rear but may, on occasions, influence the direction of movement by passing alongside the group, "deflecting" the other members away from him (Fig. 3 in Klingel, 1967).

Each family unit inhabits a home range that may overlap substantially with home ranges of other families. These ranges measured between 80 and 250 km^2 in the relatively stable environment of Ngorongoro Crater in Tanzania. In the adjacent Serengeti NP zebra are migratory, utilizing seasonal ranges of around 500 km^2, separated by distances of 100–150 km covered twice annually in the migrations (Klingel, 1969a; cf. Table 3).

No part of the home ranges is used exclusively by either a group or an individual, the plains and mountain zebras thus being strictly nonterritorial. No integrative organization above the level of the family groups is evident. Numerous family groups habitually concentrate on certain areas for the night ("sleeping grounds"), perhaps forming local subpopulations. The large herds of zebra found in various locations are purely aggregations in areas of favorable feeding conditions, in which individual families retain their cohesion and identity.

The social organization of plains and mountain zebras is unique among ungulates in that there are stable groups including one adult male, unrelated to any unit of space. This is the only case reliably described of an actual "harem system," so often reported as existing in most antelopes in the older literature. Male zebras thus compete socially over the "possession" of a female group. However, the zebra family is not held together by any kind of coercion on the part of the male (as the term harem might imply), but rather the female/young segment is an entity (a closed group) to which basically any adult male can be joined to complete the social unit. But once a stallion is attached to a group, he remains with it permanently. Only rarely is one stallion replaced by another before his death. [Grévy's zebra has an entirely different social organization, being territorial (Klingel, 1969b, 1974a, b).]

SO-type 1d. Social units are relatively large herds containing animals of both sexes and all ages; some, particularly older, males may live singly or in small groups of "peers."

This system has been found in the African buffalo, studied in Queen Elizabeth (now Ruwenzori) NP of Uganda (Grimsdell, 1969) and in the Serengeti NP, Tanzania, with supplementary observations in Lake Manyara and Arusha NPs (Sinclair, 1970, 1974). Its social organization is characterized primarily by the large and relatively cohesive herds that almost always contain a number of adult males, and the close interindividual spacing within the herds.

Herd size depends to a considerable extent on environmental conditions, primarily rainfall and/or the availability of drinking water, but also on vegetation structure (see Chap. 17). For instance, in the relatively open Serengeti NP, herd sizes ranged from 50 to 2,000, the mean being about 350, whereas on the densely forested Mt. Meru (Arusha NP) buffalo herds averaged only 50 head. In relatively dry areas herds are also smaller (e.g., Tsavo NP, see Chap. 17, B, III).

The herds usually contain mainly females and young, but adult and subadult males are almost always present, too. Their proportion within a herd varies seasonally, in relation to climatic factors and the breeding pattern, being highest during the peak mating season (usually during periods of high rainfall). It appears that entire groups of males may enter or leave a herd from time to time as units. They break away primarily during the dry season, when herd-splitting occurs most often; at this time, both the absolute number of bachelor males and their mean group size are highest, whereas overall mean herd size reaches a low point, reflecting mainly a decrease in size of "breeding" herds. The converse happens during the rainy seasons.

Although herds may split or join at different times of the year, the composition of the main groups, in terms of individual animals, appears to remain largely constant over long periods of time. This was confirmed through observations of known individuals by both Grimsdell and Sinclair, and also for a herd in Tsavo NP (Leuthold, 1972). Grimsdell reports a few instances in which different herds intermingled temporarily, but always separated out again into their original composition.

Within large herds animals of the same or similar sex/age classes may form loose subgroups, particularly subadult males (3–4 years old). Watching a herd resting in Ngurdoto Crater (Arusha NP) from the rim, Sinclair was able to determine nearest-neighbor relationships. His analysis revealed that all classes tended to avoid close company of adult males, whereas young animals of both sexes as well as adult females associated preferably with females. Sinclair concluded that young animals remain closely attached to their mothers up to about two years of age, at which time the males begin to break away. By 3–4 years of age, this process is largely completed, and these subadult males form relatively "pure" groups, from which they gradually enter the ranks of adult males, either within the breeding herds or in separate bachelor groups. In young females, the association with the mother may last much longer, but this is difficult to document without long-term observations of many known individuals.

Older males (those over 10–12 years) leave the herd more or less permanently and tend to lead a very sedentary life, sometimes in the company of other old males. They apparently select certain habitats, particularly riverine, in which they can fulfil their requirements more or less the year around. By contrast, the breeding herds, including the males associated with them, move about considerably and utilize a variety of habitats in the course of the year (see below).

Relations between individuals in a herd are governed by an absolute hierarchy. Primary criteria for rank are sex (males are usually dominant over females) and age, but within the same sex/age classes other characteristics must determine an individual's rank. In a relatively small herd of mostly known individuals Grimsdell found a linear hierarchy among 15 adult males. Among females, which are generally much more numerous, a linear hierarchy would be very difficult to demonstrate, and indeed even difficult to visualize. One criterion that affects a female's rank is her reproductive status: females accompanied by calves tend to rank higher than those without (Sinclair).

The highest-ranking adult males associate most closely with the female herds; Grimsdell found that the most dominant males achieved most matings. Lower-ranking males may be expelled from the breeding herd and relegated to existence in bachelor groups. Subadult males are generally tolerated as long as they behave as subordinates.

Each herd inhabits a spatially more or less fixed home range, the size of which varies locally as well as seasonally, and probably also in relation to herd size. Grimsdell gave the home range of a herd of 130 animals as measuring about $10 \, km^2$; a herd of about 400 head in Tsavo NP had a home range of at least $85 \, km^2$ (Leuthold, 1972); one herd (size not given) in Serengeti NP roamed over ca. $450 \, km^2$ in the course of three years (derived from Fig. 33 in Sinclair, 1970; cf. Table 3). Home ranges of two Serengeti herds were considerably larger in the wet than in the dry season; casual observations of mine suggest that this may also be so in Tsavo NP. During the dry season the area that can be utilized is limited by the availability of drinking water and adequate grazing.

Grimsdell found that, within its home range, a herd used specific areas for certain activities, particularly for resting, and travelled over established routes between such localities (space-time system, see Chap. 6, D, I). He reported average daily movements of about 9 km (range 5–13 km); Sinclair recorded herd movements of up to 30 km in a day.

Year-round home ranges of neighboring herds overlap extensively but, at least in the Serengeti, their contraction during the dry season results in almost exclusive use by each herd of its own range at that time. Thus, the attachment of each herd to a given home range may be the basis of a spacing mechanism and may have important ecological implications (see Chap. 18).

SO-type 1e. Social units are ill defined; apparently, no lasting associations exist between individuals. Females and young may form quite large herds, at least temporarily, whereas fully adult males tend to be solitary, except for transient associations with other males and/or female herds.

The eland, as far as is known at present, has approximately this type of social organization.

Eland are generally described as being nomadic, prone to considerable movements, seasonal or otherwise. Moreover, the species tends to be particularly shy and wary, compared to other ungulates, making it difficult to study in the wild. Two field studies of social organization and other aspects of eland biology have been conducted very recently, one in a small reserve in South Africa (Underwood, 1975), and one on free-ranging populations in Kenya, partly in Nairobi NP (Hillman, 1976). At the time of writing (1975), the results have not yet been published. The following account is based on information kindly made available to me by the two authors and must be regarded as preliminary.

In the Kenya population, recognizable individuals inhabited fairly large (up to 350 km^2: Table 3) and mutually overlapping home ranges; perhaps it would be more appropriate to speak of communal home ranges shared by members of the same subpopulation. No exclusive use of space by individual animals was evident, although some adult males tend to live solitarily in rather small home ranges for much of the year. However, their social relations with others are clearly governed by an absolute hierarchy, which becomes evident when they join other males and/or female herds temporarily.

A feature of the sociospatial organization of eland are the considerable differences between adult males and females in this respect. These are manifest not only in home range size (males' ranges are, on average, only about one-fourth the size of females': Table 3), but also in habitat preference and herd size. Fully adult males, at least, tend to inhabit more woody vegetation types in river valleys ("korongos"), etc., whereas females generally prefer more open plains. Partly as a consequence (cf. Chap. 19), males generally occur in very small groups only, while females and young may aggregate into herds numbering 200 or more, at least temporarily. Mean group size tends to vary seasonally, particularly in the female/young segment of the populations, being largest in the wet season. With considerable generalization one may say that the male eland is much more of a "true Tragelaphine," inhabiting a relatively small home range in fairly woody habitats, whereas the female tends to be a "plains animal" of somewhat nomadic habits, with seasonal movements of up to 55 km recorded so far. These may even be exceeded considerably during periods of extreme climatic conditions such as drought, as some indirect evidence indicates (Hillman and Hillman, 1977).

The information currently available suggests that there are few, if any, lasting bonds between individual animals (although perhaps insufficient observations of known animals have been made to date to permit firm conclusions). The eland social system thus shows, and combines, some features of that of giraffe (e. g., more or less open groups) with that of buffalo (formation of large herds, although only temporary; solitary adult males). The solitary males are, however, not "outcasts" but, in fact, the actual breeding males that will mate with any estrous females that enter their home range. Several adult males may be present in a female herd at any one time, and access to estrous females is governed by the absolute hierarchy referred to above.

Another characteristic feature of eland social organization is the strong tendency of young animals to aggregate into large herds of peers. The hiding phase (if any) appears to be extremely short in eland, and calves soon associate with others (crèche groups, see Chap. 14, E). It is not uncommon to see eland herds containing considerably more young than adult animals. The cow-calf bond seems to last for a rather short time only and is soon supplanted by strong intercalf bonds that bring about the marked cohesion of the calf groups. As they grow older, the young animals go through various stages of association with other eland, of different ages, and a period of considerable wandering, before adopting the way of life of adults, as described above.

To my knowledge, the eland is the only African antelope studied so far that is definitely not territorial (but some *Tragelaphus* species may not be territorial either; see Chap. 16, D).

B. Nonexclusive Home Range but Exclusive Home Site

This category must be considered as tentative for the time being, as information on the species included in it is rather incomplete. It is confined to species that actually nave a spatially fixed home site, a relative rarity among ungulates. The best example—and by coincidence also the best-studied species—is the warthog with its burrows (Fig. 46). Other suids may approach this type but not enough is known about their social and spatial organization; the same is true for the hippopotamus.

SO-type 2a. Social units consist of one or several females and their young living in overlapping home ranges. A group may monopolize one or several burrows within its home range. The sexes are generally segregated; adult males associate temporarily with a female group.

This type of social organization apparently exists in the warthog. While some general observations on this species have been reported relatively early from East (Geigy, 1955) and West Africa (Guiraud, 1948; Bigourdan, 1948), more intensive studies have recently been conducted in Kenya (Frädrich, 1965,

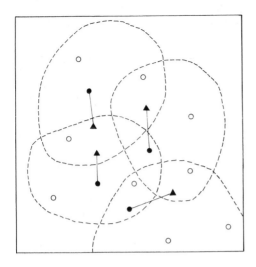

Fig. 46. Social units inhabiting nonexclusive home ranges, but each with its own (exclusive) home site.
------: home range boundary; ▲: social unit; ●: defended (exclusive) home site; ○: unoccupied potential home site

1967; Bradley, 1968), Uganda (Clough, 1969), Rwanda (Monfort, 1974) and southern Africa (Child *et al.*, 1968; Cumming, 1975). The following account is based primarily on the work of Bradley (1968) who spent most time on his study, was able to identify a considerable number of animals individually, and whose conclusions on the social organization, therefore, appear to be best documented (Cumming's study became available to me only after most of this book had been written).

An important feature of warthog biology, not only in Nairobi NP, Bradley's study area, is that reproduction is restricted to one short period per year. This produces certain seasonal variations in the basic pattern of social organization.

One, two or rarely three females and their young of the year, and occasionally one or several subadults, presumably young of the previous year, form the basic social unit of warthog. Group sizes ranged from 1–10 in Nairobi NP (Bradley, 1968), 1–10 in the Serengeti NP (Hendrichs, 1972), 1–12 in Tsavo NP (Leuthold and Leuthold, 1975a) and 1–18 in Queen Elizabeth NP, Uganda (Clough, 1969). Each group inhabits a fairly fixed home range (mean size in Nairobi NP = 133 ha: Bradley, 1968), within which it uses one or several burrows. These serve as sleeping (?) sites at night, as well as refuges from predators in daytime. The home ranges of different female groups overlap considerably; no portion is defended, with the possible exception of a burrow (Bradley's observations were not entirely conclusive on this point; there may also be seasonal variations related to reproduction).

Females in advanced pregnancy apparently chase away their young of the previous year, giving birth to a new litter in isolation in a burrow. Yearling females may join their mothers again later on. Occasionally, two gravid females may use the same burrow to give birth, and they often raise their young communally (Frädrich, 1965). Suids differ from most other ungulates in that (1) they produce several young at a time (3–4 in the warthog), and (2) the young may be suckled by more than one lactating female, whereas in most other ungulates the mother–young bond is fairly exclusive (see Chap. 14, D).

Male warthog live singly or in small groups of up to five animals, the composition of which may change from day to day. Individual males also inhabit mutually overlapping home ranges which, in turn, coincide partly or entirely with the home ranges of several female groups. At any time, but particularly during the mating season, a mature male may associate temporarily with a female group. Such association is not restricted to any given group; Bradley found some of his males wandering irregularly between up to six different female groups. Conversely, he observed one known female being accompanied by four different males within a two-month period.

During the mating season, males defend whichever female group they happen to be with. Interestingly, "the male that was with the females was always dominant, regardless of his size" (Bradley, 1968, p. 125). Perhaps "possession" of a female group provides the "owner" with a similar psychological advantage over potential rivals as a territory holder appears to enjoy over a challenger in other species (another example of relative dominance?). However, the objects and modes of social competition among male warthog remain unclear.

[In some contrast to the above, Monfort (1974) asserts that an adult male is commonly an integral member of the social unit, and that males are primarily responsible for the exclusive use of a burrow by a given group; his study was conducted in the Akagera NP, Rwanda. This view is, however, at variance with other recent studies.]

SO-type 2b. Social units are groups of females and young, with males probably segregated but in close proximity. Home ranges are temporally differentiated, with possibly group-specific areas being inhabited by day, and (probably) overlapping feeding ranges being used at night.

This type of social organization, possibly applying to the hippopotamus, is even more tentative than the preceding one, as the available literature presents conflicting interpretations of relatively limited field observations (Hediger, 1951; Verheyen, 1954). Verheyen's observations were generally more detailed and extended over a longer period of time than Hediger's, but neither author, nor both together, presented sufficient information to provide a clear picture of the social organization of the hippopotamus. This is obviously a consequence of the difficulties of observing these animals, given their amphibious and primarily nocturnal way of life.

Provisionally, the situation appears to be as follows: hippopotami spend most of the daylight hours in the water, mainly inactive (resting). In the evening they go on land to feed (almost exclusively on grass), moving considerable distances away from water, depending on feeding conditions (over 3 km according to Verheyen). What happens at night, in terms of social groupings and interactions, is virtually unknown, except that extensive trail systems are maintained and used, along which numerous marking points exist. In the water, during the day, there are relatively tightly bunched groups ("schools") consisting mainly of females and young (Verheyen calls them "crèches"). Hediger states that a large male attends, and dominates, each of these groups, whereas Verheyen denies this, saying instead that most adult males live singly or in small groups, the single ones being noticeably intolerant of others approaching them. If this is correct, one may infer—as Verheyen did—that some adult males "defend" a small home area in the water, perhaps comparable to the burrow of the warthog (as a territory?). Some of these home sites appear to be situated in the immediate vicinity of important exits from the water, where the trail systems for the nocturnal feeding trips on land begin. Perhaps easy access to, and some measure of control over these exits, is related to the social status of the males concerned. Hediger, on the other hand, considered the entire complex of aquatic home site and terrestrial trail system to constitute the territory of a male-dominated group. A more detailed study of social organization in the hippopotamus has recently been started in the same area by H. Klingel; its results are awaited with interest.

The above observations were made along lake shores in the Virunga (formerly Albert) NP, Zaire, with a very high density of hippopotami. In a recent brief study of the species along the Mara River in north-western Serengeti NP, Olivier and Laurie (1974) arrived at a rather different picture, although conclusions on social organization remained tentative only. Groups contained several adult males alongside females and young, but were somewhat unstable in size and composition. Individually recognized animals were seen in widely separated parts of the river, and no evidence for either individual or group territoriality was found. These observations were made in a very different environment, where considerable seasonal fluctuations in the amount of available aquatic habitat occurred. Possibly, the differences in external conditions are responsible for at least part of the discrepancies between the accounts of the various authors (see also Monfort, 1972). Until more detailed information is available, we can only speculate on the actual form of social organization in the hippopotamus and its potential for adjustment to different environments.

Even less is known of the pygmy hippopotamus, which inhabits river systems in tropical lowland forest of West Africa. It is said to live singly or in pairs and not to form larger groups (Dorst and Dandelot, 1970; Lang, 1972).

C. Exclusive Home Ranges in Both Sexes

The social units of species in this category inhabit home ranges that do not usually overlap (except perhaps between animals of different sex) and may be actively defended, i.e., the entire home range constitutes a territory. This may apply to completely solitary ungulates as well as to those living in pairs or even slightly larger social units. This category corresponds to social class A of Jarman (1974; see Chap. 19).

SO-type 3a. The social units are single adult animals living solitarily in exclusive home ranges which may, however, overlap with those of the opposite sex (Fig. 47). Females may be accompanied by immature offspring. The sexes generally associate only for mating.

To my knowledge, this system has not yet been conclusively documented in a wild population, but it is generally inferred to apply to a number of

Fig. 47. Individuals living in exclusive home ranges (=territories).
♂: solitary adult male; —: boundary of male's territory; ·····: boundary of male's home range; ♀: solitary adult female (with or without juvenile: j); -----: boundary of female's home range (=territory?)

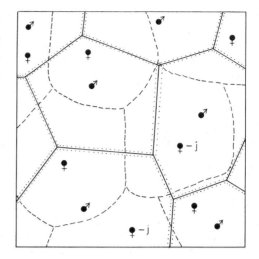

small, mainly forest-living artiodactyls, in which studies of free-ranging animals present considerable difficulties. Such species are the water chevrotain (Tragulidae) and some small bovids, such as duikers of the genera *Cephalophus* and *Sylvicapra*, perhaps steinbuck and other *Raphicerus* spp., and possibly bushbuck under certain conditions. None of these species have, so far, been studied in sufficient detail to permit firm conclusions. Inferences on the nature of their social organizations are based on circumstantial evidence, such as records of group size and composition, as well as some observations on captive animals (e. g., Aeschlimann, 1963; Ralls, 1973, 1974 on *Cephalophus maxwelli*; Elder and Elder, 1970, and Allsopp, 1971, on bushbuck, but see also Waser, 1975a, b; Dubost, 1975, on water chevrotain; Hendrichs, 1972, and Jarman, 1974, on several species).

In passing, it may be noted that some of the small cervids of southern Asia (e. g., *Muntiacus*), which resemble duikers in many respects, appear to have a social organization largely corresponding to the type described here (Dubost, 1970, 1971; Eisenberg and Lockhart, 1972).

SO-type 3b. The social unit is a pair, with or without immature offspring, living in a fixed territory (Fig. 48). Both sexes may take part in territorial activities such as defense and marking.

This type of social organization has been well documented in Kirk's dikdik (Hendrichs and Hendrichs, 1971; Hendrichs, 1975a; see also Simonetta, 1966, and Tinley, 1969):

One adult male and one adult female live together, as a more or less permanent pair, in a home range measuring 2–10 ha, which is defended in its entirety (occasional exceptions may be related to unusual conditions, e. g., drought, fire, etc.). Offspring of the pair (normally one at a time) live in the parental territory until they reach maturity, or until the birth of the following young, when they are generally evicted by one or both of the parents. Territories are marked, by both sexes, by means of the tarlike secretion of the antorbital glands, which

211

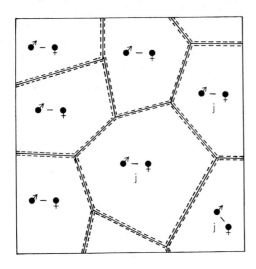

Fig. 48. Pairs living in exclusive home ranges (= territories).
♂–♀: ±permanent pair (with or without juvenile: j); ═══: boundary of pair's home range/territory

is deposited on the tips of dry twigs or other plant stalks (Fig. 7 in Hendrichs and Hendrichs, 1971). In addition, localized urination and defecation also appear to serve as a marking technique, resulting in the formation of large dung heaps, primarily at or near the territorial boundaries.

Unusual among ungulates is the exclusive and relatively long-term pair bond. If one partner dies, the other may remain alone for quite some time, until a new partner appears, presumably a grown-up young evicted from its parental territory.

Mainly circumstantial evidence suggests that this type of social organization also occurs, perhaps with minor variations, in some duikers, the klipspringer, possibly steinbuck, oribi, and one or two species of reedbuck, at least locally (Hendrichs, 1972; Jarman, 1974; Estes, 1974; Bigalke, 1974).

Under certain conditions, e.g., high density, the pair may be extended to include more than one female, while the overall sociospatial system remains the same. In the field, such a situation has been recorded for klipspringer in the Zambezi valley (Jarman, 1974). Observations on captive animals suggest that it can also occur in Maxwell's duiker, the natural social organization of which is not definitely known (Aeschlimann, 1963; Ralls, 1973, 1974). An interesting detail is the fact that, when two or more females are kept together with one male, one of them is clearly "preferred" by the male. This conclusion is based on considerable differences in the frequency of mutual face-rubbing (mutual marking with antorbital glands) between the male and different females. One female received by far the greater share of the male's attention while the other was reduced to little more than "wallflower" status. Similar behavior was also recorded in captive steinbuck in the context of mating (Chalmers, 1963).

These observations, although so far made on captive animals only, suggest a tendency toward pair formation in the species concerned and, furthermore, point to a possibly important role of antorbital secretions in interindividual recognition, in addition to the more widespread use in marking of external objects (cf. Jarman, 1974).

212

The cases of "extended pairs" may be viewed as an intermediate situation between strict pair territoriality, as in dikdik, and the formation of small female groups, as in SO-type 4 (see below). The exact manifestation of social organization depends on many factors (see Chap. 17) and, as mentioned earlier, clear-cut categorization of all types may not be possible, nor perhaps realistic.

D. Exclusive Home Range in Males Only: Home Range Coincides with Territory

In this—as in the following—category only the adult male is concerned with the establishment and maintenance of a territory, which includes most or all of his normal home range. Home ranges of females may coincide with the territory of only one male, but may also overlap, at least partially, with several male territories (Fig. 49). At any rate, the females are essentially independent in their movements, not restricted to any male's territory. They tend to form small groups with which territorial males associate temporarily, sometimes almost permanently, according to local circumstances.

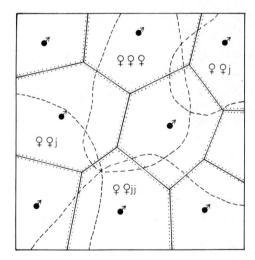

Fig. 49. Adult males inhabiting exclusive home ranges (= territories).
♂: adult male; ┅: boundary of male's home range/territory; ♀♀: small female group; j: juvenile(s) with female group; -----: home range of female group

Interindividual bonds are often more apparent than real, depending largely on spatial arrangements. The male on the one hand and the female group on the other may be attached more firmly to the area they inhabit than to one another although, of course, this is difficult to prove. Support for this statement comes from the observation (e. g., my own on gerenuk) that, in the adult male, "concern" for territorial affairs usually takes precedence over attachment to a female group, but this is not as obvious as in some species of SO-type 5 (see below).

Groups are generally small, rarely exceeding ten animals, and relatively unstable in their composition. This category corresponds to social class B of Jarman (1974).

SO-type 4. There are two kinds of social units: (1) the adult, usually territorial, male, (2) small groups of females and young. These social units, although often seen associated, are relatively independent of each other. Each inhabits a home range that may or may not coincide with that of the other.

This type of social organization has been described in some detail for the southern reedbuck (Jungius, 1971) and the gerenuk (Leuthold, 1971 c, and unpubl.). As I am more familiar with the gerenuk, I will use it as the principal example (the study was made in Tsavo NP):

Fully adult males are almost always found singly, with or without females, and generally well spaced out. The home ranges of a few individually known adult males measured $4-6 \, km^2$; they overlapped only slightly, if at all, and it was extremely rare to see another adult male within the home range of a given known one. From this and other evidence I concluded that most or all adult males in the population studied were territorial, each defending his entire home range, with minor exceptions. All groupings of more than one male consisted of subadult animals only; bachelor groups including nonterritorial adult males, common in some other antelope species (see below), were not observed. Whether this might be different in populations of higher density, remains an open question.

Females generally associate in small groups, with or without young animals, but a considerable proportion was recorded singly. Group sizes, including subadult males often attached to female groups, varied from 1–12, groups of 3–5 animals being most common. As only few females could be recognized individually, the stability of groups could not be adequately determined. What little evidence is available suggests that the groups are only loosely organized, that individual females, perhaps with their latest young, join and part "at will," and that the only coherent groupings consist of a female and her young, at least up to the time of the following parturition.

Home ranges of the few known females were of similar sizes as those of adult males. In two cases, they coincided more or less entirely with that of the "resident" male, but another female's home range included portions of two neighboring territories, although perhaps not permanently. On superficial observation one might gain the impression of a fairly stable male–female group (a small "harem") inhabiting the same home range. However, repeated and long-term observations indicate that (1) the female groups themselves are far from stable, and (2) the male is often observed alone, away from the females. This supports the statement made above that the territorial male and "his" female group represent two or more separate social units that are relatively independent of each other. In general, the male appears to be more "concerned" about maintaining contact with the females than vice versa; he often follows them when they move, while the females "couldn't care less" about the male's movements (Leuthold, 1971 c, p. 33).

A situation generally resembling that in gerenuk was found in the southern reedbuck (Jungius, 1971), but groups were rather smaller, often including one female only, so that the social system approached that of pair territories (see above, SO-type 3b). Again, the exact manifestation of the social organization is likely to be influenced by various environmental factors, in the reedbuck particularly by the availability and spatial distribution of suitable habitat. Nevertheless, I agree with Jarman (1974) in placing the species, and perhaps the other reedbucks as well (particularly R. redunca, see Hendrichs, 1975b), into this category of social organization.

The same may further apply to oribi (A. Monfort, 1972; Monfort and Monfort, 1974), rhebok (Pelea), and possibly bushbuck under certain conditions (Jarman, 1974). In the bushbuck of Nairobi NP Allsopp (1971) recorded no overlap of home ranges of adult males (although this point may not have received sufficient attention) but, on the other hand, he found no signs of overt defense of area. In Ruwenzori (Queen Elizabeth) NP, Waser (1975a, b) found a similar situation. It is, therefore, still not clear to which category of social organization the bushbuck conforms best.

The same is true for the other Tragelaphus species. Field research on these has begun only recently, probably at least partly because of the difficulties of observation in their normal habitat. Sufficiently detailed studies published to date (1975) include one on lesser kudu in Tsavo NP (Leuthold, 1974) and one on nyala in Mozambique (Tello and Van Gelder, 1975), while other research on nyala (J. L. Anderson, pers. comm.) and on greater kudu in Kruger NP (N. Owen-Smith, pers. comm.) has not yet been published. Owen's (1970) work on sitatunga provides at least a general picture of the species' social organization which, in any event, may be influenced somewhat by the very specific habitat it occupies.

Jarman (1974) placed lesser kudu, "and possibly bushbuck and sitatunga," in his class B (corresponding to our SO-type 4), nyala and greater kudu in class C (SO-type 5a, see below), the latter on the basis of his personal observations in southern Africa.

Both lesser kudu and nyala show several attributes of SO-type 4 (e. g., adult males usually found singly, or with female groups, fairly well spaced out), but home ranges of adult males overlap considerably, and no overt signs of defense of an area, or of advertizement, have been noticed. Thus, these species apparently do not show territoriality, as defined earlier (Chap. 15, C, II), in the strict sense. They may have other means—not yet identified—than spatial separation to establish and maintain a social organization based, presumably, on some system of dominance. Waser's (1975a, b) findings on bushbuck largely agree with those of other authors on lesser kudu and nyala. In view of these differences (then based only on my own work on lesser kudu) I tentatively placed the Tragelaphus species in a social category intermediate between territorial and nonterritorial bovids (Leuthold, 1974, p. 230 and Fig. 8). However, this interpretation needs to be substantiated by further studies, before it can be accepted as fully valid.

Nevertheless, in their general grouping patterns the smaller Tragelaphines largely correspond to SO-type 4, even though their relations to space may be somewhat different.

[In passing, we note that, if the separate status of Tragelaphines with respect to social organization and, particularly, territoriality, is confirmed, the social organization of the eland (see Chap. 16, A) would not differ as markedly from that of other antelopes as it appears at present.]

Territories discussed up to here have been "resource-based" ("resource" here being used in a relatively narrow sense): as they coincide with an individual's entire home range, they are likely to include more or less all basic necessities for life, such as food, water, shelter, etc. The occupant of such a territory can, theoretically, spend all his time within its boundaries without suffering any physical deprivations. Exceptions from this general rule are usually related to the nature and distribution of suitable habitat. The tall grass patches favored by the southern reedbuck may be temporarily unavailable, e.g., after a grass fire; this induces the animals to move outside their normal home range or territory (Jungius, 1971). Similar movements may result from temporary shortages of water.

E. Only Part of Home Range Exclusive, in Males Only: Mating Territory

Adult males establish territories usually comprising only a part—sometimes quite a small one—of their home range. These territories are not resource-based but rather of more or less exclusively social significance.

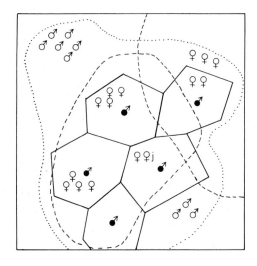

Fig. 50. Adult males using individual portions of their (often communal) home range exclusively (=mating territory). ●: adult male, territorial; ♂: adult male, nonterritorial ("bachelor"); —: territorial boundary; ·····: boundary of communal home range of all males; ♀♀♀♀ : female group/herd, with or without juveniles (*j*); -----: communal or overlapping home range(s) of female groups

SO-type 5a. The "Normal" Mating Territory. There are three kinds of social units: (1) single adult males on territories, (2) groups of females and young of variable size and composition, (3) groups of males, including some adult ones that are—temporarily at least—not territorial (bachelor herds). Except for more or less temporary associations between either territorial males or bachelor herds and female groups, the sexes are largely segregated. Home ranges of units (2) and (3) usually overlap and extend over several territories of (1); they may also include areas not occupied by territorial males (Fig. 50).

In a number of characteristics this type resembles the preceding category; the main differences are that, firstly, a male's territorial activities are usually restricted to part of his home range only; secondly, a variable but often substantial proportion of adult males, at any one time, is not territorial but, together with subadult males, forms bachelor herds; and thirdly, female groups are larger and generally more fluid in composition. They are basically free to move between different territories, although the territorial males make efforts to keep females within their boundaries ("herding"). No case is reliably reported of a permanent association between an adult male and a given female group (the so-called "harem" system) being the norm. Cases approaching such a situation may occasionally develop under certain conditions, such as the local existence of a small herd isolated from the range of a more coherent population (e. g., in impala of Nairobi NP: Leuthold, 1970b, p. 716).

This type of social organization is found in the majority of medium-sized and larger African antelopes, excepting those already mentioned in another context, with greater or lesser variations:

Waterbuck (Kiley-Worthington, 1965; de Vos and Dowsett, 1966; Spinage, 1969a, 1974; Hanks *et al.*, 1969; Child and von Richter, 1969); lechwe (de Vos and Dowsett, 1966, Child and von Richter, 1969); puku (same authors, and de Vos, 1965); Grant's gazelle (Walther, 1965a; 1968, 1972a, b; Estes, 1967); Thomson's gazelle (Brooks, 1961; Walther, 1964b, 1968; Estes, 1967); springbok (Bigalke, 1966, 1970, 1972); impala (Leuthold, 1970b; M. V. Jarman, 1970, 1973; Jarman and Jarman, 1973b, 1974; Anderson, 1972); Coke's hartebeest (Gosling, 1969, 1974, 1975); tsessebe (S. Joubert, 1972); topi (Vesey-Fitzgerald, 1955; N. Monfort-Braham, 1975; Monfort *et al.*, 1973; Jarman, 1974; Duncan, 1975); bontebok (David, 1973), blesbok (Lynch, 1971; Rowe-Rowe, 1973); blue wildebeest (Estes, 1966, 1969); black wildebeest (von Richter, 1971a, 1972).

Jarman (1974) also lists greater kudu and nyala as belonging to this type (his class C), but territoriality has not been established in these species (see above).

Jarman (1974) further treated most or all Alcelaphinae as a separate category (his Class D), primarily on the basis of their "facility for aggregation" (Fig. 51) and related propensity for nomadism. However, these traits, while prevalent in some species/populations, are neither characteristic of nor peculiar to the Alcelaphines. Under certain environmental conditions Thomson's gazelles (in the Serengeti), springbok (in South and South West Africa, at least formerly), white-eared kob (in the Sudan), and possibly other species form large aggregations and undertake considerable migrations or other movements. On the other hand, all Alcelaphines also occur in sedentary populations where their social organiza-

217

Fig. 51. Aggregation into very large herds is characteristic of migratory wildebeest, such as these in the Serengeti NP (from Kruuk, 1972)

tion essentially conforms to our category 5a. From the point of view of the social organization alone I therefore see no reason to treat the Alcelaphinae as a separate category (Jarman also took into consideration their feeding ecology, see Chap. 19).

Sable and roan are difficult to classify within the framework adopted here. Adult males of both species appear to be territorial (Estes and Estes, 1969, 1974; Grobler, 1974; S. Joubert, 1974), but densities are often so low that males are very widely spaced and territorial behavior may not be readily evident. Also, they may defend most or all of their normal home range, and bachelor herds are very small, if present at all. Female groups are usually larger than those in SO-type 4 (e. g., gerenuk), but tend to be more stable in composition than in many species of SO-type 5a. It is, therefore, difficult to assign the two species unequivocally to one or the other category. Similar situations sometimes occur in other species, e.g., Grant's gazelle (Walther, 1972a, b), or some Alcelaphinae; they serve to emphasize that a rigorous classification of social organizations accommodating all ungulate species is difficult, if not impossible, to achieve.

In addition to the antelopes mentioned above, one or two species of African Equidae also have territories that serve primarily for mating: Grévy's zebra, and probably the Somali wild ass (Klingel, 1969b, 1974a, b, 1975). A peculiarity of Grévy's zebra is the high degree of tolerance normally shown by a territorial male toward other adult males (cf. white rhinoceros, Chap. 16, F). Only when an estrous mare is present does he chase other males away; otherwise they are often free to move around on his territory. Here "exclusiveness" of the territory is clearly equivalent to "preventing others from engaging in certain activities" (see Chap. 15, C, II). Grévy's zebra represents one of very few cases

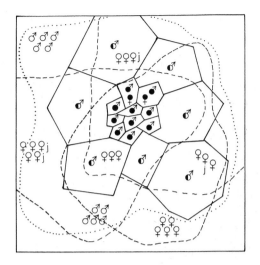

Fig. 52. The lek situation in the Uganda kob. Symbols as in Fig. 50 except that the ♂ denotes a male on a lek territory, ♂ one on a "single" territory and ♀ an estrous female on the lek

where species belonging to the same genus differ substantially in their social organization (cf. plains and mountain zebras, Chap. 16, A).

SO-type 5b. Arena or Lek Territoriality. Mating territories are very small and locally aggregated in dense clusters (arenas or leks: Fig. 52) that are maintained by tradition over considerable periods of time. Females in estrus leave their groups and enter an arena, where they mate with one or several territorial males. Social units are the same as in the preceding category.

This situation (Fig. 53) is definitely known only in the Uganda kob (Buechner, 1961, 1963; Buechner and Schloeth, 1965; Buechner and Roth, 1974; Leuthold, 1966a; Floody and Arnold, 1975). The lek system resembles that of some birds, e. g., several species of the Phasianidae and Tetraonidae, as well as a few seals, e. g., the northern fur seal (*Callorhinus ursinus*: Bartholomew and Hoel, 1953). Of particular interest is the fact that, in the Uganda kob, the arena system exists within a framework of normal territories corresponding more to those of SO-type 5a—the "single territories" of Leuthold (1966a)—from which it

Fig. 53. Part of arena of Uganda kob in Toro GR, Uganda. Note spacing between territorial males and short grass within arena

219

probably evolved (see Fig. 52). Indeed, under conditions of high density, some other antelope species may develop something approaching an arena system, the individual territories being relatively small and closely aggregated in "fields," e. g., in Thomson's gazelle and blue wildebeest in Ngorongoro Crater, Tanzania (Walther, 1964b, 1968; Estes, 1967, 1969). Territories of topi also occur in a similar arrangement locally (the "stamping grounds" of Vesey-Fitzgerald, 1955; see also N. Monfort-Braham, 1975, and Duncan, 1975), and those of puku in the Luangwa Valley, Zambia (de Vos, 1965) may also resemble a lek-type situation. For this reason, the arena system of the Uganda kob could justifiably be regarded as simply an extreme development within the category of mating territories described above (SO-type 5a), with which it shares most important attributes other than the spatial arrangement of the territories.

Among these attributes are the facts that (a) nonterritorial males are generally excluded from mating, (b) relations to environmental resources are different from those in the social systems described earlier, and (c) relative and absolute dominance occur within as well as between different social classes.

(a) Holding a territory is, with rare exceptions, the precondition for reproductive success. Under normal circumstances, males in bachelor herds hardly ever get an opportunity to mate with an estrous female. Holding a territory is thus tantamount to acquiring mating rights. It appears that the females themselves enforce this principle to a large extent through their reactions to sexual advances by males of different social status. While nonterritorial males often initiate premating behavior toward a (presumably) sexually attractive female, the latter usually avoids continuation of the sequence by running away, active rebuttal or, sometimes, lying down (see Chap. 13, A, II). On the other hand, estrous females generally tolerate approaches by territorial males much better, or they may even actively seek territorial males for mating, as is normal in the Uganda kob with its arena system. This state of affairs also helps to explain a feature of territoriality that has sometimes puzzled human observers with an anthropomorphically biased outlook, namely the fact that territorial defense usually takes precedence over sexual activities. For the male involved, preservation of his social status is more important in the long run than mating with a given female at a given moment, as holding a territory is itself the "key" to further matings (cf. Chap. 18).

(b) Whereas territories of SO-type 4 (gerenuk) usually contain all resources to fulfill at least the territorial male's requirements, and sometimes even those of the resident females, this often is not the case with mating territories of SO-type 5. In general, we may say that males establish territories in areas where females are "likely to occur because of attractive resources" (Jarman, 1974). However, since territories in this category are often small, and female groups relatively large, the latter have to move about to fulfill their own requirements. We may view the system as a combination of essentially stationary males spaced out at certain intervals, and mobile units of females and young wandering about within this network. The occurrence of females in any territory at any one time depends in large measure on the territory's contents of resources or—in other words—its location with respect to the most preferred habitat. Thus, there may be qualitative differences between individual territories, and

220

there is some evidence suggesting that these differences are reflected among the males holding the territories. Expressed crudely, the "fittest" (mainly in the physical sense) males tend to occupy the "best" territories (e. g., in impala: Jarman, 1974). However, this is certainly a great oversimplification, and the picture is complicated, firstly, by seasonal fluctuations in resource availability that may affect some territories differently than others and, secondly, by the attachment some males show for certain localities. In several species, individually known males tended to re-occupy the same territories that they held earlier, after a "spell" with the bachelor herd, e. g., in impala (Leuthold, 1970b; M. V. Jarman, 1973), wildebeest (Estes, 1969), hartebeest (Gosling, 1974), Uganda kob, on the leks and outside (Leuthold, 1966a; Buechner, Leuthold, unpubl.). Male waterbuck evicted from "prime" territories do not usually join a bachelor herd but establish themselves on "inferior" territories in less favorable habitat (Spinage, 1969a).

In the specialized arena system of Uganda kob the gradation in "quality" or "desirability" of different territories is particularly pronounced and readily evident. Single territories (Leuthold, 1966a; cf. Fig. 52) rank lowest in this scale, peripheral arena territories higher, and central arena territories highest. This is reflected in (1) the number of estrous females visiting the different territories, and (2) the intensity of male competition over them, as indicated by the frequency with which territory holders are exchanged. On a central arena territory a male may be able to hold his own for only one or a few days, while males on more peripheral and single territories may remain there for weeks or even months. Occasionally, a male that occupied a peripheral territory for some time "graduates" to become holder of a more central territory, but then risks being evicted much sooner than he would have been on his former territory. Again, it is the females who enforce this "value system" through their preference for the central arena territories. As a result, the frequencies of both sexual activity and agonistic encounters are highest on these central territories (Buechner and Schloeth, 1965; Buechner, Leuthold and Roth, unpubl.; Floody and Arnold, 1975).

(c) A male within his territory is normally dominant over all other conspecifics, except in the case of a challenge for territorial ownership. However, his dominance is relative, tied to his piece of land; once he leaves that he is compelled to "maintain a low profile" when encountering other territorial males. On the other hand, he may still be dominant over bachelor males, at least as long as he is not defeated and finally evicted from his territory. Recent studies have shown an absolute hierarchy to exist within bachelor herds of impala (M. V. Jarman, 1973) and hartebeest (Gosling, 1974), and it is not unreasonable to assume that this is the case in other species, too (as has sometimes been suspected, e. g., for Grant's gazelle: Estes, 1967). A male that has been defeated and driven off his former territory normally enters the bachelor hierarchy at a low level (at least with respect to other adult males, younger ones may still rank lower). As he recuperates from the strains of territorial life, developing into prime physical condition (cf. Stanley Price, 1974, with respect to hartebeest), he gradually advances in rank until, eventually, he reaches the top of the hierarchy. From there, he will go on to seek territorial status again, i. e., the leaves the absolute

221

hierarchy of the bachelor herd (without relinquishing his high status vis-à-vis the remaining bachelors) and re-enters the relative one of the territorial system. He enters, as it were, a different stratum in the overall social hierarchy; high rank in the bachelor herd is the "stepping stone" to establishing a territory. Behavior patterns associated with territoriality are exhibited with increasing frequency by males near the top of the bachelor hierarchy (M. V. Jarman, 1973).

Changes in territorial ownership are effected almost exclusively through fighting. Only rarely will a presumably "exhausted" male yield to another one without combat. Contests over territories are, in fact, the principal occasions on which serious fights occur (contrary to popular opinion, females are rarely the direct object of fighting). The victor in the fight will stay on the territory in question, the loser will have to leave and either join the bachelor herd (impala, kob, etc.) or set up a territory elsewhere (waterbuck). In a number of species the cycle outlined here may be repeated several times during a male's lifetime.

Interindividual relations in female groups may also be governed by an absolute hierarchy. Its expression is likely to be inversely related to herd size and cohesion, i. e., to be less pronounced in species commonly forming relatively large aggregations (e. g., impala, Uganda kob, Thomson's gazelle), but particularly well developed where groups tend to be relatively small and more stable in composition (e. g., sable, roan, Grant's gazelle). However, for most species insufficient information is available on this point.

In summary, we can say that there are probably as many variations of the basic pattern described here as there are species exhibiting this type of social organization. The range of variation is augmented even further by differences between local populations of the same species, related to environmental conditions (see Chap. 17). Nevertheless, three traits apply almost universally and thus characterize the pattern as a whole:

1. Territorial defense usually overrides sexual motivation in any given situation.
2. No female group is the exclusive property of any male, territorial or otherwise, i. e., males compete for possession of territories, not females.
3. Nonterritorial males are largely excluded from reproduction.
   Some of these features will be discussed further in Chapter 18.

F. Territory and Absolute Hierarchy Combined

SO-type 6. Exclusive home ranges in a portion of the adult males, with other adult males resident as subordinate "satellites" on some of the territories (Fig. 54). Social units are (1) adult territorial males, (2) adult satellite males, and (3) small female/young groups.

This interesting social system has only recently been discovered in the white (square-lipped) rhinoceros in South Africa (Owen-Smith, 1971, 1972, 1973, 1974, 1975).

222

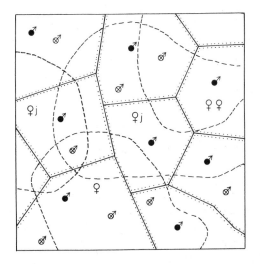

Fig. 54. Male territories combined with absolute hierarchy.
●: dominant territorial male; ♂: subordinate territorial male ("satellite"); ——: boundary of male territory/home range; -----: boundary of female home range

About two thirds of the adult males occupy territories incorporating their entire home ranges (areas of about 2 km²). Small groups of one or two females with their most recent offspring (up to six animals) inhabit overlapping home ranges of 10–12 km², covering parts or all of six to eight male territories. Temporary groups of two to five adolescent animals use similar home ranges, but some also range farther afield. So far, the system corresponds closely to our SO-type 4 (gerenuk). The important, and characteristic, difference lies in the behavior of the remaining one-third of adult males. Also living solitarily, each of them remains within the territory of another bull whom he accepts as dominant by either simply avoiding encounters, or by exhibiting specific submissive behavior. Up to three of these "satellite" bulls (Owen-Smith calls them "subsidiary" or β-males) may live on one territory. They exist as "social castrates," i. e., access to females in estrus is denied to them by the dominant territory owner; they can be regarded as the social equivalent of the bachelor herd in SO-type 5. This parallel is suggested by the fact that, occasionally, a satellite bull moves elsewhere to become territorial. Conversely, territorial bulls defeated by a rival may remain on their former territory but assume the role of satellite to the new occupant.

Of particular interest are some behavior patterns associated with different social status, suggesting important psychic changes accompanying the step from satellite to dominant bull, or vice versa. Dominant bulls urinate in a characteristic manner, emitting urine "in the form of a fine spray in three to five spasmodic bursts" (Owen-Smith, 1971, p. 297). They also scatter their dung, deposited at fixed sites, by kicking movements with their hindlegs. Satellite bulls neither spray their urine nor scatter their dung. Also, "a defeated territorial bull immediately ceases spray urination, and more gradually eliminates dung scattering" (Owen-Smith, 1974, p. 346). Such clear-cut behavioral correlates to social status have, to my knowledge, been recognized only rarely.

The white rhinoceros' social organization, although having various attributes in common with that of many other ungulates, nevertheless appears to be unique in its combination of well-defined relative dominance (territorial male vs other territorial males) and absolute dominance (a given territorial vs his satellite male).

For the black rhinoceros, results and interpretations of several field studies are at variance. Goddard (1967), working mainly in Ngorongoro Crater, Tanzania, found male home ranges (see Table 3) overlapping widely, with no evidence for territoriality. Schenkel (1966b; also Schenkel and Schenkel-Hulliger, 1969) concluded from studies in Kenya that the black rhino was not territorial. More recently, however, Hitchins (1971) presented observations from South Africa which suggest that the black rhino has a social organization closely resembling that of the white rhino. The existence of satellite males would have obscured actual territorial relationships to observers not aware of this possibility. Patterns of ritualized urination and defecation of the two species appear to be virtually identical, but it is not yet known how they are distributed among different social classes in the black rhinoceros.

There is a certain similarity between the social system of the white rhinoceros and that of Grévy's zebra. However, an important difference is that, in the latter species, the territorial male may tolerate virtually any other—nonterritorial—males on his territory, not just one or two specific individuals. The reason for this tolerance may lie in the large size of the territories (up to 10 km²: Klingel, 1974a, b), which makes it impractical to defend them against all other males.

Part 5
Behavior and Ecological Adaptation

In the preceding chapters I have reviewed certain behavioral categories in relative isolation, as if they were discrete and relatively immutable features developing to a typical form in each ungulate species. This approach has facilitated a comparative treatment, but it does not take into account the fact that behavior, just as morphological or physiological attributes, is part of the overall adaptive complex characterizing each species, or even each discrete population. Certain behavioral manifestations are, indeed, relatively constant within a species, particularly those that serve the more basic functions such as reproduction (e. g., mating behavior, mother-young relations and, to some degree, agonistic behavior). However, all those behaviors that are directly involved in an animal's interactions with its environment can be profoundly influenced and modified by local conditions and can, therefore, vary to a considerable extent between different populations of the same species. I have drawn attention to the influence of environmental factors on feeding behavior, activity patterns, etc., in the respective contexts (Chaps. 5 and 6). It now remains to examine the adaptability of the spatial and social organizations of African ungulates.

Increasing interest in the interrelationships between ecological conditions and behavior, including social organization, has led to the emergence of a relatively new discipline in biology. Depending on which aspects are emphasized most, it is variously called behavioral ecology, socio-ecology (Crook, 1970b) or sociobiology. Under the latter title Wilson (1975) has recently provided a comprehensive and in-depth review of this field of study. With respect to African ungulates, efforts to relate social behavior and organization to ecology have begun only recently, partly because the necessary descriptive information has not been available earlier. Jarman (1974) and Estes (1974) endeavored to draw together ecological and ethological observations on African bovids into a unified theoretical framework (see also Geist, 1974).

In the following chapters I attempt to review the importance of sociospatial behavior as an adaptive and/or adaptable feature, with regard to both the generalized species characteristics and the more specific circumstances of any given environment. Firstly, I will present some information on the variability of the spatial and social organization of African ungulates, in relation to different ecological conditions (Chap. 17). Then there will be a brief discussion of the probable functions of certain aspects of the social organization (Chap. 18), followed by consideration of socio-ecological hypotheses pertaining to African ungulates (Chap. 19). Finally I will present some examples and suggestions on how ethological information can be put to practical use in the management of wild and captive ungulates (Chap. 20).

Chapter 17

The Influence of Environmental Factors on the Spatial and Social Organization

In this chapter I will summarize information on how the spatial and/or social organization may vary within and between populations of the same species, under the influence of the local environment. This will demonstrate the flexibility of certain behavioral complexes that gives the species concerned a measure of adaptability, allowing it to thrive under sometimes quite different environmental conditions.

It is perhaps worth recalling here that virtually all of the best-studied African ungulates are savanna species. Even within this group, studies on the same species in different parts of its range are comparatively rare, so that the basis for discussing the degree of adaptability is still rather narrow. Next to nothing is known, in this respect, on both forest and desert ungulates.

A. Movements and Home Range

Changes in the distribution and abundance of food and water supplies largely determine the nature and extent of movements, and with them the size of the home range of any individual, group, or population of ungulates. The resultant patterns of habitat utilization vary according to whether the underlying changes are relatively regular in their spatial and temporal occurrence, and according to their magnitude in terms of both quantity and quality. In the final anlysis, these patterns can almost always be related to climatic conditions, in particular the amount and distribution of rainfall, and the resultant pattern of plant growth.

A good example to illustrate this point is the elephant, in which home ranges of family groups vary from 15–50 km^2 in Lake Manyara NP, with favorable and relatively stable conditions (though home ranges may be unnaturally constricted, due to human settlement around the park). By contrast, in Tsavo East NP, with a rather harsh and unstable environment, they may measure up to, and even over, 3000 km^2 (Table 3). Generally, no large-scale displacements occur in Manyara NP (Douglas-Hamilton, 1972, 1975), whereas in Tsavo East movements over 40–50 km within a few days are not unusual, but entirely unpredictable. They occur in fairly direct response to the often very localized rainstorms characteristic of that area (Leuthold and Sale, 1973) and may thus be termed "opportunistic." They contrast with the more regular migrations of wildebeest, zebra and some other species in the Serengeti area, which are largely—though not entirely—predictable in time and in space (Fig. 11). In those species, there are pronounced differences in home range sizes and extent of movements between the Serengeti populations and those in the nearby Ngorongoro Crater. In the latter, zebra (Klingel, 1967, 1969a) and wildebeest (Estes, 1969, in press) live in home ranges rarely exceeding 200–250 km², whereas the Serengeti animals range over several thousand km² in the course of a year (Table 3). Buffalo in Manyara NP remain within less than 50 km² throughout the year, while the annual home range of a herd in the Serengeti covered approximately 450 km² (derived from Fig. 3 in Sinclair, 1974), some portions being used primarily in the wet, others mainly in the dry season.

Seasonal variations in location and size of home ranges are, in fact, very common; some examples have been given earlier (Chap. 6). The nature and extent of such variations depend largely on environmental conditions. In the elephant, again, we find relatively little seasonal change in the extent of home ranges in Lake Manyara NP, whereas such changes are very marked in Tsavo NP. Here, individual elephants and/or groups tend to remain within a small area (a few hundred km² at most) during the dry season, from which they disperse into much larger (1000–2000 km² and more) wet-season ranges according to the rainfall pattern (Leuthold and Sale, 1973, and unpubl.).

Comparative information on home ranges in different populations of individual ungulate species is still relatively scarce (cf. Table 3), but the examples given above suffice to substantiate the point made here: certain behavioral traits—in this case movements and home range size—are highly flexible and can be adapted to a considerable range of environmental conditions.

B. Social Organization

In a number of instances, different populations of a given species differ to a greater or lesser extent in their social organization, or at least in some of its aspects. Such differences are generally also related to environmental conditions. In other cases, the social organization within a given population may change in the course of the year, usually on a seasonal basis related to climatic cycles.

I. Sedentary versus Migratory Populations

The blue wildebeest, and a few other ungulate species, exist in sedentary populations inhabiting the same area throughout the year, and migratory ones moving over several hundred kilometers annually. Sedentary and migratory populations differ markedly in several aspects of their social organization. Perhaps the best-documented example is that of the Serengeti and Ngorongoro wildebeest. A substantial proportion of the Ngorongoro wildebeest is sedentary; a network of mating territories (corresponding to the impala type, see Chap. 16, E) is maintained throughout the year, even though breeding is strictly seasonal. Females and their young form fairly coherent groups numbering about ten animals each, which sometimes coalesce into larger aggregations. Nonterritorial males live in bachelor herds that are normally segregated from the female groups. This social organization remains more or less the same throughout the year, with minor variations at the times of rutting and calving; a few males are known to have remained on the same territories for over two years (Estes, 1966, 1969). In the Serengeti, by contrast, wildebeest are migratory, spending only a few months at a time in the same area (Fig. 11; see also Pennycuick, 1975). They tend to form large aggregations numbering tens and occasionally hundreds of thousands (Fig. 51; see Inglis, 1976) and containing animals of both sexes, with little or no apparent segregation. Territoriality is largely confined to the relatively short rutting season during which the herds are migrating, and is considerably attenuated, compared to the sedentary populations. Adult males, while moving along with the main herds, set up temporary territories from time to time, in which they try to herd females and mate with them. After a few hours, or at the most a few days, they abandon these territories, move on to catch up or even get ahead of the migrating aggregations, and establish new, equally temporary, territories at their next "stop-over" (Walther, 1966a; Estes, 1969). Thus, territoriality, as a means of obtaining mating rights, is practiced, one might say, to the "minimum extent necessary." Overall, the social organization of the Serengeti wildebeest appears quite different from that of the sedentary population in Ngorongoro, being characterized particularly by the huge aggregations, in conjunction with high mobility. (The situation is complicated somewhat by the fact that a small migratory population also uses Ngorongoro Crater, mainly during the dry season, and that a small sedentary population exists in the western portion of the Serengeti: Estes, 1969; see Fig. 11). Similar differences between separate wildebeest populations have also been found in southern Africa; but this should not be taken to imply that there is a fundamental divergence between such populations. Rather, the two forms of social organization described here probably represent extremes of what may be a continuum of adaptive responses. Some evidence indicates that migratory populations, or portions of them, can become sedentary if environmental conditions improve sufficiently. Estes (1969, p. 364) sums up this situation as follows: "the duration and amplitude of nomadism is flexibly adapted to long- and short-term environmental influences; these same influences govern the expression of territorial behavior."

Similar, but considerably less pronounced differences are evident between Ngorongoro and Serengeti populations of Grant's and Thomson's gazelles. In both species, males occupy mating territories the year round in Ngorongoro Crater, the population as a whole being sedentary. In the Serengeti, some portions of the populations are migratory to a greater or lesser extent; males also occupy mating territories but in many cases only for part of the year. While migrating, Thomson's gazelles in Serengeti form large aggregations including animals of both sexes, as do the migratory wildebeest and, to a lesser extent, also Grant's gazelle. Both gazelle species show a whole range of gradations between entirely sedentary and markedly migratory populations—or population segments— within the Serengeti ecosystem, as well as year-to-year variations related to climatic conditions (Walther, 1968, 1972a).

Interestingly enough, corresponding differences do not occur between zebra populations of Ngorongoro and Serengeti, or are at least far less obvious, even though one is essentially sedentary and the other migratory, as in wildebeest. At the most, there is a greater tendency toward forming large aggregations in the Serengeti, but this may simply be a consequence of the considerably larger size of the population involved. Most likely, this lack of differences is related to the zebra's particular type of social organization: the system of stable family groups is equally well suited to a sedentary as to a migratory way of life. By contrast, the marked territoriality of the sedentary bovid populations mentioned above cannot be feasibly maintained in a migratory population, and the necessary modifications have pronounced effects upon general grouping patterns. In those species, the differences between populations in social organization are clearly interrelated with those in home ranges and movements, all being ultimately caused by differences in environmental conditions, acting presumably through the food supply and perhaps other features of the local environments (competition from other herbivores, predation pressure, etc.).

II. Seasonal Changes Within Populations

In some ungulate populations, the social organization undergoes profound changes in the course of the year, while in others there may be less pronounced seasonal variations. In many cases, there are clear-cut, in others less obvious relationships to reproduction, particularly where the latter is markedly seasonal. Most or all these changes are ultimately related to seasonal fluctuations in food and water supplies and thus indirectly to environmental factors such as rainfall.

A good example to illustrate such a situation is the impala. In southern Africa, under subtropical conditions, there is a pronounced annual cycle, characterized by a short lambing season in November and a correspondingly short rutting season in April/May. During the latter, a proportion of the adult males is territorial, but for the rest of the year most territories are abandoned and the males concerned join bachelor groups that may intermingle with female herds (Anderson, 1972; Jarman and Jarman, 1973b, 1974). By contrast, in the tropical climate of East Africa impala breed throughout the year (though with seasonal peaks in some areas) and males occupy mating territories the year round (Leuthold, 1970b; Jarman and Jarman, 1973b, 1974). Only under unusually adverse conditions, such as prolonged drought, does the territorial system occasionally break down, but as soon as conditions return to normal, it is re-established much as before (M. V. Jarman, 1970). But even though the system as a whole appears quite stable on an annual basis, there are seasonal variations in grouping patterns that can be related to the temporal distribution of rainfall (Jarman, 1974, see below).

In some ways, the situation of impala in southern Africa is comparable to that of the migratory wildebeest in that territoriality, the behavioral mechanism governing and distributing mating rights (see Chap. 18), is "invoked" only when it is "needed," i.e., at rutting time, and is dispensed with for the rest of the year, when it might interfere with movements and dispersion patterns related to environmental conditions. This intraspecific flexibility of the social organization enables the species concerned to successfully occupy habitats that they could not thrive in, if they had only one more or less fixed pattern at their disposal.

In many ungulate populations, relatively minor changes in social organization occur seasonally; the easiest to measure are variations in mean group size. The direction and magnitude of such changes differ from species to species, and from one population to another, being part of the overall adaptation to a given environment.

For instance, herds of buffalo in the Serengeti NP, numbering several hundred and up to 2,000 head, tend to split up in the dry season, so that mean herd size becomes significantly lower than in the wet season. This is explained chiefly as an adaptation to a diminished and more localized food supply in the dry season (Sinclair, 1970, 1974; see also Pienaar, 1969). Similarly, mean group size of elephants in Tsavo NP tends to be lower in the dry than in the wet season. During the latter, elephants often congregate in large numbers in areas of temporarily abundant food supplies; many family units and bull groups may join up to form temporary herds numbering several hundred and occasionally over 1,000 animals. As the dry season progresses, these herds gradually split up again, eventually to the level of individual family units in most cases. The variations in mean group size are correlated with rainfall, at least in parts of Tsavo NP (Leuthold, 1976).

Corresponding changes in mean group size, during the course of the year, have been recorded in wildebeest and impala of the Selous Game Reserve, Tanzania (Rodgers, 1977) and for impala in the Serengeti NP and some other areas (Jarman and Jarman, 1974). In all cases, they are correlated with rainfall in one way or another, with a different time lag in different areas. The real cause underlying the variations is, most likely, the changing food supply, but since measurements of food supply are only rarely available and since, in any event, plant growth is governed largely by rainfall, the "secondary" correlation with rainfall is a useful substitute for the (presumed) "primary" one with the food supply. The seasonal changes in mean group size probably reduce intragroup competition for food during the dry season, while allowing some as yet largely unexplained social interactions to take place in times and areas of abundant food supply.

In other species, and under different circumstances, groups may be larger in the dry season. For instance, in Grant's gazelle of the Serengeti originally segregated male and female groups coalesce into mixed groupings during parts of the dry season; this process is usually associated with migration (Walther, 1972a). Waterbuck in parts of Tsavo NP are forced to concentrate in a relatively small area of suitable habitat that remains in the dry season. This results in a significant increase in mean group size over wet-season values (Leuthold and Leuthold, 1975a). Corresponding changes have been recorded in other waterbuck populations (e. g., Hanks et al., 1969). In fact, when food and water become restricted to small areas, various ungulates may aggregate in such localities in considerable numbers, reversing the otherwise prevalent trend toward smaller groups in the dry season.

Another factor that may influence group size seasonally and/or locally is fire, through its effect on the vegetation. When the grass is burned in the dry season, the new vegetation emerging there later is usually more nutritious for some time than that in adjacent areas. This may lead to local and temporary concentrations of ungulates, which can also obscure otherwise existing seasonal trends in mean group size and their relation to such environmental factors as rainfall.

III. Influences of the Local Environment on Social Organization

This title requires a word of explanation as, of course, the two preceding sections have also been concerned with environment. However, in the first one (Chap. 17, B, I) we have dealt with the relatively specific situation of a given species forming sedentary and migratory populations, while in the second one (Chap. 17, B, II) we have examined the effects of seasonal climatic changes on the social organization within a given population. In the following, we will consider how certain environmental features, such as vegetation structure, relative aridity, etc., affect some aspects of the social organization, so as to produce more or less marked differences between conspecific populations.

1. Vegetation Structure

Several African ungulates tend to form larger herds in open country, i. e., grassland, etc., than in bushed or wooded habitats. Grant's gazelle in the Serengeti NP sometimes assembled in herds of up to 400 individuals on the open short-grass plains, while the largest herd seen in the bush/woodland areas numbered 37 (Walther, 1972a). A similar relationship was found for impala in Nairobi NP (Leuthold, 1970b) and apparently applies throughout the species' range (Jarman, pers. comm.; see also Monfort et al., 1973). In Tsavo NP, four out of seven ungulate species studied in this respect formed significantly larger groups in an area with more open vegetation; in two other species mean group size was also higher in the more open area, but the differences were not statistically significant (possibly due to inadequate sample sizes); only the warthog showed no difference in mean group size between open and more bushy vegetation (Leuthold and Leuthold, 1975a). In elephants of Tsavo NP, too, groups tended to be smaller in the wooded parts of the park, and larger in more open vegetation types (Leuthold, 1976). On a different geographic scale, this relationship is perhaps most pronounced in buffalo, with herds numbering only 20–50 head in dense forest but several hundred animals in more open habitats (Sinclair, 1970, 1974).

Apparently, this principle not only applies within, but also between species: ungulates living primarily in forest and bush habitats form smaller groups, in general, than those inhabiting mainly open country (Jarman, 1974; Estes, 1974; see Chap. 19). Thus, vegetation structure obviously has an important effect on grouping patterns of ungulates. It is, of course, easy to visualize how woody vegetation may interfere with the formation and cohesion of large groups, particularly where visual communication is important in this context (see also Chap. 19).

Obstruction of visual contact by woody vegetation may also be responsible for some variations in the expression of certain social behavior patterns. For instance, in topi of the Akagera NP, Rwanda, Monfort *et al.* (1973) and N. Monfort-Braham (1975) reported considerable variations in the manifestation of territoriality, which were apparently related to vegetation structure. In more wooded areas territories were comparatively large, and each contained a more or less stable female group along with the territorial male. In areas of open grassland, territories were very small and locally aggregated, in a manner similar to the arenas of Uganda kob, and individual females left their herds and moved to these "arenas" to consort with territorial males. At the same time, the two areas supported quite different densities of topi, and it is not clear whether the observed differences in sociospatial organization were related primarily to density or to vegetation type per se (see further discussion below). In topi of the Serengeti NP, Duncan (1975) found a virtually identical situation, with corresponding differences between different vegetation types.

The effects of vegetation structure on several aspects of the social organization combine to produce the sometimes considerable differences found between individual populations, or population segments, of the same species. For instance, the impala of Somali Ridge in Nairobi NP, an area of open grassland with few bushes and trees, were usually concentrated in only two female herds of approximately 50 animals, each normally associated with a territorial male, and one bachelor herd of 30–40 males. By contrast, in the Forest area—only 3–4 km away—where patches of forest and bush were interspersed with small grassy areas, impala occurred in much smaller groups that also varied considerably in composition, and a substantial proportion of female groups, at any one time, were not associated with a territorial male (Leuthold, 1970b). These differences between the two areas can be attributed mainly to the differences in vegetation cover. Not only were groups basically smaller in the Forest area, because of the forest, but also the herding activities of territorial males may have been impeded by the woody vegetation; the overall effect was a general fragmentation and fluidity with regard to group formation. On Somali Ridge, unrestricted visibility favored the generally marked tendency of impala toward gregariousness and allowed territorial males a maximum of "control" over the females' movements; all this resulted in relatively large and stable herds.

2. Rainfall and Degree of Aridity

Given similar vegetation structure, certain ungulate species tend to form larger groups in areas of higher rainfall than in more arid ones. Comparative information on this point is still rather scarce, but the following examples support this statement: in the Serengeti NP (annual rainfall 800–1,000 mm) herds of buffalo commonly number over 300–400, and occasionally up to 2,000 animals (Sinclair, 1970, 1974), whereas in Tsavo NP (annual rainfall 400–600 mm) herds of over 300 animals are relatively rare and the largest herd recorded in recent years comprised about 500 head. In impala, I found similar differences between Serengeti and Tsavo populations, and the relationship between rainfall and mean group size has been documented over large portions of the species' range (Jarman, pers. comm.). Klingel (1967) commented that the small group size of plains zebra in the Etosha NP of South-West Africa was perhaps related to the "harsh" conditions there.

Obviously, rainfall per se is unlikely to have a direct effect on group size, but rather an indirect one, via the food supply. Rainfall is the main determinant of primary productivity, in many areas, and thus probably acts through the overall "resource levels" available to different populations. We may look at this relationship between geographically distant areas as a parallel to the process operating seasonally within a given area, as described earlier.

However, rainfall also has some influence on vegetation type and structure, and it may be difficult to identify the relative importance of different factors in the environment which, in any case, may be interrelated in various ways. This applies to the following section as well.

3. Population Density

Various aspects of the social organization may also be influenced by population density, for instance group size, the expression of territoriality, etc. Quantitative information on such relationships is as yet very sparse, but several authors at least suspect their existence from qualitative observations.

In waterbuck of Ruwenzori (Queen Elizabeth) NP, Uganda, Spinage (1969a) found a positive correlation between density and mean size of female groups. Laws (1974) presented data suggesting a similar relationship in elephants of Kabalega (Murchison Falls) NP. Estes (1974) listed several differences in home range size, movement patterns and herd sizes between different populations of sable antelope, some of which appear to be related to population density. Territorial behavior is usually most pronounced in populations of high density, partly because competition for the available territories tends to be more severe. The development of lek behavior in the Uganda kob may also depend on density and/or absolute population size (Leuthold, 1966a).

Of course, population density is itself determined largely by environmental conditions. It may, therefore, often be difficult to decide which factor is responsible for which phenomenon, and in many cases a separation of influences may be impossible altogether. Thus, certain differences in social organization of local impala populations in the Akagera NP were attributed primarily to population density by Monfort et al. (1973), whereas they connected similar differences among topi with both vegetation structure and population density (see above). However, whilst it is always desirable to identify the factor(s) operating in any given situation, the salient point here is that spatial and social organizations are flexible and can be adjusted to a considerable range of environmental conditions (a "side effect" of this flexibility may be the sometimes conflicting statements in the literature concerning the social organization of a given species!).

As a final, and most interesting, example I wish to mention the Bohor reedbuck. Though not studied yet in detail, it is generally thought (e. g., Dorst and Dandelot, 1970; Jarman, 1974) to have a sociospatial organization similar to that of the southern reedbuck, with groups rarely exceeding three or four animals (Jungius, 1971; see Chap. 16, D). Yet in the Dinder NP in southeastern

Sudan, this species was found to form large herds, several of them numbering over 100 animals, the largest comprising about 400 head (Holsworth, 1972). Whether this was a normal situation or only a temporary phenomenon remains to be established, but I received similar reports nearly 10 years earlier from A. C. Brooks (pers. comm.). Perhaps more such cases of intraspecific variation will be discovered once field research is extended to the more remote, up to now neglected areas of Africa, such as the Sudan, much of Central and West Africa, the Saharan and Sahelian zones, Angola, etc. Further comparative studies on individual species in different parts of their geographic range, along the lines of those on impala by Jarman and Jarman (1973b, 1974), are likely to be rewarding.

Chapter 18

Functional Aspects of Certain Social Behaviors

While reviewing the various behavioral categories earlier on, I have repeatedly discussed functional aspects in the respective contexts, particularly with regard to behaviors operating primarily at the level of the individual (e. g., home range, activity patterns, sexual and mother-young behavior). It remains now to do the same for certain aspects of social behavior and social organization, which have important ecological implications at higher levels, i.e., those of the group, herd or population.

A. Gregariousness

In the review of social organizations (Chap. 16) we have seen that African ungulates occur in a wide variety of social groupings, ranging from solitary individuals to herds of several thousands. The question immediately arises as to what governs the size of groups formed by the various species. While this question will be dealt with more extensively below (Chap. 19) we may, for the time being, briefly discuss the question of why groups and herds are formed at all. Since a considerable number of ungulates lead largely solitary lives or form pairs only, it is not immediately evident why others should unite in larger groups or herds.

Most ethologists agree that gregariousness—in ungulates as well as in other mammals, birds or fish—is primarily an antipredator adaptation (e. g., Eibl-Eibesfeldt, 1967/70; Ewer, 1968), and this idea has been elaborated with respect to African ungulates by Jarman (1974). The main lines of reasoning are that (1) several animals together have a higher probability of detecting a predator before it is ready to attack (improved predator detection), (2) an individual's chance of being singled out for attack and caught by a predator is lower in a group than when it is alone ("safety in numbers"), (3) at least in some species, a group may successfully defend itself against a predator in a concerted action, where a single animal could not (communal defense). These arguments, though still largely hypothetical, appear even more plausible when seen in the overall context of each species' socio-ecological adaptations, to be discussed in Chapter 19. For instance, it is primarily the small-bodied species of closed habitats that live singly or in pairs and rely mainly on cryptic behavior as an antipredator strategy. By contrast, those forming larger groups are mainly species of greater body size and inhabiting open habitats; they tend to flee rather than hide from predators. Herd formation therefore appears to be primarily an adaptation to life in open country, with special regard to antipredator behavior (Jarman, 1974; Estes, 1974). One may go even as far as to say that, functionally, herd formation is equivalent to seeking cover, as an extension of argument (2) above (Hamilton, 1971, in Estes, 1974).

While much of this functional explanation of gregariousness remains hypothetical, a few recent field studies have produced evidence supporting these hypotheses. Both Kruuk (1972) and Schaller (1972) emphasized the importance of protection through group formation, particularly in relation to cursorial predators such as spotted hyena, cheetah and wild dog. In many cases, these predators abandoned a chase if they failed to isolate an individual from its group. Schaller (1972, p. 257 and Table 61) further found that, with respect to Thomson's gazelle, zebra and wildebeest, lions hunting single animals generally were more successful than when stalking animals in groups. Sinclair (1970, 1974) found that among old male buffalo that lived singly or in small groups, rather than in the large breeding herds, significantly more were killed by lions than would have been expected on the basis of their proportions in the total population (the age structure being similar in both samples). The inference is that large herds provided better protection against predation than the small bachelor groups. Several studies on predation mention that male ungulates fall prey to carnivores more often than females, at least partly because males generally live in smaller and less coordinated herds than females. However, in such studies it is not always possible to eliminate certain biases, e.g., the fact that the remains of horned males are found relatively more often than those of hornless females (where applicable), and that old males may be in relatively poor physical condition, which may make them a priori more vulnerable to predation, in addition to being excluded from the presumed protection afforded by a herd.

Further evidence for the protective function of a herd has emerged from the study of calf mortality in blue wildebeest of Ngorongoro Crater. Calves born in large herds suffered proportionally lower predation (mainly by spotted hyaenas) than those born in smaller herds. The rate of predation was further affected by the degree of synchrony of births which, in turn, was also related to some extent to herd size (Estes, 1976). In impala, females with small young tend to rejoin a herd sooner after parturition if there are already several calves in the herd than if there are none. This involves a reduction of the hiding period and is interpreted as ensuring that the calf is not an "outstanding member" of the herd (Jarman, 1974).

Estes (1974) further suggests the existence of a purely psychological basis for the formation of a group which, by implication, affords the animal a feeling of "security," analogous to being in cover. As supporting evidence he quotes the general "uneasiness" often noted in isolated individuals of gregarious species, and specific instances where single animals (in his example sable antelopes) looked up considerably more often while grazing than did animals in a group. In my view, this "psychological factor" may be a secondary consequence of the antipredation benefits of gregariousness: the uneasiness reinforces the individual's efforts to rejoin the group and partake in those benefits.

While antipredation effects have almost certainly provided the main evolutionary impetus toward gregariousness, at least in open-country species, other benefi-

237

cial consequences of group formation can be envisaged, too. For instance, a patchily dispersed food source can possibly be exploited more efficiently by a group than by single individuals who might spend relatively more time actually locating the patches. Also, animals grazing together in some number may keep the herb layer (especially grasses) in a continually growing condition, and thus in a state offering better nutrition, than single dispersed individuals. One could further imagine that traditional information on features of the habitat (e.g., migration routes, emergency food and/or water supplies) can be transmitted more efficiently and more securely within larger social units than within single mother-young pairs. It is probably no coincidence that virtually all migratory, or otherwise highly mobile, ungulates are also fairly to very gregarious (although this may have other main causes).

B. Dominance

We have defined dominance (Chap. 15, C, I) as an attribute according the "holder" preferential access to certain resources. We must now examine what resources are involved and discuss the ecological implications of differential apportionment of such resources within a population. As these implications are more readily evident in the context of space-related dominance, I will begin by discussing some of the ecological aspects of territoriality.

I. Territoriality

I wish to make clear right at the outset that much of what follows is still largely hypothetical, as it is very difficult to demonstrate conclusively any ecological consequences of territoriality, however plausible these may appear. We need only look at the ornithological literature, where the subject has been discussed for much longer than with respect to ungulates, to realize that functional interpretations of territoriality are far from settled.

One of the most prominent hypotheses that emerged from the ornithological literature (e.g., Kluyver and Tinbergen, 1953) was the idea that territoriality can regulate population density (for reviews see Wynne-Edwards, 1962; Watson and Moss, 1970). One qualification is immediately necessary in this context, if we look at ungulates: population density can only be regulated through territoriality under a system where the territory encompasses more or less the entire home range, i.e., includes all resources necessary for the occupant(s) to survive and reproduce. Such systems are relatively rare among African ungulates (see Chap. 16); if, as is possible, one may further have to stipulate monogamy to envisage self-regulation of the population through territoriality (via the food supply monopolized by each territory holder), then the "eligible" cases become very few (e.g., dikdik, see Chap. 16, C). Therefore, while a regulatory effect on population may possibly occur in a few species, it is highly unlikely to be of general importance to the majority of African ungulates, most of which have polygynous to promiscuous mating systems and territories (if present) that do not conform to the stipulations made above. A recent study in which the possible regulatory influence of territoriality on population density in water-buck was critically evaluated led to the conclusion that such influence was either absent or unimportant (Spinage, 1974). Thus, the main functions of ungulate territoriality must be looked for in other contexts.

Among males of territorial species, mating is virtually confined to territory holders, whereas members of bachelor herds, or other nonterritorial males, achieve very few if any copulations. This suggests that holding a territory is a prerequisite to successful reproduction. In other words, possession of a territory provides its occupant with exclusive mating rights with respect to any females that may be present on the territory. This has been confirmed, at least by implication, in many field studies. The situation is particularly clearcut in the extreme case of the Uganda kob where the territories, clustered tightly on spatially fixed leks, serve no other detectable function than that of mating stations which are visited by estrous females. In other species, territories may be less exclusively oriented toward mating only, but serve other functions as well; we shall review them shortly.

For the time being, we may ask what advantages accrue by restricting mating to established territorial males. Two main points are normally considered impor-tant in this context:
1. Limitation of interference in reproductive activities
2. Selection of the "fittest" males for breeding

A territory holder is, ipso facto, normally dominant over other males that may be on his territory. This makes it relatively easy for him to control their activities, at least to a certain extent, and in particular to restrict their access to any estrous females that may also be present. We have seen that the events leading to successful mating are often complicated and drawn-out behavioral sequences (Chap. 13). Any interference by other animals present, and particularly by other males, is likely to interrupt this sequence and therefore prevent mating. Although this seems plausible enough in theory, there are relatively few actual observations documenting such situations. Klingel (1974b, p. 127) describes one as follows: "I observed an estrous mare (of Grévy's zebra) in an area without territories. For two hours she was courted by up to nine stallions at a time. These stallions were practically continuously fighting each other and therefore none of them succeeded in copulating with the mare. The group eventually moved into a territory where the territorial stallion took over. The other stallions moved away while he copulated with the mare." In impala, I observed a similar situation when a territorial male, on whose territory there was a female herd, became engaged in a fight with another adult male. A nearby bachelor herd "took advantage" of his absence and started mingling with the females, approach-ing and chasing some of them in courtship postures, creating considerable commo-tion and disorder (Leuthold, 1970b). While there was no obviously estrous female among the impala, the implication was clearly that the males were "looking for" one, but they succeeded only in frightening the females and creating chaos temporarily. In both of these cases it is fairly clear that the presence of the territorial male suppressed courting behavior in the other males. Thus, the idea of territories serving to limit interference in mating is supported by these observations (see also Gosling, 1975).

Another function of territories has often been postulated but remains to be properly substantiated (difficult though this may be): that of selection of the physically fittest males for breeding purposes, through competition for territories. In a number of field studies it has become evident that, among male ungulates, there is little if any direct competition over females, but that such competition is directed primarily at attaining high social status, i.e., dominance (absolute or relative, as the case may be). The offshoot of this is that competition, or conflict, over territories almost always overrides that over females. In practical terms, this means that a territorial male normally will not intrude upon another male's territory to gain access to an estrous female there; or if he has an estrous female on his territory, he will interrupt courtship and leave her to threaten or fight another male that may have entered his territory. Assertion of territorial "sovereignty" thus takes precedence over utilizing opportunities for mating. Again, this is most clearly demonstrated in the Uganda kob, where females may wander more or less at will from one territory to another, without the respective territory holders following them beyond the territorial boundary (although each may attempt to prevent the females from leaving his territory).

Thus, the occupancy of a territory is the prime objective of social competition among males, and opportunities for reproduction result secondarily from success in this competition. The latter is therefore highly likely to act as a strong selective force among the males. This assumption is supported by the facts that (1) in the more gregarious species only a fraction of the adult males usually hold a territory at any one time (e.g., "about one third" in impala: Jarman and Jarman, 1973b; less than 50% in Uganda kob: Leuthold, 1966a), and (2) displacements of territory holders by other, previously nonterritorial males occur with varying frequency in many species. Where territoriality lasts throughout the year, but breeding is seasonally restricted, as in blue wildebeest in Ngorongoro Crater, the frequency of such interchanges is highest during the rutting period (Estes, 1969, 1974). Jarman and Jarman (1974, p. 875) suggested that, in impala of the Serengeti, "prime-age males," i.e., presumably the "fittest," tended to occupy most territories during periods of highest conception frequency. These last examples also emphasize the link between territoriality and reproductive activities, while nevertheless supporting the basic tenet that males compete primarily for territories.

Male ungulates are subject to the effects of this competition from a very early age, often from the time of weaning (at about six months in many species). Territorial males tend to harass these young males to the extent that they eventually leave their mothers' groups and may wander around alone until they can join a bachelor herd. In the latter, they will be the lowest-ranking members and therefore probably subject to more harassment. Thus, during this transitional period, their food intake may be somewhat reduced, their resting time may be less than for others, while they may incur a relatively high energy expenditure through continually avoiding contacts with higher-ranking males. In addition, the fact that they may wander alone, or be with a relatively small

240

and loosely knit male group, may expose them to higher risks of predation than if they had stayed with a female herd. All these factors combine to produce an age/sex-specific mortality rate considerably higher than in females; this has been well documented in impala (Jarman and Jarman, 1973b) and is likely to apply to other species with a similar social system. This high mortality in juvenile and/or subadult males may well be the primary cause of the unbalanced adult sex ratio commonly found in gregarious bovids (adult ♂♂ : adult ♀♀ often ca. 0.5–0.7 : 1).

This influence on the sex ratio is one of the additional effects that territoriality may have on the population practicing it. Others are related to the dispersion of the population within its habitat. For instance, a network of relatively evenly spaced territorial males may contribute to breaking up potentially large and dense aggregations of females and young that might exert too much pressure on the local food supply. There is an upper limit to the size of a female herd that a male can "manage" on his territory; in very dense populations the activities of territorial males will, therefore, tend to space out female herds in a pattern similar to their own spacing (e. g., Estes, 1969, 1974).

By analogy, Buechner (1963) suggested that the spacing of leks in the Toro Game Reserve, Uganda, might contribute to a relatively even dispersion of the Uganda kob population over the available habitat and help to prevent local overutilization of the food supply. This is, however, less directly related to territoriality as such than the situation in, e. g., wildebeest.

Furthermore, male territoriality may bring about a differential distribution of population segments with respect to available resources (food, water). This has been demonstrated in the impala (Jarman and Jarman, 1973b) where male herds were absent from certain parts of the area used by females, for no other apparent reason than as a consequence of activities of territorial males. The inference here is that "prime" territorial males tend to occupy the best portions of habitat, in terms of resource availability, which are normally also those used preferentially by females. Bachelor herds being excluded from these areas, at least to some extent, are automatically relegated to somewhat inferior habitat. Several authors have commented that, under a territorial system, bachelor herds, single nonterritorial males, and also some less successful territorial ones, generally live in habitat less favorable than that occupied by prime territorial males (e. g., Kiley-Worthington, 1965; Estes, 1969, 1974; Spinage, 1969a; Monfort et al., 1973; Gosling, 1974). A major consequence of such differential distribution is that the most favorable parts of the habitat are made available primarily to the female/young segment of the population, and this may have the effect of maximizing reproductive success (Jarman and Jarman, 1973b). However, under adverse conditions (e. g., drought) the territorial system may break down temporarily (where it is otherwise permanent), as for instance in impala in the Serengeti (M. V. Jarman, 1970), and all animals may then intermingle and utilize available resources as best they can. This latter situation obtains for much of the year in populations where territoriality is markedly seasonal, e. g., in southern Africa.

To summarize, we may say that the primary effects of territoriality are to provide a framework within which individual males compete to win exclusive mating rights in a given area and, once established, can exert these rights with a minimum of disturbance by other males. Secondary effects are an indirect influence on the adult sex ratio and a contribution to the spacing and dispersion of the population over the available habitat. These latter effects operate primarily in those territorial systems that are combined with polygynous mating systems (impala type, Chap. 16, E), but probably not, or in a different manner, in those species that have individual or pair territories comprising more or less the entire home range (duiker and dikdik types, Chap. 16, C). In these latter cases, territories may serve to apportion the available habitat, and with it the food supply, among the social and/or reproductive units constituting a population. Under these circumstances a regulatory influence on population density is at least conceivable.

In plains and mountain zebras, the family group functionally takes the place of the territory, as far as mating rights are concerned. This is an exceptional situation among ungulates as it is the only known case of male competition being directly oriented toward possession of a female group (harem) without reference to space.

II. Absolute Dominance

In the context of reproduction, absolute dominance as an individual attribute appears to have much the same consequences as territory occupancy in other species, as discussed above. For instance, Grimsdell (1969) found that in buffalo the majority of matings were performed by the two or three highest-ranking males in a herd. In less gregarious species it is more difficult to establish a relationship between dominance status and reproductive activity. Thus, although we repeatedly saw a certain male giraffe drive others away from an estrous female he was guarding, we had no other criteria by which to establish that such males were the highest-ranking in the local population, simply because we observed very few other interactions from which dominance relationships could have been determined. We can therefore only assume, by analogy to other species, that the males successfully guarding estrous females were also the highest-ranking in other contexts.

The establishment of a dominance hierarchy subjects the males involved to a similar process of selection as competition for territories does in other species. There is, however, little evidence in this context on possible effects that this competition may have on the sex ratio. In buffalo, the adult sex ratio appears to be near-unity, although a proportion of low-ranking males is temporarily or permanently excluded from the breeding herds. In this case, low-ranking males are not relegated to inferior habitat, but are apparently exposed to a higher predation risk, related to the smaller size of all-male groups, and suffer increased mortality. This seems to apply, however, mainly to old males that are no longer reproductively active (Sinclair, 1970, 1974). In giraffe, adult sex ratio seems to vary considerably between areas; in Tsavo NP, for instance, there is even a slight preponderance of males (Leuthold and Leuthold, in press).

The other effects of territoriality, particularly those relating to the dispersion of the entire population, can be less readily visualized under a social system with absolute dominance only. Yet some degree of spacing is achieved in the species concerned as well, but we still do not know how it is brought about. For instance, entire herds of buffalo in the Serengeti NP were spaced more regularly than at random, each inhabiting a home range overlapping only little with that of other herds (Sinclair, 1970, 1974). This suggests that, at the herd level, some social mechanism is operating to effect this spacing. In other nonterritorial species (e. g., elephant, giraffe, plains zebra), some spacing mechanisms are likely to exist, too, but nothing is known about them yet.

C. Social Organization

As the social organization is essentially the product of grouping patterns, spatial and dominance relations among the members of a given population, some of its ecological implications can be understood in relation to the "constituent components," i. e., gregariousness and dominance, as discussed above. However, the social organization is more than just the sum of its constituent components, and many ecological adaptations can only be understood in the context of a species' overall adaptive complex. "Social organization thus expresses the complex evolutionary response of a species to numerous variables of the environment" (Crook, 1965, p. 207). To review these interrelationships between social organization and ecological conditions for African ungulates is the aim of Chapter 19; for the moment, I will just mention two other points relating to social organization.

Recent findings that the highest-ranking males in a bachelor herd are those likely to acquire a territory soon (e. g., in impala: Jarman and Jarman, 1974; Coke's hartebeest: Gosling, 1974), indicate that territoriality and a rank hierarchy are not radically different forms of organization, but rather different applications, or manifestations, of one basic phenomenon: dominance (see Chap. 15, C, I). While in a bachelor herd, males compete for absolute dominance within the bachelor-male segment of a given population. During this time they use a home range similar in size to that of females and usually much larger than individual territories existing in the same area. They are subordinate to any territorial male whose territory they may enter. Heaving reached the top of the bachelor hierarchy, a male is, so-to-speak, one rung on the ladder below territorial males, in social status. To move from that to the top rung involves several important changes in "life style": firstly, he will have to acquire a territory for himself, and then defend it; secondly, he will have to restrict his own activities, more or less, to within the new territory, as he is likely to be attacked by neighboring males, or lose his territory, if he wanders outside; thirdly, he will now have opportunities for undisturbed mating, if he succeeds in keeping any estrous females on his territory. The change from bachelor to territorial male thus greatly affects his "budgets" in space (smaller area, different resource distribution), time (less feeding and resting) and energy expenditure (more agonistic and sexual activity; for details see Jarman and Jarman, 1973a, on impala, also Chap. 6).

These changes will influence his physical condition and, in turn, his continued ability to occupy a territory in the face of competition from other males.

With respect to the remaining bachelors, our territorial male's social status remains largely unchanged. At least in theory, he can still maintain his high absolute rank although, by virtue of his spatial confinement, contacts with bachelors are likely to become less frequent. With respect to other territorial males, there is an important change in that he is no longer inferior to them everywhere (as he was as a bachelor) but in fact superior to all the others within his own territory. For the sake of simplicity we may therefore say that he is dominant over all other males, bachelors and territorial alike, while within his territory (relative dominance). When he loses it to a competitor, he will rejoin the bachelor herd, but at a comparatively low rank, and revert to a considerably different activity pattern in a larger area, the bachelor home range. As he recuperates physically (and perhaps psychologically as well) from the strains of territorial life, he may gradually move upward in the bachelor hierarchy, until he reaches the top again, the jumping-off point for another period on a territory.

This generalized description of the "life cycle" of an adult male bovid of a territorial and gregarious species shows how the two forms of dominance—absolute and relative—coexist in one population, in different social segments, and are complementary in their functional aspects. It further shows that the coexistence of the two forms, and the change from one to the other, has important consequences for individual animals, not only for the whole population as discussed earlier. Male ungulates compete, within groups of peers, for high social status which, in turn, is the prerequisite for successful reproduction. The main difference between territorial and nonterritorial systems is that, in the latter, high dominance status remains an individual attribute (i.e., absolute), whereas in the former the high status is "transferred" to, and contingent upon, a piece of land (i.e., relative).

Furthermore, the social organization, and particularly the resultant spacing pattern, may affect the genetic make-up and, in the long run, the evolution of an ungulate population. Detailed study has shown a number of outwardly homogeneous populations to be subdivided into relatively small localized units, socially determined, which may function as local inbreeding units (demes), reproductively isolated from each other to a considerable extent. Such situations are readily visualized in species that live in relatively large, well-spaced herds, such as buffalo (Sinclair, 1974), but apparently exist in many other species as well. Examples are the sable which, e.g., in the Shimba Hills of Kenya, form relatively discrete herds occupying distinct home ranges with little or no overlap (Estes and Estes, 1969; Estes, 1974); the impala which, e.g., in Nairobi NP, occur in local population units between which there is little interchange (Leuthold, 1970b); and the Uganda kob in which a large population in the Toro Game Reserve is subdivided into local units, each associated with one of some 15 leks (Buechner, 1963, 1974; Buechner and Roth, 1974).

From a genetic point of view, such population units are analogous to island populations, and the overall effect of the subdivision into local demes is probably increased genetic heterogeneity in what might otherwise be a genetically homogeneous population (cf. Wilson, 1975). This interpretation is still largely hypothetical, but Buechner and Roth (1974) presented some evidence (mainly body measurements) suggesting that there are indeed minor genetic differences between Uganda kob "demes" attached to different leks.

Some gene flow is obviously necessary to maintain the genetic integrity of the population, and ultimately the species concerned. This may come about in two ways: (1) periodic intermingling of animals from different demes, and (2) a relatively constant but low rate of interchange of individuals between different demes. Periodic intermingling may occur regularly where there are marked seasonal changes in the social organization (as in impala in southern Africa: Jarman and Jarman, 1973b), or irregularly under extreme environmental conditions, when drought, floods, etc., may lead to a temporary collapse of an otherwise stable social system. Infrequent movements of individuals between different population units have been recorded in several of the species mentioned above (impala, Uganda kob, buffalo). In general, it appears that males tend to move more between demes (e. g., in buffalo: Grimsdell, 1969), but movements of females have also been observed. It may be an important function of the "wanderings" of subadult males to contribute to genetic exchange between different population units. The extraordinary abduction of young female plains zebra from their family units may also be primarily a behavioral mechanism promoting outbreeding, as an alternative to potentially harmful close inbreeding within the small and stable family units.

Chapter 19

Relationships Between Morphology, Ecology, and Social Organization of African Ungulates

The past two decades have brought a great increase in our knowledge on the ethology of African ungulates. Much of the information accumulated has, of necessity, been largely descriptive, with occasional speculations on functional aspects and relatively rare attempts at substantiating such speculations by accurate observational data. An important next step in expanding our understanding of ungulate biology, and particularly the interrelationships between behavioral and ecological adaptations, was to collate the available information in an evolutionary framework and to formulate hypotheses that could be tested by further observation and, if possible, experimentation.

Reviews of this kind on the relationships between—mainly—social organization and ecology in major vertebrate groups have been presented for birds by Crook (1965), for mammals generally by Eisenberg (1966), for primates by Gartlan (1968), Crook (1970a), Kummer (1971), and for both primates and birds, with more general discussions, by Crook (1970b), Crook and Goss-Custard (1972) and by Wilson (1975). Partly following these models, two attempts have been made recently to synthesize relevant information on African bovids, one by Estes (1974) and one by Jarman (1974), the latter being an expansion of material and ideas presented several years earlier in an unpublished thesis (Jarman, 1968).

The present chapter is based largely on these two papers, dealing only with the Bovidae rather than with all African ungulates. The main reasons for this restriction are that (1) the bovids comprise the great majority of African ungulates anyway (cf. Chap. 2 and Appendix), and (2) while the bovids constitute a relatively homogeneous group showing pronounced radiation, the remaining ungulates form a rather heterogeneous collection of taxa with different evolutionary histories, as far as these are known. In the following, I will discuss the role of social organization in the framework of the overall adaptive complex characteristic of each species. In contrast to Chapter 17, where intraspecific variations of social organization in relation to ecological factors were reviewed, emphasis will be placed on comparisons between species. I should perhaps stress that most of what follows remains somewhat speculative, although much of the available information fits the predictions made by the various hypotheses presented below.

"In general, an ungulate species has two major problems, to feed itself and to avoid being fed upon" (Eisenberg and Lockhart, 1972, p. 87). Although applicable to *individuals* rather than species, this about sums up the basic requirements that ungulates have to meet in order to survive. The main concern of the *species*, self-propagation, in turn depends on the success with which individuals cope with these demands. The social organization, as well as some other behavioral (and nonbehavioral) attributes of a species are, therefore, closely integrated into an adaptive complex "designed" to solve these basic problems. In essence, they amount to a compromise strategy enabling the animals to fulfill their overall energy requirements for maintenance, growth and reproduction without undue exposure to risks of predation or other sources of mortality.

In Chapter 18, I have already mentioned briefly that herd-forming ungulates tend to be relatively large and live mainly in fairly open habitats, whereas solitary species are generally small and live mostly in bush or forest (see also Chap. 16). At the time, these relationships were explained primarily in terms of antipredator behavior, but there is more to them than that, and we shall now examine other aspects of these relationships. Before doing so, however, we have to consider briefly the ways in which certain "basic" characteristics such as body size, physiology, etc., affect the ecological and behavioral capabilities of African bovids. Caution should be exercized in interpreting the following statements in terms of cause-effect relationships.

Body size is to a certain extent determined by a species' taxonomic position which, in turn, is related to its phylogeny. For instance, all gazelles are relatively small, whereas all Alcelaphinae are upper-medium to large size. In other groups, differences within a subfamily are more marked, particularly so in the Tragelaphines. In any event, in the present context we may consider body size as a predetermined characteristic of each species. Body size, in turn, is a major determinant of several ecological and behavioral traits. For instance, the absolute quantity of food required is broadly related to body size, although this relationship is complicated by differences in metabolic rates, which tend to be higher in small animals. An animal requiring a relatively small total amount of food may either spend less time overall on feeding or, alternatively, spend more time per unit energy intake, i.e., be more selective. A smaller-bodied animal, generally, is also less mobile than a larger one, both with respect to short-term (daily) and long-term (seasonal/annual) movements. It therefore ought to be able to meet its energy requirements within a relatively small area. A small animal is also vulnerable to a greater variety of predators than a larger one and, as its escape and defensive capabilities are limited, it has to rely more on crypsis (i.e., making itself inconspicuous) than on flight and/or defense to avoid predation. This antipredator strategy is likely to be more effective in a well-structured (i.e., closed) than in an open habitat, and single animals can employ this strategy more successfully than large groups. All these effects of body size, taken together, can largely explain why small antelopes should occur solitarily, or in small groups only, and mainly in closed habitats such as bush or forest. With regard to larger bovids, and their social organization, further explanations are, however, necessary (see below).

Physiology (including anatomical features) may be assumed, for the present argument, as being a predetermined trait of each species, as body size. In our context, three types of physiological adaptations are important: (1) the degree of dependence on free water, (2) the ability to subsist on poor-quality food, (3) the thermoregulatory capabilities. They may have the following effects on ecology and behavior of ungulates:

1. An animal largely independent of drinking water may be able to live in a relatively small area, provided it can find sufficient food there. A water-dependent animal, on the other hand, needs to find drinking water at regular intervals, often daily, and may have to move over considerable distances to do so, depending on the availability of food. Thus, water requirements affect home range size, daily and/or seasonal movements, the activity pattern, as well as food selection, since animals can only be independent of free water, if they obtain sufficient water from their food. In this context it is interesting to note that certain dry-country ungulates tend to feed primarily at night, when the water content of the otherwise dry plants is highest (through hygroscopic absorption), e.g., Grant's gazelle in northern Kenya (Taylor, 1972).

2. The ability to extract nutrients (mainly protein) from poor-quality plant food, in combination with the kind of food normally taken (i.e., whether grass or browse), also plays an important role in determining movements and, to some extent, activity patterns. These are further related to the dispersion of food items, as is typical group size (see below).

3. Thermoregulatory efficiency, or tolerance of heat stress, also affect activity patterns to a considerable degree. Animals with a low heat tolerance may have to spend much of the daytime inactive, resting in whatever shade is available, and move and feed primarily at night. These patterns may also vary seasonally, depending on seasonal changes in mean temperatures and/or solar radiation. Nocturnal activity alters an animal's risk of contacting predators, which may, in turn, affect certain aspects of the social organization. Heat tolerance, on the other hand, depends to some extent on body size (surface/volume ratio) and/or qualities of the skin and hair coat (e.g., Finch, 1973).

Of course, the various relationships just enumerated form a complicated web of interdependent features and adaptations, and some of the features mentioned are further affected by other factors, intrinsic and extrinsic to the animal(s) concerned. Activity patterns, for instance, while greatly influenced by the basic needs of food, water and thermoregulation, are also shaped by antipredator measures (e.g., avoidance of vegetation types in which predators may hide, or shift of certain activities to times when predators are least active), by reproductive condition (e.g., a female with a newborn young may have an activity pattern very different from one with older or no offspring), by social status (e.g., a territorial male may spend much less time feeding than a nonterritorial one), etc., as discussed in Chapter 6.

We may now proceed to examining the relationships between ecology and social organization in African bovids in more detail, primarily on the basis of the papers by Estes (1974) and Jarman (1974). The two authors used rather different approaches: Estes based his arguments and conclusions primarily on a generalized dichotomy between solitary, forest-dwelling antelopes on one hand, and gregarious, open-country species on the other hand, whereas Jarman used "feeding styles" as the starting point and attempted to relate most other features to them. In the process, he subdivided the African bovids into five "classes" with different features of social organization, apparently related to the different feeding styles.

In essence, Estes attempted to follow the lines that bovid evolution may have taken, assuming that primitive forms were more or less solitary forest-dwellers and that gregarious species are phylogenetically more advanced; he placed considerable emphasis on the "socialization process" associated with the transition from closed to more open habitats. Jarman, by contrast, formulated a number of hypotheses, based on existing information, designed to relate the various aspects of a species' biology into a strictly functional, more ecologically oriented framework (see also Geist, 1974).

Neither approach is fully satisfactory; nor can perhaps any such endeavor be, since, in Jarman's own words, "any attempt at subdividing a continuum creates problems." Whereas Estes perhaps overemphasized the distinction between solitary and "social" species, without fully taking into account the many more or less intermediate forms, Jarman faced considerable difficulties in assigning each species definitely to one of his five classes. These shortcomings should, however, not detract from the basic usefulness of the two papers as attempts to formulate a theoretical framework for existing information. As Jarman's approach is more similar to my own, as far as classification of social organizations is concerned (see Chap. 16), I will follow his more closely than that of Estes without, however, implying that one paper is necessarily better than the other.

As Jarman based his arguments primarily on the feeding styles of different bovids, we will have to refer briefly to some aspects of feeding behavior and ecology (cf. Chap. 5). Probably the most important point to consider is the difference between monocotyledonous (i. e., primarily grasses) and dicotyledonous plants (browse) with regard to their spatial distribution, seasonal availability and nutrient contents. Particularly in open savannas, where the majority of African bovids occur (cf. Chap. 2), browse items are rather widely dispersed, whereas grasses grow in "blanket" form. Given similar quality of food items, browsers have to move about more, and spend more time and energy, to ingest a similar quantity of food than grazers may have to do. However, the salient point is that of food quality. Grasses tend to grow in a highly synchronized manner, following substantial rainfall, and then dry out evenly within a fairly short period of time after cessation of rains. By contrast, browse plants, particularly woody ones, while often showing a spurt of growth immediately following rain, too, tend to continue growing small shoots, leaves, flowers and fruits long after growth has ceased in grasses. Thus, freshly produced browse items are usually available at times when grasses are at or near their lowest level of nutrient contents. In addition, browse items (leaves, flowers, etc.) contain generally less fiber, and thus a larger proportion of directly utilizable nutrients, than grasses. Overall, therefore, browse tends to be of higher nutritive quality than grasses, but is available in relatively small quantities only, in the form of widely dispersed individual items.

The exploitation of browse calls for a considerably different feeding strategy than utilization of grasses. Browsers should have relatively low requirements with regard to food quantity, as the dispersed nature of browse food militates against substantial bulk intake within the time available for food gathering (although this is partially offset by the high quality of individual food items). On the other hand, the continued production of browse items through much of the year makes it possible for an animal with low quantitative requirements to find sufficient food within a relatively small area over long periods of time. A corollary of this last point is that browse is most economically exploited by single animals, or at most very small groups, as otherwise intragroup competition could severely interfere with the fulfillment of individual energy needs (cf. Fig. 3 and accompanying discussion in Jarman, 1974).

As a consequence of the above, and taking into account the earlier discussion related to body size, it is not at all surprising to find that most pure browsers are small in size (note that we are discussing bovids only!) and live singly or in small groups (e. g., duikers, dikdiks, pygmy antelopes, klipspringer, gerenuk). Most of them also live in fairly dense bush or forest, habitats which lend themselves best to exploitation by pure browsers.

Ecological conditions, and resultant feeding strategies, are radically different for species feeding primarily or exclusively on grasses. While grass is green, they have no problem in finding sufficient food, in terms of both quantity and quality. Potential food is densely distributed and there is virtually no limit to the amount that can be found and ingested. However, once the grass starts drying out, the problem of food quality becomes increasingly pressing, as outlined above. An important adaptation in this context is mobility, enabling animals to take advantage of irregularly distributed rainfall and associated grass growth. Mobility, in turn, requires relatively large body size, partly related to morphology (length of legs, etc.) and to energetics, partly to possibly increased risk of predation associated with high mobility and thus conspicuousness. In the latter context, gregariousness is also of advantage, particularly in open habitats, and as intragroup competition over food is less likely to be serious in grazers than in browsers, herd-formation will be favored. We may, therefore, expect the most pronounced grazers to be large, gregarious, and relatively mobile. This is indeed the case; examples are wildebeest, oryx and buffalo (however, a major exception is the eland, which is large, gregarious and highly mobile, but a browser).

Up to here, I have described only the two extremes in feeding styles which, to a considerable extent, correlate with extremes in body size. However, the majority of African Bovidae fall somewhere between these extremes. On the basis of available information Jarman (1974) divided them into five categories, each showing somewhat different feeding habits:

Class A. Exclusive browsers that search selectively for small, highly nutritious food items (young leaves, flowers, fruits; occasionally also animal matter: Kurt, 1963; Grimm, 1970). Species in this class tend to have a small home range that they occupy the year round; it usually lies within only one major vegetation type. Examples are most duikers, dikdiks, pygmy antelopes and klipspringer, all among the smallest bovids.

Class B. Browsers or grazers that also select strongly for nutritious individual food items (i.e., plant parts). They have a somewhat larger home range, within which they may show small-scale seasonal displacements, but they tend to utilize only one major vegetation type, or at most very few similar ones. Examples are the three reedbuck species, oribi, sitatunga, bushbuck and gerenuk; they are all somewhat larger than most species in Class A.

250

Class C. A rather heterogeneous collection of browsers, grazers and mixed feeders (for qualifications of these terms see Chap. 5, A). They have fairly large home ranges, within which they may move seasonally between different vegetation types but, on the whole, they are still relatively sedentary. Their diet may change considerably over the seasons, which usually means a decreasing proportion of grasses as the dry season progresses. Examples include impala, several gazelle species, several kob and waterbuck species; most of them are of intermediate size, although the range of sizes is rather large within the class.

Class D. These are fairly exclusive grazers, selecting to a considerable extent for growth stage and plant part, particularly preferring leaf over stem material. In adaptation to the great fluctuations in availability of suitable food, some of these species are highly mobile, having some of the largest annual home ranges recorded in African ungulates (cf. Table 3). They are essentially bulk feeders and comparatively less selective than species in classes A–C. Examples include several Alcelaphinae and probably oryx.

Class E. Species feeding on a wide variety of grasses, or grasses and browse, moving over quite large areas, and between different vegetation types, in the course of the year. Examples are buffalo and eland.

Obviously, it is impossible to strictly categorize the wide range of feeding styles found in African bovids into just five classes. As a consequence, the above classification is not fully satisfactory, in various ways. For instance, Class E combines two (or maybe more) species with very different feeding habits. On the other hand, a number of species are difficult to fit into any of the classes described, partly because of their specializations in feeding and habitat preference, and partly because not enough is known about them (e.g., bongo, mountain nyala, most Hippotraginae, Hunter's hartebeest). The best-defined classes are A and D, representing two extremes in feeding styles. The behavior of the species assigned to them conforms best to the theory, taking into account the earlier discussion on the effects of body size, physiology and type of food eaten. Classes B and E comprise mainly species which, so-to-speak, deviate somewhat but not very much from those in Classes A and D, respectively, while Class C includes virtually all species well removed from either extreme.

These criticisms should not detract from the overall usefulness of the classification given by Jarman, the basic justification of which will, however, only become apparent when the various correlates in social organization are taken into account, too.

Turning to grouping patterns, Jarman (1974) suggested that, within limits, two main factors act to determine typical group size of any one species. An upper limit on group size is imposed by the likelihood of intragroup competition in feeding which, in turn, is related to feeding style. With some simplification we can say that the more selectively a species feeds (i.e., the more dispersed its usual food items are), the fewer animals can associate closely without interfering with each other's feeding. This would explain why the most selective feeders (i.e., Class A) tend to be solitary on the whole. Conversely, animals feeding relatively unselectively on a fairly evenly dispersed food supply may congregate in quite large numbers without entering into serious competition. This obviously

251

applies to grazers and, since the availability of palatable grass fluctuates considerably in the course of a year, marked seasonal changes in group size are a feature of many grazing ungulates (some Class C and Class D species and, to a lesser extent, buffalo). On the whole, there is good agreement between the group size typical of a species and its feeding style, class B feeders usually occurring in groups of about 2–5, and up to 10 or 12 in the extreme, while Class C feeders form groups numbering between about 5 and 50, occasionally over 100, and Class D and E feeders may aggregate in herds of several hundreds or even thousands. Together with antipredator considerations which, to some extent, account for the lower limits of typical group size (see Chap. 18), these relationships between feeding style and group size go a long way toward explaining typical grouping patterns of African bovids in terms of ecological constraints. As a corollary, they also provide an explanation for the inverse relationship between habitat "density" (e. g., degree of woody cover) and group size referred to earlier (Chapters 17, B and 18, A). In the more wooded habitats, food items tend to be dispersed more than in open (grassy) habitats, thereby impeding the formation of large groups on account of competition. Difficulties in communication, especially in maintaining group cohesion, and in remaining inconspicuous to predators additionally favor the formation of relatively smaller groups in closed habitats. This principle appears to apply both within and between species (see Chap. 17, B, III for examples of intraspecific variations).

The above discussion also provides the answer to the question as to why small species tend to be solitary, whereas the larger ones are generally more gregarious. As we have seen, most or all of the smallest bovids are highly selective feeders, mainly browsers, and—largely as a consequence—live in relatively closed habitats, so group formation is not advantageous to them, both from the feeding and the antipredator point of view. *Mutatis mutandis*, the converse applies to larger species, as outlined above.

There are, however, still other interrelationships between ecological and behavioral traits. Probably mainly as a consequence of the basic grouping patterns described above, there are also correspondences between feeding style and other features of social behavior and organization, particularly the mating system.

Class A species tend to have individual or pair territories coinciding with the entire home range (duiker and dikdik types, see Chap. 16, C) and to occupy them the year round, as far as is known. In keeping with their overall antipredator strategy, which relies on inconspicuousness, they do not advertize territorial ownership through visual or auditory displays, but use primarily olfactory marking, by means of antorbital glands and/or dung heaps (e. g., dikdik, klipspringer, steinbuck).

Class B species are also mostly territorial, but differ from Class A in that females are somewhat more gregarious and do not take part in territorial activities. The males' territories encompass most or all of their home range and tend to be fairly stable throughout the year. These species, too, rely primarily on crypsis as an antipredator mechanism and, accordingly, use almost exclusively olfactory means for territorial marking (if any). This system corresponds to the type described for gerenuk (Chap. 16, D), and probably also applies to the reedbucks and the oribi.

In most Class C species males are also territorial, for part or all of the year, but their territories constitute only a relatively small portion of their home range (impala type, Chap. 16, E). Other major differences to Classes A and B are the considerable gregariousness of females and the fact that a variable proportion of adult males do not hold a territory at any one time ("bachelors"). The main feature of this system and, particularly, the many variations, both inter- and intraspecifically, have been described earlier and need not be elaborated further here. In keeping with the generally more open nature of the habitat occupied by the species concerned and resultant differences in antipredator behavior (flight rather than crypsis), more conspicuous visual and auditory displays are used in territorial advertizement. While olfactory marking is still important in some species (e. g., antorbital glands in Thomson's gazelle, dung heaps or linked urination/defecation ceremonies in several species), visual and auditory signals are more prominent, such as the conspicuous stance of a territorial male ("static-optic" advertizement), the whistling of Uganda kob or the grunting of wildebeest (see Chap. 8).

Class D species differ little from Class C in their basic social organization, except that some of them show a distinct propensity toward forming large seasonal aggregations and to be migratory to a greater or lesser degree, particularly the wildebeest. Under these circumstances a territorial system, which is probably the original condition in these species as well, may become attenuated to a considerable extent. Overall, this phase can perhaps be looked upon as a transitional stage between a Class C and a Class E system, with partial emancipation from a localized territorial system providing greater flexibility in exploiting an irregular food supply. In this context, it would be interesting to have more information on the oryx and its desert-inhabiting relatives.

Class E species differ from all others in that no animals are territorial, and that the probable function of territoriality in other species (to apportion mating rights) is taken over by a system based on absolute dominance. Males and females may move in unison in fairly to very large herds, without any individual showing pronounced attachment to a specific piece of ground (except, perhaps, for certain portions of the dry-season home range which are, however, not used exclusively). This, or a similar situation, has so far been documented only in buffalo and eland.

When discussing the various interrelationships between morphology, ecology and social organization, as outlined above, it is difficult to avoid circular reasoning or inferring cause-effect relationships that are by no means substantiated. In many cases we have no way of knowing in which direction a currently extant relationship evolved, i. e., which of its constituent traits affected another one, and to what extent. Quite probably, different traits influenced each other mutually, and what we see today may be a compromise result of sometimes conflicting influences.

Keeping in mind these pitfalls and limitations in arguing, it may nevertheless be useful to attempt a schematic representation of the different factors that have shaped the socio-ecological evolution of African bovids (Fig. 55). For want of a better alternative, I have assumed (as above) that body size, general morphology and physiology are largely predetermined, and that the ecological

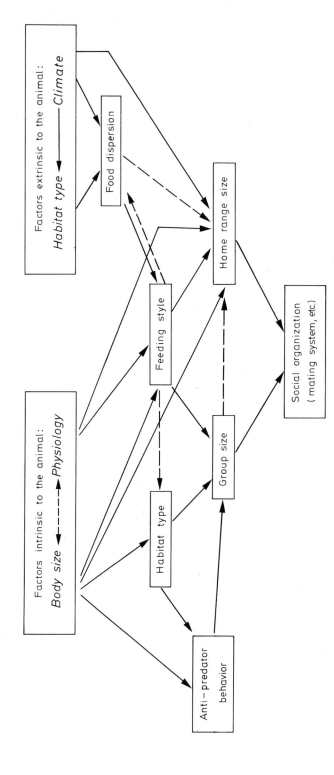

Fig. 55. Interrelationships between morphology/physiology, ecology and social organization in African bovids

and behavioral characteristics considered here are secondary adaptations. However, this need not necessarily be so. Also, the actual interplay of different factors and influences is likely to be considerably more complex than the simple graphic representation in Figure 55 implies; several additional factors may also affect different aspects of the ecology and/or social organization of any given species. Figure 55 should, therefore, be looked upon as nothing more than a crude attempt at illustrating some of the relationships discussed in this chapter.

One factor that I have not yet mentioned but which exerts considerable influence on the details of social organization, particularly with regard to intraspecific variations, is the general resource level in any given area. By this term I mean the magnitude of primary productivity, its temporal fluctuations and, perhaps, the availability of open water. In Africa, the general resource level is determined primarily by rainfall, its quantity and temporal distribution. This is what is meant by "Climate" in Figure 55. In general, rainfall acts indirectly, through the type and/or state of vegetation that it generates.

It will be noted that "Habitat type" occurs in two positions in Figure 55. This is primarily because I have found no other way of expressing the dual role of the habitat in this context: on the one hand, any habitat can be considered as being a predetermined environmental factor resulting from the interactions of topography, soil, rainfall, etc.; on the other hand, a species' body size and related feeding style, and its antipredator behavior a priori restrict the types and number of habitats it can successfully occupy, out of the total range available. This illustrates that many of the interrelationships represented in Figure 55 are not necessarily "one-way streets," although most of them are indicated as such, mainly for want of adequate knowledge.

For easy reference, the five classes of African bovids, as defined by Jarman (1974) and discussed above, are listed in Table 7, with their ecological and social characteristics. I should emphasize again that a considerable amount of simplification has to be used to arrive at this classification, and that many species do not fit it all too well. However, it would be unrealistic to expect a strict categorization to be possible in a biological context where flexibility may be an asset anyway. Such flexibility is amply demonstrated by a number of species that have been studied in more than one area (see Chap. 17). Thus, while I have constantly talked about species-specific characteristics in this chapter, such characteristics may, in reality, be highly variable under different environmental conditions, with the possible exception of the species in Class A.

Overall, however, the information currently available conforms reasonably well with the hypotheses underlying the above-mentioned classification. The hypotheses may, therefore, be accepted, at least provisionally and until considerably more knowledge has been obtained, which might either confirm them or subject them to revision.

Although taking a different approach, as explained earlier, Estes (1974) came to similar conclusions in many respects, but his analysis is somewhat less ecologically oriented. However, his review should be consulted by anyone with an interest in bovid social organization and its evolutionary aspects.

So far, we have dealt exclusively with the Bovidae, as the two reviews on which this chapter is based confined themselves to this family. But what about

Table 7. Summary of relationships between morphology, ecology, spatial organization and social behavior of African bovidae (after Jarman, 1974)

	Class A	Class B	Class C	Class D	Class E
Body size	mostly small	small to medium	medium, but wide variation	(medium-) large	large to very large
Main habitat	forest or dense bush (closed)	bush, tall grass (fairly closed)	medium to open bush or grassland (very variable)	savanna (mainly open) and grassland	savanna, mostly open
Feeding style	"delicate" browsing, highly selective	browsing or grazing, fairly to highly selective	browsing or grazing, fairly selective; marked seasonal changes	mainly grazing, selection for plant parts	grazing or browsing, relatively unselective
Social groupings	solitary or pairs; rarely over 3 in group	commonly 3–6; adult males often solitary, young males in small groups	very variable; 5–50 (-several hundred); adult males often solitary; young males in herds[a]; seasonal changes	very variable; 5–50 (-several thousand); adult males often solitary; young males in herds[a]; seasonal aggregations	± permanent[c] herds of 50–500 (-2,000); adult males often solitary or in small groups

256

Group stability	no groups, or strong pair bond	generally high	variable; groups often ± open	variable; groups often ± open	relatively high[c]
Home range	small, stable	small, rel. stable	medium to large; some seasonal movements	large to very large, with large-scale seasonal movements in some cases	large to very large, mobility quite high
Territory	+ + individual or pair; "resource" type; ± coincides with home range	+ +[b] male only; may encompass entire home range; resource type	+ +[b] male only; part of home range only; mating territory	+ + as Class C	— absolute dominance hierarchy; several adult males may associate
Antipredator behavior	concealment, freezing	concealment, freezing, but also flight	flight (defense of young only)	flight; occasionally group defense	flight; individual and communal defense
Representative species	duikers, dikdik, several other Neotragini	reedbucks, bushbuck, sitatunga, lesser kudu, gerenuk	impala, waterbuck, (Uganda) kob, Grant's and Thomson's gazelle, greater kudu	wildebeest and some other Alcelaphinae	savanna buffalo; eland, oryx (?)

[a] Male herds also include nonterritorial adult males.
[b] Territoriality not confirmed in Tragelaphines.
[c] Substantiated only for buffalo; eland may be quite different.

the other African ungulates? Are similar relationships between social organization and ecology evident in other groups, too? The answer to this question is: partially. For instance, the close correlation between body size, habitat and food habits, and social structure has its parallels in at least two other ungulate families that have representatives in different habitat types. Both the pygmy hippopotamus and the okapi live in lowland rain forest, are essentially solitary (perhaps pair-forming) and are considerably smaller than their savanna counterparts, the common hippopotamus and the giraffe. (The giraffe presents a special problem in the present context, being a very large-bodied and fairly gregarious browser; perhaps the key to the apparent puzzle lies in its height, which enables it to utilize a much greater proportion of the potential browsing zone than any other ungulate except the elephant). A similar relationship apparently also exists between the forest and savanna varieties of elephant and buffalo, although the forest forms are not really solitary but live in smaller groups than the savanna representatives, as far as is known (see Dorst and Dandelot, 1970; and Sinclair, 1970, 1974, for buffalo).

In the Suidae, by contrast, almost the reverse seems to be true. The open-country warthog is the smallest of the three African species and also seems to form the smallest groups, whereas the bush pig and the giant forest hog are both larger, tend to occur in larger groups, yet inhabit decidedly more closed habitats (Dorst and Dandelot, 1970). Very little detailed information is, however, available on the latter two species.

Among the Equidae, all four African species are essentially adapted to life in open country; the main differences between species-specific habitats lie in the degree of aridity. There is an interesting dichotomy in social organization between those species inhabiting the drier habitats, which are territorial (Grévy's zebra and wild ass), and those occupying somewhat less arid areas, which are "spatially emancipated" and form permanent harem groups (plains and mountain zebra). At first sight, this is rather puzzling, as territoriality would seem rather maladaptive in semidesert areas with strong fluctuations in food supplies. The only plausible explanation currently available is that territoriality is an original condition among the Equidae and has been retained by the more primitive (?) species, whereas the more advanced species have abandoned territoriality and thereby gained greater mobility (Klingel, 1972b, 1974b, 1975), often coupled with the facility to aggregate temporarily into very large herds as, for instance, in the Serengeti area. In some ways, the plains zebra has thus taken an evolutionary course similar to that of the most gregarious Alcelaphinae and the buffalo within the Bovidae.

No pronounced differences in social organization are evident between the black and the white rhinoceroses, although the former is a browser and tends to be somewhat more solitary than the latter, which is primarily a grazer and sometimes forms groups of 5–6 animals; it is also larger in body size (e.g., Owen-Smith, 1974, 1975).

The apparent absence of clear-cut relationships between ecology and social organization among a number of nonbovids need not come as a surprise. African nonbovid ungulates comprise only 15 species (versus 75 bovids, see Appendix), belonging to phylogenetically very different taxa, each of which includes only a small number of species. Within the Bovidae, which all share a similar basic organization (i. e., morphology, etc.), the ecological constraints that appear to have influenced their social evolution are much more readily evident. For the other ungulate groups, although there are a few cases of apparent convergent evolution, as in the pairs pygmy hippo/hippopotamus and giraffe/okapi, it appears that each "lineage" has found its own distinct solutions to the common problem facing all ungulates: "To eat and not be eaten."

Chapter 20

Applications of Ethological Information to Management

"At certain stages of man's prehistory a practical knowledge of the behaviour of such animals as the ungulates ... was probably a condition of survival" (Kalmus, 1965, pp. 1, 2).

"Since man first pursued animals he has been a student of animal behaviour" (Cowan, 1974, p. 921).

These two statements emphasize the practical value that knowledge of at least certain features of animal behavior has entailed for man ever since he emerged as a potential competitor and, more particularly, a hunter of other animals, including ungulates. As man's relationships with such animals have grown more complex, from initial predation to domestication of a few selected species, to husbandry and ranching of wild ungulates for economic exploitation, and to maintenance and propagation of wild animals in captivity for recreational and educational purposes (zoos, etc.), behavioral information has become increasingly more useful and necessary to the success of these various endeavors. In the following, I will review some of the instances in which ethological knowledge has already been put to practical use, and indicate where such knowledge should be taken into account in future planning. This review, of necessity, cannot be comprehensive, as the exact details of application vary from case to case, according to external circumstances as well as the animal species involved. At the current state of knowledge, application of behavioral principles to management has reached only a fairly elementary level, as far as African ungulates are concerned. It has progressed somewhat further with respect to temperate-zone species, and I will mention some examples to indicate the direction that this development has taken (see, in particular Geist, 1971a, b). Moreover I wish to emphasize, again, that behavioral factors should not be considered in isolation, but as integral parts of the complete set of adaptations that any one species possesses. And, above all, the primary condition for successful management of ungulates is the provision of suitable living space, in terms of ecological requirements. Only when this condition has been met can behavioral information begin to play a useful role (Cowan, 1974).

For convenience, we may subdivide the overall continuum of management practices, according to their principal objectives, into the following three major fields:

1. Hunting and conservation, where animals remain essentially free in their natural environment.
2. Ranching and other forms of commercial exploitation, where the animals may remain in largely natural habitats but are subjected to various constraints and manipulations.

3. Maintenance in captivity, where animals are transplanted into partly or entirely artificial surroundings.

Success in ventures in these three fields is judged by different criteria, and the behavior of the animals involved must, therefore, be taken into account from different points of view, depending on the goal in any given instance.

A. Conservation and Hunting

Under this heading we may combine, for present purposes, all endeavors to maintain populations of ungulates in as nearly natural environments as may be available, for sport hunting or nonconsumptive uses (recreation, education, scientific studies, etc.). While the detailed goals in different cases may diverge considerably, the overall general objective is largely the same: to maintain free-ranging populations, as diverse as possible (or as desired), in balance with their habitat and avoiding conflicts with other human interests, such as agriculture, etc. The latter condition imposes certain constraints on what may be practicable under any given circumstances, but it does not—or to a lesser degree only—apply to such "nature reserves" as national parks, integral game reserves, wilderness areas, etc.

With regard to management, it is a cardinal principle that animals develop best in a "predictable environment" (Geist, 1971 a, b; Cowan, 1974). Any influence that reduces "predictability," i.e., anything one could call a "disturbance," is likely to impair the performance of a population in terms of energetic efficiency. This may manifest itself in animals losing condition, in reduced rates of reproduction and/or recruitment, or in higher mortality, or a combination of these factors. As animals perceive and respond to disturbances primarily by behavioral means, it is in this general context that ethological information, and its application, may be most useful in management.

The behavior of ungulates in a wild state affects management in three major contexts:
1. The reactions to environmental conditions and the degree of adaptability to different circumstances.
2. Reactions to, and tolerance of, man-made disturbances.
3. Implications of specific behavioral characteristics for research and management.

We will consider these separately, although they may be interrelated in many ways.

I. Reactions to Environmental Conditions

It may appear self-evident that an area in which wild ungulates are to live and prosper should contain all their "basic necessities" for life. Yet, in many instances, very little is known on the actual importance that certain components

261

of the environment may have for part or all of a single-species population or a multi-species community. We may have certain vague ideas about what habitats may be suitable for one species or another, but we may not know just why this is so. Detailed studies on the mode of feeding, the selection of certain items from the available vegetation, the frequency and locations of drinking (Jarman, 1972a; Jarman and Mmari, 1971), day-to-day and seasonal movements, as well as the use of space in social contexts, will provide the knowledge that, in the long run, may be essential for the successful management of wild ungulates.

With respect to African ungulates, our information on these topics is still far from adequate in most cases. Moreover, contrary to the views of many, if a species has been studied, however thoroughly, in one area, that does not mean that one then has all the knowledge needed and that it can be applied to all situations in which the species occurs. It is not "duplication of research" if several studies are carried out on the same species in different areas, or even in the same area at different times, as conditions may vary both in time and in space. Studies on one species in several areas may, in fact, considerably increase our understanding of its various behavioral and other adaptations. A good example is the work on impala in eastern and southern Africa by Jarman and Jarman (1973b, 1974).

Also, while many people would consider the topics of research enumerated above as being primarily ecological rather than ethological, it is obviously impossible to draw a line between the two disciplines, and each must complement the other. This is particularly evident with respect to movements. In Robinette's (1966) words: "A knowledge of movements is basic to the management of any game species." There are, however, many different kinds of movements, with a great variety of underlying causations. Some may be related simply to the availability of certain resources (food, water) and might therefore be considered as purely "ecologically" determined. Yet in some cases they may be governed, proximately, by such behavioral factors as leadership and tradition, as has been well documented for some temperate-zone ungulates, e. g., bighorn sheep (Geist, 1971b) and red deer or wapiti (Schloeth, 1961a; Altmann, 1956). It is highly likely that such mechanisms are also involved in the movements and/or migrations of certain African ungulates, particularly those with a closely knit social structure (e. g., elephant, plains zebra, buffalo).

The regularity and/or scale of movements, i. e., the distances involved, in any near-natural system may point to the limiting factors operating on any given ungulate population, usually food and/or water. A good example is the migration of wildebeest, and a few other species, in the Serengeti area. These ungulates move more or less regularly along a rainfall gradient coinciding with a vegetation zonation ranging from short-grass plains in the south-east to fairly densely wooded savanna in the north-west (Pennycuick, 1975; see Fig. 11). These migrations are timed in such a way that the animals are in the "poorest" habitats (short grass areas) in the rainy season, i. e., at the time of highest plant productivity. Similar in principle, but considerably different in detail are the movements of elephants in Tsavo NP between more or less fixed dry-season ranges and a variety of irregularly used wet-season areas determined primarily by the highly erratic distribution of rainfall (Leuthold and Sale, 1973, and unpubl.). Whereas ecological necessities undoubtedly lie at the root of these movements, behavioral factors probably play an important part in their execution. For instance, the locations of dry-season ranges are likely to be transmitted from older to younger animals by tradition, as may be localized food or water resources; cues as to when to move, and where, may also be acquired and refined through experience. While much remains unknown about the actual mechanisms involved in such movement and/or migration systems, the importance of the older animals in this context can hardly be overemphasized, particularly in elephants. The consequences for management, especially hunting, are obvious.

Other instances of movements may have entirely behavioral causes, particularly those where only certain sex/age groups are involved. Most commonly, these are subadult males that have been driven out of their mothers' herds by territorial males, as in impala (Jarman and Jarman, 1973b, 1974) and probably many other antelope species. While some of them may succumb to predators or other sources of mortality, the survivors may play one or two biologically important roles. Firstly, if they move away from their original range permanently, they contribute to gene flow between different population segments that might otherwise become genetically isolated from each other. Secondly, if there is suitable but unoccupied habitat in the vicinity of a given population, males may be the first to (re)colonize it, as has been described for impala in South Africa (Hitchins and Vincent, 1972). Few females participated in the dispersal, and those that did appeared to be nonbreeding (possibly subadult) ones. In giraffe, too, males tend to move more than females (Foster and Dagg, 1972; Hitchins and Vincent, 1972; Leuthold and Leuthold, in press), and this may be true of other species. Knowledge of such details of dispersal mechanisms can be very important for management in certain contexts, such as the spontaneous or artificial restocking of areas depleted of game. On the other hand, a high degree of attachment to a fixed home area may impede spontaneous dispersal into understocked areas and, if animals are forcibly translocated, may lead to homing and thus defeat the purpose of the operation.

Other aspects of the use of space, and certain resources, include those where space plays a definite part in social interactions, particularly where territoriality may have a limiting effect on population density (cf. Joubert, 1974, referring to roan antelope). In this context it is necessary to know what factors determine territory size, and how these factors can perhaps be modified or eliminated, if it is desired to increase population density. On the other hand, one may simply have to recognize that density cannot be increased above a certain level, due to sociospatial limitations.

Overall, therefore, the reactions of ungulates to certain features of their environment, and specifically the degree of plasticity and adaptability shown in this context, are—or should be—of the highest interest to those concerned with management.

II. Reactions to Man-Made Disturbances

For present purposes, I wish to define as a disturbance any human activity that is not normally—or was not in the recent past—part of the natural environment of the animals involved. This comprises, for instance, tourism in its various forms (vehicular traffic, walking, camping), construction (buildings, roads, etc.), alteration of the physical environment (e. g., dams, fences), hunting, trapping, etc. In many contexts it is useful to know in advance, or at least to judge approximately, what reactions to and what degree of tolerance of disturbances can be expected in any given situation. To this end, a knowledge of the normal behavior of the animals involved, and of the extent to which they can adapt to new circumstances, is often essential.

Ungulates, as most other mammals, possess considerable learning abilities which can be utilized to "educate" the animals (Geist, 1971a), to make them accept certain changes in their environments. A very basic learning process is that of habituation, particularly to vehicles and/or people. The main point in this context is that few, if any, ungulates are inherently "wild" with respect to man; "the behavior of 'wild' ungulates toward human beings is largely a consequence of our behavior toward them; they are as 'wild' as we teach them to be" (Geist, 1971a, p. 416). In other words, if they have had no bad experiences with man, or with vehicles, they come to accept him (them) as normal components of their environment and hardly react to their presence. The validity of this statement is amply demonstrated by the high degree of habituation that most ungulates show, at least toward vehicles, in many African national parks. Moreover, the extent of habituation bears some relationship to the time an area has been under protection, as well as to the density of traffic. The opinion has been advanced repeatedly that this habituation may be facilitated by a certain similarity in appearance between motor vehicles and such large mammals as rhinoceroses (e. g., Cowan, 1974), but it is really unnecessary to adduce this kind of explanation. Habituation occurs simply as a result of the sum total of positive (or at least harmless) and negative experiences with a given class of objects (in this case vehicles). Recognition of this fact is behind the regulation that tourists should not leave their cars when near animals in a national park; the car, in effect, serves as a mobile hide for observation and photography. Unfortunately, many tourists do not look at it this way but get annoyed about being denied the opportunity to "stalk their game" and are highly surprised at the meagre photographic results they usually get out of such stalks, when they break the regulations! Apart from considerations of "sportsmanship," the same principle is probably behind the rule, contained in the game laws of several African countries, that no shooting is allowed within a certain distance of a vehicle.

However, there is no reason why habituation should be confined to vehicles, although this is often a first step. In fact, a number of investigators have demonstrated that it is possible to educate free-ranging ungulates, and other mammals, to the point of accepting man even unconcealed. In Geist's words, again (1971a, p. 414): "It is up to us to act in such a manner that we become acceptable, and remain a harmless part of that species' environment." Geist himself gave an impressive demonstration of this practice in his work with bighorn sheep, eventually reaching the point where he could hand-capture and tag some of the sheep, or read their tag numbers, on the open range. More recently, Douglas-Hamilton and Douglas-Hamilton (1975) achieved a similar relationship with

264

one or two wild elephants in Lake Manyara NP, Tanzania (though opinions among their colleagues on the wisdom of this undertaking are divided!). Another example are one or two old male buffaloes that took up residence near a rangers' post in Kabalega (Murchison Falls) NP and eventually became so tame that the rangers' children were able to play with them and even ride on their backs (Parker and Graham, 1971).

The speed and extent of habituation depend in some degree on species-specific or individual characteristics that are best termed "temperament." Although they cannot be described fully objectively, temperamental differences undoubtedly exist, both between species (e. g., wild eland are notoriously shy, whereas waterbuck tend to have "strong nerves") and between individuals within species (cf. Bigalke, 1974; Cowan, 1974).

Habituation is generally a slow process, and the initial introduction of a disturbance into the animals' habitat usually elicits adverse reactions at first. If a disturbance is localized, the locality concerned can be avoided. This may amount to some loss of available habitat, at least temporarily, but overall the effects of the disturbance may not be overly serious. If, on the other hand, disturbances are frequent and unpredictable with respect to locality, they may adversely affect the performance of the ungulate population involved. This has been experimentally established in domestic ungulates (references in Geist, 1971 a) and there is every reason to believe that similar effects can occur in wild ungulates, too. Such effects include neurosis, loss of appetite and weight, reduced growth, decreased reproduction, and even death. This is an extension of the principle, mentioned earlier, that animals develop best in a predictable environment. Any decrease in predictability causes excitation which, in turn, induces a rise in metabolic rate, i. e., "raises the energy cost of living" (Geist, 1971 a), thus diverting energy from growth and reproduction. Although all examples given by Geist in this context refer to temperate-zone and/or domestic ungulates and, to my knowledge, little if any comparable information exists as yet with regard to African ungulates, the potentially deleterious effects of man-made disturbances should always be kept in mind.

Apart from the more indirect (i. e., physiological, etc.) effects of disturbances on wild ungulates, man-made structures may also present more directly detrimental hazards to them. Obvious examples are roads and highways through game areas, but Cowan (1974) quoted some other instances in which ungulates perished because they were unable to cope with certain properties of man-made structures that differed from those of their natural counterparts, in particular canals and/or dams. Thus, provisions should be made to avoid such losses wherever developments of this nature are planned (e. g., irrigation schemes, realignment and correction of small rivers and streams, hydroelectric and other dams, etc.). The needs of game animals to approach and/or cross such structures should be kept in mind and allowance made in their design. This is particularly important where such construction projects are likely to interfere with long-established movements of ungulates.

Whereas wild ungulates may react to an increased disturbance level by simply withdrawing from an area (which would amount to a loss of available habitat), they can also respond in other ways. In particular, they may adjust their activity patterns, or their entire space-time systems, so as to minimize contact with the source(s) of disturbance. The commonest way of doing this—since man is basically a diurnal creature—is to shift the major activities to the night, or to visit certain areas only or mainly at night. A variety of large ungulates, such as elephant, buffalo, rhinoceros, etc., feed in the immediate vicinity of human habitations (park headquarters, tourist lodges, unprotected gardens and croplands) at night, but withdraw from the areas during the day. Where they are heavily hunted, some normally diurnal animals may become partly or entirely nocturnal in their activities, e. g., the warthog (Shortridge, 1934). Conversely, animals that tend to be crepuscular or nocturnal in unprotected areas may show essentially diurnal activity patterns in reserves or national parks, in the absence of serious disturbances.

Even if animals appear to be fully habituated to the presence and movements of vehicles, tourist traffic in a national park, particularly indiscriminate cross-country driving, can still have detrimental effects. In Thomson's gazelle, for instance, territorial males have a considerably lower flight distance from cars than females (Walther, 1969a). They will, therefore, tolerate much more traffic, without leaving their territories, than females which are disturbed more easily. This difference in reactions may, in the long run, lead to a lower reproductive rate, as potential matings are disturbed by unrestricted traffic. A simple remedy, to prevent such a situation from turning into a decline of the population involved, would be to restrict vehicular traffic to prescribed roads.

There are several good reasons for doing so anyway (destruction of vegetation, soil erosion, etc.); an additional one is also related to a behavioral characteristic of a number of African ungulates: the hiding of newborn young. To small fawns that lie on the ground for long periods, often far from the nearest adult conspecifics, indiscriminate cross-country driving constitutes a considerable danger. The very youngest fawns, in particular, tend to remain lying until being touched (cf. Fig. 44), rather than to jump up and run at the last moment, as some of the older ones do. They are, therefore, exposed to a considerable risk of being run over by vehicles moving across country. Moreover, even if they did escape that danger by running off, the very act of leaving their hiding place would increase the risk of their not being found again by their mothers, and thus impair their chances of survival. We have seen that the hiding place is an important link in the formation of the mother–young bond initially.

Additionally, a young antelope flushed from its hiding place is sometimes caught by tourists, on the erroneous assumption that it is abandoned or "orphaned." It is then off-loaded onto the nearest conservation officer who is expected to look after it. The tourists leave in the elevating belief of having saved the "orphan," whilst the park warden, or whoever it happens to be, is left with the often thankless task of catering for a young antelope that may be exhausted from the capture and the trip in the vehicle and, moreover, "determined" not to touch any food that one may attempt to force on it. Even under the best of circumstances, the survival chances of such young animals are rarely improved, and the best advice one can give to people coming across an apparently abandoned young antelope is to leave it alone. The outcome of the experiment I once performed with a newborn lesser kudu (see Chap.

14, D, II and Leuthold, 1971 d), and many other observations, indicate that lone antelope fawns may be less abandoned than they look.

So far, I have reviewed the effects of various man-made disturbances on free-ranging ungulates in general. It now remains to evaluate the specific influence of hunting through which certain individuals are killed. In many respects, the same considerations apply as discussed above; for instance, if hunting is heavy and fairly localized, animals may react by avoiding the area involved. The net result may be a loss of available habitat, and perhaps a decrease in the overall game population, if dispersal opportunities are limited. Probably the most important point to be made in this context is that hunting should be carried out in such a way that it would be difficult or impossible for the game to associate it with specific stimuli, such as cars, people, etc., so as not to interfere with a more general process of habituation to such objects (if desired at all). If such precautions are not observed, game animals will respond in some of the ways described earlier (e. g., general wildness, withdrawal from certain areas, changes in activity patterns, etc.), so that future hunting may become more and more difficult. Such situations have repeatedly arisen in the context of game eradication schemes designed to combat trypanosomiasis; this is one of the reasons why no such scheme has ever been fully successful.

The impact of hunting as a disturbance can further be lessened by restricting it in time, i. e., by having specified hunting seasons as is, in fact, being done in many areas. Such temporal restrictions of hunting should take into account the reproductive cycle of the animals concerned, so as to minimize interference with mating, parturition and care for the young. However, many tropical African ungulates breed throughout the year, making such considerations difficult or impossible to apply.

Hunting can further affect the performance of ungulate populations, in a manner at least partly related to behavior, through selective removal of certain sex/age classes. Sport hunting is traditionally directed primarily toward "trophies" and, as a consequence, mainly at adult—and often prime—males. If such selective hunting pressure becomes too great, the entire behavioral mechanism that operates in the distribution of mating opportunities (e. g., territoriality and other dominance relationships, see Chap. 18) may break down. As a result, relatively young males could obtain mating opportunities at an age at which they might still be subject to strong selective forces in an undisturbed population. This might have undesirable long-term consequences, particularly with respect to the genetic make-up of the population concerned.

Selective removal of older individuals—males or females—may also affect the maintenance of behavioral traditions, such as knowledge about seasonal home ranges, migration routes, etc. (cf. Leuthold, 1970c).

At the present state of knowledge on behavior and ecology of African ungulates we have, to date, only circumstantial evidence on many of the possible effects of disturbances, as discussed above, or we can only make inferences by analogy with other ungulates, or with less closely related mammals. In many situations, the effects of certain disturbances can only be determined empirically. However, it is certainly useful, for those concerned with management, to have at least a general idea of what may happen in any given circumstances, and what precautions could possibly be taken to minimize the impact of man-made disturbances, in the interest of healthy ungulate populations.

III. Specific Implications for Research and Management

After dealing with a number of rather generalized relationships between ungulate behavior and management, I now wish to review some more specific behavioral characteristics that have to be taken into account in the context of research and management.

1. Censusing

Certain behavioral features of ungulates affect the feasibility and/or accuracy of censuses and have to be considered when census methods are devised. The exact details may vary from one situation to another, but the following factors may be important:

1. Habitat preference and, particularly, its daily and/or seasonal changes. Obviously, the main type of habitat that a species normally occupies has a bearing on census methods, through conditions of visibility, etc. Perhaps even more important are the movements between different habitat types that are undertaken by some ungulates on a daily or seasonal basis. Only when these are known reasonably well, can a meaningful census be carried out.

2. Differential distribution of sex/age groups. In some ungulate species, particularly territorial ones, different sex/age classes may be spatially segregated to a considerable extent (see Chap. 18). If total population figures only are required, this may not matter, but if information on sex and age structure is desired, the census (particularly sampling) has to be distributed in such a way as to cover all habitats occupied by members of the population concerned.

3. Daily activity patterns can also affect the outcome of censuses, particularly in species that tend to have very restricted periods of activity (e. g., crepuscular). In theory, the best time for censusing would be the time of most intensive activity. In practice, however, it is often impossible to follow this guideline. As an alternative, animals may be flushed from resting areas for census purposes, e. g., small antelopes such as dikdik or bushbuck, but such methods are applicable only over small areas. In cases where large areas have to be covered, prolonged periods of inactivity can present serious obstacles to accurate counting. A case in point are elephants, which tend to rest in tightly bunched groups under trees for a considerable proportion of the daylight hours, particularly in hot weather, and are then difficult to count from the air. In any event, at least a general knowledge of a species' activity pattern is important in relation to censusing.

4. The tendency of many young bovids to remain hidden during their first few days or weeks creates a further difficulty for certain kinds of censuses, i. e., determination of the number of small young in a population. Hiding behavior, coupled with the fact that many African bovids produce young throughout

the year, thus presents considerable obstacles to the assessment of reproductive rates, natality and juvenile mortality in free-ranging ungulates.

2. Capture and Marking

For many types of study the possibility of recognizing individual animals is essential. While some species have permanent natural markings (e. g., giraffe, zebra, several Tragelaphines), others have to be artificially marked with visual tags and/or radio-transmitters. In this context, two potential hazards related to behavior have to be taken into account: reactions to the process of capture and handling, and responses to tags, etc., affixed to the animals.

Reactions to capture may include emotional stress, such as fear, etc., which in turn may lead to physiological disorders, a negative reaction to the place of capture and subsequent withdrawal from it, or loss of contact with the animal's social unit. The severity of such effects is likely to vary greatly, both within and between species, depending on circumstances in any given case. If an animal, after having been marked, leaves the area where it was caught, this may defeat the whole purpose of the operation. Such reactions usually cannot be predicted, but care should be taken that the animal(s) are not exposed to easily identifiable stimuli before and during handling, to minimize the possibilities for emotional upset and/or negative conditioning. It is difficult to evaluate the actual frequency of such reactions, as they may not always be reported. I have personal experience of the following two cases: in female Uganda kob, ovulation appeared to be suppressed in some cases where estrous females were immobilized on a lek; it is not clear whether this was an indirect consequence of emotional upset or a direct effect of the drugs used in the operation (Buechner et al., 1966). On the other hand, well over two hundred kob were captured during that study with no obvious ill effects in most cases (e. g., Buechner and Roth, 1974), and estrous females may have been especially sensitive to disturbance. One female elephant that was immobilized and radio-collared in Tsavo NP completely lost contact with her original group by wandering steadily away from the place of capture. This probably happened at a time when the animal was still under the influence of the drugs, though able to walk. Observations on such animals are obviously of dubious value. However, this female eventually joined another cow-calf group in another area. In most other cases of female elephants having been immobilized (11), there is at least circumstantial evidence that they rejoined their original groups within a few days (Leuthold and Sale, 1973, and unpubl.). Nevertheless, the possibility of aberrant behavior following capture has to be kept in mind when artificial marking is undertaken.

A special case of disturbance by capture is that involving newborn young, which may be caught by hand for marking during their hiding phase, or otherwise soon after birth. There is a certain danger that the establishment of the mother-young bond may be disrupted in the process. This is most likely to happen if (1) the female does not re-accept her young after it has been handled, or (2) if the young, after release, runs so far from its original hiding place that the mother does not find it again. The main precautions that can be taken to prevent either from happening are, firstly, to work quickly and to reduce the amount of actual handling of the young to the minimum, and, secondly, to release the young as close to the capture site as possible, and preferably near vegetation suitable for hiding again (tall grass, bush clumps, etc.). On the whole, the danger of disrupting the mother–young bond is probably exaggerated sometimes; in a number of studies many newborn young were caught and marked, the majority of which were resighted later. For instance, in the study of Uganda kob quoted above, of 34 fawns marked soon after birth 22 (71 %) were reobserved later (Buechner, 1963). Given the generally high juvenile mortality in bovids, this suggests that interference with the mother–young bond was not a serious factor in this case. However, again, the possibility must always be kept in mind.

The placing of artificial markers (ear tags, collars, radio-transmitters, etc.) could conceivably also affect the behavior of the animals concerned, either directly by causing discomfort, irritation, etc., or indirectly, through the responses of conspecifics to the "decorations." The best way to determine possible bias due to this source is to make comparative observations on naturally identifiable individuals, a few of which can almost always be found if looked for. On the whole, experience indicates that aberrant behavior directly attributable to artificial markers is rare and, if it does occur, usually confined to a short period immediately after marking.

3. Translocation and Restocking Operations

With the accelerating decrease of suitable habitat for ungulates, it happens more and more frequently that a remnant population becomes isolated in a small area unsuitable for its continued survival, or planned changes in land use threaten its further existence. Recent examples in Kenya include Uganda kob, roan antelope and Rothschild's giraffe. In such cases, translocation of part or all of the remnant population to another, "safer" area is often considered and sometimes carried out. However, there are a number of constraints that affect the success of such operations, some of which have largely behavioral causes.

In the process of translocation the animals are exposed to a number of stressful situations: the capture, contact with people around holding pens and vehicles, the actual transport, release and adjustment to the new area in terms of climate, food availability and other features. Thus, simple survival may be rather difficult, breeding and increase in numbers even more so. Therefore, the chances of success in such endeavors are a priori not very high, and the record of recent translocations confirms this: some Uganda kob translocated from western Kenya to the Mara Game Reserve (Kenya Game Department, 1963) have not been recorded recently; a number of Rothschild's giraffe moved from western to north-central Kenya in 1967/68 (Nesbit Evans, 1970) eventually dispersed and are now unaccounted for; some 35 roan taken to the Shimba Hills Reserve in 1969 decreased to 12 by 1974 and, although reproducing, lead a very tenuous existence; the latter also applies to some Hunter's hartebeest and Grévy's zebras introduced into Tsavo NP in 1963. On the other hand, translocation of white rhinoceroses from the Umfolozi GR in South Africa to a variety of other areas has been very successful. Also, a number of ungulate species have been introduced to various South African ranches, generally with reasonable success.

How, then, can these differences in success be explained, particularly as far as behavioral characteristics are concerned? The following factors may be important in this context:

Difficulties in Adjusting Food Habits. As we have seen (Chap. 5), the development of specific food habits can be a long and complex process, and readjustment may be difficult, particularly for adult animals. However, the very survival of at least some translocated ungulates indicates that this obstacle can be overcome with time, although there may be variations between species in the ease with which they adjust to new food sources.

Lack of Familiarity with Home Range. When discussing the concept of home range, we have seen that intimate familiarity with one's living space may be vital for survival in several respects, such as knowledge of food and water resources, antipredator behavior, etc. Lack of knowledge about seasonal changes in the environment, and possible movements to cope with them, may further expose the animals to increased stress. Absence of such knowledge in newly translocated animals is likely to impair not only individual survival but also reproduction and recruitment.

Lack of Social Cohesion. In the course of a translocation exercize it is quite likely that members of different social groups are caught and later released together. This may lead to fragmentation of the translocated herd and scattering of individuals as, in fact, has happened repeatedly. This can have two major consequences: firstly, the absence of more or less coherent groups may increase the risk of predation; secondly, lack of constant contact between males and females may prevent, or at least retard, reproduction.

Lack of Dispersal. Even if a translocation turns out to be basically successful, in terms of survival of individuals and subsequent reproduction, it may still fail to achieve its main objective, if the animals do not disperse and colonize available habitat farther afield. While there is no clear evidence in this respect for any African ungulates to date, such behavior has been very marked in bighorn sheep in the USA and Canada (Geist, 1968, 1971 b).

Other behavioral factors that may affect the success of translocation and restocking operations are the sensitivity of animals to capture and handling (partly a matter of temperament) and the tendency for homing. Perhaps the latter can be effectively neutralized if translocation is undertaken over a sufficiently great distance.

There are many additional factors that affect the outcome of such operations, mostly ecological ones such as the general suitability of the new habitat, the occurrence of predators, parasites and other organisms causing diseases, the security of the area with regard to hunting and other disturbances.

Obviously, the success of a translocation does not depend on one factor alone, but on a combination of several of those mentioned above, and perhaps others. In the white rhinoceros, the fact that it is virtually invulnerable to predators, at least when adult, may have played a big part in the successful outcome of a number of translocations. In smaller species, especially bovids, the crucial factor may well be simply the number of animals involved; if a sufficiently large stock can be moved initially, it can absorb considerable losses and still eventually establish a viable population in the new habitat.

4. Other Contexts

Activity Patterns. Like censusing, other aspects of research can be affected by an animal's activity pattern. For instance, Foster and Dagg (1972) reported that young giraffes seemed to be weaned and/or to separate from their mothers at only one or a few months of age. More recent studies (e. g., Mejia, 1972; Langman, pers. comm.; B. Leuthold, unpubl.) showed, however, that suckling often takes place at or near dawn and dusk and is generally very brief, but several young giraffes were being suckled until over one year old. If Foster's field work did not regularly include the dawn and dusk periods, he could easily have missed these interactions and consequently arrived at erroneous conclusions, particularly since young giraffes are often separated from their mothers by considerable distances during the daytime.

Traditions. If certain areas are regularly used for certain activities, care should be taken that such places are disturbed as little as possible. This applies especially to traditional calving and/or mating grounds (Cowan, 1974). While I know of no reports of fixed calving grounds in African ungulates (except possibly in blue wildebeest: Estes, 1966), the leks of the Uganda kob are a good example of localized, traditionally maintained mating areas (e. g., Buechner and Roth, 1974). Serious disturbances of such localities could have adverse effects on the population concerned.

Reactions to Light at Night. Kruuk (1972) reported that various ungulates tended to become disoriented when exposed to strong light beams at night and sometimes attracted attacks from predators under such circumstances. This reaction would probably also affect the value of any behavioral observations that might be made with the aid of car headlights, etc. In fact, the response is sometimes exploited for capture or shooting of ungulates dazzled by spotlights (see below).

Reactions to Physical Obstacles. Most ungulates hesitate to jump over an obstacle beyond which they cannot see. This behavior has been successfully exploited for the capture of relatively large numbers of ungulates (for translocation or other purposes). Opaque plastic material has been used to construct the wings of funnel traps into which the animals were then driven, by helicopter, men on horseback, etc. Even the walls of holding pens have been made from such plastic and, although the material could easily have been torn by the ungulates involved, it effectively contained them (e. g., Oelofse, 1970).

B. Game Ranching and Cropping

In enterprizes of this kind originally wild ungulates are left in more or less natural surroundings, but subject to various manipulations, and exploited for commercial gain. Economic considerations are therefore paramount, and a major goal is to avoid any condition that may adversely affect growth (weight gain). Behavioral characteristics and responses are relevant mainly in the following four broad contexts:

(a) food selection and intake; (b) activity patterns; (c) social relationships; (d) spatial constraints and the animals' reactions to them.

Interest in these relationships between behavior and productivity has awakened only recently, and relatively little well-documented information is available yet. A few detailed studies have been conducted recently, however (e. g., Lewis, 1975), and more are underway; some research on related topics has also been directed at domesticated ungulates under different systems of management (e. g., Kiley, 1974), the results of which may be relevant in our present context, too. The following is, of necessity, somewhat generalized and rather sketchy, and more detailed information is clearly needed in this field.

I. Food Selection and Intake

Under certain conditions of ranching various constraints are imposed on the animals involved, in terms of movement patterns, vegetation types available, and time spent feeding. In other words, the animals cannot follow their own inclinations and regulate their food intake and selection at will. In some cases, particularly where large predators still occur, ungulates are enclosed in stockades at night, with little or no food available during that time. All these constraints are likely to affect production adversely, particularly in animals that have not had time to fully adapt to them. Adverse effects may come about in the following ways:

1. Restriction of total intake, through insufficient time being available for feeding overall
2. Intake of qualitatively inferior food, through insufficient time and/or unsuitable vegetation types being available to enable proper selection to be made
3. A combination of both through various causes, including overutilization of the pastures to which the animals have access, soiling of the vegetation by dung (which can be a problem in cattle; see, e. g., Kiley, 1974), etc.
4. Disturbance of the natural rhythm of food intake and rumination, which may result in incomplete or inefficient utilization of the food actually ingested
5. Interference with the normal processes of water balance and intake mechanisms (for instance, some dry-country ungulates tend to feed primarily at night, taking advantage of higher relative humidity and water absorption by plants; e. g., Grant's gazelle: Taylor, 1972)
6. The effects of social interactions (see below).

II. Activity Patterns

As we have seen in Chapter 6, activity patterns of wild animals are finely adjusted to a number of environmental conditions, such as food, water, weather, etc. The main function of such adaptations is to optimize the animals' energy balance. If natural activity patterns are severely disrupted and artificial ones imposed under conditions of ranching, this is likely to have adverse effects on production, too. Some of these influences operate through the rhythms of feeding and rumination, actual time available for feeding and/or drinking, as outlined above. Activity patterns may further affect production via thermoregulation, e. g., if the animals subjected to an artificial timetable have to spend more energy on heat and water balance than if left to their own devices. Again, the distribution of activities between day and night may play an important part in this context (cf. Lewis, 1975).

III. Social Interactions

Where animals are herded or confined in relatively compact groups, attention must be paid to aspects of social compatibility. For instance, species that tend to be solitary and strongly territorial, such as dikdik, some duikers, etc., have to be considered as largely unsuitable for such treatment. In more gregarious species, dominance relationships within herds may affect individual well-being; for example, some animals may be "terrorized" by others and consequently be prevented from obtaining sufficient food and/or water, or from adjusting their activity pattern to external conditions in the most efficient way. This, in turn, will affect their performance in terms of production.

Individual distance will dictate the maximum density at which animals can be kept together (e. g., in enclosures, etc.), as well as the maximum number that it is practicable to herd together (Lewis, 1975). Engagement in certain social activities, such as the maintenance of a territory (where applicable), herding of females, etc., may take up too much time and energy in adult males to permit them to function efficiently in terms of food assimilation, reproduction, etc. Under natural conditions, "exhausted" males are replaced by "fresh" ones from time to time; this possibility should also be considered in ranching operations. Unless the functioning of the natural social organization is recognized and simulated as far as possible, certain behaviorally based problems in ranching (e. g., injuries caused by frequent social strife) can only be countered by extreme measures, such as de-horning.

A special problem is posed by the mother–young relationship. This bond is vital for the survival and development of young ungulates, and its formation depends on certain conditions. The most important of these, in the majority of species, is the isolation of the parturient female from other conspecifics. Care should therefore be taken that this condition can be met as far as may be possible under the circumstances prevailing in any given case. Otherwise, "misattachment" of young may easily occur which, in turn, could jeopardize their survival.

274

IV. Effects of Spatial Constraints

The design of fences and other barriers constructed to contain ungulates must take into account not only the physical abilities of the animals concerned, but also their behavioral reactions to them and the effects of confinement in general. Lack of space may be a cause of injuries or of malnutrition, if certain animals are harassed by others and cannot withdraw sufficiently. Also, normal development of the mother–young bond may not be possible, as mentioned above. On the other hand, animals may adapt so completely to certain spatial constraints that they will not leave an enclosure even after the fence has been removed (Bigalke, 1974)! Such behavior may present obstacles to the implementation of, e. g., rotational grazing schemes.

All the constraints referred to above, and the animals' reactions to them, can have detrimental effects on the performance of the ungulates involved, and thus on the economic return they provide. Those in charge of game ranching projects should, therefore, endeavor to take into account the behavioral characteristics of ungulates in their care and to see how they can best cope with them in each particular situation.

The above remarks apply primarily to ranching projects with fairly intensive management and manipulation of the animals involved. In other circumstances essentially free-roaming ungulates are exploited commercially through regular shooting and utilization of products, such as meat and skins (sustained-yield cropping). In such situations many of the points mentioned earlier in the context of sport hunting apply equally, viz. minimization of disturbances, consideration of the social structure, differential habitat preferences and/or dispersion of different sex/age classes, mobility and/or local attachment (fidelity to a given home range), etc. The aim will have to be to spread utilization more or less equally through the population concerned, both geographically and sociologically, unless a change in the original population structure is desired. In this context, differences in flight distances between sex/age classes, as demonstrated in Thomson's gazelle by Walther (1969a) and probably prevailing in many ungulate species, have to be taken into account, too. Unless a conscious effort is made to randomize collections, those animals with the shortest flight distances are in danger of becoming overexploited. One possible way to avoid this is to hunt at night, using powerful spotlights which dazzle the animals (Chap. 20, A, III, 4). Night hunting has the additional advantage that it tends to minimize disturbances to the animals and, particularly, is less likely to result in negative conditioning toward certain stimuli (vehicles, people, etc.) than daytime hunting (cf. Cowan, 1974; Bigalke, 1974).

In the case of the elephant, overall disturbance can also be reduced by shooting entire family units (e. g., Laws and Parker, 1968). The tightly knit structure of these groups results in their remaining together and clustering around the leading cow, which it is advantageous to shoot first. This is probably the most effective and, relatively speaking, most humane method of shooting comparatively large numbers of elephants, particularly where reduction cropping is desired and where no selectivity with regard to sex and age is intended.

Other considerations of some importance with respect to game utilization concern more basic traits of species, such as their habitat preference, gregariousness, body size, etc. As we have seen (Chap. 19), these attributes are interrelated to a considerable extent, and some species lend themselves better than others to exploitation on a sustained-yield basis. An important factor in this context is the input (man-hours, etc.) required per unit product. From this point of view most species that combine small body size with largely solitary life in dense vegetation (dikdik, duikers, etc.) are unsuitable for commercial cropping and can be exploited more profitably through sport hunting, provided the necessary market exists (for further discussion on this subject, and specific examples, see Bigalke, 1974).

C. Management in Captivity

This is not the place to deal with this subject in depth; others more qualified have done this before, in particular Hediger (1942/50), who emphasized the behavioral requirements of wild animals kept in captivity. I will, therefore, only mention a few points briefly.

The principal concerns in maintaining wild animals in captivity, primarily in zoos and zoolike establishments, are their survival, good health and, if possible, reproduction. The first two of these aspects relate mainly to physical health which, in turn, can be assured largely through suitable food and adequate conditions of hygiene, veterinary care and protection from accidents, as far as may be possible. Reproduction, however, depends in much larger measure on the overall, including behavioral, well-being of the animals concerned; indeed, reproduction is often the ultimate criterion by which well-being (as opposed to mere survival) can be judged.

In this context, the quality of the space provided may play an important part, as Hediger (1942/50) first pointed out. A certain diversity in the structure of enclosures provides possibilities for the establishment of specific space-time systems. Since food and water are provided and there are no predators to guard against, captive ungulates have very little "to do." Unless preventive measures are taken, this may lead to the development of stereotyped action patterns, which are not only repulsive to watch but also difficult to get rid of once they are established. Variety in the equipment of enclosures can go a long way toward alleviating possible "boredom." A further step in the same direction is to engage the animals in regular exercizes, performance of work, "tricks," etc., as is frequently done with such active and versatile animals as elephants. In the same context, it is also advantageous to keep ungulates in groups rather than singly, so that there are opportunities for social interactions, always provided that their natural social organization makes them suitable for group-living.

Keeping several animals, whether conspecifics or not, in the same enclosure raises other problems, related perhaps more to quantity than to quality of

276

the space provided. Harassment of low-ranking animals by others, including interference with feeding, and attendant problems of injuries can be eliminated, or at least alleviated, if sufficient space is made available, and/or if the space provided is suitably subdivided so that the "persecuted" animal(s) can withdraw from the attacker. Sufficient space is also necessary in the context of mother–young relations, as discussed earlier, and care has to be taken to ensure that the mother–young bond is properly developed before young animals are brought into contact with others. Dittrich (1968) reported an instance of utter confusion arising when two young hartebeests were released into a large open-air enclosure with their mothers, as well as some other animals, before they had learned to recognize their mothers individually. Panic resulting from such situations could easily lead to losses of young animals.

The exclusiveness of the mother–young bond in most ungulates may create difficulties when a young animal has to be reared artificially. If it has already had some contact with its mother, it may refuse to take food from humans. Alternatively, if it has been fed by one particular person since birth, it may not accept food from anybody else. These difficulties can be overcome, in most cases, if the scent of the real or foster mother is presented along with the new source of food (Walther, 1969b; Leuthold, 1967). The effect may be enhanced by such "maternal" activities as rubbing the perineal area of the young, simulating licking by the mother.

For those in charge of captive ungulates, at least a basic knowledge of their behavior can be useful, occasionally even vital, particularly with regard to expressive behavior. As animals tend to use their intraspecific behavior in interactions with other species, including man, as well (Hediger, 1965), familiarity with such behavior is likely to facilitate handling of the animals and, especially, to prevent "misunderstandings" and possible accidents resulting from them. This is most important with respect to threat behavior that may precede an attack, but may also be useful in other contexts, e. g., to recognize imminent parturition from the behavior of a female seeking to isolate herself from conspecifics.

Further problems and details of keeping wild ungulates in captivity have been discussed by Walther (1965c), in addition to the broader treatments of the subject by Hediger (1942/50) and Crandall (1964).

D. Conclusion

The information and discussions presented in this chapter have, I hope, made clear that knowledge of the behavior of wild ungulates can be a very useful, even essential, tool in management. The main difficulty that prevents a more widespread application of such knowledge at the present time is that much remains unknown about the interrelationships between ecological conditions and behavioral adaptations of ungulates. Up to now, students of the biology of African ungulates have endeavored mainly to accumulate basic information about as many species as possible. While much still remains to be done in this respect—especially regarding forest and desert ungulates—it is at least as important now to conduct comparative studies on the same species in different areas, under different environmental conditions, as has been done with, e. g., impala. Only in this way will it be possible to arrive at sound conclusions regarding the functional relationships between behavior and ecology which, in turn, can be applied to management.

The ultimate aim in this context should be to develop behavioral criteria that can be used to assess ecological performance. This would be particularly useful in relation to national parks and other reserves, as it might obviate—or at least reduce—the need to collect animals for ecological investigations, such as monitoring the status of populations (cf. Geist, 1971 a). The following case provides a crude example: in a situation where southern reedbuck were suffering from overcrowding and consequent starvation, they adopted unusual activity patterns, such as exposing themselves to the sun in the open areas in daytime; they also gave indications of heavy tick infestation by very frequent scratching (Ferrar and Kerr, 1971). The animals were by then in very poor condition and later died in considerable numbers. Obviously, this is an extreme case, where ecological deterioration had already progressed very far and the behavior of the animals bordered on the pathological. However, it is entirely conceivable that more subtle behavioral manifestations could eventually provide an assessment of the ecological "health" of ungulate populations. Possible fields of investigations in this direction include all those behaviors that can be directly or indirectly affected by environmental conditions, e. g., the extent of movements, dispersal of different sex/age classes, activity patterns, frequency of aggressive interactions, the intensity of maternal care, etc. This approach has, to my knowledge, hardly been tried yet, but I feel some research to investigate its feasibility would be worthwhile.

References

Note: A considerable number of papers quoted below were published in the context of a symposium on ungulate behavior held in November 1971 in Calgary, Canada. To avoid repetition, this will be referred to simply as "Calgary-Symposium." The full citation is as follows:

Geist, V., Walther, F. R. (eds.): The Behaviour of Ungulates and its Relation to Management. Morges: IUCN Publications New Series No. 24 (1974)

Papers referred to but which I did not see in the original are marked with an asterisk (*).

Ables, E. D., Ables, J.: Home-range and activity studies of impala in northern Kenya. Trans. N. Amer. Wildl. Nat. Res. Conf. **34**, 360–371 (1969)

Ables, E. D., Ables, J.: Radio-tracking studies of a Kenya hartebeest. E. Afr. Wildl. J. **9**, 145–146 (1971)

Adams, L., Davis, S. D.: The internal anatomy of home range. J. Mammal. **48**, 529–536 (1967)

Aeschlimann, A.: Observations sur *Philantomba maxwelli* (Hamilton-Smith), une antilope de la forêt éburnée. Acta Trop. **20**, 341–368 (1963)

Allee, W. C.: The Social Life of Animals. Boston: Beacon Press (revised ed.), 1958

Allsopp, R.: The population dynamics and social biology of bushbuck (*Tragelaphus scriptus* Pallas). Unpubl. M. Sc. Thesis, Univ. Nairobi, 1971

Altmann, D.: Harnen und Koten bei Säugetieren. Neue Brehm-Bücherei No. 404. Wittenberg-Lutherstadt: Ziemsen, 1969

Altmann, D.: Zur Geburt beim Buntbock, *Damaliscus dorcas dorcas*. Zool. Garten NF **40**, 80–96 (1971)

Altmann, M.: Patterns of herd behavior in free-ranging elk of Wyoming, *Cervus canadensis nelsoni*. Zoologica (N. Y.) **41**, 65–71 (1956)

Altmann, M.: Naturalistic studies of maternal care in moose and elk. In: Maternal Behavior in Mammals. Rheingold, H. L. (ed.). New York: Wiley, 1963, 233–253

Anderson, J. L.: Seasonal changes in the social organization and distribution of the impala in Hluhluwe Game Reserve, Zululand. J. Sth. Afr. Wildl. Manage. Assoc. **2**, 16–20 (1972)

Ansell, W. F. H.: Proboscidea, Perissodactyla, Artiodactyla. Parts 11, 14 and 15. In: The Mammals of Africa—An Identification Manual. Meester, J., Setzer, H. W. (eds.). Washington: Smithsonian Institution, 1971

Antonius, O.: Über Herdenbildung und Paarungseigentümlichkeiten der Einhufer. Z. Tierpsychol. **1**, 259–289 (1937)*

Astley Maberly, C. T.: Animals of East Africa. Cape Town: Timmins, 1960

Attwell, R. I. G.: Oxpeckers and their associations with mammals in Zambia. Puku **4**, 17–48 (1966)

Ayeni, J. S. O.: Utilization of waterholes in Tsavo National Park (East). E. Afr. Wildl. J. **13**, 305–323 (1975)

Backhaus, D.: Beitrag zur Ethologie der Paarung einiger Antilopen. Zuchthygiene **2**, 281–293 (1958)

Backhaus, D.: Beobachtungen über das Freileben von Lelwel-Kuhantilopen (*Alcelaphus buselaphus lelwel*) und Gelegenheitsbeobachtungen an Sennar-Pferdeantilopen (*Hippotragus equinus bakeri*). Z. Säugetierk. **24**, 1–34 (1959)

Backhaus, D.: Über das Kampfverhalten beim Steppenzebra. Z. Tierpsychol. **17**, 345–350 (1960)

Backhaus, D.: Beobachtungen an Giraffen in zoologischen Gärten und in freier Wildbahn. Bruxelles: Inst. Parcs Nat. Congo, 1961

Balch, C. C.: Sleep in ruminants. Nature (Lond.) **175**, 940–941 (1955)

Baldwin, H.: Instrumentation for remote observation of physiology and behaviour. Proc. Symp. Biotel. S. Afr. C. S. I. R. (1971; quoted in Douglas-Hamilton, 1972)*

Balinsky, B. I.: Patterns of animal distribution on the African continent. Ann. Cape Prov. Mus. **2**, 299–310 (1962)

Bartholomew, G. A., Hoel, P. G.: Reproductive behavior of the Alaska fur seal *Callorhinus ursinus*. J. Mammal. **34**, 417–436 (1953)

Bell, R. H. V.: A grazing ecosystem in the Serengeti. Sci. Amer. **224**, 86–93 (1971)

Bigalke, R. C.: The Springbok. Nat. Hist. **75**, 20–25 (1966)

Bigalke, R. C.: The contemporary mammal fauna of Africa. Quart. Rev. Biol. **43**, 265–300 (1968)

Bigalke, R. C.: Observations on springbok populations. Zool. Afr. **5**, 59–70 (1970)

Bigalke, R. C.: Observations on the behaviour and feeding habits of the springbok, *Antidorcas marsupialis*. Zool. Afr. **7**, 333–359 (1972)

Bigalke, R. C.: Ungulate behaviour and management, with special reference to husbandry of wild ungulates on South African ranches. Calgary Symposium, 830–852 (1974)

Bigourdan, J.: Le phacochère et les Suidés dans l'Ouest africain. Bull. IFAN (Dakar) **10**, 285–360 (1948)*

Blunt, D. E.: Elephant. London: East Africa, 1930

Bradley, R. M.: Some aspects of the ecology of the warthog (*Phacochoerus aethiopicus* (Pallas)) in Nairobi National Park. Unpubl. M. Sc. Thesis, Univ. East Africa, Nairobi, 1968

Bradley, R. M.: Warthog (*Phacochoerus aethiopicus* Pallas) burrows in Nairobi National Park. E. Afr. Wildl. J. **9**, 149–152 (1971)

Brooks, A. C.: A study of the Thomson's gazelle (*Gazella thomsoni* Günther) in Tanganyika. London: Col. Res. Publ. No. 25 (1961)

Brown, J. L., Orians, G. H.: Spacing patterns in mobile animals. Ann. Rev. Ecol. Syst. **1**, 239–262 (1970)

Brown, L. H.: Africa, a Natural History. New York: Random House, 1965. German ed.: Afrika. München, Zürich: Droemer Knaur, 1966

Buechner, H. K.: Territorial behavior in Uganda kob. Science **133**, 698–699 (1961)

Buechner, H. K.: Territoriality as a behavioral adaptation to environment in Uganda kob. Proc. 16th Intern. Congr. Zool. **3**, 59–63 (1963)

Buechner, H. K.: Implications of social behavior in the management of Uganda kob. Calgary Symposium, 853–870 (1974)

Buechner, H. K., Harthoorn, A. M., Lock, J. A.: Recent advances in field immobilization of large mammals with drugs. Trans. N. Amer. Wildl. Conf. **25**, 415–422 (1960)

Buechner, H. K., Morrison, J. A., Leuthold, W.: Reproduction in Uganda kob with special reference to behavior. Symp. Zool. Soc. London **15**, 69–88 (1966)

Buechner, H. K., Roth, H. D.: The lek system in Uganda kob antelope. Amer. Zool. **14**, 145–162 (1974)

Buechner, H. K., Schloeth, R.: Ceremonial mating behavior in Uganda kob (*Adenota kob thomasi* Neumann). Z. Tierpsychol. **22**, 209–225 (1965)

Buechner, H. K., Stromann, H. R., Xanten, W. A.: Breeding behavior of sable antelope *Hippotragus niger* in captivity. Int. Zoo Yb. **14**, 133–136 (1974)

Burckhardt, D.: Kindliches Verhalten als Ausdrucksbewegung im Fortpflanzungszeremoniell einiger Wiederkäuer. Rev. suisse Zool. **65**, 311–316 (1958)

Burke, C. B.: Zebrastute packte Löwin am Genick. Tier **14**, 7–9 (1974)

Burt, W. H.: Territorial behavior and populations of some small mammals in southern Michigan. Misc. Publ. Univ. Michigan Mus. Zool. **45**, 1–58 (1940)

Burt, W. H.: Territory and home range concepts as applied to mammals. J. Mammal. **24**, 346–352 (1943)

Burt, W. H.: Territoriality. J. Mammal. **30**, 25–27 (1949)

Buss, I. O.: Some observations on food habits and behavior of the African elephant. J. Wildl. Manage. **25**, 131–148 (1961)

Buss, I. O., Estes, J. A.: The functional significance of movements and positions of the pinnae of the African elephant. J. Mammal. **52**, 21–27 (1971)

Buss, I. O., Smith, N. S.: Observations on reproduction and breeding behavior of the African elephant. J. Wildl. Manage. **30**, 375–388 (1966)

Chalmers, G.: Breeding data: Steinbok (*Raphicerus campestris* Thunberg). E. Afr. Wildl. J. **1**, 121–122 (1963)

Child, G., le Riché, J. D.: Recent springbok treks (mass movements) in south-western Botswana. Mammalia **33**, 499–504 (1969)

Child, G., von Richter, W.: Observations on ecology and behaviour of lechwe, puku and waterbuck along the Chobe River, Botswana. Z. Säugetierk. **34**, 275–295 (1969)

Child, G., Roth, H. H., Kerr, M.: Reproduction and recruitment patterns in warthog (*Phacochoerus aethiopicus*) populations. Mammalia **32**, 6–29 (1968)

Cloudsley-Thompson, J. L.: The Zoology of Tropical Africa. London: Weidenfeld and Nicolson, 1969

Cloudsley-Thompson, J. L.: The expanding Sahara. Environm. Cons. **1**, 5–13 (1974)

Clough, G.: Some preliminary observations on reproduction in the warthog, *Phacochoerus aethiopicus* Pallas. J. Reprod. Fert., Suppl. **6**, 323–337 (1969)

Clough, G., Hassam, A. G.: A quantitative study of the daily activity of the warthog in the Queen Elizabeth National Park, Uganda. E. Afr. Wildl. J. **8**, 19–24 (1970)

Coe, M. J.: "Necking" behaviour in the giraffe. J. Zool., Lond. **151**, 313–321 (1967)

Cowan, I. McT.: Management implications of behaviour in the large herbivorous mammals. Calgary Symposium, 921–934 (1974)

Crandall, L. S.: The Management of Wild Mammals in Captivity. Chicago: Univ. Chicago Press, 1964

Crook, J. H.: The adaptive significance of avian social organizations. Symp. Zool. Soc. Lond. **14**, 181–218 (1965)

Crook, J. H.: The socio-ecology of primates. In: Social Behaviour in Birds and Mammals. Crook, J. H. (ed.). London and New York: Academic Press, 1970a

Crook, J. H.: Social organization and the environment: Aspects of contemporary social ethology. Anim. Behav. **18**, 197–209 (1970b)

Crook, J. H.: Sources of cooperation in animals and man. In: Man and Beast, Smithsonian Annual III. Eisenberg, J. F., Dillon, W. S. (eds.). Washington: Smithsonian Institution, 1971, pp. 237–260

Crook, J. H., Goss-Custard, J. D.: Social ethology. Ann. Rev. Psychol. **23**, 277–312 (1972)

Croze, H.: The Seronera bull problem.—I. The elephants. E. Afr. Wildl. J. **12**, 1–27 (1974)

Cumming, D. H. M.: A field study of the ecology and behaviour of warthog. Museum Memoir No. 7, Salisbury: 1975

Dagg, A. I.: External features of giraffe. Mammalia **32**, 657–669 (1968)

Dagg, A. I.: *Giraffa camelopardalis*. Mammal. Species **5**, 1–8 (1971)

Dagg, A. I., Taub, A.: Flehmen. Mammalia **34**, 686–695 (1970)

Darling, F. F.: Wild Life in an African Territory. London: Oxford Univ. Press, 1960

David, J. H. M.: The behaviour of the bontebok, *Damaliscus dorcas dorcas* (Pallas 1766), with special reference to territorial behaviour. Z. Tierpsychol. **33**, 38–107 (1973)

David, J. H. M.: Observations on mating behaviour, parturition, suckling and the mother–young bond in the Bontebok (*Damaliscus dorcas dorcas*). J. Zool., Lond. **177**, 203–223 (1975)

Davis, D. H. S.: Distribution patterns of Southern African Muridae, with notes on their fossil antecedants. Ann. Cape Prov. Mus. **2**, 56–76 (1962)

Dittrich, L.: Absetzen von Voraugendrüsensekret an den Hörnern von Artgenossen bei Gazellen und Dikdiks. Säugetierkundl. Mitt. **13**, 145–146 (1965)

Dittrich, L.: Erfahrungen bei der Gesellschaftshaltung verschiedener Huftierarten. Zool. Garten NF **36**, 95–106 (1968)

Dittrich, L.: Beitrag zur Fortpflanzungsbiologie afrikanischer Antilopen im Zoologischen Garten. Zool. Garten NF **39**, 16–40 (1970)

Dorst, J., Dandelot, P.: A Field Guide to the Larger Mammals of Africa. London: Collins, 1970

Douglas-Hamilton, I.: On the ecology and behaviour of the African elephant.—The elephants of Lake Manyara. Unpubl. D. Phil. Thesis, Univ. Oxford, 1972

Douglas-Hamilton, I.: On the ecology and behaviour of the Lake Manyara elephants. E. Afr. Wildl. J. **11**, 401–403 (1973)

Douglas-Hamilton, I., Douglas-Hamilton, O.: Among the Elephants. London: Collins and Harvill Press, 1975

Dubost, G.: Un ruminant à régime alimentaire partiellement carné: Le chevrotain aquatique (*Hyemoschus aquaticus* Ogilby). Biol. Gabon. **1**, 21–23 (1964)

Dubost, G.: Quelques traits remarquables du comportement de *Hyemoschus aquaticus* (Tragulidae, Ruminantia, Artiodactyla). Biol. Gabon. **1**, 283–287 (1965)

Dubost, G.: L'organisation spatiale et sociale de *Muntiacus reevesi* Ogilby 1839 en semi-liberté. Mammalia **34**, 331–355 (1970)

Dubost, G.: Observations éthologiques sur le Muntjak (*Muntiacus muntjak* Zimmermann 1780 et *M. reevesi* Ogilby 1839) en captivité et semi-liberté. Z. Tierpsychol. **28**, 387–427 (1971)

Dubost, G.: Le comportement du Chevrotain africain, *Hyemoschus aquaticus* Ogilby (Artiodactyla, Ruminantia). Z. Tierpsychol. **37**, 403–501 (1975)

Dubost, G., Terrade, R.: La transformation de la peau des Tragulidae en bouclier protecteur. Mammalia **34**, 505–513 (1970)

Duncan, P.: Topi and their food supply. Unpubl. Ph. D. Thesis, Univ. Nairobi, 1975

Eaton, R.: Hunting behavior of the cheetah. J. Wildl. Manage. **34**, 56–67 (1970)

Eibl-Eibesfeldt, I.: Grundriss der vergleichenden Verhaltensforschung. München: Piper, 1967. English ed.: Ethology, the Biology of Behavior. New York: Holt, Rinehart and Winston, 1970

Eisenberg, J. F.: The social organizations of mammals. Handb. Zool. **8** (10/7, 39. Lfg.), 1–92 (1966)

Eisenberg, J. F., Kleiman, D. G.: Olfactory communication in mammals. Ann. Rev. Ecol. Syst. **3**, 1–32 (1972)

Eisenberg, J. F., Lockhart, M.: An ecological reconnaissance of Wilpattu National Park, Ceylon. Smithsonian Contrib. Zool. 101. Washington: Smithsonian Institution, 1972

Elder, W. H., Elder, N. L.: Social groupings and primate associations of the bushbuck (*Tragelaphus scriptus*). Mammalia **34**, 356–362 (1970)

Emlen, J. T.: Defended area?—a critique of the territory concept and of conventional thinking. Ibis **99**, 352 (1957)

Erkert, H. G.: Der Einfluss des Mondlichtes auf die Aktivitätsperiodik nachtaktiver Säugetiere. Oecologia (Berl.) **14**, 269–287 (1974)

Esser, A. H. (ed.): Behaviour and Environment. New York: Plenum Press, 1971

Estes, R. D.: Behaviour and life history of the wildebeest (*Connochaetes taurinus* Burchell). Nature **212**, 999–1,000 (1966)

Estes, R. D.: The comparative behavior of Grant's and Thomson's gazelles. J. Mammal. **48**, 189–209 (1967)

Estes, R. D.: Territorial behavior of the wildebeest (*Connochaetes taurinus* Burchell, 1823). Z. Tierpsychol. **26**, 284–370 (1969)

Estes, R. D.: The role of the vomeronasal organ in mammalian reproduction. Mammalia **36**, 315–341 (1972)

Estes, R. D.: Social organization of the African Bovidae. Calgary Symposium, 166–205 (1974)

Estes, R. D.: The significance of breeding synchrony in the wildebeest. E. Afr. Wildl. J. **14**, 135–152 (1976)

Estes, R. D.: Behavior of Large African Mammals—I. Ungulates. Cambridge USA: Harvard Univ. Press (in press)

Estes, R. D., Estes, R. K.: The Shimba Hills sable population. Unpubl. Progress Report, Nat. Geogr. Soc., 34 pp. (1969)

Estes, R. D., Estes, R. K.: The biology and conservation of the giant sable antelope, *Hippotragus niger variani*, Thomas, 1916. Proc. Acad. Nat. Sci. Philadelphia **126**, 73–104 (1974)

282

Estes, R. D., Goddard, J.: Prey selection and hunting behavior of the African wild dog. J. Wildl. Manage. **31**, 52–70 (1967)

Etkin, W. (ed.): Social Behavior and Organization Among Vertebrates. Chicago: Univ. Chicago Press, 1964

Ewer, R. F.: Adaptive features in the skulls of African Suidae. Proc. Zool. Soc. Lond. **131**, 135–155 (1958)

Ewer, R. F.: Ethology of Mammals. London: Logos Press, 1968

Ferrar, A., Kerr, M.: A population crash of the reedbuck *Redunca arundinum* (Boddaert) in Kyle National Park, Rhodesia. Arnoldia (Rhod) **5** (16), 1–19 (1971)

Field, C. R.: The food habits of some wild ungulates in Uganda by analyses of stomach contents. E. Afr. Wildl. J. **10**, 17–42 (1972)

Finch, V. A.: Energy exchanges with the environment of two East African antelopes, the eland and the hartebeest. Symp. Zool. Soc. Lond. **31**, 315–326 (1972)

Finch, V. A.: Thermoregulation and heat balance in some East African herbivores. Unpubl. Ph. D. Thesis, Univ. Nairobi, 1973*

Fisler, G. F.: Mammalian organizational systems. Los Ang. County Mus. Contrib. Sci. no. **167**, 32 pp. (1969)

Floody, O. R., Arnold, A. P.: Uganda kob *(Adenota kob thomasi)*: Territoriality and the spatial distributions of sexual and agonistic behaviors at a territorial ground. Z. Tierpsychol. **37**, 192–212 (1975)

Foster, J. B.: The giraffe of Nairobi National Park: Home ranges, sex ratios, the herd, and food. E. Afr. Wildl. J. **4**, 139–148 (1966)

Foster, J. B., Dagg, A. I.: Notes on the biology of the giraffe. E. Afr. Wildl. J. **10**, 1–16 (1972)

Frädrich, H.: Zur Biologie und Ethologie des Warzenschweines (*Phacochoerus aethiopicus* Pallas), unter Berücksichtigung des Verhaltens anderer Suiden. Z. Tierpsychol. **22**, 328–393 (1965)

Frädrich, H.: Das Verhalten der Schweine (Suidae, Tayassuidae) und Flusspferde (Hippopotamidae). Handb. Zool. **8** (10/26), 1–44 (1967)

Frädrich, H.: A comparison of behaviour in the Suidae. Calgary Symposium, 133–143 (1974)

Fraser, A. F.: Reproductive Behaviour in Ungulates. London and New York: Academic Press, 1968

Gaerdes, J. H.: The impala of South West Africa. Afr. Wild Life **19**, 108–113 and 145 (1965)*

Gartlan, J. S.: Structure and function in primate societies. Folia primatol. **8**, 89–120 (1968)*

Geigy, R.: Observations sur les phacochères du Tanganyika. Rev. suisse Zool. **62** (suppl.), 139–163 (1955)

Geist, V.: The evolution of horn-like organs. Behaviour **27**, 175–214 (1966)

Geist, V.: Welchen Wert hat die Verhaltensforschung in Wildnisgebieten für eine moderne Wildverwaltung? Tag.ber. **104**, 9–15, Beiträge zur Jagd und Wildforschung. Berlin: Deutsche Akademie der Landwirtschaftswissenschaften, 1968

Geist, V.: A behavioural approach to the management of wild ungulates. In: The Scientific Management of Animal and Plant Communities for Conservation. Duffey, E., Watt, A. S. (eds.). Oxford: Blackwell Sci. Publ., 1971 a, pp. 413–424

Geist, V.: Mountain Sheep. A Study in Behavior and Evolution. Chicago: Univ. Chicago Press, 1971 b

Geist, V.: On the relationship of social evolution and ecology in ungulates. Amer. Zool. **14**, 205–220 (1974)

Gentry, A. W.: Genus *Gazella*. Part 15.1 In: The Mammals of Africa; an Identification Manual. Meester, J., Setzer, H. W. (eds.). Washington: Smithsonian Institution, 1971

Glover, P. E.: An ecological survey of the proposed Shimba Hills National Reserve. Mimeographed Report, Nairobi: Kenya National Parks, 1968

Goddard, J.: Mating and courtship of the black rhinoceros. E. Afr. Wildl. J. **4**, 69–75 (1966)

Goddard, J.: Home range, behaviour and recruitment rates of two black rhinoceros *Diceros bicornis* L. populations. E. Afr. Wildl. J. **5**, 133–150 (1967)

283

Goddard, J.: Food preferences of two black rhinoceros populations. E. Afr. Wildl. J. **6,** 1–18 (1968)

Goddard, J.: Food preferences of the black rhinoceros in the Tsavo National Park. E. Afr. Wildl. J. **8,** 145–161 (1970)

Gosling, L. M.: Parturition and related behaviour in Coke's hartebeest, *Alcelaphus buselaphus cokei* Günther. J. Reprod. Fert., Suppl. **6,** 265–286 (1969)

Gosling, L. M.: The construction of antorbital gland marking sites by male oribi (*Ourebia ourebi* Zimmermann, 1783). Z. Tierpsychol. **30,** 271–276 (1972)

Gosling, L. M.: The social behaviour of Coke's hartebeest (*Alcelaphus buselaphus cokei*). Calgary Symposium, 488–511 (1974)

Gosling, L. M.: The ecological significance of male behaviour in Coke's hartebeest, *Alcelaphus buselaphus cokii,* Günther. Unpubl. Ph. D. Thesis, Univ. Nairobi, 1975

Grimm, R.: Blauböckchen (*Cephalophus monticola,* Thunberg, 1798; Cephalophinae, Bovidae) als Insektenfresser. Z. Säugetierk. **35,** 357–359 (1970)

Grimsdell, J. J. R.: Ecology of the buffalo, *Syncerus caffer,* in Western Uganda. Unpubl. Ph. D. Thesis, Univ. Cambridge, 1969

Grobler, J. H.: Aspects of the biology, population ecology and behaviour of the sable *Hippotragus niger niger* (Harris, 1838) in the Rhodes Matopos National Park, Rhodesia. Arnoldia (Rhod.) **7** (6), 1–36 (1974)

Grubb, P., Jewell, P. A.: Social grouping and home range in feral Soay sheep. Symp. Zool. Soc. London **18,** 179–210 (1966)

Grzimek, M., Grzimek, B.: A study of the game of the Serengeti Plains. Z. Säugetierk. **25** (Sonderheft), 1–61 (1960)

Guggisberg, C. A. W.: Man and Wildlife. London: Evans Bros., 1970

Guiraud, M.: Contribution à l'étude du *Phacochoerus aethiopicus* (Pallas). Mammalia **12,** 56–66 (1948)*

Gwynne, M. D., Bell, R. H. V.: Selection of vegetation components by grazing ungulates in the Serengeti National Park. Nature (Lond.) **220,** 390–393 (1968)

Haas, G.: Untersuchungen über angeborene Verhaltensweisen beim Mähnenspringer (*Ammotragus lervia* Pallas). Z. Tierpsychol. **16,** 218–242 (1959)*

Hagen, H.: Zum Trinkverhalten der Giraffengazellen (Gerenuk), (*Litocranius walleri* Brooke, 1878). Z. Säugetierk. **40,** 54–57 (1975)

Haltenorth, T.: Klassifikation der Säugetiere: Artiodactyla. Handb. Zool. **8** (32), 1–167 (1963)

Hamilton, P. H., King, J. M.: The fate of black rhinoceroses released in Nairobi National Park. E. Afr. Wildl. J. **7,** 73–83 (1969)

Hanks, J.: Puku translocation. Black Lechwe **7,** 10–13 (1968)

Hanks, J., Stanley Price, M. R., Wrangham, R. W.: Some aspects of the ecology and behaviour of the defassa waterbuck (*Kobus defassa*) in Zambia. Mammalia **33,** 471–494 (1969)

Harthoorn, A. M.: Application of pharmacological and physiological principles in restraint of wild animals. Wildlife Monographs **14,** 1–78 (1965)

Harthoorn, A. M.: The Flying Syringe. London: Bles, 1970

Hassenberg, L.: Verhalten bei Einhufern. Neue Brehm-Bücherei 427. Wittenberg Lutherstadt: Ziemsen, 1971

Heath, B. R., Field, C. R.: Elephant endurance on Galana ranch, Kenya. E. Afr. Wildl. J. **12,** 239–242 (1974)

Hedberg, I., Hedberg, O. (eds.): Conservation of vegetation in Africa south of the Sahara. Acta phytogeogr. suecica **54,** 1–320 (1968)

Hediger, H.: Zur Biologie und Psychologie der Flucht bei Tieren. Biol. Zentralbl. **54,** 21–40 (1934)

Hediger, H.: Zum Begriff der biologischen Rangordnung. Rev. suisse Zool. **47,** 135–143 (1940a)

Hediger, H.: Über die Angleichungstendenz bei Tier und Mensch. Naturwiss. **20,** 313–315 (1940b)

Hediger, H.: Biologische Gesetzmäßigkeiten im Verhalten von Wirbeltieren. Mitt. Naturf. Ges. Bern (1941)*

Hediger, H.: Wildtiere in Gefangenschaft. Basel: Schwabe, 1942. English ed.: Wild Animals in Captivity. London: Butterworth, 1950

Hediger, H.: Säugetier-Territorien und ihre Markierung. Bijdr. Dierkunde **28**, 172–184 (1949)

Hediger, H.: Observations sur la psychologie animale dans les Parcs Nationaux du Congo Belge. Bruxelles: Inst. Parcs. Nat. Congo, 1951

Hediger, H.: Skizzen zu einer Tierpsychologie im Zoo und im Zirkus. Zürich: Büchergilde Gutenberg, 1954. English ed.: Studies of the Psychology and Behaviour of Captive Animals in Zoos and Circuses. London: Butterworth, 1955

Hediger, H.: Tierpsychologie im Zoo und im Zirkus. Basel: Reinhardt, 1961

Hediger, H.: Man as a social partner of animals and vice-versa. Symp. Zool. Soc. Lond. **14**, 291–300 (1965)

Hediger, H.: Tierstrassen im Zoo. In: Die Strassen der Tiere. Hediger, H. (ed.). Braunschweig: Vieweg, 1967, pp. 4–18

Hendrichs, H.: Freilandbeobachtungen zum Sozialsystem des Afrikanischen Elefanten, *Loxodonta africana* (Blumenbach, 1797). In: Dikdik und Elefanten. Hendrichs, H., Hendrichs, U. Munich: Piper, 1971, pp. 77–173

Hendrichs, H.: Beobachtungen und Untersuchungen zur Ökologie und Ethologie, insbesondere zur sozialen Organisation, ostafrikanischer Säugetiere. Z. Tierpsychol. **30**, 146–189 (1972)

Hendrichs, H.: Changes in a population of dikdik, *Madoqua (Rhynchotragus) kirki* (Günther, 1880). Z. Tierpsychol. **38**, 55–69 (1975 a)

Hendrichs, H.: Observations on a population of Bohor reedbuck, *Redunca redunca* (Pallas, 1767). Z. Tierpsychol. **38**, 44–54 (1975 b)

Hendrichs, H., Hendrichs, U.: Freilanduntersuchungen zur Ökologie und Ethologie der Zwerg-Antilope *Madoqua (Rhynchotragus) kirki* (Günther, 1880). In: Dikdik und Elefanten. Hendrichs, H., Hendrichs, U. Munich: Piper, 1971, pp. 9–75

Henshaw, J.: Notes on conflict between elephants and some bovids and on other inter-specific contacts in Yankari Game Reserve, N. E. Nigeria. E. Afr. Wildl. J. **10**, 151–153 (1972)

Hersher, L., Richmond, J. B., Moore, A. U.: Maternal behavior in sheep and goats. In: Maternal Behavior in Mammals. Rheingold, H. L. (ed.). New York, London: Wiley, 1963, pp. 203–232

Hillman, J. C.: The ecology and behaviour of free-ranging eland (*Taurotragus oryx* Pallas) in Kenya. Unpubl. Ph. D. Thesis, Univ. Nairobi, 1976

Hillman, J. C., Hillman, A. K. K.: Mortality of wildlife in Nairobi National Park during the drought of 1973–74. E. Afr. Wildl. J. **15**, 1–18 (1977)

Hitchins, P. M.: Preliminary findings in a radio-telemetric study on the black rhinoceros in Hluhluwe Game Reserve, Zululand. Proc. Symp. Biotel. S. Afr. C. S. I. R., 1–15 (1971)

Hitchins, P. M., Behr, M. G.: Parental care in impala. Lammergeyer **9**, 43 (1968)

Hitchins, P. M., Vincent, H.: Observations on range extension and dispersal of impala (*Aepyceros melampus* Lichtenstein) in Zululand. J. Sth. Afr. Wildl. Manage. Assoc. **2**, 3–8 (1972)

Hofmann, R. R.: Comparisons of the rumen and omasum structure in East African game ruminants in relation to their feeding habits. Symp. Zool. Soc. Lond. **21**, 179–194 (1968)

Hofmann, R. R.: The ruminant stomach. E. Afr. Monogr. Biol. **2**. Nairobi: East African Lit. Bureau, 1973

Hofmann, R. R., Stewart, D. R. M.: Grazer or browser: A classification based on the stomach structure and feeding habits of East African ruminants. Mammalia **36**, 226–240 (1972)

Holsworth, W. N.: Reedbuck concentrations in Dinder National Park, Sudan. E. Afr. Wildl. J. **10**, 307–308 (1972)

Hummel, H.: Beiträge zur Kenntnis der Pheromone. Unveröff. Dissertation, Univ. Marburg, 1968

Huth, H. H.: Zum Verhalten der Rappenantilope (*Hippotragus niger* Harris, 1838). Zool. Garten NF **38**, 147–170 (1970)

Inglis, J.: Wet season movements of individual wildebeests of the Serengeti migratory herd. E. Afr. Wildl. J. **14**, 17–34 (1976)

285

Innis, A. C.: The behaviour of the giraffe, *Giraffa camelopardalis*, in the eastern Transvaal. Proc. Zool. Soc. Lond. **131**, 245–278 (1958)

IUCN (International Union for the Conservation of Nature and Natural Resources): United Nations list of national parks and equivalent reserves. IUCN Publ. New Ser. No. **27** (1973)

Jarman, M. V.: Attachment to home area in impala. E. Afr. Wildl. J. **8**, 198–200 (1970)

Jarman, M. V.: The quintessential antelope. African Wildlife Leadership Foundation News **8**, 3–7 (1973)

Jarman, M. V.: Impala social behaviour.—Birth behaviour. E. Afr. Wildl. J. **14**, 153–167 (1976)

Jarman, P. J.: The effects of the creation of Lake Kariba upon the terrestrial ecology of the Middle Zambezi Valley, with particular reference to the large mammals. Unpubl. Ph. D. Thesis, Univ. Manchester, 1968*

Jarman, P. J.: Diets of large mammals in the woodlands around Lake Kariba, Rhodesia. Oecologia (Berl.) **8**, 157–178 (1971)

Jarman, P. J.: The use of drinking sites, wallows and salt licks by herbivores in the flooded Middle Zambezi Valley. E. Afr. Wildl. J. **10**, 193–209 (1972a)

Jarman, P. J.: Seasonal distribution of large mammal populations in the unflooded Middle Zambezi Valley. J. Appl. Ecol. **9**, 283–299 (1972b)

Jarman, P. J.: The development of a dermal shield in impala. J. Zool., Lond. **166**, 349–356 (1972c)

Jarman, P. J.: The social organization of antelope in relation to their ecology. Behaviour **48**, 215–267 (1974)

Jarman, M. V., Jarman, P. J.: Daily activity of impala. E. Afr. Wildl. J. **11**, 75–92 (1973a)

Jarman, P. J., Jarman, M. V.: Social behaviour, population structure and reproductive potential in impala. E. Afr. Wildl. J. **11**, 329–338 (1973b)

Jarman, P. J., Jarman, M. V.: Impala behaviour and its relevance to management. Calgary Symposium, 871–881 (1974)

Jarman, P. J., Mmari, P. E.: Selection of drinking places by large mammals in the Serengeti woodlands. E. Afr. Wildl. J. **9**, 158–161 (1971)

Jewell, P. A.: The concept of home range in mammals. Symp. Zool. Soc. Lond. **18**, 85–109 (1966)

Jewell, P. A.: Social organisation and movements of topi *(Damaliscus korrigum)* during the rut at Ishasha, Queen Elizabeth Park, Uganda. Zool. Afr. **7**, 233–255 (1972)

Johnson, R. P.: Scent marking in mammals. Anim. Behav. **21**, 521–535 (1973)

Joubert, E.: Activity patterns shown by mountain zebra, *Equus zebra hartmannae*, in South West Africa, with reference to climatic factors. Zool. Afr. **7**, 309–331 (1972a)

Joubert, E.: The social organization and associated behaviour in the Hartmann zebra, *Equus zebra hartmannae*. Madoqua Ser. I **6**, 17–56 (1972b)

Joubert, E., Eloff, F. C.: Notes on the ecology and behavior of the black rhinoceros, *Diceros bicornis* Linn. 1758, in South West Africa. Madoqua Ser. I **3**, 5–53 (1971)

Joubert, S. C. J.: Territorial behaviour of the tsessebe *(Damaliscus l. lunatus* Burchell) in the Kruger National Park. Zool. Afr. **7**, 141–156 (1972)

Joubert, S. C. J.: The social organization of the roan antelope *Hippotragus equinus* and its influence on the spatial distribution of herds in the Kruger National Park. Calgary Symposium, 661–675 (1974)

Joubert, S. C. J.: The mating behaviour of the tsessebe *(Damaliscus lunatus lunatus)* in the Kruger National Park. Z. Tierpsychol. **37**, 182–191 (1975)

Jungius, H.: Studies on the breeding biology of the reedbuck *(Redunca arundinum* Boddaert, 1785) in the Kruger National Park. Z. Säugetierk. **35**, 129–146 (1970)

Jungius, H.: The Biology and Behaviour of the Reedbuck *(Redunca arundinum* Boddaert, 1785) in the Kruger National Park. Mammalia Depicta. Hamburg and Berlin: Parey, 1971

Kalmus, H.: Origins and general features. Symp. Zool. Soc. Lond. **14**, 1–12 (1965)

Kaufmann, J. H.: Ecology and social behavior of the coati *(Nasua narica)* on Barro Colorado Island, Panama. Univ. Calif. Publ. Zool. **60**, 95–222 (1962)

Kaufmann, J. H.: Is territoriality definable? In: Behavior and Environment. Esser, A. H. (ed.). New York: Plenum Press, 1971, pp. 36–40

Keay, R. W. J.: Vegetation Map of Africa South of the Sahara. London: Oxford Univ. Press, 1959*

Kenya Game Department: Translocation of Uganda kob. E. Afr. Wildl. J. **1**, 126 (1963)

Kiley-Worthington, M.: The waterbuck (*Kobus defassa* Rüppell 1835 and *K. ellipsiprymnus* Ogilby 1833) in East Africa: Spatial distribution. A study of the sexual behaviour. Mammalia **29**, 177–204 (1965)

Kiley, M.: The vocalizations of ungulates, their causation and function. Z. Tierpsychol. **31**, 171–222 (1972)

Kiley, M.: Behavioural problems of some captive and domestic ungulates. Calgary Symposium, 603–617 (1974)

Kingdon, J.: East African Mammals, Vol. I. London and New York: Academic Press, 1971

Kirchshofer, R.: Das Verhalten der Giraffengazelle, Elenantilope und des Flachland-Tapirs bei der Geburt; einige Bemerkungen zur Vermehrungsrate und Generationenfolge dieser Arten im Frankfurter Zoo. Z. Tierpsychol. **20**, 143–159 (1963)

Klingel, H.: Soziale Organisation und Verhalten freilebender Steppenzebras. Z. Tierpsychol. **24**, 580–624 (1967)

Klingel, H.: Soziale Organisation und Verhaltensweisen von Hartmann- und Bergzebras (*Equus zebra hartmannae* und *E. z. zebra*). Z. Tierpsychol. **25**, 76–88 (1968)

Klingel, H.: Social organisation and population ecology of the plains zebra (*Equus quagga*). Zool. Afr. **4**, 249–263 (1969a)

Klingel, H.: Zur Soziologie des Grévy-Zebras. Zool. Anz., Suppl. **33** (Verh. Dtsch. Zool. Ges.), 311–316 (1969b)

Klingel, H.: Reproduction in the plains zebra, *Equus burchelli boehmi*: Behaviour and ecological factors. J. Reprod. Fert., Suppl. **6**, 339–345 (1969c)

Klingel, H.: Dauerhafte Sozialverbände beim Bergzebra. Z. Tierpsychol. **26**, 965–966 (1969d)

Klingel, H.: Das Verhalten der Pferde (Equidae). Handb. Zool. **8** (10/24), 1–68 (1972a)

Klingel, H.: Social behaviour of African Equidae. Zool. Afr. **7**, 175–185 (1972b)

Klingel, H.: Soziale Organisation und Verhalten des Grévy-Zebras (*Equus grevyi*). Z. Tierpsychol. **36**, 37–70 (1974a)

Klingel, H.: A comparison of the social behaviour of the Equidae. Calgary Symposium, 124–132 (1974b)

Klingel, H.: Die soziale Organisation der Equiden. Verh. Dtsch. Zool. Ges., 71–80 (1975)

Klingel, H., Klingel, U.: Die Geburt eines Zebras (*Equus quagga boehmi*). Z. Tierpsychol. **23**, 72–76 (1966)

Kluyver, H. N., Tinbergen, L.: Territory and the regulation of density in titmice. Arch. néerl. Zool. **10**, 265–289 (1953)

Knappe, H.: Zur Funktion des Jacobsonschen Organs. Zool. Garten NF **28**, 188–194 (1964)*

Kraft, T.: (Buffalo kill lion). Africana (Nairobi) **5**, 36–37 (1973)

Kruuk, H.: Predators and anti-predator behaviour of the black-headed gull (*Larus ridibundus* L.). Behaviour, Suppl. **11**, 1–130 (1964)*

Kruuk, H.: The Spotted Hyena. A Study of Predation and Social Behavior. Chicago and London: Univ. Chicago Press, 1972

Kühme, W.: Beobachtungen am afrikanischen Elefanten (*Loxodonta africana* Blumenbach 1797) in Gefangenschaft. Z. Tierpsychol. **18**, 285–296 (1961)

Kühme, W.: Ergänzende Beobachtungen an afrikanischen Elefanten (*Loxodonta africana* Blumenbach 1797) im Freigehege. Z. Tierpsychol. **20**, 66–79 (1963)

Kummer, H.: Primate Societies. Chicago and New York: Aldine Atherton Inc., 1971

Kurt, F.: Zur Carnivorie bei *Cephalophus dorsalis*. Z. Säugetierk. **28**, 309–313 (1963)

Kurt, F.: Das Sozialverhalten des Rehes (*Capreolus capreolus* L.). Mammalia Depicta. Hamburg and Berlin: Parey, 1968

Kurz, J. C., Marchinton, R. L.: Radiotelemetry studies of feral hogs in South Carolina. J. Wildl. Manage. **36**, 1,240–1,248 (1972)

287

Lang, E. M.: The birth of an African elephant *Loxodonta africana* at Basel Zoo. Int. Zoo Yb. **7**, 154–157 (1967)

Lang, E. M.: The pygmy hippopotamus. In: Grzimek's Animal Life Encyclopedia. New York: Van Nostrand Reinhold Co., 1972, Vol. 13, pp. 110–116

Langman, V. A.: Radio-tracking giraffe for ecological studies. J. Sth. Afr. Wildl. Manage. Assoc. **3**, 75–78 (1973)

Laws, R. M.: The Tsavo Research Project. J. Reprod. Fert., Suppl. **6**, 495–531 (1969a)

Laws, R. M.: Aspects of reproduction in the African elephant *Loxodonta africana*. J. Reprod. Fert., Suppl. **6**, 193–217 (1969b)

Laws, R. M.: Elephants as agents of habitat and landscape change in East Africa. Oikos **21**, 1–15 (1970)

Laws, R. M.: Behaviour, dynamics and management of elephant populations. Calgary Symposium, 513–529 (1974)

Laws, R. M., Parker, I. S. C.: Recent studies on elephant populations in East Africa. Symp. Zool. Soc. Lond. **21**, 319–359 (1968)

Laws, R. M., Parker, I. S. C., Johnstone, R. C. B.: Elephants and their Habitats. London: Oxford Univ. Press, 1975

Lent, P. C.: A preliminary study of the Okavango lechwe (*Kobus leche leche* Gray). E. Afr. Wildl. J. **7**, 147–157 (1969)

Lent, P. C.: Mother-infant relationships in ungulates. Calgary Symposium, 14–55 (1974)

Leuthold, B. M., Leuthold, W.: Food habits of giraffe in Tsavo National Park, Kenya. E. Afr. Wildl. J. **10**, 129–141 (1972)

Leuthold, B. M., Leuthold, W.: Ecology of giraffe in Tsavo National Park, Kenya. Z. Säugetierk. (in press)

Leuthold, W.: Variations in territorial behavior of Uganda kob, *Adenota kob thomasi* (Neumann, 1896). Behaviour **27**, 214–257 (1966a)

Leuthold, W.: Homing experiments with an African antelope. Z. Säugetierk. **31**, 251–255 (1966b)

Leuthold, W.: Beobachtungen zum Jugendverhalten von Kob-Antilopen. Z. Säugetierk. **32**, 59–63 (1967)

Leuthold, W.: Preliminary observations on food habits of gerenuk in Tsavo National Park, Kenya. E. Afr. Wildl. J. **8**, 73–84 (1970a)

Leuthold, W.: Observations on the social organization of impala (*Aepyceros melampus*). Z. Tierpsychol. **27**, 693–721 (1970b)

Leuthold, W.: Ethology and game management. Trans. 9th Intern. Congr. Game Biol. (Moscow), 78–88 (1970c)

Leuthold, W.: Studies on the food habits of lesser kudu in Tsavo National Park, Kenya. E. Afr. Wildl. J. **9**, 35–45 (1971a)

Leuthold, W.: A note on the formation of food habits in young antelopes. E. Afr. Wildl. J. **9**, 154–156 (1971b)

Leuthold, W.: Freilandbeobachtungen an Giraffengazellen (*Litocranius walleri*) im Tsavo-Nationalpark, Kenia. Z. Säugetierk. **36**, 19–37 (1971c)

Leuthold, W.: Observations on the mother-young relationship in some antelopes. E. Afr. Wildl. J. **9**, 152–154 (1971d)

Leuthold, W.: On the association between antelopes and baboons. Bull. E. Afr. Nat. Hist. Soc. Dec. 1971, 195–196 (1971e)

Leuthold, W.: Home range, movements and food of a buffalo herd in Tsavo National Park. E. Afr. Wildl. J. **10**, 237–243 (1972)

Leuthold, W.: Observations on home range and social organization of lesser kudu, *Tragelaphus imberbis* (Blyth, 1869). Calgary Symposium, 206–234 (1974)

Leuthold, W.: Group size in elephants of Tsavo National Park and possible factors influencing it. J. Anim. Ecol. **45**, 425–439 (1976)

Leuthold, W., Leuthold, B. M.: Notes on the behaviour of two young antelopes reared in captivity. Z. Tierpsychol. **32**, 418–424 (1973)

Leuthold, W., Leuthold, B. M.: Patterns of social grouping in ungulates of Tsavo National Park, Kenya. J. Zool., Lond. **175**, 405–420 (1975a)

Leuthold, W., Leuthold, B. M.: Parturition and related behaviour in the African elephant. Z. Tierpsychol. **39**, 75–84 (1975b)

Leuthold, W., Sale, J. B.: Movements and patterns of habitat utilization of elephants in Tsavo National Park, Kenya. E. Afr. Wildl. J. **11**, 369–384 (1973)

Lewis, J. G.: A comparative study of the activity of some indigenous East African ungulates and conventional stock under domestication. Unpubl. Ph. D. Thesis, Univ. London, 1975

Leyhausen, P.: The communal organization of solitary mammals. Symp. Zool. Soc. Lond. **14**, 249–263 (1965)

Leyhausen, P.: Dominance and territoriality as complements in mammalian social structure. In: Behaviour and Environment. Esser, A. H. (ed.). New York: Plenum Press, 1971, pp. 22–33

Lind, E. M., Morrison, M. E. S.: East African Vegetation. London: Longman, 1974

Lindsay, D. R.: The importance of olfactory stimuli in the mating behaviour of the ram. Anim. Behav. **13**, 75–78 (1965)

Lorenz, K.: Der Kumpan in der Umwelt des Vogels. J. Ornithol. **83**, 137–213, 289–413 (1935)

Lynch, C. D.: A behavioural study of blesbok, *Damaliscus dorcas phillipsi*, with special reference to territoriality. Unpubl. M. Sc. Thesis, Univ. Pretoria, 1971*

Maloiy, G. M. O. (ed.): Comparative Physiology of Desert Animals. Symp. Zool. Soc. London **31**. London: Academic Press, 1972

McBride, G.: Theories of animal spacing: The role of flight, fight, and social distance. In: Behaviour and Environment. Esser, A. H. (ed.). New York: Plenum Press, 1971, pp. 53–68

McKay, G. M.: Behavior and ecology of the Asiatic elephant in Southeastern Ceylon. Smithsonian Contrib. Zool. 125. Washington: Smithsonian Institution, 1973

Meester, J.: The origins of the southern African mammal fauna. Zool. Afr. **1**, 87–95 (1965)

Mejia, C.: (Social behaviour and organization of giraffe in the Serengeti National Park). Unpubl. Report, Serengeti Research Institute, 1972 (quotes in: Moss, 1975)

Metzgar, L. M.: An experimental comparison of screech owl predation on resident and transient white-footed mice *(Peromyscus leucopus)*. J. Mammal. **48**, 387–391 (1967)

Monfort, A.: Densités, biomasses et structures des populations d'ongulés sauvages au Parc National de l'Akagera. Terre et Vie **26**, 216–256 (1972)

Monfort, A.: Quelques aspects de la biologie des phacochères *(Phacochoerus aethiopicus)* au Parc National de l'Akagera, Rwanda. Mammalia **38**, 177–200 (1974)

Monfort, A., Monfort, N.: Notes sur l'écologie et le comportement des oribis *(Ourebia ourebi* Zimmermann, 1783). Terre et Vie **28**, 169–208 (1974)

Monfort, A., Monfort, N., Ruwet, J. C.: Eco-éthologie des ongulés au Parc National de l'Akagera (Rwanda). Ann. Soc. Roy. Zool. Belg. **103**, 177–208 (1973)

Monfort-Braham, N.: Variations dans la structure sociale du topi, *Damaliscus korrigum* Ogilby, au Parc National de l'Akagera, Rwanda. Z. Tierpsychol. **39**, 332–364 (1975)

Moore-Berger, E.: Utilisation of the habitat by the reticulated giraffe *(Giraffa camelopardalis reticulata* Linnaeus) in northern Kenya. Unpubl. M. Sc. Thesis, Univ. Nairobi, 1974

Moreau, R. E.: The Bird Faunas of Africa and its Islands. New York and London: Academic Press, 1966

Morgan-Davies, A. M.: The association between impala and olive baboon. J. E. Afr. Nat. Hist. Soc. **23**, 297–298 (1960)

Moss, C.: Portraits in the Wild. Behavior Studies of East African Mammals. Boston: Houghton Mifflin Co., 1975

Mukinya, J. G.: Density, distribution, population structure and social organisation of the black rhinoceros in Masai Mara Game Reserve. E. Afr. Wildl. J. **11**, 385–400 (1973)

Müller-Schwarze, D.: Complexity and relative specificity in a mammalian pheromone. Nature **223**, 525–526 (1969)

Müller-Schwarze, D.: Pheromones in black-tailed deer *(Odocoileus hemionus columbianus)*. Anim. Behav. **19**, 141–152 (1971)

Müller-Schwarze, D.: Social functions of various scent glands in certain ungulates and the problems encountered in experimental studies of scent communication. Calgary Symposium, 107–113 (1974)

Naaktgeboren, C.: Untersuchungen über die Geburt der Säugetiere. Bijdr. Dierkunde **32**, 1–50 (1963)

Naaktgeboren, C., Slijper, E. J.: Biologie der Geburt. Hamburg und Berlin: Parey, 1970

Nesbit Evans, E. M.: The reaction of a group of Rothschild's giraffe to a new environment. E. Afr. Wildl. J. **8**, 53–62 (1970)

Ngere, L. O., Dzakuma, J. M.: The effect of sudden introduction of rams on oestrus patterns of tropical ewes. J. Agric. Sci., Camb. **84**, 263–264 (1975)

Nice, M. M.: The role of territory in bird life. Amer. Midl. Nat. **26**, 441–487 (1941)

Noble, G. K.: The role of dominance in the life of birds. Auk **56**, 263–273 (1939)

Norton-Griffiths, M.: Serengeti Ecological Monitoring Program. Report, 26 pp. Nairobi: Afr. Wildl. Leadership Foundation, 1972

Odum, E. P.: Fundamentals of Ecology. 2nd ed. Philadelphia and London: W. B. Saunders Co., 1959

Oelofse, J.: Plastic for game catching. Oryx **10**, 306–308 (1970)

Olivier, R. C. D., Laurie, W. A.: Habitat utilization by hippopotamus in the Mara River. E. Afr. Wildl. J. **12**, 249–271 (1974)

Owen, R. E. A.: Some observations on the sitatunga in Kenya. E. Afr. Wildl. J. **8**, 181–195 (1970)

Owen-Smith, R. N.: Territoriality in the white rhinoceros (*Ceratotherium simum* Burchell). Nature **231**, 294–296 (1971)

Owen-Smith, R. N.: Territoriality: The example of the white rhinoceros. Zool. Afr. **7**, 273–280 (1972)

Owen-Smith, R. N.: The behavioural ecology of the white rhinoceros. Unpubl. Ph. D. Thesis, Univ. Wisconsin, 1973*

Owen-Smith, R. N.: The social system of the white rhinoceros. Calgary Symposium, 341–351 (1974)

Owen-Smith, R. N.: The social ethology of the white rhinoceros, *Ceratotherium simum* (Burchell, 1812). Z. Tierpsychol. **38**, 337–384 (1975)

Parker, I. S. C., Graham, A. D.: The ecological and economic bases for game ranching in Africa. In: The Scientific Management of Plant and Animal Communities for Conservation. Duffey, E., Watt, A. S. (eds.). Oxford: Blackwell Sci. Publ., 1971, pp. 393–404

Pennycuick, L.: Movements of the migratory wildebeest population in the Serengeti area between 1960 and 1973. E. Afr. Wildl. J. **13**, 65–87 (1975)

Petrusewicz, K.: Further investigations of the influence exerted by the presence of their home cages and own populations on the results of fights between male mice. Bull. Acad. Polon. Sciences, Ser. Sci. Biol. VII, **8**, 319–322 (1959)

Pienaar, U. de V.: Observations on developmental biology, growth and some aspects of the population ecology of African buffalo (*Syncerus caffer caffer* Sparrman) in the Kruger National Park. Koedoe **12**, 29–52 (1969)

Pilters, H.: Untersuchungen über angeborene Verhaltensweisen bei Tylopoden, unter besonderer Berücksichtigung der neuweltlichen Formen. Z. Tierpsychol. **11**, 213–303 (1954)*

Plessis, S. S. du: Ecology of blesbok with special reference to productivity. Wildl. Monogr. No. 30 (1972)

Pocock, R. I.: On the specialized cutaneous glands of ruminants. Proc. Zool. Soc. Lond. 840–986 (1910)

Poppleton, F.: An elephant birth. Afr. Wild Life **11**, 106–108 (1957)

Rahm, U.: Territoriumsmarkierung mit der Voraugendrüse beim Maxwell-Ducker (*Philantomba maxwelli*). Säugetierkundl. Mitt. **8**, 140–142 (1960)

Ralls, K.: Mammalian scent marking. Science **171**, 443–449 (1971)

Ralls, K.: *Cephalophus maxwellii*. Mammal. Species No. **31**, 1–4 (1973)

Ralls, K.: Scent marking in captive Maxwell's duikers. Calgary Symposium, 114–123 (1974)

Ralls, K.: Agonistic behaviour in Maxwell's duiker, *Cephalophus maxwelli*. Mammalia **39**, 241–249 (1975)

Richter, W. von: The black wildebeest (*Connochaetes gnou*). Orange Free State Nature Conserv. Misc. Publ. No. 2 (1971 a)

Richter, W. von: Observations on the biology and ecology of the black wildebeest (*Connochaetes gnou*). J. Sth. Afr. Wildl. Manage. Assoc. **1**, 3–16 (1971 b)

Richter, W. von: Territorial behaviour of the black wildebeest, *Connochaetes gnou*. Zool. Afr. **7**, 207–231 (1972)

Robbins, B.: (Nyala defends young against bateleur eagle). Lammergeyer **15**, 80 (1972)

Robinette, W. L.: Mule deer home range and dispersal in Utah. J. Wildl. Manage. **30**, 335–349 (1966)

Rodgers, W. A.: Seasonal diet preferences of impala in the Selous Game Reserve, Tanzania. E. Afr. Wildl. J. **14**, 331–334 (1976)

Rodgers, W. A.: Seasonal change in group size amongst five wild herbivore species. E. Afr. Wildl. J. **15** (1977)

Root, A.: Fringe-eared oryx digging for tubers in Tsavo National Park (East). E. Afr. Wildl. J. **10**, 155–157 (1972)

Rowe-Rowe, D. T.: Social behaviour in a small blesbok population. J. Sth. Afr. Wildl. Manage. Assoc. **3**, 49–52 (1973)

Rowe-Rowe, D. T.: Flight behaviour and flight distances of blesbok. Z. Tierpsychol. **34**, 208–211 (1974)

Sanderson, G. C.: The study of mammal movements—a review. J. Wildl. Manage. **30**, 215–235 (1966)

Sauer, E. G. F.: Interspecific behaviour of the South African ostrich. Ostrich, Suppl. **8**, 91–103 (1970)

Schaffer, J.: Die Hautdrüsenorgane der Säugetiere. Berlin und Wien: Urban und Schwarzenberg, 1940

Schaller, G. B.: The Serengeti Lion. A Study of Predator-Prey Relations. Chicago and London: Univ. Chicago Press, 1972

Schenkel, R.: On sociology and behaviour in impala (*Aepyceros melampus suara* Matschie). Z. Säugetierk. **31**, 177–205 (1966a)

Schenkel, R.: Zum Problem der Territorialität und des Markierens bei Säugetieren – am Beispiel des Schwarzen Nashorns und des Löwen. Z. Tierpsychol. **23**, 593–626 (1966b)

Schenkel, R., Lang, E. M.: Das Verhalten der Nashörner. Handb. Zool. **8** (10/25), 1–56 (1969)

Schenkel, R., Schenkel-Hulliger, L.: Ecology and Behaviour of the Black Rhinoceros (*Diceros bicornis* L.). Mammalia Depicta. Hamburg and Berlin: Parey, 1969

Schloeth, R.: Zur Psychologie der Begegnung zwischen Tieren. Behaviour **10**, 1–79 (1956)

Schloeth, R.: Markierung und erste Beobachtungen von markiertem Rotwild im Schweizerischen Nationalpark und dessen Umgebung. Ergebn. wiss. Untersuch. Schweiz. Nationalpark **7** (NF 45), 199–227 (1961a)

Schloeth, R.: Das Sozialleben des Camargue-Rindes. Z. Tierpsychol. **18**, 574–627 (1961b)

Schneider, K. M.: Das Flehmen. I. Zool. Garten **3**, 183–198 (1930); II. Zool. Garten **4**, 349–364 (1931); III. Zool. Garten **5**, 200–226 (1932); IV. Zool. Garten **5**, 287–297 (1932); V. Zool. Garten **7**, 182–201 (1934)

Schomber, H. W.: Die Giraffengazelle und Lamagazelle. Neue Brehm-Bücherei No. 358. Wittenberg Lutherstadt: Ziemsen, 1966

Sekulic, R., Smulders, H., Smulders, A., Estes, R. D.: Birth and perinatal behavior of sable antelope. Unpubl. Report, Nairobi, 1976

Short, R. V.: Oestrous behaviour, ovulation and the formation of the corpus luteum in the African elephant, *Loxodonta africana*. E. Afr. Wildl. J. **4**, 56–68 (1966)

Shortridge, G. C.: The Mammals of South West Africa. London: Heinemann, 1934

Sikes, S. K.: The Natural History of the African Elephant. London: Weidenfeld and Nicolson, 1971

Simonetta, A. M.: Osservazioni etologiche ed ecologiche sui dikdik (gen. *Madoqua*; Mammalia, Bovidae) in Somalia. Monit. Zool. Ital. **74** (Suppl.), 1–33 (1966)

Simpson, C. D.: Observations on courtship behaviour in warthog (*Phacochoerus aethiopicus* Pallas). Arnoldia **1** (20), 1–4 (1964)

Simpson, C. D.: An evaluation of seasonal movements in greater kudu populations—*Tragelaphus strepsiceros* Pallas—in three localities in southern Africa. Zool. Afr. **7**, 197–205 (1972)

Sinclair, A. R. E.: Studies of the ecology of the East African buffalo. Unpubl. Ph. D. Thesis, Univ. Oxford, 1970

Sinclair, A. R. E.: The social organization of the East African buffalo (*Syncerus caffer* Sparrman). Calgary Symposium, 676–689 (1974)

Sinclair, A. R. E., Gwynne, M. D.: Food selection and competition in the East African buffalo (*Syncerus caffer* Sparrman). E. Afr. Wildl. J. **10**, 77–89 (1972)

Smuts, G. L.: Home range sizes for Burchell's zebra *Equus burchelli antiquorum* from the Kruger National Park. Koedoe **18**, 139–146 (1975)

Smythe, N.: On the existence of "pursuit invitation" signals in mammals. Amer. Nat. **104**, 491–494 (1970)

Spinage, C. A.: A quantitative study of the daily activity of the Uganda defassa waterbuck. E. Afr. Wildl. J. **6**, 89–93 (1968)

Spinage, C. A.: Territoriality and social organization of the Uganda defassa waterbuck *Kobus defassa ugandae*. J. Zool., Lond. **159**, 329–361 (1969 a)

Spinage, C. A.: Naturalistic observations on the reproductive and maternal behaviour of the Uganda defassa waterbuck, *Kobus defassa ugandae* Neumann. Z. Tierpsychol. **26**, 39–47 (1969 b)

Spinage, C. A.: Territoriality and population regulation in the Uganda defassa waterbuck. Calgary Symposium, 635–643 (1974)

Stanley Price, M. R.: The feeding ecology of Coke's hartebeest, *Alcelaphus buselaphus cokii* Günther, in Kenya. Unpubl. D. Phil. Thesis, Univ. Oxford, 1974

Stewart, D. R. M.: The epidermal characters of grasses, with special reference to East African plains species. Bot. Jb. **84**, 63–116 (1965)

Stewart, D. R. M., Stewart, J.: Comparative food preferences of five East African ungulates at different seasons. In: The Scientific Management of Animal and Plant Communities. Duffey, E., Watt, A. S. (eds.). Oxford: Blackwell Sci. Publ., 1971, pp. 351–366

Talbot, L. M., Lamprey, H. F.: Immobilization of free-ranging East African ungulates with succinylcholine chloride. J. Wildl. Manage. **25**, 303–310 (1961)

Talbot, L. M., Talbot, M. H.: Food preferences of some East African wild ungulates. E. Afr. Agric. For. J. **27**, 131–138 (1962)

Talbot, L. M., Talbot, M. H.: The wildebeest in western Masailand, East Africa. Wildl. Monogr. No. 12 (1963)

Taylor, C. R.: The eland and the oryx. Sci. Amer. **220**, 88–95 (1969)

Taylor, C. R.: Strategies of temperature regulation: effect on evaporation in East African ungulates. Amer. J. Physiol. **219**, 1,131–1,135 (1970 a)

Taylor, C. R.: Dehydration and heat: effects on temperature regulation of East African ungulates. Amer. J. Physiol. **219**, 1,136–1,139 (1970 b)

Taylor, C. R.: The desert gazelle: a paradox resolved. Symp. Zool. Soc. Lond. **31**, 215–227 (1972)

Tello, J. L. P. L., Gelder, R. G. van: The natural history of nyala, *Tragelaphus angasi* (Mammalia, Bovidae), in Mozambique. Bull. Amer. Mus. Nat. Hist. **155** (4), 319–386 (1975)

Tinbergen, N.: The function of sexual fighting in birds; and the problem of the origin of "territory". Bird Banding **7**, 1–8 (1936)

Tinbergen, N.: Die Übersprungbewegung. Z. Tierpsychol. **4**, 1–40 (1940)*

Tinbergen, N.: The Study of Instinct. London: Oxford Univ. Press, 1951

Tinbergen, N.: Einige Gedanken über "Beschwichtigungsgebärden." Z. Tierpsychol. **16**, 631–665 (1959)*

Tinley, K. L.: Dikdik *Madoqua kirki* in South West Africa: Notes on distribution, ecology and behaviour. Madoqua **1**, 7–33 (1969)

Trumler, E.: Beobachtungen an den Böhm-Zebras des Georg-von-Opel Freigeheges für Tierforschung, e. V. 1. Das Paarungsverhalten. Säugetierkundl. Mitt. **6**, 1–48 (1958)

Trumler, E.: Das "Rossigkeitsgesicht" und ähnliches Ausdrucksverhalten bei Einhufern. Z. Tierpsychol. **16**, 478–488 (1959)

Tschanz, B.: Über die Beziehung zwischen Muttertier und Jungen beim Mouflon *(Ovis aries musimon)*. Experientia **18**, 187–191 (1962)

Underwood, R.: Social behaviour of the eland *(Taurotragus oryx)* on Loskop Dam Nature Reserve. Unpubl. M. Sc. Thesis, Univ. Pretoria, 1975

Verdcourt, B.: The arid corridor between the north-east and south-west arid areas of Africa. Palaeoecology of Africa **4**, 140–144 (1969)

Verheyen, R.: Monographie éthologique de l'hippopotame (*Hippopotamus amphibius* L.). Bruxelles: Inst. Parcs Nationaux Congo, 1954

Vesey-Fitzgerald, D. F.: The topi herd. Oryx **3**, 4–8 (1955)

Vesey-Fitzgerald, D. F.: Grazing succession among East African game animals. J. Mammal. **41**, 161–172 (1960)

Vos, A. de: Territorial behavior among puku in Zambia. Science **148**, 1,752–1,753 (1965)

Vos, A. de, Dowsett, R. J.: The behaviour and population structure of three species of the genus *Kobus*. Mammalia **30**, 30–55 (1966)

Walther, F.: Zum Kampf- und Paarungsverhalten einiger Antilopen. Z. Tierpsychol. **15**, 340–380 (1958)

Walther, F.: "Antilopenhafte" Verhaltensweisen im Paarungszeremoniell des Okapi (*Okapia johnstoni* Sclater, 1901). Z. Tierpsychol. **17**, 188–210 (1960)

Walther, F.: Entwicklungszüge im Kampf- und Paarungsverhalten der Horntiere. Jahrb. G. von Opel Freigehege für Tierforsch. **3**, 90–115 (1960/61)

Walther, F.: Zum Kampfverhalten des Gerenuk (*Litocranius walleri*). Natur u. Volk **91**, 313–321 (1961)

Walther, F.: Über die Möglichkeiten der Verhaltensforschung in Tiergärten. Säugetierkundl. Mitt. **11**, 62–68 (1963 a)

Walther, F.: Einige Verhaltensbeobachtungen am Dibatag (*Ammodorcas clarkei* Thomas, 1891). Zool. Garten NF **27**, 233–261 (1963 b)

Walther, F.: Verhaltensstudien an der Gattung *Tragelaphus* de Blainville (1816) in Gefangenschaft, unter besonderer Berücksichtigung des Sozialverhaltens. Z. Tierpsychol. **21**, 393–467 (1964 a)

Walther, F.: Einige Verhaltensbeobachtungen an Thomsongazellen (*Gazella thomsoni* Günther, 1884) im Ngorongoro-Krater. Z. Tierpsychol. **21**, 871–890 (1964 b)

Walther, F.: Zum Paarungsverhalten der Sömmeringgazelle (*Gazella soemmeringi* Cretzschmar, 1826). Zool. Garten NF **29**, 145–160 (1964 c)

Walther, F.: Verhaltensstudien an der Grantgazelle (*Gazella granti* Brooke, 1872) im Ngorongoro-Krater. Z. Tierpsychol. **22**, 167–208 (1965 a)

Walther, F.: Psychologische Beobachtungen zur Gesellschaftshaltung von Oryx-Antilopen (*Oryx gazella beisa* Rüpp.). Zool. Garten NF **31**, 1–58 (1965 b)

Walther, F.: Ethological aspects of keeping different species of ungulates together in captivity. Int. Zoo Yb. **5**, 1–13 (1965 c)

Walther, F.: Mit Horn und Huf. Hamburg und Berlin: Parey, 1966 a

Walther, F.: Zum Liegeverhalten des Weissschwanzgnus (*Connochaetes gnou* Zimmermann, 1780). Z. Säugetierk. **31**, 1–16 (1966 b)

Walther, F.: Huftierterritorien und ihre Markierung. In: Die Strassen der Tiere. Hediger, H. (ed.). Braunschweig: Vieweg, 1967 a, pp. 26–45

Walther, F.: Tierstrassen in Afrika. *Ibidem*, 19–25 (1967 b)

Walther, F.: Verhalten der Gazellen. Neue Brehm-Bücherei No. 373. Wittenberg Lutherstadt: Ziemsen, 1968

Walther, F.: Die Hornträger. – Ducker, Böckchen und Waldböcke. – Kuhantilopen, Pferdeböcke und Wasserböcke. – Die Gazellen und ihre Verwandten. 11., 12., 14., 15. Kap. In: Grzimek's Tierleben. Grzimek, B. (ed.). Zürich: Kindler, 1968, Vol. XIII, pp. 301–364, 437–492. English ed.: Grzimek's Animal Life Encyclopedia. New York: Van Nostrand Reinhold Co., 1972, Vol. XIII, pp. 272–330, 399–448

Walther, F.: Flight behaviour and avoidance of predators in Thomson's gazelle (*Gazella thomsoni* Günther, 1884). Behaviour **34**, 184–221 (1969 a)

Walther, F.: Ethologische Beobachtungen bei der künstlichen Aufzucht eines Blessbockkalbes (*Damaliscus dorcas phillipsi* Harper, 1939). Zool. Garten NF **36**, 191–215 (1969 b)

Walther, F.: Social grouping in Grant's gazelle (*Gazella granti* Brooke, 1872) in the Serengeti National Park. Z. Tierpsychol. **31**, 348–403 (1972 a)

Walther, F.: Territorial behaviour in certain horned ungulates, with special reference to the examples of Thomson's and Grant's gazelles. Zool. Afr. **7**, 303–307 (1972 b)

293

Walther, F.: Round-the-clock activity of Thomson's gazelle (*Gazella thomsoni* Günther, 1884) in the Serengeti National Park. Z. Tierpsychol. **32**, 75–105 (1973)

Walther, F.: Some reflections on expressive behaviour in combats and courtship of certain horned ungulates. Calgary Symposium, 56–106 (1974)

Warren, H. B.: Aspects of the behaviour of the impala male *Aepyceros melampus* during the rut. Arnoldia (Rhod.) **27** (6), 1–9 (1974)

Waser, P.: Diurnal and nocturnal strategies of the bushbuck *Tragelaphus scriptus* (Pallas). E. Afr. Wildl. J. **13**, 49–63 (1975a)

Waser, P.: Spatial associations and social interactions in a "solitary" ungulate: the bushbuck *Tragelaphus scriptus* (Pallas). Z. Tierpsychol. **37**, 24–36 (1975b)

Watson, A., Moss, R.: Dominance, spacing behaviour and aggression in relation to population limitation in vertebrates. In: Animal Populations in Relation to their Food Resources. Watson, A. (ed.). Oxford: Blackwell Sci. Publ., 1970, pp. 167–220

Watson, R. M.: Reproduction of wildebeest, *Connochaetes taurinus albojubatus* Thomas, in the Serengeti region, and its significance to conservation. J. Reprod. Fert., Suppl. **6**, 287–310 (1969)

Wecker, S. C.: The role of early experience in habitat selection by the prairie deer mouse, *Peromyscus maniculatus bairdi*. Ecol. Monogr. **33**, 307–325 (1963)

Wecker, S. C.: Habitat selection. Sci. Amer. **211**, 109–116 (1964)

Weir, J. S., Davison, E. C.: Daily occurrence of game animals at water holes in dry weather. Zool. Afr. **1**, 353–368 (1965)

Wilson, E. O.: Competitive and aggressive behavior. In: Man and Beast, Smithsonian Annual III. Eisenberg, J. F., Dillon, W. S. (eds.). Washington: Smithsonian Institution, 1971, pp. 183–217

Wilson, E. O.: Sociobiology—The New Synthesis. Cambridge USA: Harvard Univ. Press, 1975

Wing, L. D., Buss, I. O.: Elephants and forests. Wildlife Monogr. No. 19 (1970)

Woodford, M. H., Trevor, S.: Fostering a baby elephant. E. Afr. Wildl. J. **8**, 204–205 (1970)

Wynne-Edwards, V. C.: Animal Dispersion in Relation to Social Behaviour. London: Oliver and Boyd, 1962

Young, E.: Observations on the movement patterns and daily home range size of impala, *Aepyceros melampus* (Lichtenstein), in the Kruger National Park. Zool. Afr. **7**, 187–195 (1972)

Zeeb, K., Kleinschmidt, A.: Beobachtungen zum Paarungsverhalten von Grévy-Zebras in Gefangenschaft. Z. Tierpsychol. **20**, 207–214 (1963)

Ziegler-Simon, F.: Beobachtungen am Rüsseldikdik (*Rhynchotragus kirki* Günther). Zool. Garten NF **23**, 1–13 (1957)*

Zinderen Bakker, E. M. van: Botanical evidence for quaternary climates in Africa. Ann. Cape Prov. Mus. **2**, 16–31 (1962)

Zinderen Bakker, E. M. van, Coetzee, J. A.: A reappraisal of late-Quaternary climatic evidence from tropical Africa. Palaeoecology of Africa **7**, 151–181 (1972)

Appendix

Scientific and common names of African ungulates mentioned in the text, and an outline of their classification, following Ansell (1971) and Gentry (1971). Figures in parentheses indicate the number of species in each family, subfamily or tribe, according to the above classification, that occur in the area considered here (see Chap. 1).

Order: Proboscidea

Family: Elephantidae (1)
Loxodonta africana   African elephant

Order: Perissodactyla

Family: Rhinocerotidae (2)
Ceratotherium simum   Square-lipped ("White") rhinoceros
Diceros bicornis   Black rhinoceros

Family: Equidae (4)
Equus africanus   (African) Wild ass
E. grevyi   Grévy's zebra
E. zebra   Mountain zebra (incl. Hartmann's zebra)
E. burchelli   Plains (Burchell's) zebra

Order: Artiodactyla

Family: Suidae (3)
Potamochoerus porcus   Bush pig
Phacochoerus aethiopicus   Warthog
Hylochoerus meinertzhageni   Giant forest hog

Family: Hippopotamidae (2)
Hippopotamus amphibius   Hippopotamus
Choeropsis liberiensis   Pygmy hippopotamus

Family: Tragulidae (1)
Hyemoschus aquaticus   Water chevrotain

Family: Giraffidae (2)
Giraffa camelopardalis   Giraffe
G. c. reticulata   Reticulated giraffe
Okapia johnstoni   Okapi

Family: Bovidae (75)
Subfamily: Bovinae
Tribe: *Bovini* (1)
Syncerus caffer   African buffalo
Tribe: *Tragelaphini* (9)
Tragelaphus euryceros   Bongo
T. buxtoni   Mountain nyala
T. spekei   Sitatunga

	T. angasi	(Lowland) Nyala
	T. scriptus	Bushbuck
	T. strepsiceros	Greater kudu
	T. imberbis	Lesser kudu
	Taurotragus oryx	Eland
	T. derbianus	Giant eland
Subfamily:	Cephalophinae (16)	
	Cephalophus monticola	Blue duiker
	C. maxwelli	Maxwell's duiker
	C. jentinki	Jentink's duiker
	C. sylvicultor	Yellow-backed duiker
	C. spadix	Abbott's duiker
	C. zebra	Banded duiker
	Sylvicapra grimmia	Bush duiker (common duiker)
Subfamily:	Reduncinae (8)	
	Redunca arundinum	(Southern) Reedbuck
	R. redunca	Bohor reedbuck
	R. fulvorufula	Mountain reedbuck
	Kobus ellipsiprymnus	Waterbuck
	K. megaceros	Nile lechwe (Mrs. Gray's waterbuck)
	K. leche	Lechwe
	K. kob	Kob (incl. Uganda kob)
	K. vardoni	Puku
Subfamily:	Hippotraginae (5)	
	Addax nasomaculatus	Addax
	Hippotragus equinus	Roan antelope
	H. niger	Sable antelope
	H. n. variani	Giant sable
	Oryx dammah	Scimitar-horned oryx
	O. gazella	Oryx (incl. "gemsbok," Beisa and fringe-eared oryx)
Subfamily:	Alcelaphinae (6)	
	Connochaetes gnou	Black wildebeest
	C. taurinus	Blue wildebeest
	Alcelaphus lichtensteini	Lichtenstein's hartebeest
	A. buselaphus	Hartebeest
	A. b. cokii	Coke's hartebeest (kongoni)
	Damaliscus dorcas dorcas	Bontebok
	D. d. phillipsi	Blesbok
	D. lunatus	Tsessebe, topi
Subfamily:	Aepycerotinae (1)	
	Aepyceros melampus	Impala
Subfamily:	Antilopinae	
Tribe:	*Antilopini* (10)	
	Antidorcas marsupialis	Springbok
	Gazella dama	Dama gazelle, Mhorr
	G. soemmerringi	Soemmerring's gazelle
	G. granti	Grant's gazelle
	G. dorcas	Dorcas gazelle
	G. spekei	Speke's gazelle
	G. thomsoni	Thomson's gazelle
	Litocranius walleri	Gerenuk (Waller's gazelle)
Tribe:	*Ammodorcadini* (1)	
	Ammodorcas clarkei	Dibatag (Clarke's gazelle)

296

Tribe:	*Neotragini* (14)	
	Oreotragus oreotragus	Klipspringer
	Madoqua kirki	Kirk's dikdik
	M. phillipsi	Phillips' dikdik
	Dorcatragus megalotis	Beira
	Ourebia ourebi	Oribi
	Raphicerus campestris	Steinbuck (Steenbok)
	Neotragus pygmaeus	Royal antelope
	N. moschatus	Suni
Subfamily:	Peleinae (1)	
	Pelea capreolus	Rhebok (Vaal ribbok)
Subfamily:	Caprinae (3)	
	Capra (Ammotragus) lervia	Barbary sheep

Subject Index

Italics concern references in Figures or Tables.
Boldface indicates more substantial parts of the text.

301

Mother-young bond, see bond (mother-young)
— — relations 102, 103, 108, 158, **167–183,** 274, 277
Mounting 130, 144, *147,* 149–156
  see also, mating behavior
Movements 28, 40–42, 46, **51–53,** 61, 64–70, 107, 108, **227–230,** 248, 251, 262, 263, 268
  see also, migrations

Neck-fighting, -wrestling 114, *115,* 116, 144, 154
"Necking" (giraffe) *129,* 130, 198
Nest, — building (in suids) 49, 158, 159
Nursing, see suckling

Olfactory marking, see scent-marking
— signals, see signals (olfactory)

Parasites 35, 38, 73, 74, 76, 271
Parturition 158, 159, **161–163,** 166, 167, **181,** 183
Pawing, see scraping the ground
Personal area, — field 189
  see also, individual distance
Pheromones 94
  see also, signals (olfactory)
Play 39, 62, 173, 174
Postcopulatory behavior 139, **150,** 152–157
Postpartum behavior **163–167, 181–183**
Prancing (gait) 90, *146,* 155, 156
Precopulatory behavior 139, **140–149, 151–157**
Predation, predator 50, 63, 65, 74, **76–83,** 92, 105, 111, 112, 162, 177, 178, **181–182,** 236–237, 247, 250–252, 271, 272
  see also, antipredator behavior
Premating behavior, see courtship behavior, precopulatory behavior
Prepartum behavior **158–160**
— isolation 62, **159–160, 181,** 182
Pronking 81
  see also, stotting

Radio-tracking 14, 56, 201, 269
Rain, reaction to 58, *59,* 60, 69
— posture 69
Rainfall, influence of 46, 51–53, 66–70, **227–234,** 255, 262
  see also, season
Rank (social) 109, 190, 200, 205
— order, see hierarchy (social)
Regulation (of population size) 238–242
Reproductive condition, — status 62, 64, 80, 95, 142, 205, 248

Resting area 49, 65
— phase 56, 57, 105
Rumination 56, 61, 63, 273, 274
Rutting 61, 66, 185, 191, 195, 229, 230, 240

Scent-marking 32–34, **94–100,** 123, 138, 155, 156, 194, 252, 253
  see also, signals (olfactory)
— —, function **99–100**
— —, interindividual **98–99,** 132, 156, 212
— —, sites of *47,* 49, 65, 97–99
Scraping the ground, with forefoot 33–35, 91, 96, 138, 166
— — —, with hind foot 33, 34, 91, 127, 223
Season, influence of 23, 40, 51–53, 55, **57–61, 64–67,** 76, 139, 191, 197, **227–234,** 250–252
  see also, food supply, migration, movements, rainfall
Sex ratio 241, 242
Sexual behavior 39, **139–157**
  see also, mating behavior
Signal(s) **87–101,** 116, 117, 176
  see also, communication, expression
—, auditory 88, **91–94,** 171, 253
  see also, vocalization
—, olfactory 88, **94–100,** 140, 171
  see also, scent-marking
—, tactile 88, **100–101,** 144, 145
  see also, allogrooming
—, visual 79, 82, **88–91,** 93–94, 125, 145, 170, 253
  see also, display, expression
Single territory (Uganda kob) 62, 63, 219, 221
Size, see body size
Sleep 56, 57
Social distance 189, 190
— environment, influence on activity 55, 58, 62
— facilitation 62, 105, 107
  see also, allelomimetic behavior, contagious behavior
— group 187, 188
— organization 64, 77, 140, 180, **185–194,** 195–224, 246–259, 274
— —, functions of **243–245,** 246–259
— —, types of **195–224,** *196,* 246–259
— —, variations in 195, 222, **225–235**
— status 62, 87, 95, 98–100, 139, 189–193, 240–244, 248
  see also, dominance, rank
— structure, see social organization
— subphase 189
— system, see social organization

Systematic Index

Italics concern references in Figures and Tables.
Boldface indicates more substantial parts of the text.
Asterisks (*) indicate numerous references in the text, of which only the more important ones are listed in the Index.

Aardvark *Orycteropus afer* 49
Addax *Addax nasomaculatus* 11, 14, *22*, 51
Aepycerotinae, see impala
Alcelaphinae, Alcelaphines* 40, **133–137,**
  155, 217–218, 251, *257*
Alcelaphus 141, 155
  see also, hartebeest
Antilopini **137–138, 156**
  see also, gazelles
Ass, wild (African) *Equus africanus* 218, 258
Axis deer, see deer (Axis)

Baboon *Papio* sp. 73, 74
Bateleur eagle *Terathopius ecaudatus* 83
Beira *Dorcatragus megalotis* 11
Beisa oryx, see oryx
Bighorn sheep *Ovis canadensis* 130, 183, 262,
  264, 271
Bison 112
Blesbok *Damaliscus dorcas phillipsi* *10*, 68,
  69, 98, *170, 176,* 217
Boar, wild *Sus scrofa* 112
Bongo *Tragelaphus euryceros* 10, *13*, 22, 251
Bontebok *Damaliscus dorcas dorcas* *10*, 22,
  68, *125, 135, 136,* 137, *143,* 144, 148, 174,
  175, 188, 217
Bos 112
Bovidae, bovids* 37, 87–93, 111–116, 120–
  126, *131–138,* 139–145, 149, **154–156,**
  166–173, **204–207, 210–222, 246–259**
Buffalo, African *Syncerus caffer*** 22, *44,* **131,**
  154, *196,* **204–206,** 231–233, 237, 242–243,
  250–253, *257,* 258
Bushbuck *Tragelaphus scriptus* 10, *22,* 42,
  44, 63, 65, 71, 72, 80, 188, 211, 215, 250,
  257, 268
Bush pig *Potamochoerus porcus* 10, *13,* 49,
  116, 127, 128, 158, 258

Caribou *Rangifer tarandus* 161
Cattle egret *Bubulcus ibis* 74
Cavicornia 111
  see also, Bovidae

Cephalophinae, see duikers
Cervidae, cervids 113, 116, 160
  see also, deer
Cheetah *Acinonyx jubatus* 83, 177, 237
Chevrotain, water, see water chevrotain
Clarke's gazelle, see dibatag
Coke's hartebeest, see hartebeest
Crocodile *Crocodylus* sp. 79

Damaliscus 90, 141, 155, 168
  see also, blesbok, bontebok, topi, tsessebe
Deer, Axis *Axis axis* 73, 83
—, red *Cervus elaphus* 183, 262
—, roe *Capreolus capreolus* 183
—, Wapiti *Cervus canadensis* 183, 262
—, white-tailed *Odocoileus virginianus* 50
Dibatag (Clarke's gazelle) *Ammodorcas clar-*
  kei 11, *13,* 22, 25, 35, 98
Dikdik *Madoqua* sp.* 22, 32, 33, 96, 99,
  112, 250, 252, *257*
—, Kirk's *M. kirki* 10, *31,* **34–35,** 45, 97,
  126, **138,** *141,* **156,** *175, 196,* **211–212**
—, Phillips' *M. phillipsi* 156
Drongo *Dicrurus adsimilis* 74
Duiker, Abbot's *Cephalophus spadix* 10
—, banded *C. zebra* 10, 11
—, bush (common) *Sylvicapra grimmia* 10,
  22, 40, 80, 211
—, Jentink's *Cephalophus jentinki* 10, 11
—, Maxwell's *C. maxwelli* 98, 100, *132,* 211,
  212
—, yellow-backed *C. sylvicultor* 10
Duikers (Cephalophinae)* 22, 25, 40, 97,
  112, **131–132,** 154, *196,* **211–212,** 250, *257*

Eland, common *Taurotragus oryx** 10, 22,
  44, 93, 96, 178–179, *196,* **206–207,** 250–
  253, *257*
—, giant *T. derbianus* 10
Elephant, African *Loxodonta africana** 22,
  24, 28, 36–38, *43,* 46, 51–53, 75, 90–98,
  102–108, *121,* 122, **126–127, 151,** 159–166,

Zoophysiology and Ecology

Editors: D. S. Farner (Coordinating Editor), W. S. Hoar, B. Hoelldobler, H. Langer, M. Lindauer

Springer-Verlag
Berlin
Heidelberg
New York

Behavioral Ecology and Sociobiology

publishes original contributions and short communications dealing with quantitative studies and with the experimental analysis of animal behavior on the level of the individual and of the population. Special emphasis will be given to the functions, mechanisms and evolution of ecological adaptations of behavior.

Aspects of particular interest are:

- Orientation in space and time
- Communication and all other forms of social and interspecific behavioral interaction, including predatory and anti-predatory behavior
- Origins and mechanisms of behavioral preferences and aversions, e.g. with respect to food, locality, and social partners
- Behavioral mechanisms of competition and resource partitioning
- Population physiology
- Evolutionary theory of social behavior

Subscription information available upon request. Write to: Springer-Verlag, 3 Heidelberger Platz, D-1000 Berlin 33. Ask for your sample copy.

Editors:

John H. Crook
Department of Psychology
University of Bristol
8-10 Berkeley Square
Bristol BS8 1HH, Great Britain

Bert Hölldobler
Department of Biology
Harvard University
MCZ Laboratories
Oxford Street
Cambridge, Mass. 02138, USA

Hans Kummer
Ethologie und Wildforschung
Zoologisches Institut
und Museum der Universität Zürich
Birchstraße 95
CH-8050 Zürich, Switzerland

Edward O. Wilson
Department of Biology
Harvard University
MCZ Laboratories
Oxford Street
Cambridge, Mass. 02138, USA

Managing Editor:

Hubert Markl
Fachbereich Biologie
Universität Konstanz
D-7750 Konstanz
Postfach 7733
Federal Republic of Germany

Springer-Verlag
Berlin
Heidelberg
New York